JUN 20

Praise for *Deadly Deceit*

"[Walters] crafts chilling antagonists and irresistible protagonists who illuminate the crux of human desperation, including how far people will go to hide a mistake and to expose another's weakness. Its fast and entwined plot lines, exciting twists, and electrifying conclusion will appeal to fans of suspenseful inspirational romances."

Booklist

Praise for *Living Lies*

"Walters's fresh new voice pulls readers into an edge-of-your-seat plot with more than a few surprises."

Family Fiction

"Natalie Walters has masterfully woven an emotionally charged suspense and love story. It's the perfect book for the avid romantic-suspense reader. Look for more novels to come from this new author!"

DiAnn Mills, author of *Burden of Proof*, www.DiAnnMills.com

"*Living Lies* is a nail-biter that will make you play hooky from your day job, feed your children cereal for supper, and not stop reading until the last page. Natalie Walters's debut novel is intriguing and enticing, with a romance that will make you believe not only in love but also that you are worth being loved. It gripped me from the first chapter and didn't let go until the end!"

Jaime Jo Wright, author of *The Reckoning at Gossamer Pond* and the Christy Award–winning novel *The House on Foster Hill*

"A deftly written, compulsive page-turner of a read from cover to cover, *Living Lies* showcases author Natalie Walters's genuine flair for originality and a narrative storytelling style that keeps her reader's rapt attention from beginning to end."

Midwest Book Review

SILENT
SHADOWS

HARBORED SECRETS
BOOK THREE

SILENT SHADOWS

NATALIE WALTERS

Revell

a division of Baker Publishing Group
Grand Rapids, Michigan

© 2020 by Natalie Walters

Published by Revell
a division of Baker Publishing Group
PO Box 6287, Grand Rapids, MI 49516-6287
www.revellbooks.com

Printed in the United States of America

Library of Congress Cataloging-in-Publication Data
Names: Walters, Natalie, 1978– author.
Title: Silent shadows / Natalie Walters.
Description: Grand Rapids : Revell, a division of Baker Publishing Group, 2020. |
    Series: Harbored secrets; Book 3
Identifiers: LCCN 2019028660 | ISBN 9780800735340 (paperback)
Subjects: LCSH: Women nurses—Fiction. | Single mothers—Fiction. | Disabled
    veterans—Fiction. | Soldiers' homes—Fiction. | GSAFD: Love stories. | Christian
    fiction.
Classification: LCC PS3623.A4487 S55 2020 | DDC 813/.6—dc23
LC record available at https://lccn.loc.gov/2019028660

ISBN 978-0-8007-3781-8 (casebound)

Scripture quotations are from the Holy Bible, New International Version®. NIV®. Copyright © 1973, 1978, 1984, 2011 by Biblica, Inc.™ Used by permission of Zondervan. All rights reserved worldwide. www.zondervan.com. The "NIV" and "New International Version" are trademarks registered in the United States Patent and Trademark Office by Biblica, Inc.™

20   21   22   23   24   25   26   7 6 5 4 3 2 1

To the three who call me Mom—
you are the treasure I'm most proud of. I love you.

For I know the plans I have for you . . .
plans to give you hope and a future.

Jeremiah 29:11

ONE

PECCA GALLEGOS never thought she'd be turning down a marriage proposal—much less four of them. Of course, the average age of the men proposing was sixty-seven, but still. In her short time working as a rehabilitation nurse at Home for Heroes in Walton, Georgia, Pecca had found it impossible to resist the sweet affection of the military veterans in her care. And right now, the deep blue eyes of the octogenarian staring up at her held amused hope.

"I'm sorry, Sergeant Kinkaid." Pecca wheeled the retired Army veteran down the hall and into his room. "But my heart belongs to another."

As she set the brake on the wheelchair, a warm hand covered hers. She looked up into the veteran's wistful and wise eyes. "That little boy is lucky to have a sweet mama raising him."

The kind sentiment turned her vision glassy. "Thank you, sir."

After she situated "Sarge" in his room to watch Fox News, Pecca made her way back through the halls of the Georgian plantation–style home turned rehab facility. She loved that it wasn't a large, overcrowded place but rather the perfect size to offer the type of personalized assistance the veterans needed.

The bright-colored walls, lightly stained oak floors, and large picture windows in every room made the place feel more like a home than a medical facility. It didn't matter whether the veterans needed help dressing themselves or using their prosthetics—or, all too often, learning to cope with the anguish that sometimes followed them home from war—Home for Heroes was a place of acceptance and healing.

Passing the second-floor lounge, Pecca noted the time on her smartwatch and picked up her pace. She headed for the grand stairway that led to the main floor, dividing the house in half and offering a dramatic welcome to anyone coming in for the first time. She took the steps down two at a time.

"Whoa, honey." Shirley Perkins, a robust woman with dark skin, rose up from behind the wraparound desk anchoring one side of the foyer. She eyed Pecca with deep brown eyes that held all the authority of a no-nonsense woman. "You run down those steps like that and you're going to end up with a broken ankle and leave me dealing with the ornery vets in D-Wing."

Pecca's foot hit the last step. "The guys in D-Wing love you." She winked, thinking of the cantankerous veterans from all branches of the military who occupied the west wing rooms and filled the hallways with battle tales that grew more exaggerated with every retelling. "They like giving you a hard time because you react."

Shirley arched an eyebrow and opened her mouth to respond, only to be interrupted when the phone at her desk rang. She reached across and answered it while Pecca picked up the clipboard that held her schedule. She needed to check on two patients to see how they were recovering from their therapy sessions before beginning the in-processing paperwork for the new arrival.

Captain Colton Crawford. US Army. Pecca's cheeks pinched into a smile, as she was keenly aware that the dynamics in D-Wing were about to shift, giving the Army veterans a one-man advantage. She flipped the page and began scanning Captain Crawford's information. Pecca liked having a general idea about her patients before they arrived to help make their transition as easy as possible. Her eye was immediately drawn to the picture in the corner. Chiseled jaw, straight nose, sharp hazel eyes that seemed to stare straight through her. *Hmm, good-looking too.*

Heat blossomed in her chest, and Pecca forced her eyes from his photo to take in the rest of the information. Thirty-two years old put him not much older than she was, yet if he was coming here it was likely he had the lifelong scars of war etched into his skin and bones—or perhaps his mind, except . . . *Hmm.* No physical injuries indicated. Only PMD. Was it a mistake? A typo? Pecca was familiar with PTSD but had never heard of PMD.

Maybe Shirley would know, but the second Pecca's gaze caught sight of the grim look etching the receptionist's face, she forgot her question.

"It's Principal Webb." Shirley held out the phone.

Pecca's pulse jumped as her fingers closed around the receiver. Maceo? "Hello, Mrs. Webb, this is Pecca Gallegos. Is Maceo okay?"

"Oh, yes, Ms. Gallegos, he's fine." Principal Webb's voice was reassuring, though Pecca heard some hesitation. "I'm sorry to bother you at work, but Maceo's in my office. He's in a bit of trouble, and I'd like it if you could come over to discuss it further."

Trouble? Pecca checked the time. Her new patient was late and it was her job to check him in, but she had no one else she could call to pick up Maceo. Frustration turned into emptiness. This was yet another stinging realization that, even though her life was good here in Walton, she was still mostly alone. Her gaze traveled to Shirley, who took the clipboard from Pecca's hand and gave a nod of empathy.

"I'll be there shortly." Pecca handed the receiver back to Shirley. "I've gotta go. Maceo's gotten into some kind of trouble."

"Go on, honey. Your shift ends in half an hour anyway. I'll get your patient settled in and the paperwork started. You can take care of the rest in the morning."

Pecca's anxiety rocketed through her at the idea of leaving work early. She loved this job and didn't want to let anyone down—especially her patients. But the whole reason Pecca was here, working hard, was for Maceo. She had no choice—he came first.

"Thank you, Shirley." After grabbing her keys and purse, Pecca hurried out the large front door and down the steps of the wraparound porch. The large limbs of the live oaks stretching over the small parking lot did little to smother the warm September day. The heat brought with it the memory of Texas in the fall. And with that, a pang of longing.

Pecca climbed into her car and adjusted the air-conditioning to full blast. She refused to allow herself to reflect on everything she'd left behind. Instead, her focus turned to her son and getting to the school as quickly as possible. *What could Maceo possibly have done to warrant a visit to the principal's office?*

She was so focused on leaving that she didn't see the figure that had stepped out of the brush and in front of her car until she was already pressing the gas. Pecca screamed and stomped on her brakes just as the man jumped back. The man's dark gaze speared her, his shadowed expression partially hidden behind a thick beard. *What in the world?*

Heart pounding, she pressed the button to roll down her window. Before she could apologize, the man stepped back into the copse of live oaks bordering the back half of the Home for Heroes property. The next moment he was gone.

Releasing a shaky sigh, Pecca flexed her knuckles, which had whitened over the steering wheel. Who was that guy? His sudden appearance had rattled her nerves. She needed to get a grip. There was nothing to be afraid of here. She gingerly pressed on the gas and steered toward the elementary school. Annoyance replaced the fear trying to root itself within her. She hated that any variance in her life sent her mind careening to her past. Coming to Walton was supposed to be a fresh start. One Pecca had to make out of necessity rather than desire. Necessity driven by the fierce instinct to protect Maceo at all costs.

The shrill ring of her phone startled her, sending her pulse racing all over again. She glanced at the screen. Adrian? Why would her brother be calling in the middle of the day? He worked nights and should be sleeping. Unless . . .

There was only one reason he would be calling at this time—South Side Barrio. Adrian worked undercover in the gang unit in southern New Mexico but kept tabs on the gang activity in El Paso, especially when it related to Javier Torres, her ex and Maceo's father.

The road blurred ahead as a sickening wave of panic paralyzed her. She blinked quickly to clear her vision, forcing herself to focus on the road. Pecca bit her lip as she flicked the screen, then she spoke into the air as Bluetooth projected the conversation through the vehicle's speaker.

"Adrian?" Her voice sounded small, wounded. And yet, wasn't that the truth? She had been wounded, but not as badly as Maceo. "What is it?"

"Hey, *Pequeña*, I didn't want to bother you, but I've been hearing some things out in the field and think you should know." Adrian's voice held no emotion. "Javier is up for early parole. He has to go before the board, but the chatter out on the streets is that the SSB is very interested in his release. They're looking for you and Maceo."

Pecca felt dizzy and considered pulling the car over. "What do you mean they're looking for us?"

"What better reason to release a prisoner than hearing from his girlfriend and child who need him?"

"I'm not his girlfriend, and we don't need him." It had taken Pecca too long to come to that conclusion, to realize her mistake, but by then it was too late. Javier was already facing jail time and she was already pregnant. Maceo was the only good thing to come from her mistake.

Suddenly, the road ahead was too dark. She peeked over her shoulder to the line of trees that marked the edge of the road. Shadows held imaginary faces staring back at her, and her mind flashed to the scruffy face of the man she almost hit in the parking lot. A shudder ran down her spine. She flicked on her turn signal and pulled onto the shoulder, hitting the locks as an instinctive precaution.

"Do you think they know where we are?"

"I don't think so. I spoke with a friend in El Paso's gang unit, and he said Javier's cousin, Felix, is leading the charge. Seems the SSB isn't as strong as it was with Javier in control."

"What should I do?" Panic threatened to strangle her. Felix's gang nickname, "Spider," fit him well. He trapped people in a web of lies until they were forced to do his bidding.

"Nothing. You aren't thinking about going to the parole hearing, are you?"

"What? No." Pecca thought back to her last conversation with Javier. "I don't want Maceo anywhere near the SSB. That's why I left El Paso."

"Good. Because I've been in the job long enough to know that it's hard for any prisoner to maintain a clean record when they're released from prison, but it's even harder for gang members."

"Do you think they're going to let him out?"

"Hard to say. My commanding officer is doing what he can to get some details from the prison, but getting through the bureaucracy hasn't been easy. The information we've got so far is off the street and through back channels, but I'll let you know as soon as we can confirm anything."

"Okay." Pecca rubbed her eyes as her car purred in idle. "I've gotten close to the sheriff here, and a few of the deputies. Do you think I should let them know?"

"Can't hurt."

That admission made Pecca's gut churn. Adrian didn't exaggerate.

"Stay safe, sis. And give Mac a fist bump from his *tio*."

"I will."

Pecca ended the call and let the phone sit in her cold hands. *Javier might get out and the SSB was looking for her and—*

A horn blasted from behind her. Pecca jumped and sent visual daggers at the car speeding past hers. Heart pounding, she checked her mirrors and pulled back into the road. Fear curdled around her shoulders as she resumed her journey to the school.

She'd left everything behind to protect Maceo and would do it again if necessary. How desperate was the South Side Barrio? Or Felix? What would they do if they found her? She shuddered, already knowing the answer. They'd do whatever it took.

TWO

COLTON CRAWFORD ground his molars as the tremor in his right arm curled his fingers into a fist. With his left hand, he swiped the hair from his forehead. His breaths came in shallow gasps. He focused his quick steps around the curve of the asphalt trail, trying hard to ignore the sting of sweat dripping in his eyes. Ahead he saw a large boulder shaded by the long branches of live oaks and aimed for it, clutching his arm against his stomach.

Just a few more steps. He pushed through the brush, ignoring the sharp twigs scratching at his skin and wishing away what he knew was coming. A foot away from the large rock, the tremor in his shoulder twitched into a convulsion that wracked his upper body, thrusting his chin upward. He grunted in pain, dropping to his knees.

Clenching his teeth, Colton squeezed his eyes shut. He tried to regain control over his body, but the muscles in his arms, shoulders, chest, and neck disobeyed. They continued to seize for what felt like minutes but truthfully were only mere seconds. The worst seconds of Colton's life . . . well, maybe not the worst.

A second later, his mutinous muscles relaxed and he drew in his first free, deep breath. Pain radiated through him as if he'd just finished a vigorous workout session. He gripped the rough surface of the rock and heaved himself up. He swiped the salty sweat from his scruffy face and wished he'd thought to bring a bottle of water with him. He used to think Dallas was humid. He was wrong. Very wrong.

That was becoming a theme for his life lately.

Colton forced himself to practice the breathing techniques one of his therapists had taught him and took in the view. He scanned the horizon. Trees lined the river on the other side of the bank, which had a topography that reminded him a little of his home in Texas.

"Heard this place has a million-dollar view. Lucky you get to enjoy it." Those were the parting words of the Uber driver who dropped him off in front of Home for Heroes yesterday.

Lucky? Not even close.

He was here for only one reason—and it wasn't to enjoy the views. He was looking for answers. Healing. The chance to get back the life that was stolen from him. Or at least understand.

The morning sun glinting off the river he couldn't pronounce the name of had inspired him to put on his running shoes this morning and do the one activity he could still sort of control. And now it seemed that was going to be taken from him too. He studied the tremor moving his fingers. He clenched his fist, but the tremor wouldn't be controlled and the muscle twitched in his arm, causing it to jerk.

He growled. Low and angry, grinding his teeth together until his jaw ached. Why? Why was this happening to him?

Anger coursed through him. Nothing in his life was going the way he planned, and all he could feel was anger. He shouldn't be here. He should be with his unit back in Bragg—halfway through a promising career. But no. Instead of living the life he worked hard for, his body had betrayed him, forcing him to find a specialist who could offer him something no one else had been able to—a solution.

Releasing a long sigh, Colton studied his arm. The jerks, twitches, and uncontrollable movements were getting worse. The unofficial-official diagnosis was a movement disorder—a vague, all-encompassing answer his puzzled doctors offered when they could find no other medical reason to explain how or why he was experiencing these symptoms. *Except one.*

Colton walked toward the edge of the embankment and stared out over the water. *Psychogenic.* The word still burned him. No way was this movement all in his head. There had to be an explanation, something that could be cured with a pill or a procedure. Anything to give him back control over his life.

Dr. Mike Kelly.

Colton's final hope rested in the therapist who'd been using some kind of brain therapy to help patients with post-traumatic stress disorder. Due to his late arrival at Home for Heroes yesterday, his in-processing was delayed and he had missed his first appointment with the man he was praying could reverse the disorder plaguing him.

Praying. Colton snorted. Praying was supposed to bring peace. Hope. Answers. As of yet, the only thing praying did was make him feel utterly forgotten.

Thunk!

Colton froze.

The noise echoed from over his right shoulder. He turned slowly to find nothing but dense trees and overgrown brush. Birds chirped overhead, the branches swaying as they swooped in and out. Maybe it was a squirrel or— *Thunk.* Instinctively, Colton's breathing slowed. His senses had no reason to be on alert, but the habits he'd acquired after a decade in the Army didn't just go away once the discharge papers were signed.

Taking careful steps, Colton had to pause every few feet and reorient himself to the direction the noise was coming from. Adrenaline caused his arm to jerk more frequently. He needed to get back to his room and take his morning medications, but he couldn't ignore the noise, which was beginning to sound more like . . . sniffling?

The faint sounds of someone talking drifted on the first breeze Colton had felt all morning. Stepping over a root, he shifted around a tree and found the source of the noise. A small boy with black hair sat perched on a fallen log. When he wasn't chucking rocks at the trees, he was wiping at his face with the back of his hand.

Colton glanced around the dense foliage. It was still pretty early in the morning—too early for a child to be out here by himself. The defeated slump in the boy's shoulders was too familiar to ignore, but indecision kept Colton planted where he was. If he suddenly emerged out of the tree line, he could scare the kid, and they were close enough to the steep embankment that one wrong step could have him falling into the river below. But he couldn't just leave the kid there. The boy's quiet mumblings of sorrow pulled at Colton.

He cleared his throat and the little boy's face swung around, dark eyes wide with fear as Colton stepped into full view and put his hands in front of him.

"I didn't mean to scare you. Just making sure you're okay."

"I'm fine," the boy mumbled before turning his attention back to the stick in his hand.

"You're sure?"

"Did my mom send you to get me?"

Colton frowned. This kid *was* here by himself. "No. Is your mom nearby?"

"Works at—"

"Ughhh!" Colton clutched his right arm to his stomach as the seizing pulled his neck backward.

"Hey, are you okay, mister?"

Even if Colton wanted to assure the kid he was, there was no way he could push the words out. Gritting his teeth, he forced himself to take in slow breaths until the muscle spasm finished. *In. Out. Slow.*

Colton's eyes were clamped shut, but he felt the presence of the boy next to him. The muscles in Colton's neck, back, and arm began to relax. When he was able, he opened his eyes. He peered down into the boy's face, expecting to see fear or worry, but instead saw simple curiosity.

"Sorry. I have, uh . . ." He licked his lips and forced himself to say the words. "It's a movement disorder. Causes my muscles to seize."

The boy gave a one-shoulder shrug. "Thought maybe you were Bruce Banner."

"No, I'm Colton. Colton Crawford."

"Are you kidding?" The boy arched an eyebrow. "You don't know who Bruce Banner is?"

There was so much disbelief in the kid's tone, Colton wanted to lie and say that he did. "Should I?"

"You just get out of jail or something?"

Colton smirked. "No." His hand twitched. "Though it felt like one."

"What's up with your hand?"

"I told you."

"Movement disorder." His dark brown eyes followed the tremor in Colton's arm. "So it just moves whenever it wants?"

"Yeah."

He eyed Colton's hand for a second longer before offering another nonchalant shrug like nothing was unusual about a man's hand or body twisting uncontrollably.

It was the strangest thing. Ever since his diagnosis, people stared at his movements and then avoided him. Like whatever he had was contagious. Even kids, though they stared out of simple curiosity, which he could deal with until their parents whispered and dragged them away. But not this kid. He seemed . . . like he couldn't care less.

Except there was obviously something he cared about enough to lead him into the woods in the early morning hours all by himself. Colton looked around and saw a football peeking out of an open backpack. He remembered passing an elementary school a half mile back, and there was nothing up ahead except for the rehab facility. "Are you out here alone?"

"No." The boy looked up. "You're here."

Colton's lip quirked. "What's your name?"

"Maceo."

"Should you be in school right now?"

Maceo dropped his gaze to his shoes, and that's when Colton

noticed it. Where there should've been two scratched-up, knobby knees, there was only one. The other was the familiar metal tube of a prosthesis.

"You said your name was Maceo, but with that piece of metal, you're clearly one of Tony Stark's inventions."

Maceo lifted his chin, surprise lighting his eyes. "You know Marvel?"

"That's the name of the comics, right?" Colton hated how lame he sounded, but the truth was that he wasn't much into comics *or* movies. He'd dated a girl who wanted to see the new *Iron Man* movie when it came out, and he obliged. "And Bruce Banner is . . . ?"

"The Hulk," Maceo said, walking back over to the log.

The Hulk. Yeah, he could see how he might've resembled the Hulk's transformation when his muscles were seizing. "Isn't the Hulk kind of mean?"

"Misunderstood." Maceo reached for his backpack. "How would you feel if something was happening to your body and you didn't know why?" His small fingers traced the white lacing of the football. "Or it stopped you from having friends and doing the things you want."

Colton couldn't ignore the wobble in Maceo's voice. It didn't take a genius to figure out that this kid, who couldn't be more than ten years old, had experienced more than his fair share of disappointment, and it put Colton's self-pity into place. "You like football?"

"Yeah," he said, lacking enthusiasm.

"Ever heard of Vincent James?"

Maceo glanced up with an expression that said Colton was crazy. "He's the wide receiver for the Mustangs, and like, the greatest receiver of all time."

Colton smiled. "Did you know Vince broke his leg in eighth grade? Pretty bad. The doctors told him he would never play ball again."

"Because of a broken leg?"

"It was a bad break. His femur." Colton tapped the top of his right thigh. "Biggest bone in the leg. He had to have surgery. It took an entire year of physical therapy before Vince could even run full speed on it."

"But it's better now." Maceo began spinning the football between his hands. "Bet no one told him he couldn't play football."

"They did."

Maceo's eyebrows lifted in disbelief.

"Doctors, physical therapists, coaches, even his mom and dad told him that if he played football, he could reinjure his leg and maybe one day not be able to walk without a cane or wheelchair."

"What did he do?"

Colton held out his hands and Maceo tossed him the ball. "He didn't listen to them." The familiar look of rebellion filled Maceo's face, and Colton thought better of what he'd said. "What I mean is, Vince didn't let the doctors' fear become his. He listened to what they told him and followed their instructions for physical therapy so he could make his leg stronger. He worked hard. Harder than anyone else I've ever known, and when it was time, he began to practice again. He worked on the skills he could until . . ." Colton lifted the ball over his shoulder and aimed it toward Maceo, who opened his hands, palms facing out. Colton threw it, and with just a quick step to the side, Maceo received it. "He became the greatest receiver of all time."

Maceo looked from the football in his hands to Colton. "So, did you read all that stuff about Vincent James or something?"

"Nope. Vince and I went to school together."

The ball fell from Maceo's hands. "You *know* Vincent James?"

Colton laughed. "Who do you think taught him the Saint James Fake?"

"*You* taught Vincent James the Saint James Fake?" Maceo's eyes burned brighter than the sun. "The Mustangs won the Super Bowl with that play." Again disbelief furrowed the kid's brows. "Are you lying?"

"I don't lie, little man." Colton nodded toward the trail. "There's a big lawn near Home for Heroes. You got some time to toss the ball around before school?"

Maceo eyed Colton's arm, uncertainty in his expression.

"Hey"—Colton flexed the fingers on his right hand—"there's no sympathy on the field. If you don't see my weakness, I won't see yours."

A smile spread across Maceo's face, pulling his cheeks into deep dimples. "Deal."

THREE

"HE *SHOVED* A KID. To the ground." Pecca rubbed her eyes. "In this day and age, I'm surprised we're not being sued."

Shirley gave a soft laugh of understanding before handing Pecca the schedule for the day. "Honey, I raised four boys, and if there's one thing I know about them it's this: they gonna fight and then it's over. Your boy is gonna be just fine."

"I don't know." Pecca sighed, remembering the silent drive home from school and the way Maceo slammed his door when they got there. Not hard enough to get into trouble but just enough to make a point. "He's seven and suspended from school. I really thought he was finally settling in here."

"Baby, Maceo's faced more difficulties in his little life than some of our patients. He just needs some understanding right now. Needs his mama to make his favorite meal. Maybe watch one of those superhero movies with him."

Pecca looked at Shirley, sure the disbelief was written all over her face. "Doesn't that send the wrong message, rewarding bad behavior?"

Shirley's brown eyes deepened with wisdom. "It's called grace. Put yourself in his place. Deputy Ryan Frost, who was basically his playmate, moved away, then he found out Noah, his best friend—the one who's actually his age—is not in the same class as him at school." Shirley raised her eyebrows. "Seems the child needs a little compassion this time around."

"He needs to talk to me," Pecca said. "He wouldn't tell Principal Webb or me why he did it. I thought moving here was the right decision but—"

"Don't you go second-guessing yourself. You're doing the best

23

you can given the circumstances." Shirley placed her hand over Pecca's and gave it a squeeze. "Now, go take that young man of yours into the kitchen. I picked up some of Lane's famous cinnamon rolls this morning."

Pecca's stomach growled in anticipation. "Maybe later. I've got to catch up on the work I missed yesterday. Did Captain Crawford ever show up?"

"Sure did. You're gonna need some grace for that one too."

"A hard one, huh?"

"I'll let you decide." Shirley feigned innocence before leaning over the counter between them. "Let's just say Maceo might not be the most difficult male you deal with today. Now, where's Maceo so I can feed him some love?"

Pecca smiled. "He's reading in the library." As Shirley shuffled off after her son, Pecca picked up the file on Captain Crawford. After dealing with Maceo and the news about Javier, the last thing she needed was a difficult patient.

All last night her thoughts had circled between Maceo's behavior and what the SSB would do if they really wanted Pecca to testify on Javier's behalf. She thought about telling Sheriff Huggins, but part of her felt like Adrian might've been exaggerating. His work in the gang unit made him hypervigilant. In fact, he was the one who suggested that Pecca move away—to do whatever was necessary to keep Maceo away from the gang life that had put his father in a jail cell for the last eight years.

"Honey, did you say Maceo was supposed to be in the library?" Shirley's steps stopped at the threshold of the foyer and the east wing.

"Yes. I told him he had to stay there and read for an hour so I could do my rounds." Pecca set down the file. "He's not there?"

Shirley didn't need to answer. It was all over her face.

Pecca pressed her lips together. Maceo's disobedience was at an all-time high. She passed the library, a list of punishments growing in her mind, and it was empty. What was she going to do with him? She walked down the hall toward the dining room and kitchen, only finding a few residents and staff there.

Adrian's words from yesterday tore through her mind. *"They're looking for you."* A chill skirted across her shoulders as she picked up her pace. Pecca's thoughts went to a hundred different possibilities as memories of what the SSB was capable of colored every scenario. Stop. She had to stop. The SSB didn't know where she was—she was jumping to conclusions. That should've comforted her, but as she started for the side door leading to the gym, swimming pool, and lawn, she could feel the panic starting to rise.

Pecca exited Home for Heroes, the morning air cool but still humid and suffocating. Or was that fear? Taking a breath, she forced herself to remain calm. Maceo was mad at her. And probably doing this to make her worry. Like she needed another reason to worry. She was probably going to find him sulking in the gym or by the pool or—

A scream captured her attention. *Maceo?*

Another scream, and Pecca took off in the direction she thought it had come from. Rounding the front corner of the detached building that held the gym, she caught sight of her son running across the lawn. Relief slowed her pounding pulse—until a man emerged from the hedgerow.

The man, his arms held out wide, barreled after Maceo. Pecca blinked as her mind tried to make sense of what she was seeing. It was him. The man she almost ran over yesterday. With Adrian's warning echoing in her ears, Pecca charged across the lawn, her feet barely touching the carefully manicured grass as she aimed for the grizzly man twice her size.

"Maceo!" Her scream grabbed the attention of her son, who froze at the sight of her running full speed. She closed the distance, glaring into the man's hazel eyes seconds before her body collided with his.

Oof!

What she lacked in weight and strength, she'd made up for in speed as the man, caught off guard, was thrown sideways to the ground. The only problem was, Pecca hadn't accounted for the momentum and found herself rolling on the grass alongside him. Somehow she had become tangled in his arms, the strength of them cocooning her from the ground.

"Mama!"

"Stay back, Maceo." Pecca disentangled herself and winced. *Ouch*. Her shoulder screamed, but she couldn't let pain keep her from protecting her son. "Go . . . get Ms. Shirley."

But Maceo didn't move. His eyes shifted quickly between her and the man moaning next to her.

Scooting up to her knees, Pecca scrambled backward, putting herself between Maceo and the man pushing himself up. Fear squeezed her lungs. Who was this guy? She watched him rub a hand over the side of his ribs, blood oozing from a scrape on his elbow.

"Mom, we were just—"

"Why were you chasing my son?" Pecca said, pushing Maceo behind her. The man raised a dark gaze on her. She swallowed. "Who are you?"

"Pecca!" Shirley was nearly sprinting toward them.

Pecca turned her attention back to the man, who was now standing, giving her a good look at him. Or . . . up at him. The man was several inches taller than her, which wasn't difficult, given she was only five-two. Her eyes traveled the length of his body. Running shorts, T-shirt. The jerk of his right arm grabbed her attention. He tucked it to his side quickly, causing her eyes to meet his annoyed expression. "Who are you?" she repeated.

"Honey . . . are you . . . okay?" Shirley said, breathless. "Oh, you're . . . bleeding."

Pecca swung her gaze between Shirley and the man she'd just plowed into. The woman was examining his elbow. Wait. "You know this guy, Shirley?"

Amusement lit a sparkle in Shirley's eyes. "Sweetie, this is Captain Colton Crawford. Your new patient."

No, no, no, no, no. This couldn't be happening. Had she really just smashed her new patient into the ground? Pecca swallowed as she searched the face of the bearded man in front of her, trying to reconcile him with the picture of the clean-cut Army officer in her file.

Flaming heat burned in her cheeks. She was mortified. And probably going to lose her job. "Captain Crawford, I am sooo sorry. I don't know what I was thinking . . . well, I do. I saw a strange man chasing my son and I was like, *Oh, stranger danger,* and you look like—" Her eyes met his, and she clamped her lips closed. *Can I make this any worse?*

Shirley stifled a giggle, and Pecca shot her a look before returning her focus back to the man she'd just assaulted. "I'm incredibly sorry, and I totally understand if you want to file a complaint. I mean, I would. You came here to get treatment, *not* knocked out by your nurse and—"

"Captain Crawford"—Shirley put a hand on Pecca's arm to silence her—"let me introduce you. This is—"

"The defensive end for the Atlanta Falcons?"

Pecca gave an awkward laugh. If Captain Crawford was trying for humor, it was only with his words. Nothing was humorous about the way he was looking at her. This was bad. If Shirley thought this patient was going to be difficult before, Pecca had just made it a hundred times worse.

<hr />

A chaplain?

Colton sank further into the leather sofa as he stared at the man behind the desk. According to the framed degree hanging on the wall, Dr. Michael Kelly was a retired Army chaplain and a licensed therapist. Colton's mother and her prayer group would be giddy given this fact. She was always telling him how much she prayed God would prove he was in control and everything would work out.

He rubbed the ache growing in his shoulder, his thoughts

returning to the pint-size nurse who had bulldozed him on the Home for Heroes lawn an hour and a half ago. So far nothing about his arrival here was working out.

"You want me to stop taking the medications that help my movements?"

Colton sharpened his focus on Chaplain Kelly, who had to be in his late fifties. He was bald except for wispy hairs that crowned his head. Hands spotted with age held Colton's file and a pair of silver glasses that he probably only wore when reading off lengthy reports penned by a dozen psychiatrists, psychologists, and therapists.

"I've spoken with your neurologist, and she agrees it's unlikely the medications are really doing anything more than sedating your muscles. We'll start with a clean slate. Wean you off slowly."

Colton looked down at his arm. Fingers shaking, his hand curled and uncurled of its own accord, as his whole arm jerked like it was being electrocuted. *Hmm, would that help?* If it had been an option, Colton would've done it. He was willing to try anything to make the movements stop, but going off his meds . . .

"Won't that make my movements worse? I mean, shouldn't we wait until we see if the whole CBT thing works first?"

"It is my hope that Cognitive Brain Therapy will be part of the solution." Chaplain Kelly set down the file. "Given the extent of bloodwork, scans, and specialists, it doesn't appear that what's causing your movement is organic, which means the medications might treat the symptoms, but they're not treating the cause."

"What do you mean?"

"Psychogenic movement disorders often emerge as the result of a conversion disorder. In my experience with other patients, it's possible you're harboring something that's forced your body to respond this way—"

"You're saying this is my fault?" Heat surged through Colton's body. He'd long ago lost count of the number of pokes, prods, and assessments he'd been subjected to, only to leave without a single answer as to why this was happening or how to fix it. But the one thing he knew was that this was not in his head.

"Not at all." Chaplain Kelly's demeanor remained calm. "Patients suffering from PMD have no control over their movements. It's a coping mechanism, usually as a result of suffering from extreme stress or a painful experience. It's safe to presume that as a military intelligence officer with multiple deployments under your belt, you've likely experienced both."

"Nothing more than the next soldier," Colton said through gritted teeth. He looked down at his tremoring hand. "My doctors at Reed told me I needed to begin the CBT as soon as possible if I don't want this to become permanent. That's why I'm here."

"I agree." Chaplain Kelly crossed his arms. "But CBT alone isn't the answer. We're going to need to address the underlying cause of the condition—"

"There's no underlying cause." Colton's angry declaration echoed in the room, and he was instantly embarrassed. He blew out a long exhale. "I'm sorry, sir."

"There's no need to apologize for the frustration you must be feeling. I can't imagine what it must be like to have your whole life shift so dramatically."

That's right, you can't. Anger swelled, and Colton let his gaze travel around the office space where presumably he'd be spending most of his time. Mahogany wainscoting contrasted warmly with the light cream color on the wall. A military print was on one side of the room and on the other were all of Chaplain Kelly's degrees and certificates. Colton's eyes locked on one in particular—the "Certificate of Retirement from the United States Army for Major Michael Kelly."

Major. Colton's chest seized. He was so close. His board was only a year away. He sucked in a breath. "I want my life back."

"Captain Crawford, I believe in order to reach that goal, we must work through all aspects of the psychological impact—"

"I don't have PTSD, if that's what you're implying. My mind is fine. I was fine. I was serving my country, and yes, I saw horrible things. But if you've got boots on the ground, you're going to see things you don't want to and you're going to try to make sure . . ."

The muscles in his right arm grew rigid. The tremor was building. Colton wiped the beads of sweat dampening his forehead. Standing, he pulled his arm close to his body. He knew what was coming next, and he needed to get out from underneath Chaplain Kelly's penetrating gaze. "I need to go."

Colton rushed to the door and out into the hallway. *Just get to your room.* His pace tripled until he rounded a corner, nearly knocking over the friendly receptionist.

"Well, hello, handsome." Shirley flashed a bright smile. "Fancy running into you."

The tightness climbing through his arm and into his shoulder and chest refused him the option of responding in kind. He tried to move around her, vowing to apologize when he—

"Gah!" The painful yelp escaped Colton's lips as his right arm jerked outward. The muscles in his chest squeezed so tightly he couldn't exhale.

The playfulness in the receptionist's eyes vanished. "Hold on, baby. I'm going to get you some help."

Colton couldn't have stopped her if he wanted to. He watched her scurry down the hall before squeezing his eyes shut. *Please, God, make it stop.* But the prayer, like all the rest, did nothing to ease the spasm. He had to wait it out. *"You've got to breathe, Colton."* Easy for the doctor to say when his muscles weren't twisting and writhing in pain.

The sound of footsteps approaching pulled Colton's focus from the breath that wouldn't come. Strong hands gripped his good arm and shoulder. He opened his eyes and found Chaplain Kelly's pale blue eyes locked on his.

"It's going to be okay, Colton. I want you to match your breaths with me as I count." It took everything in him to comply, but he finally nodded. "Okay, here we go. Inhale, one, two, three . . ."

As Chaplain Kelly continued to count, Colton fought to regain control of his breath, but the chaplain's words from earlier came rushing back. *"We're going to need to address the underlying cause."*

But just like the doctors, Colton didn't have a clue. He had no idea what he did to deserve this or why he was being punished—only that if this was his life sentence, he would've chosen the alternative.

FOUR

"I'D SAY YOU'RE PART MARINE."

"Bah!" The gnarled and age-spotted hand of Sergeant Kinkaid swiped the air at Gunnery Sergeant Hugo Flores. "You don't know anything, Gunny. The lady has Army grit running in her blood."

"Hooah!" Two voices echoed in unison behind Pecca.

It hadn't taken long for the news of her collision with the newest resident to find its way into the hallway of D-Wing.

"I heard the newbie is Army." Gunny tapped his cane against the floor. "An officer. Only a Marine has the brass to take out an officer."

"Oorah!" Buddy Collins appeared in the hallway, fist raised in the air.

Great. This was getting out of control, and if she didn't put an end to it . . . who was she kidding. These guys lived for the challenge of proving who was tougher and which branch of service was more heroic. It had taken her a solid month to memorize the rank for each of the branches for fear she'd accidentally demote someone or, heaven forbid, link them to the wrong one. A flicker of admiration warmed her chest. All the men sitting in the upstairs lounge inspired her. They were all heroes. Equally brave for their service. She'd tell them that, but she knew it would incite another round of measuring that she didn't have time to referee.

"Now, gentlemen." Pecca eyed each of them. She grabbed a walker and placed it in front of Sarge. "What happened with Captain Crawford was my fault."

"See." Gunny slapped his hand against his thigh. "Took out an officer. That's a Marine."

"It was a misunderstanding," Pecca said before they could get started again. "And I feel bad—"

"Nah." A towering man with rich, dark skin pushed himself off the couch and reached for his walker. "I'd give half my retirement to have a pretty gal like you run me over." Murmurs of agreement echoed. And Lance Corporal Franklin "Sticks" Bowie smiled. "And I'd give the other half of my retirement to be able to get up and walk afterward."

Howling laughter filled the lounge.

"Alright, boys. Time to get you downstairs for lunch."

Lunch seemed to be the magic word. Despite their replaced hips and knees, arthritic joints, and slow gaits, all the members of D-Wing began making their way toward the elevator or, for those who were able, the stairs.

After making sure the men were settled into the dining room, Pecca moved down the hall to the library and found her son slouched in a club chair, flipping pages of a chapter book faster than he could read.

"Good book, huh?"

Maceo rolled his head to the side, his eyes landing on her. He shrugged.

Back to the silent treatment. "Are you hungry? I think they're serving macaroni and cheese with the chicken today."

"I don't like macaroni and cheese."

"Since when?"

He shrugged.

Pecca took a leveled breath, counting silently to herself. She didn't want to argue with Maceo, but there had to be an explanation for what was going on in his head that made him so . . . insubordinate. He still had offered no explanation for his behavior at school, and Pecca wouldn't entertain any possibility that Maceo was exhibiting a natural inclination toward violence. She had moved him away from that environment before he was old enough to see it—or experience it. Something else had to be going on.

"Honey, do you have a minute?"

Shirley's soft voice made Pecca turn around. She gave a nod before planting a kiss on top of Maceo's dark hair. "I brought caldo de res if you get hungry. It's in the staff kitchen refrigerator."

Maceo barely acknowledged her, and she heaved a sigh. She'd take the ornery arguments of the D-Wing men over her son's moodiness. Pecca found Shirley waiting in the hallway, a worried expression on her face.

"Everything okay?"

"It is now, but I wanted to let you know that Captain Crawford had an episode earlier, after his appointment with Chaplain Kelly."

"Is he alright?"

"The doctors checked him out again, but it seems like he is. He's waiting for you inside the gym."

Again. It was her fault Captain Crawford had to be checked out the first time. Pecca bit her lip. Had his episode been an aftereffect of her hitting him? She groaned, feeling the weight of guilt pile up.

"I feel *so* bad, Shirley." Pecca closed her eyes. "What am I going to say?"

"Start with 'I'm sorry,' and then speak your truth."

Pecca opened her eyes to find Shirley looking at her with curiosity. "To my defense, the man I tackled did *not* look like the Colton Crawford in the file." She dragged up the image of his face and the scruffy beard in her mind. "More like Grizzly Adams, but I doubt he'll share my sense of humor, huh?"

Shirley laughed loudly enough that it filled the hallways. "I'd say that's probably not the way you'd want to start, but you never seem to have a problem winning over our residents." She handed Pecca the file she'd been holding. "If your humor doesn't work, flash him one of your pretty smiles. He won't be able to resist that."

"Are you suggesting I *flirt* with him?" Pecca whispered sharply, checking her surroundings.

"A little flirt never hurts. How do you think I get those old coots in D-Wing to mind me?" And with that, Shirley turned and headed back toward her post, hips swaying the entire way.

Pecca laughed and carried the momentary joy with her like a shield as she made her way to the gym. Humor hadn't worked the first time.

And she wasn't going to flirt.

Grunting met her at the door. She slipped in and through a reflection in the mirrors caught sight of Captain Crawford bent over a barbell weighted on both sides. She stopped at the door. His shirt was off and muscles rippled across his back. Not in a bulky way like bodybuilders. His muscles were long and lean—the kind that reflected agile strength.

With another grunt, he pulled the bar up to his hips in a dead lift, giving her a good look at his face. Dark brown hair fell over his forehead almost to his brows. His beard covered the lower half of his face but didn't hide the strong angles of his jaw. She noticed the wireless earbud in his ear, which she thought accounted for why he hadn't heard her enter, but as soon as the thought crossed her mind, the barbell dropped to the ground with a loud *thunk* and his steely gaze shifted, pinning her beneath it.

Maybe she did need to flirt her way through this. "Uh, hi, Captain Crawford." She walked toward him and almost tripped on a mat someone had left out. Righting herself, she looked up and smiled. And then stopped. *Was that a flirty smile?* Ugh. Shirley had gotten into her head. Squaring her shoulders, she continued forward.

He tugged an earbud out of his ear but didn't respond.

Okay.

"I see you started without me." She felt her eyes drifting down to his bare chest. Pecca blinked and forced herself to look anywhere but there. Unfortunately, her eyes were drawn to his right arm. It twitched and shook so much that he dropped it to his side in an attempt to hide it, and she felt bad. *Good job, Pecca!* She chastised herself as she moved to a counter and set his file down.

"That's okay. This first meeting is really an assessment to see what you can do."

"Does your assessment normally include running down your patients?"

And there it was. She pivoted around and found him walking toward her, earbuds hanging over his *still* bare shoulders, shirt in hand. "I'm *really, really* sorry about what happened earlier. I don't know what came over me. I think it was just seeing you chase after my son, and he told me you were just playing ball with him but—"

"Stranger danger."

Pecca swallowed, her gaze lost beneath his penetrating one. "R-right."

"I've been hit lighter than that by guys who play in the NFL."

Was that humor? His expression was unreadable. Pulling a clipboard off the wall, she grabbed a pen out of her pocket and clicked it. She needed to turn this around. Be the professional she was and do her job. She turned on her heel and offered a wide smile that was definitely *not* flirtatious.

"First thing I need to ask is if everything is okay after your, um, episode?"

"I'm fine." His lips pressed into a thin line. Gripping his shirt, he started to tug it over his head but was having trouble.

"Can I help?"

"I've got it," he growled as he pulled the shirt the rest of the way over his torso. His right hand clenched and jerked to the side. His eyes flashed to hers and then down. He tucked the arm to his side as it continued to jerk.

Pecca put as much cheer as she could into her voice. "Captain Crawford, I'm really sorry for what happened this morning, but I'd like to start over again. I'm here to help you in any way possible—"

"Great. Let's get started."

She blew out a slow breath, her eyes finding Captain Crawford's rehab schedule. *Great.* Eight weeks. Eight excruciatingly long weeks. This was going to be painful.

"Arghh." The handlebar of the weight machine snapped out of Colton's grip and crashed against the panel with a loud crack.

"Why don't we take a little break." Pecca handed him a bottle of water, but when he reached for it, his arm jerked and knocked it to the ground. "I'll get it—"

"I've got it." The words escaping his lips were harsher than he had intended. Colton twisted around, keeping his right arm close to his side, and used his left hand to pick up the bottle. When he straightened, he avoided meeting her eyes. Partly because he was embarrassed he'd been unable to hide the way his movements prohibited him from doing even the simplest tasks, but also because it was becoming clearer just how weak he was.

"You're doing really well."

Colton opened the bottle of water and brought it to his lips to avoid responding. What was he supposed to say, thanks? He had nothing to be grateful for when his body was failing him. He glanced at the clock and realized that maybe he did have something to be thankful for—their session was over.

"That's him!"

Colton and Pecca turned to see Maceo pushing his way through the door, a man limping in behind him.

"Maceo." Pecca gave Colton an apologetic smile before stepping around a rack of dumbbells to meet him at the door. "You know you're not supposed to interrupt me when I'm with a patient."

"That guy knows Vincent James." Maceo stopped, arms folded over his chest. He tilted his chin toward Colton. "Isn't that right?"

It took Colton a second to realize Maceo wasn't sharing his relationship with Vince for Pecca's benefit but for the man leaning on a cane behind Maceo.

"Tell him," Maceo prodded. "Tell him you know Vincent James and taught him the Saint James Fake."

"Sorry, Pec, he insisted," said the man who looked much too young to be using a cane. Early thirties, sandy brown hair, strong build. Was he another resident? A veteran?

"Captain Crawford, this is David Turner. He was also in the Army." Pecca turned to David. "A sergeant, right?"

"I guess I should call you sir." David shifted, stretching out his hand. Then he noticed Colton's arm moving and let his hand fall back to his side.

"Colton will be just fine."

Maceo tugged on the hem of Colton's shirt. "Tell him you know Vincent James. He doesn't believe me. Tell him the story about how you helped him get better."

"I didn't say you didn't know him." David lifted his hand, palm out as though he'd been caught. "I said it was unlikely."

"Tell him."

"Maceo." Pecca grabbed her son's hand. "That's enough."

"It's okay." Colton nodded at Maceo. "Vince and I grew up together in Jasper, Texas. Played football together in middle and high school. I have his number in my cell phone if you want to give him a call, but I'd suggest waiting until the season's over or he gets cranky."

"See." Maceo's chin jutted forward toward David. "Now you owe me a double scoop from Sandy's."

"You got it, kid," David said, ruffling Maceo's hair.

A weird feeling settled in Colton's gut at the man's affection for Maceo and the way he looked at Pecca. She hadn't introduced David as her husband, but he wondered if maybe they were a couple.

Colton's hand spasmed and clenched. He needed to get back to his room. "Nice to meet you," he said to David and started for the door. Then he stopped and said to Maceo, "Next time, always bet for the triple-scoop sundae with extra toppings."

Orange pill bottles lay on his bed. *"We'll start with a clean slate. Wean you off slowly."* After Colton's disastrous session with Pecca, the last thing he was going to do was come off his medications. They helped. Or why else would his doctors prescribe them?

Colton shook two yellow pills from one bottle and a large white one from another and stared at them. Before arriving in Walton, he'd had his prescriptions filled to make sure he had plenty. Chaplain Kelly would never know—except Colton would. He dropped one of the yellow pills back into the bottle before screwing the top back on. With a swig of water, he swallowed the meds—he wouldn't allow the movement disorder to take his integrity too.

Tap-tap-tap.

The light knock on the door echoed against the whirring of the ceiling fan, and Colton froze. He did a quick scan across the corners of his room, searching for a camera. He closed his eyes and shook off the paranoia caused by his insubordinate thoughts a second ago.

Tap-tap-tap. "Captain Crawford?"

It was a male voice. Sounded familiar. The day already felt too long, and he'd skipped dinner in the dining room on purpose. Eating had become a messy challenge, so he'd saved himself the embarrassment and stopped by the kitchen to get a sandwich he could eat in his room. Maybe if he didn't answer, whoever it was would go away.

"Captain Crawford, it's Chaplain Kelly. Just came to check on you."

Colton's eyes darted to the bottles of pills on his bed, a weird feeling penetrating his gut. Chaplain Kelly's timing seemed . . . fortuitous. Had he expected Colton's resistance and wanted to check on him to make sure he had obeyed? He pinched his eyes closed at his ridiculous thoughts. He quickly gathered the pill bottles, shoved them into his sock drawer, and went to the door.

Chaplain Kelly smiled. "I'm sorry to bother you, but I wanted to see how you were recovering from earlier."

"I'm better, thanks."

"If you're not busy, I'd like you to come meet a couple of the other residents in the lounge."

He had a dozen excuses at the ready, but one look at Chaplain Kelly's humble expression and Colton didn't have the courage to use any of them. Colton pulled his door shut and followed the chaplain down the hall, wishing the day would just end already.

Loud voices and laughter greeted Colton and Chaplain Kelly as they stopped near the threshold of the lounge. The gathering place took up a quarter of the second floor and was filled with long sofas and chairs. A large television was attached to a wall at the end of the room and a long table filled the space at the other end. Bookshelves were covered with board games and books. A media console held a half dozen remote controls, along with game consoles.

"Well, if it ain't the daisy who got his boots licked right out from under him by a gal."

Colton's gaze swung to an older African American man sitting in one of the club chairs, a wide smile lighting his face.

"Son, I didn't realize you were so big. That hot tamale nurse must be a lot stronger than I thought." This came from another older man with feathery silver hair combed over a bald head. He was holding a cup of coffee with gnarled, age-spotted hands, a crossword puzzle lying discarded on the table in front of him.

A man rolled up in a wheelchair, a tin of dominoes on his lap. He squinted up at Colton from beneath a black hat with big white lettering that spelled out ARMY. "You better speak up, boy. Put those grunts and fly-boys in their place." The hissed words barely escaped the man's lips as he rolled past him.

"Bah, I told you he was soft." The African American man smirked. "Don't make 'em like they used to, eh, Sarge?"

The man in the wheelchair—Sarge—responded with a withering look etched into his features. "What are you talking about, Sticks? I'd bet Cap here has seen more action than you on the battlefield and"—with a slick smile spreading across his face, Sarge looked at Colton—"off the battlefield."

The room filled with hoots and howls as Sticks swiped his hand in the air as if he were batting away the insult.

Colton swallowed. Cap? Were they referring to him? He looked over his shoulder at Chaplain Kelly, who was smiling.

"Welcome to D-Wing."

FIVE

HE TICKED OFF THE HOURS on his fingers before picking up his cell phone and dialing. After walking into the living room, he settled himself onto the couch and put his feet on the coffee table. When no one picked up after the fourth ring, he frowned.

"*Hola.*"

A breath of frustration left his lips. "*Hello*, Beatriz."

"Oh, hello, sir." The maid's tone shifted nervously. "I am sorry. I was getting the meal ready—"

"Do not let it happen again," he said, interrupting Beatriz's uneven English. "When you are in my home, you will speak English only. Especially in front of Diego."

"Yes, sir."

"Good. Now please get Alicia."

"Yes, sir."

He leaned over his legs and grabbed the remote control from a bowl. Flipping through the channels, he paused on the local news for a minute before continuing until he finally settled on a sports channel. The Dallas Mustangs were playing, and he had money on them.

"Hello."

"*Mi amor.*" Juan smiled. The sound of his wife's voice was refreshing. "Hello, my love. How are you?"

"Tired. Diego had soccer practice and insisted we take the team out for pizza afterward. Do you know how hard it is to wrangle seventeen eight-year-old boys?"

Juan chuckled, imagining the scene. "Is he there?"

Alicia released a sigh into the phone, and Juan pictured her crossing the Calacatta marble flooring he'd brought in simply

43

because she saw it used on a luxury home improvement show. His wife had impeccable—but expensive—taste. And he loved indulging her.

"He's taking his bath. I will bring him to the phone when he's done, but first I want to hear about your day."

Vincent James, the star receiver for the Mustangs, made a touchdown, putting the score in their favor and guaranteeing a payout. Juan barely smiled. "My work is boring and not worth the breath to repeat it."

"Then why do you stay? Quit. Come home. We can move into one of those tiny log homes up in the mountains, and I will make jam or something. Maybe tamales?"

The image of his wife in a plaid shirt, her long hair pulled back with strands framing her face, folding masa and red chile into cornhusks, made him smile—and long to draw her into his arms. "Would you really give up your Pilates classes and mommy-group lunches for me?"

"*Amor*, you make me sound pretentious."

Juan turned off the television and closed his eyes. "Not you."

Alicia laughed, and the melodious sound sparked an internal warming that reminded him just how long he'd been away from her. "How about when I return home, you and I escape to one of those islands with the little huts in the middle of the azure seas? The ones you have to take a boat just to get to? And we can make plans for our cabin in the woods."

"Mmm, that would be lovely," Alicia wistfully whispered into the phone, and he wondered if she missed him as badly as he missed her. "Ah, here is your son. Diego, your father is on the phone."

"*Bonjour*, Papa."

Juan sat forward. "Have you begun your French classes, *mijo*?"

"*Oui*, Papa, but I don't know very much yet."

"But you will and then you will be able to speak the language of sophistication."

"*Que es soph . . . sophisti—*"

"Sophistication," Juan said it again, slowly. "And in English, please. Or French," he added with a smile. "Sophistication means confidence. When you speak English, and soon French, you show your friends that you have confidence."

"Why not Spanish?"

Juan inhaled deeply. His son had yet to learn that many in this world had a polluted opinion of those who spoke his mother language. Alicia, with her tanned skin and chocolate-colored eyes, had enchanted Juan the second he saw her. Diego had been gifted his mother's beautiful Hispanic features, but along with it—the long history of prejudice.

"Spanish is in your heart, Diego. One day when you are a man, you will be able to win the adoration of a beautiful woman with the language of soul."

"Eww, Papa. Girls are gross."

"You won't always feel that way." Juan laughed. "Now, tell me about your soccer game this weekend. Are you going to win?"

"Will you be there?"

The ache in his chest was palpable. "I am sorry, mijo, but I have work—"

"For how long?" Diego whined. "You've already missed two games, and all the other dads come and help my friends warm up on the field before the game starts. I only have Victor."

"And is he good?" Juan asked, thinking of the aged driver he had hired for Diego and Alicia. "Does he know how to do a jump cut?"

"No. He's old. And out of shape. He said I should play golf."

"Golf is a good idea."

"No, Papa, that's boring." Diego whined again. "When are you coming home?"

Juan's cell phone beeped with an incoming call. He pulled it from his ear to check the ID, and when he saw the nameless number, he scowled.

"Soon, my boy, but for now I must work. Give your mom a kiss for me and tell her to stop watching those shows about log cabins."

"Okay, Papa."

The disappointment in Diego's voice could gut him like nothing else. "I love you, mijo. Remember, everything I do is for you and your mother."

"Yes, sir."

The incoming call beeped again in his ear. "I love you, Diego."

"I love you too, Papa."

The call with Diego ended and Juan stared at his cell phone, not sure he wanted to answer the incoming call. He clenched his jaw, his fingers tightening around the phone. If he didn't answer, there would be trouble. And that was the last thing he needed.

"Señor."

"You've kept me waiting."

"My apologies." Juan pushed himself off the couch and stalked down the narrow hallway he shared with the cockroaches. "A situation has come up at work."

Of the two depressing bedrooms, he had turned the smaller one into an office of sorts. His steps creaked across the floorboards until he was at his desk. He pulled out the chair and sat.

"I hope it will not keep you from doing your job?"

Juan looked up at the board on the wall, his eyes moving across the pictures and notes until they stopped on her face. "No."

"Then why have you not obtained the target?"

Fisting his hand, Juan leaned back, his chair squeaking. "I understand your urgency—"

"You understand nothing of my urgency!"

Juan pulled the phone from his ear. "*Lo siento*, Señor."

"I am paying you well, am I not? I brought you on because I trusted you and there is loyalty between us. You have proven yourself invaluable to the business, but do not think you cannot be replaced. That you are beyond my . . . reach."

Tension threaded into the muscles along Juan's back, and his hands shook. He was not as afraid of Señor's threat as he should have been. All Juan had to do was open a paper back home to see the handiwork of his boss's attempt to regain control of what—Juan's eyes flashed to her photo—she did.

No. It wasn't fear—it was rage.

Where one man had led with respect, his successor led with intimidation and insolence. Both were equally violent, but Juan owed his allegiance to the former and he was gone.

As calmly as he could, Juan chose his next words carefully. "Señor, I promise you will have her." He rocked his chair backward and forward, allowing the rhythmic squeak to soothe his temper. "But you must allow me to do the job you entrusted to me—my way. If not, then you might as well call the American police and give them your address."

A string of curses filled his ear until Señor finally took a breath. "*Escúchame*," he demanded. "*El tiempo se acaba.*"

The line went dead, and Juan set his phone on the desk. Yes, he would listen to Señor, but time was not running out—it was on his side. Juan stood and ran his thumb over the brown eyes staring back at him from the photo.

Time was on his side, and he would deliver.

SIX

ROUND TWO.

Today had to be better than yesterday. Pecca was determined to make sure that it was. Whatever it took, she was going to win Captain Colton Crawford over . . . or at least make up for her massive blunder.

Pecca took a deep breath and stepped into the gym. She released it when she found the room empty. Colton wasn't there yet. She looked to the spot she'd found him the day before—*shirtless*.

Squeezing her eyes shut, Pecca shoved the image out of her mind. Or tried to, anyway. It was proving to be as difficult to do as it was to get Maceo to eat his vegetables. Probably didn't help that after she got her son into bed last night, she spent hours searching the internet trying to get as much information as she could regarding movement disorders and what kind of therapy would help while an especially steamy episode of *The Bachelor* played in the background.

Pecca had sensed Colton's frustration at the end of his session yesterday and knew that if he was frustrated with his inability to do something, it would decrease his willingness to keep trying. It was a familiar cycle she'd experienced with Maceo as he continued to adjust to his prosthetic.

What she learned last night—besides how stupid easy it was to pull up a shirtless Colton in her mind when she was watching *The Bachelor*—was that body weight exercises, stretching, and aqua therapy were beneficial to patients with Parkinson's, chorea, and dyskinesia. And those were the most relatable diagnoses to Colton's PMD.

She had started to set out the TheraBands when she heard the door open and Colton walked in. Pecca swallowed. A flush of warmth fired up in her cheeks. "Good morning."

"Morning," he grumbled, his lips barely moving beneath his beard.

Ah, he wasn't a morning person. That was okay. She could do this. Pecca put on her biggest smile. "I spent all night researching a bunch of exercises that I think you're going to like. I want you to take it easy, not push yourself too hard as you get used to the routine. Then if you're up to it, I suggest we add a workout session at the pool in the afternoons."

Colton glanced toward the French doors and back. "Fine."

Fine? Was he purposely trying to be difficult? His arm jerked, and Pecca was riddled with guilt. The man was dealing with his own issues. If he didn't jump up and down for joy because of her late night, was she really going to think badly of him because of it?

Suddenly, the image of him jumping up and down, clapping his hands like a giddy cheerleader, came to mind and she almost laughed out loud. Swallowing the giggle, she steeled her expression and pointed to the colorful rubber tubing lined up on the floor.

"We'll start with the resistance bands."

Colton eyed the bands with disdain.

"I promise you'll feel it but not too bad," she added quickly when she saw his expression sour. "Just enough to know it's working, and I promise it won't be as bad as being taken down by a girl."

Pecca froze. Had she really just said that? Colton's hazel eyes shifted to her and she braced herself for his severe stare, only it wasn't there. And was that . . . ? There was a little lift to the edge of his lips. Was that the start of a smile?

Inexplicably, her heart swooped inside her chest and she smiled. Maybe round two was going to be better. She pulled a tiny remote from her pocket and clicked a button, and the large speakers mounted in the corners of the room came to life with a thumping beat. "Let's get started."

Forty-five minutes in, Pecca had nearly chewed through her lip watching Colton strain through the exercises. She knew he needed a break whether he admitted it or not, which she learned he would not, given the number of times she offered and he refused.

Pecca lowered the volume on the stereo. "You're doing great, Captain Crawford."

Colton stopped mid-exercise, letting the rubber band fall to his side. He turned to her. "I'm pretty sure that's the hundredth time you've told me that." He used the back of his hand to wipe the sweat from his brow. "On top of"—his voice pitched mockingly high—"'That's great,' 'Keep it up,' and 'Looking good,' though that last one is fine." His voice returned to normal. "Are you always this motivating?"

"I find it brings out the best in my patients." She went to the counter and grabbed a cold bottle of water from the fridge. She opened the water and tossed the cap before taking it to him. "And do I really sound that nasally?"

He shrugged and took the bottle of water with his left hand. After watching him, she learned it was his nondominant hand, which meant his condition was forcing him to relearn basic functions. Colton swigged from the bottle until it was empty.

"Would you like another?"

Wiping the wet droplets from his beard, he shook his head. "I'm good."

Pecca watched him reach for the bands again. "So, is the beard part of the whole 'let it go' movement?" She leaned her hip against the counter. "You got out of the military and now you're a hipster?"

"No." Colton ran his fingers over the scruffy hair growing along his jawline. "Putting a razor anywhere near my face or neck can be . . . dangerous, given my condition."

She closed her eyes, heat blossoming in her cheeks. Of course he couldn't shave. What was wrong with her? Opening her eyes, Pecca found him watching her. "I'm sorry, I didn't think about that."

"The hospital in DC had barbers who would come to our rooms and give a shave or haircut. My mom said she would try, but then I saw *her* hands shaking and figured I was safer to let it grow."

Pecca gave a stilted laugh. "Most of our residents ride into town in the van for haircuts. I never thought about the shaving part though."

Colton shrugged.

"I can ask Shirley about it and see if the barbers in town offer a shave, or if we can bring them here."

Colton gave another tight nod, then picked up the band and started back into his reps, but slower. The movements in his arm were more pronounced, and she could see him struggling. She needed to distract him.

"Your file says you live in Texas. Is that where you're from? Do your parents live there?"

"Yes."

Pecca frowned at his one-word answer. Maybe he didn't want to share about his life—too personal? She thought about her own life, and her mood darkened. Adrian still hadn't called her back about the SSB or Javier's cousin, and she hated to admit that the unknown had been messing with her mind.

The last couple of nights she kept finding herself looking over her shoulder, unable to shake the feeling that someone was watching her or hiding in the shadows. When Maceo got up in the middle of the night for a glass of water, the noise nearly gave her a heart attack and she yelled at him. And then she apologized all morning.

Colton cleared his throat and Pecca blinked, realizing he had finished and was watching her.

"Oh, um . . ." She looked down at her clipboard, trying to clear through the fog of her own fear to figure out what he'd asked her. "I, uh . . ."

"Your name. I was asking you about your name. It's unusual. Does it mean something?"

"Oh, yeah. Kind of. I have three siblings, all older, and I was sort of a surprise baby. The smallest and so my family started calling me Pequeña, which means small in Spanish. And that got shortened to Pecca."

"And Maceo?"

"Gift of God." Thinking of her little boy, she smiled. Despite his moodiness and the one schoolyard brawl, he truly was a gift.

"So, if Pecca isn't your real name, what is it?"

"Serena," Pecca deadpanned.

"Wow. Spoken with such enthusiasm."

She lifted her eyebrows. "Do I look like a Serena?"

Colton shrugged. "It's nice."

Pecca started to open her mouth to give him all the reasons why her personality didn't fit the calm and tranquil name, when she realized what he'd said, and suddenly there was an unexplainable uptick in her pulse. It was just a compliment. Not even a great one. *Nice.* And yet the back of her neck was growing warm just the same.

"Uh, so, Texas. What do you miss most about Texas?"

"What do you miss most about Texas?" Could that segue be any more obvious? But obvious of what? She was just trying to make conversation like she did with all her patients. Except . . . none of her other patients rattled her like this one did.

"Whataburger."

"What?"

Colton eyed her. "What I miss most about Texas right now is Whataburger."

"Oh, yes," she said quickly, tucking a loose strand of hair behind her ear. "Their honey butter chicken biscuits are the best."

"You're from Texas?"

"Mom." Maceo had walked into the gym, his attention on the iPad in his hand. "What are we having for dinner tonight, because Noah asked if—"

"Mac, watch out!"

Pecca's warning came too late. Maceo's toe caught the edge of the mat and pitched him forward, his prosthetic moving awkwardly to the side instead of in front of him. The iPad hit the ground, but before Maceo could, Colton's left arm had wrapped around him, bringing him back to standing.

"Whoa," Maceo said in awe. "That was cool."

"It was not cool." Pecca turned him so she could look him in the eye. "You could've been seriously hurt. How many times have I told you not to walk around staring at that thing? You have to watch where you're going."

Maceo's cheeks turned pink. "Sorry."

She bit the inside of her cheek. Staying mad at Maceo was nearly impossible. Kryptonite. That's what she and her family called him. "It's fine. But you need to apologize to Captain Crawford."

"Colton." A look Pecca couldn't decipher crossed over his face before he glanced down at Maceo. "And it's okay, but if you want to be good on the field, you've got to be quick on your feet." Colton bounced from side to side on the balls of his feet. "Always ready to read your QB."

Pecca frowned. "QB?"

"Quarterback, Mom," Maceo said with a roll of his eyes.

"Hey!" She playfully bumped Maceo's shoulder. "Maybe liver and onions are on the menu tonight."

"Eww." Maceo made a face. "Gross."

"I agree." Colton laughed.

The deep baritone sound woke something up in Pecca—something that had long been dormant. And it made her blush. Hard. So she flipped her wrist and checked the time. "Yikes, your session was over ten minutes ago."

Colton made a move to leave, but Maceo held up his hand.

"Wait." He mimicked Colton's move, though, due to his prosthetic, it was a little less fluid. "Like this?"

"Yep." Colton hunched, hands in front of him. The right one

jerked, but Colton wasn't focused on it—he was focused on Maceo. Facing off, Colton hopped left and Maceo mirrored the move. "See how you went right?" Colton went right and Maceo left. "That's right. You're anticipating my move. Good job."

Maceo's smile couldn't have grown any wider, and Pecca's heart twisted around in her chest. She wasn't prepared for or even willing to acknowledge the flood of emotion that hit her.

"Hey, Mom." With excitement lighting his eyes, Maceo turned to her. "Can Colton come to dinner with us tonight? I want him to meet Noah."

"Oh, um." She peeked up at Colton, who had shifted to avoid her gaze. Go to dinner with a patient? There had to be a rule about that, right? "I'm not sure we're going to the café tonight and—"

"Please, Mom," Maceo begged. "Then he can show me some more football moves." He turned to Colton. "Right?"

"Maceo." Pecca's tone held warning. "We can talk about it later."

"It's okay," Colton said. His arm jerked, and he glanced down at it before tucking it to his side. "I'd be happy to show you some moves another time."

Pecca sensed Colton's mood darken again, and at once she felt bad. Had she embarrassed him? Did he think his movements bothered her? That *she* was embarrassed? Licking her lips, she made a decision and blurted it out. "I would love to take you to dinner tonight if you're available."

Love?

Colton's gaze narrowed on her.

"I mean, to make up for yesterday." Pecca tugged Maceo back by his shoulders, taking him by surprise as he stumbled backward. "It would mean a lot to Maceo, and it would make me feel better, because I still feel really bad and the food is good and—"

"Mom?"

She took a breath, looking down at Maceo and then back to

Colton. "Sorry. Would you like to go to dinner at the Way Station Café with us tonight?"

"Please," Maceo added.

A few seconds passed between them, and Pecca could see him weighing his response. She wasn't sure if she was hoping he would refuse or accept.

"Okay."

Maceo pumped his fist. "Yes!"

Okay. He said okay. So Colton would be having dinner with her tonight. And Maceo. Yes, and Maceo. "Alright, so I'll give you the details this afternoon. I'm sorry I kept you so long this morning. You did really good today, by the way. And I'm excited to see you in the pool—I mean, swimming. For therapy." *Just stop talking.*

Colton's lip tilted into a smirk, and he released the bands into her hand. "See you this afternoon."

Watching him leave, Pecca slid down to the weight bench and closed her eyes, trying to ease the pounding in her head—or was it her heart? It was just a dinner to make up for the other day. She groaned. This couldn't go sideways at all, right?

SEVEN

"CAPTAIN COLTON CRAWFORD, I was wondering when you were going to come visit me."

The older woman with short white hair and a sparkle to her eyes smiled widely and wrapped Colton in a hug the second he stepped into the Way Station Café. He flashed a look to Pecca, who smiled with a wink.

"I've been waiting for you, honey," she said, pulling back but not letting him go. She looped her arm around his left elbow and escorted him into the café. "I'm Ms. Byrdie, and before I give you and Pecca our best table, I'm going to introduce you to everyone."

Colton swallowed and tossed a glance over his shoulder. Pecca had stopped to talk to a brunette woman carrying a pitcher and Maceo abandoned him, running up a set of stairs. His arm jerked, and Colton worried that accepting the dinner offer had been a mistake.

Thankfully, the round of introductions was quick. There was a group of regulars that included a trio of men who liked to fish, though it seemed one of them—the scrappiest of the three—actually caught more ducks with his boat than fish, giving him the moniker "Ducky"; a motorcycle-riding couple named Harley and Dottie, who had just returned from a mission trip to Haiti; and a college-aged girl working behind the counter, whose name tag said Bethany.

Most kindly obliged Ms. Byrdie with a friendly smile and a few questions about where Colton was from and if he was staying at the Mansion. Ms. Byrdie whispered that that's what most locals called Home for Heroes. She made a few more introductions, until

Colton's stomach growled, and with a quick wink, she hurried him over to a table near a large window with a view of downtown Walton.

"Ms. Byrdie, it smells delicious." Pecca walked over and gave the woman a hug before turning to Colton. "So, have you met everyone? Know their favorite food? Color? Blood type?"

"Oh, you hush now." Ms. Byrdie smiled. "It wasn't that bad, was it?"

Colton gave her a tight-lipped smile. "No, ma'am."

Ms. Byrdie beamed. "With manners like that, you're going to get a double helping of dessert."

"Ooh, and I heard it's your famous peach cobbler," Pecca said, sitting in the chair across from Colton. "You're a lucky guy."

Colton's arm hit the side of the table, sending the silverware clattering loudly. A few faces turned in his direction, and he tucked his chin. Yes, this was definitely a mistake. The worse his condition got, the more he avoided going out, especially to eat, but for whatever reason, he'd found it impossible to refuse Maceo's request. Or his mom's.

How was he going to do this? He didn't even want to eat in the dining room at Home for Heroes. Trying to eat with his left hand was proving to be hard, especially when his movements were bad. Colton looked for a menu. Maybe he could order a sandwich. Or fries. Explain he wasn't that hungry.

"Is there a menu?"

"Oh no, honey. We serve one hot meal in the evenings. Tonight's special is country fried steak." Ms. Byrdie grinned. "You two get settled, and I'll have your plates out in a few minutes. Bethany will be over with some sweet tea."

"Thank you, Ms. Byrdie."

"Thank you, ma'am."

True to her word, several minutes later Ms. Byrdie delivered to their table three home-cooked meals Colton bet were as mouth-watering as they looked. He looked at his silverware and back at the plate of fried goodness slathered in gravy. This was a disaster waiting to happen.

"You won't likely get a meal better than this anywhere within a hundred-mile radius," Pecca said as she motioned to someone over Colton's shoulder. Maceo ran up. "Did you wash your hands?"

"Yes, ma'am." Maceo held up his hands and sat. "Noah's doing homework, but he's going to come down to meet Colton when he's finished."

"See, Noah does his homework."

Maceo rolled his eyes and scooped a spoonful of mashed potatoes into his mouth.

Colton started to reach for his fork and then hesitated. It would be rude not to try and eat something, and the teasing aroma was causing his stomach to grow angry with hunger.

"Aren't you hungry?" Pecca asked, her fork paused midair. "Is something wrong?"

"Um, no." Colton balled the napkin in his lap. His right arm jerked and rattled the table, sending their sweet tea spilling over the edges of their glasses. "Sorry."

"It's okay," Maceo said around a bite. He placed his napkin over the spilled droplets as if it was the most natural thing to do. "So, do you think you could teach me the Saint James Fake?"

"Maceo."

"But Mom, if I know how to do it, maybe they'll let me on the football team."

Colton thought he saw Pecca flinch, but before she could answer, he spoke up. "I don't mind. I'm free in the afternoons after my appointments with Chaplain Kelly. If it's okay with your mom." He looked at Pecca, who was chewing on her lower lip. "I can teach you a few moves."

Maceo's fork clattered to his plate. "Please, Mom!"

Pecca looked between Maceo and Colton a few times before her shoulders relaxed. "Fine, but only if you eat your dinner and do all your homework—and promise to never, ever push another kid again."

"Unless it's for football, right?" Maceo held his finger up. "Because you have to push people in football, Mom."

Colton stifled a laugh, which earned him a harsh but playful smile from Pecca. He cleared his throat, hoping to calm the swell of feelings rushing through him. He reached for his glass of tea just as his arm twitched, sending his spoon and knife to the ground.

Without missing a beat, Maceo slid out of his chair and grabbed them, his attention still on his mom as he placed them in front of Colton. "It's called tackling."

"Well, is there such a thing as gentle tackling?"

"No, Mom," Maceo answered with exaggeration.

"You better finish, your friend is coming."

Colton turned and found the woman Pecca had been talking to earlier walking toward them with a tall man wearing a tan deputy uniform and a little boy with light brown hair who looked about the same age as Maceo.

"I'm sorry to interrupt your dinner, but I want to make sure you're saving room for dessert," the woman said. "Ms. Byrdie's cobbler is the best."

"Colton, this is my friend Lane Lynch." Pecca wiped her lips with her napkin. "She owns this lovely café, and her cinnamon rolls rival the cobbler, I can assure you."

"Well, I don't know about that." Lane blushed. "But I can send you home with a box of them to share with D-Wing, and you can judge for yourself."

Colton wasn't sure he wanted to take anything back to the men who called him Cap and kept razzing him about being sacked by his "hot tamale" nurse. He couldn't imagine what kind of heat he'd find himself under if they knew where he was and who he was with right now.

Hmm, maybe the cinnamon rolls were a good idea—a distraction to keep D-Wing off his back.

"Pleasure to meet you, Colton," the man in the uniform said. "I'm Charlie"—the man looked down at the boy in front of him— "and this is Noah."

Noah gave Colton a smile that was missing one front tooth. "What's wrong with your arm?"

"Noah!" Charlie's and Lane's voices collided, and each of them gave Colton an apologetic look.

"He's got a movement disorder," Maceo said, pushing his empty plate away. "It means his arm moves by itself."

Maceo's simple explanation, the way he didn't bat an eye adjusting for Colton's movements when he dropped or spilled something . . . it was easing some of the discomfort he had carried into the café. Somehow in his seven years of life, Maceo had mastered compassion and understanding—characteristics some adults didn't possess.

Colton's gaze slid to Pecca and an appreciation developed. At least that's how he was going to identify the feelings swimming in his chest. All afternoon he'd been trying to figure out if it was nerves, anxiousness, or something else entirely. The only conclusion he had come up with so far was that it started shortly after Pecca plowed into him the day before.

"You can't stop it?"

"Nope," Colton answered Noah. "It's like a silly puppy that can't sit still."

"Like Bane!" Noah said.

Now it was Colton's turn to be curious. He looked to Lane and Charlie.

"It's our dog."

"His dog." Lane stuck out her thumb toward Charlie. "Apparently it was a package deal."

"And I got the better deal." Charlie kissed Lane's temple while placing a protective hand on her protruding belly. "Right, buddy?"

"Colton's going to teach me some football moves," Maceo said proudly. "Maybe even the Saint James Fake."

Noah's eyes lit up and he turned to Colton. "You are? Can you teach me? Mom said I'm not allowed to play football with the other kids because she doesn't want my brains to get scrambled like eggs."

Colton laughed along with Lane and Charlie. "Your mom is pretty smart."

Noah made a face and Lane bumped him with her hip. "Hey."

"So, will you teach me too? I can throw the ball real good, right, Dad?"

Charlie scooped Noah up and lifted his arm. "The best. Now, why don't we let them finish dinner so they can have some of Aunt Byrdie's cobbler?"

"I'm already finished." Maceo pointed to his plate. "Can Noah and I have dessert together?"

"It's alright with me," Lane said, looking to Pecca, who nodded. "Alright, both of you to the counter." The words were barely out of her mouth before the boys were scrambling toward the barstools.

"I'm going to get in on that." Charlie grinned. "Great to meet you, Colton. Even if you fought on the wrong team. Oorah." He winked at Lane, who shook her head before returning her attention to Colton.

"Don't mind him. Before he wore that uniform, he wore one for the Marines."

Colton was grateful for the explanation, but it didn't explain how half the town knew who he was. He shifted in his chair. "You wouldn't happen to know if there was some kind of announcement in the paper about me moving here?"

"Welcome to Walton," Lane said with a laugh. She placed a hand at the small of her back, the other on her stomach. "I'm going to go grab you two some dessert before those guys eat it all."

"Lane's not kidding." Pecca pushed her plate aside. "I think half the town knew my name before my change of address even took effect."

"And I thought where I grew up was bad."

Bethany delivered two bowls of cobbler. The smell was too tantalizing for Colton to resist. With a purposeful movement, he grabbed his spoon and carefully scooped a bite into his mouth. The tangy sweetness took him back to his summers camping near the Brazos River with his family. He missed Texas. Missed his family.

Pecca took her first bite, closing her eyes as she chewed. Colton let his gaze wander over her features. Tiny lines edged her eyes, no doubt from the way the skin crinkled when she smiled. Her nose had a delicate slope that highlighted her cheeks, balancing the roundness of her face in a very flattering and feminine way. His eyes fell to her lips, and he swallowed as they moved—

"It's the best, isn't it?"

Colton tried for another bite, determination making his movements slow and deliberate. A good distraction from the way he was staring at his nurse. His mouth was watering by the time the spoon reached his tongue. His eyes flickered back to Pecca, and he realized she was waiting for his answer. He gave a nod, embarrassed.

"So, you're a dessert first kind of guy, huh?" Pecca said, eyeing his bowl.

He looked down. His dinner plate was barely touched. Maybe he could get it to go.

"I can wrap that up for leftovers." Lane was at their table again, a coffee pot in her hand. "Even add an extra helping of cobbler."

"I'd appreciate that, ma'am." Colton leaned forward and retrieved his wallet from his back pocket. "I'll also take the check."

"No." Pecca reached across the table and laid her hand on his arm. The heat of her touch sent his gaze right back to her lips. "I told you this was my treat to make up for the other day."

"I can't let you pay—"

"Neither of you are paying," Lane cut in with a smirk. "It's on the house."

Colton opened his wallet. "It's okay, I can pay."

"I'm sure you can, but another thing this town is known for besides its gossip is its appreciation for the men and women who serve in the military. We're grateful for the sacrifice. Giving you a home-cooked meal is the least we can do." She smiled. "Just promise you won't call me ma'am anymore. Makes me feel old."

"I can do that." Putting his wallet back into his pocket, he took in the gracious woman who couldn't have been much older than Pecca. "Thank you, I appreciate the meal." He pushed his chair back gently. "I should probably get back."

Lane handed the coffee pot to Bethany and grabbed his plate. "Let me get that wrapped for you." She shot Pecca a look before walking to the counter and disappearing into the kitchen.

"Let me get Maceo, and we'll be ready to go."

"Not necessary." Colton stood. "Home for Heroes is not that far from here. I can walk back."

Pecca looked out the window and back at him. "But it's dark."

"The trail is lit."

She frowned. "I really don't mind. We don't live far, and it's on the way."

Colton wasn't sure, and he was probably reading into her offer, but it sounded like Pecca wasn't ready for him to leave. Yeah right. He was definitely reading into it. The result of many long and lonely nights since his diagnosis.

"It's a nice night, and I could use the exercise."

Pecca gave his body a once-over and then blushed, her brown eyes wide in disbelief before she cringed. "I'm sorry. I didn't mean for that to look the way it did. It's just that you look fine—I mean, not like fine-fine, just like you don't need to run or walk or burn calories—"

"What my flustered friend is trying to say is that if you'd like a ride back, she'd be *more* than happy to take you." Lane held up a bag holding his untouched dinner as Pecca gave her a less-than-subtle jab.

"It's alright, really. It was nice meeting you and your family." He took the bag of leftovers and started toward the door, overhearing Lane's loud whisper.

"You didn't tell me he was so good-looking."

"I heard that." Charlie's voice echoed across the room and the remaining customers, hearing the exchange, laughed.

With his cheeks flaming, Colton waved a quick farewell before slipping out the door. Pecca had talked about him? When? He hadn't been in town more than forty-eight hours yet. And what had she said? He took a deep, purposeful breath. His hand clenched open and closed, the joints in his fingers aching. A walk would do him good. He could burn some energy and not think about—

"Colton, wait."

He turned and saw Pecca exiting the Way Station Café with Maceo at her side.

"Mom, I forgot my backpack."

"Hurry and go get it." Pecca tilted her head toward the café. "One minute or I'm leaving without you." She turned to Colton and held up her car keys. "You wouldn't let me drive you here, but I insist on giving you a ride back."

"It's really not necessary. I don't mind walking back."

"Maceo insists. Says it's the nice thing to do, but I think he just wants to chew your ear off about Vincent James." Pecca clicked the key fob and a horn beeped from a silver Camry. "If you don't let me give you a ride back, then he'll torture me about a game I know nothing about."

Colton found it hard not to smile. He looked over at the trail and back to her, struggling to find the willpower to refuse. "Okay."

"Thank you," she said with exaggeration as she walked toward her car. "Look," she began, turning so abruptly he almost ran into her. "Oh. Sorry."

He took a step back. "My fault."

"I'm sorry about Lane. What she said in there. I never told her you were, um . . ." She bit her lip. A loose strand of hair danced around her face on a breeze. "She's pregnant. Hormonal. And recently married. To Charlie. Which has her all 'la-la' for love or trying to match people up." Her eyes rounded. "Not that she was trying to do that with us. You and me. She knows I'm your nurse." Pecca gave a nervous laugh and then sighed, regaining her composure. "What I'm trying to say is that when she said I didn't tell her you were, um . . . well, I only told her I had a new patient and you were from Texas. *Nothing* else."

The reflection from the twinkling lights on the patio danced in Pecca's eyes, and suddenly he wanted to let his eyes drift to her lips. He might've given in to the temptation if a flash of green hadn't caught his attention.

Colton, instinctually on alert, jerked back. He swung his gaze over his shoulder, unsure if his eyes were playing tricks on him, when he caught the reflection of light again and had no doubt.

"Get down!"

"What?"

Pecca's question was muffled as he grabbed her and pulled her to the ground beneath him before a crack over their heads shattered the passenger-side window, raining glass down on them.

Thwap-thwap.

Pecca screamed, and Colton sheltered her. "Shh, just stay down."

"Wh-what's happening?" Pecca wiggled beneath him. "What's going on?"

I have no idea. Were they really just—Colton's head swiveled side to side, his eyes scanning the area, but it was too dark to see. Pecca's panicked breathing pressed against his chest rapidly and—not wanting to crush her—he shifted his weight.

"Colton—"

"Hold on." He looked around a second and third time before turning his eyes on the café. No one inside seemed aware of what had just happened, and truthfully, he was still trying to wrap his own head around it. After another quick look overhead at the missing window, his eyes trailed down to where he thought he'd find two more holes, but he didn't.

Did that just happen?

With Pecca's scream still ringing in his ears, he began analyzing the events like he always did when he was in the field. Except he wasn't in the field. He was in Walton.

"What happened?" Pecca asked. "Was it a rock or something?"

Colton rolled to his side, putting his body in front of her like a shield, and glanced over his shoulder in search of the green laser. *Nothing.* He turned to her.

"It wasn't a rock, Pecca. Someone just took a shot at us."

EIGHT

NOT JUST ONE SHOT.

Three.

Someone had taken three shots at her.

Pecca surveyed the activity in her home. Charlie was pacing in her kitchen on his cell phone. Deputy Wilson's huge frame stalked around her home, checking windows and doors. Colton . . . where was he?

The sound of voices drew her eyes to the front window, where she found him and Sheriff Huggins talking on the porch. *Someone just shot at us.* Colton had refused to let her get up until he was sure the shooter was gone. Pecca hadn't even had a chance to register his words as he helped her up and into the Way Station Café. She must've looked a mess because every eye turned to her direction, and in a dizzying blur, things started happening.

Pecca looked at her trembling fingers. Three shots. She'd had no idea what was happening when Colton pushed her to the ground the second before her passenger-side window exploded. Charlie and Sheriff Huggins located two more bullets buried in the trunk of the live oak next to her car. She hadn't heard any of them—only the explosion of glass erupting over her.

Ms. Byrdie had come to the house and was putting Maceo to bed. The town's matriarch was also Sheriff Huggins's wife and one of the gentlest souls Pecca knew. Just being in her presence evoked peace. Exactly what Pecca needed right now.

Charlie ended his call and came over to the couch just as Colton and Sheriff Huggins walked in. "How's Lane?" Pecca asked.

"She's fine." The sheriff's blue eyes remained on her. "Everyone is fine."

69

Except her. She was not fine. "Wh-what happens next?"

Sheriff Huggins sat on the couch next to her and grabbed her chenille throw and wrapped it around her shoulders. If the sheriff was well-known for anything, it was his patriarchal protectiveness, which he extended to everyone in Walton. Pecca had seen glimpses of it a few months ago with Vivian DeMarco, Ryan's girlfriend, but now she was on the receiving end.

"Well, honey, we're going to ask you some questions." His bright blue eyes peered down on her with an almost fatherly love. "Are you feeling up to it?"

Movement from the corner drew her attention to Colton. His arm was shaking. More than it had been earlier. Pecca feared it was because of her. Because of this whole ordeal. Colton came to Home for Heroes to recover—not to get shot at.

Colton shifted under her gaze. "I can leave."

"Actually," Sheriff Huggins said, turning his focus to Colton. "We need to ask you some questions too."

Confusion dimmed Colton's hazel eyes. "Like?"

"You served in military intelligence."

It wasn't a question, and Colton's expression tightened. "Yes, sir."

"Any reason you might be a target?"

"Me?"

"Him?"

Pecca's and Colton's voices collided, as did their eyes. She quickly turned hers on Sheriff Huggins. He couldn't be serious.

"Sir, with all due respect, I've been out of the Army for more than a year now and was"—Colton's arm shook—"discharged with a clear record. No one knows I'm here but family."

In that half-second explanation, Pecca watched Colton's body shift into the rigid posture of a soldier. She licked her lips. Why would Colton's career in the military make him a target? Only one person was responsible for what happened tonight and it was her. She needed to tell them the truth.

"It's me." Her voice shook. "I think I'm the target."

Three sets of eyes locked on her, and she shifted beneath the tension. Sheriff Huggins put a gentle hand on her shoulder.

"What do you mean, honey?"

Pecca looked over her shoulder toward the hallway where Maceo's room was. He had to be sleeping by now, right? She turned her attention back to the men in front of her and took a breath.

"My brother, Adrian, called me a few nights ago and told me that my ex . . ." Her eyes fluttered to Colton, and a pang of fear entered her chest. Did she really want him to hear this? What would he think of her? And why was that bothering her? She'd just been shot at and so had he. The least he deserved was to know why.

"My ex, Javier Torres, is up for parole. My brother told me members of the South Side Barrio, a gang he belonged to, might be looking for me to testify on his behalf."

"Why?"

She turned to Charlie. "Adrian said the gang wants Javier out of prison. I hadn't realized until his arrest how influential he was—it's the main reason I left El Paso. I wanted to protect Maceo from that atmosphere."

"And you think the gang members would come after you here?" Colton's face was as grim as his tone. "Shoot at you?"

Pecca ran her palms down the thin material of her scrubs. "If you'd asked me that a few hours ago, I would have said no, but now . . . I'm not sure." Her eyes lifted to Colton again, and her pulse slowed at his expression. She'd seen that look before when he was in the gym and was angry with himself, except this time— was he angry with her?

"Look, I'm having a really hard time trying to make sense of this. When I spoke with Adrian, he didn't think anyone from the SSB knew where I was and . . ." She looked at Sheriff Huggins and Charlie but avoided looking at Colton. "As crazy as this sounds, I can't imagine Javier doing this."

"Given what you've told us," Charlie said, his eyes sympathetic, "it's going to be hard to rule this out as accidental. We don't normally have random shootings—"

"Sir," Deputy Wilson said as he walked up, his attention directed to Sheriff Huggins. "Beverly Wilcox called in a complaint a few days ago. Said someone had been shooting at the old barn on her property."

"See." Pecca, feeling slightly desperate to find another explanation for what had happened tonight, latched onto that fact like a lifeline. "Maybe someone was out there shooting for fun. They do that in small towns, right?"

"Not usually with a laser scope." Colton pressed off the wall. "Or a silencer."

"Which is why we're going to investigate all possibilities." Sheriff Huggins rose to his full height. He ran a hand through his thick white hair before settling both hands on his gun belt. "Pecca, if it's alright with you, I'd like Charlie to contact Adrian and get all the information he can regarding the South Side Barrio and Javier's upcoming parole." Pecca nodded. "Until we rule them out, I'm going to leave a patrol outside your home—"

"What about when she's not at home?" Colton's voice was cold as steel. "Tonight they took the shot when she was out."

Pecca studied the man standing sentry near her door. If the SSB had found her, she had just put his life in danger too. Yet his concern was for her. Emotion burned the back of her throat. The moody man she had tried to win over was winning her over with his unassuming grit, and it felt like she'd barely scratched the surface. What else was Colton hiding beneath that gruff exterior?

Charlie shifted. "We don't have the manpower to put someone on her at all times."

"No," Pecca said. "That's too much." She looked to Sheriff Huggins. "I'm happy to give you Adrian's number and let him work with Charlie in your investigation. And if you want to put a car outside my house, I'm okay with that too, but I moved across the country because I was desperate for Maceo to grow up where he feels safe. We don't know for sure that it was the SSB that fired the shots."

Without words, the protective huddle of men around her made it clear they thought otherwise.

Sheriff Huggins's face creased in thought before he pressed his lips into a tight line. "This is an active investigation, and while I understand your feelings, Pecca, I can't allow you to tie my hands. If I feel there's a threat against you or anyone else in my town, I will respond accordingly."

Pecca's shoulders sank.

"What if I help?" Colton said. "While she's at work. I'm there. I have nothing else to do."

"No," Pecca said quickly, seeing the shadow of hurt line the edges of his eyes. Colton wasn't there to put his life in danger on her behalf. Pecca cringed, realizing he may have already done that, but she wasn't going to let him do it again. She was his nurse—his advocate—and her only job was to help him get healthy.

Not injured—or killed.

"You're my patient."

"I think it's a good idea." Charlie nodded. "Just while we're investigating."

"Wait." Pecca's brows pinched together. From the corner of her eye, she saw Colton's body go rigid. "You can't ask that of—"

"I want to help."

Pecca turned to Colton and saw something in his eyes that made her breath catch in her throat. Something about his offer sounded like it was coming from a need. A need to help maybe as much as to prove he could? And for a reason she couldn't exactly pinpoint, she wanted to give that to him.

"Okay."

Colton seemed to relax, and a flicker of emotion met his hazel eyes that caused her heart to beat faster.

"Well, that's settled then." Sheriff Huggins tilted his head toward the door. "I'll have Deputy Wilson cover your house tonight. Deputy Lynch will give Colton a ride back to the Mansion, and I'll go grab my wife and take her home so you can try to get some sleep."

"Thank you."

Charlie gave Pecca a quick hug and whispered that Lane would check in with her in the morning. Deputy Wilson followed him out the front door, passing Colton, who remained where he was. She hugged Sheriff Huggins and Ms. Byrdie, who both made promises to check in as well. *This is why I moved to Walton.* Since she'd had to uproot Maceo from his family, she had wanted to be sure that wherever they landed, he still understood the value of having people in his life who cared about him.

"We'll keep you updated on any new information." Sheriff Huggins grabbed his wide-brim hat and paused at the door to say something to Colton that earned him a tight nod.

"What did he say?"

Colton's hazel eyes fell to hers. "He assured me he would take care of you."

"He will," Pecca said, feeling her heart beating heavy in her chest. "I . . . I don't want you to feel obligated to help though." A flicker of hurt passed over his face, and Pecca immediately regretted her words. "What I mean is that you came here to get better, and I wouldn't want my mess to interfere with your progress. Or cause any setbacks."

The muscles in his jaw flinched. "Don't worry about me. It's not like I'm doing anything special. Just keeping an eye on the situation while you're at work."

Colton turned on his heel and started down the porch to Charlie's squad car. His coarse tone said she had hurt him, and that bothered her. A lot. Closing the door, she rested her forehead against it. *"Don't worry about me."* Ha. That was her job as his nurse. Only the feelings percolating inside her warned her that the line in her professional relationship with Colton Crawford had just become blurred.

Colton's gaze didn't leave the passenger-side mirror until Pecca's house disappeared from view. "Everyone knows that what happened tonight was not some hillbilly out shooting for fun, right?"

Charlie wheeled the squad car onto Ford Avenue in the direction of Home for Heroes. "We can't rule it out."

"You're a Marine. I don't need to spell out what it looks like when a laser sight is used and there's no report." That Colton hadn't heard the familiar crack of a gun firing unnerved him. "That wasn't a random incident."

"I agree, but we have to do our due diligence—and that means checking into every possibility."

The way Charlie said "checking into every possibility" brought Colton's thoughts back to Sheriff Huggins's earlier question. "Are you still thinking someone might be targeting me?"

"Can you be certain something from your career hasn't followed you?"

Colton ground his molars. "Yes, but I can reach out to a friend of mine and double-check."

"That'll help." Charlie pulled in front of Home for Heroes and parked. Colton faced him. "Tomorrow morning I'll call Pecca's brother, Adrian, and get as much information as I can regarding Javier Torres and the South Side Barrio."

Colton was planning to get some information too—only he'd be using his own resources. He had made up his mind the second Pecca started looking for another explanation for what happened tonight.

"Do you think it's strange they didn't shoot her?" The question made Colton sick. The last thing he wanted to think about was what could've happened if he hadn't seen that green beam of light.

"What do you mean?" Charlie asked.

"Someone with a scope on their rifle isn't usually a novice, and yet they missed," Colton said.

"Which means maybe it really was an accident."

Colton shot Charlie a look, and he could tell the deputy was just playing devil's advocate. "Except if what Adrian told Pecca is true—that the gang wants her to testify on her ex's behalf—why would they shoot at her?"

"Or miss, you mean?"

"Exactly. The two shots that hit the tree came after we were already on the ground. It's like they weren't even aiming at us."

"So you don't believe the shooting was random, yet you sound like you have a theory."

"I'm just trying to analyze the information."

"How come I get the feeling you're going to be doing your own investigation?"

"Would that be bad?" Colton said nervously. "I have resources that could prove to be helpful."

"Technically, you're part of the investigation." Charlie raised his eyebrows. "As long as you share your information, I don't see why we can't work together on this." He shrugged. "And you are helping us keep an eye on Pecca."

A charge of electricity zipped through him, and his arm jerked. Looking down at it, Colton remembered Pecca's insistence that he was here to get better and she didn't want him to have any setbacks. For some reason, that bothered him. Did she not think he could do something as simple as keep an eye on her?

What if he couldn't?

"If I hear back from Adrian tomorrow," Charlie said, "I'll swing by and let you know."

"Sure." Colton opened the passenger-side door and slid out of the car. "Thanks for the ride."

When Charlie pulled out of the parking lot, Colton started across the wide lawn. The memory of tossing the football around with Maceo made him smile. The memory of Pecca running him down made him chuckle. The still-fresh memory outside the Way Station Café sobered him.

He hadn't been exaggerating when he told Charlie the scenario would be a lot different if he'd missed the recognizable green beam of a scope. What if he had missed it? Colton scanned the towering live oaks lining the edge of the Ogeechee River and the back of the Mansion. So many places for a shooter to hide.

Dread coiled around his gut. Maybe tonight he'd been lucky. If there was a next time, the results might be different. If the Army didn't trust him to fulfill his oath, what made him think he could protect Pecca and Maceo?

A familiar voice filled his mind. *"If you want to win the game, you got to know who you're playing."* Colton's uncle Jack loved football as much as he did and never missed a game or an opportunity to coach him from the sidelines, much to the irritation of his actual coaches. However, Colton had carried this piece of advice with him into his career in intelligence. His job was to know how the enemy operated so he could protect his troops.

Colton tugged his cell phone from his pocket and dialed. If he wanted to protect Pecca and Maceo, then he first needed to know who their enemy was. And there was only one person Colton trusted to help him.

"Brah, do you know what time it is?"

"Lunchtime?" Colton checked the time on his phone. It was just after eleven. "Let me guess, loco moco?"

"How'd you know?"

Chief Kekoa Young was a cryptologist for the US Navy, and when Colton met him at a security summit in DC, he had brought in the island favorite and called it a "taste of home." The taste of home inside the Styrofoam container included a pile of rice and a hamburger patty slathered in brown gravy with two over-easy eggs on top.

"Lucky guess."

Colton lowered himself to the first step outside of the Mansion. It felt kind of good referring to his new residence like a local. "Late night?"

"You know I work best at night, brah."

He did, and that's why he knew it would be okay to call. "I have a favor."

"What you need, brah?"

Kekoa's pidgin was something that had taken Colton a bit of time to get used to, but once he got the gist of the island language, it quickly became a comfort whenever he spoke with his Hawaiian friend.

"I've got two favors. First, I need you to check and see if I've been marked—"

"Whoa, brah, you in trouble?"

"I don't think so, but there was a bit of an incident tonight that has me wondering if something from my past may have followed me."

"Okay, and number two?"

"I need you to use your skills to check into someone else for me."

"Name?"

Colton made a face. He had forgotten Javier's last name. "I only have a first name. Javier. He's in prison somewhere in Texas and is associated with a gang called the South Side Barrio in El Paso."

"Javier? In a gang? From El Paso?" Kekoa said, sounding like he was speaking around a mouthful. "Are you trying to make this as hard as possible?"

"Thought you said you were the Navy's best cryptologist?"

"Brah, I'm good, but you giving me kibble."

Colton leaned the back of his head against the railing post, trying to think what other information he could give Kekoa, but he didn't have much. Except, he did. Pecca. "You can try Pecca Gallegos."

"Pecca Gallegos," Kekoa repeated. "Anyone else?"

"Wait." What was he doing? If Kekoa pulled up Pecca's name, whatever information was out there would come back, and it was a violation of her privacy.

"You there?"

"Yeah. I'm just . . ." Colton stared up at the blanket of stars twinkling against the inky sky. A year ago he wouldn't have thought twice about looking into someone's background if it served the mission, but this wasn't a mission and he wasn't in the intelligence business.

Not anymore.

"So you don't want me to check into this Pecca person?"

Colton swallowed. *Know your enemy*. Pecca wasn't convinced the gang or her ex were involved tonight. If she knew . . .

"Her name is Serena. Serena Gallegos."

NINE

THE FEELING PENETRATED PECCA'S GUT, and no matter what she did, she couldn't shake it. Since Friday, she'd been jumping at the slightest noise, looking over her shoulder, and flipping on as many lights as she could, trying to extinguish the shadows messing with her mind.

"Mom!"

Pecca jerked with a cringe. This had to stop. Maceo had already started noticing her jumpiness, which she quickly blamed on Halloween being right around the corner. It was her least favorite holiday, and the stores had already begun marketing the morbid day.

"Mom! We're going to be late."

Sheesh. How many mornings had she had to light a fire under Maceo to get him out of bed and now *he* was rushing *her*? Pecca yanked up her duvet, tucking it beneath the pillows, and adjusted the books stacked on the nightstand before pausing at the threshold of her bedroom. She gave it another once-over. Everything looked the way it should, yet something felt amiss. What was it?

"Moooommm!"

Pecca shook the shudder away. If she had anything to worry about, Charlie would've said something to her when they spoke after church on Sunday. Or Adrian when he called her after speaking with Charlie. But so far they had no leads and nothing but her suspicions to indicate Javier or the SSB were involved.

"Coooommming," Pecca said, mimicking her son. Inside the kitchen she found Maceo pulling the straps of his backpack over his shoulders. Breakfast dishes were not sitting in the sink as usual. "Did you put your dishes in the dishwasher?"

"*Si*, Mama."

The Spanish reply flipped her heart. She stared down at her son. "Who are you and what have you done with my son?"

"Come on, Mom." Maceo pulled at her hand. "I don't want to be late for school."

Okay. Now she knew something was up. "What's going on, mijo?"

"Nothing." He drew the word out. "Can we go now?"

A glint in Maceo's eyes said it was more than nothing. She eyed him, grabbing her keys from the bowl by the door. "Your rush to get to school wouldn't have anything to do with a certain patient of mine knowing Victor whatever his name is, would it?"

"Vincent James." Maceo stopped dead in his tracks, sending her crashing into his back. The jolt caused him to tumble forward, his prosthetic creaking, into a bookshelf. A framed picture of her and Maceo crashed to the ground.

"I'm sorry, Mama." Maceo reached for the frame, twisting around on the ground. "It's not broken."

"Mijo, that was my fault. Are you okay?"

Maceo pulled himself up and tugged his backpack tighter over his shoulder. "Yeah."

Pecca didn't miss the scornful look he gave his prosthetic. She'd seen Colton give his own arm, though flesh and bone, a similar look whenever it jerked. Part of her believed Colton and Maceo had bonded over more than football the day she found them playing on the lawn. And on Friday she hadn't missed the flicker of boyish excitement that spread over Colton's face when Maceo asked for some help with the game. Had she really just referred to Colton as boyish? Nothing was boyish about Colton—especially when he was shirtless.

Ayyy. Pecca took the picture frame from Maceo and forced her mind back to a G rating. Colton was her patient, and it was unethical to think of him like that. Right?

Yes!

Right.

"Ready." She set down the frame on the dust-covered bookshelf and hesitated, noticing the empty space next to it. *Huh*. Her fingers brushed over an area that wasn't dusty. An area where something was missing. "Maceo, what happened to the picture that was here?"

Maceo was tying his shoe. "What picture?"

"It was right here." Pecca tapped her finger on the shelf where the picture should've been. "The one after your first surgery. With Tia Claudia, Grandma, and Grandpa." Maceo still hadn't looked up. "Maceo."

Her sharp tone sent his eyes upward. He glanced to where she was pointing and then back at her before shrugging. "I can't remember."

Pecca frowned, the odd sensation returning. "I could swear this is where I kept it." She took in the family room, scanning the shelves near the television and the side tables on either side of the couch. No picture. Was she wrong? Had she stuck it somewhere else and forgotten she moved it?

"Come on, Mom." Maceo tugged her toward the front door. "We're going to be late. You don't want me to get suspended again, do you?"

That snapped her out of her confused daze. "No. No more suspensions." Ruffling Maceo's black hair, she gave him a nudge through the front door before looking over her shoulder to the vacant space on the shelf.

I'm being ridiculous. Pecca pulled the door closed and locked it. She was allowing paranoia to take root and blossom into something she didn't want in her life—fear.

⁓⁓⁓⁓⁓⁓

Two hours later, Maceo was well into his school day, Pecca had already worked with her first patient of the morning, and now she was debating whether her nerves could handle another cup of coffee. Nerves that had nothing to do with Friday's events and everything to do with her next patient.

"Here's the kit you asked for."

Pecca jumped at Shirley's intrusion into her thoughts. She turned to find the robust receptionist in a bright poppy-colored blouse and black slacks. The color on anyone else would've been glaring, but on Shirley, it highlighted her ebony skin in a way that made it glow.

Shirley set the box on the table. "You okay?"

"I'm fine." Pecca, wanting to avoid Shirley's uncanny ability to read faces, busied herself with the coffee pot. The last thing she needed was for her to suspect Pecca had feelings for Colton—which she didn't. "Would you like some coffee?"

"No, thank you, honey." Shirley opened the fridge and pulled out the hazelnut creamer and handed it to Pecca. "The doctor says I need to cut back. I've only had two cups this morning."

"Oh?" Pecca peeked over Shirley's shoulder to the travel mug on the receptionist's desk. "Doesn't that thing hold twenty ounces? That's like three cups."

"Hush now, baby." Shirley's lips pinched into a smile. "I let you keep to your business, you let me keep to mine."

"Fair enough." Pecca raised her cup of coffee in acknowledgment. Shirley didn't have a malicious bone in her body, but she wasn't one to pass up sharing gossip. That she hadn't hounded Pecca about Friday night the second she came in to work spoke highly of Sheriff Huggins's and Charlie's abilities to keep the incident quiet.

"Your next patient is already in the gym." Shirley's eyebrows bounced above her brown eyes. "I'm *more* than happy to learn his business."

Pecca coughed as she spewed coffee across the table. Shirley's laughter was as hearty as she was, and it filled the entire staff kitchen as she grabbed paper towels from the roll. Pecca wiped her mouth and the drops that had landed on her violet scrubs.

"Shirley, if your husband heard you talking like that—"

"He'd spit his coffee out just like you, honey." Shirley finished wiping up the coffee. "He knows I ain't never gonna leave him. Thick and thin, sickness and health. All that stuff meant something when we said it. Still does." She tossed the wet towels into the trash can and turned to Pecca. Giving her a wink, she said, "But a girl can still appreciate—"

"God's handiwork or something like that," Pecca finished.

"Or something like that."

There was no mistaking Shirley's thinly veiled innuendo, but Pecca wouldn't address it or how often thoughts of Colton came to mind. When she wasn't jumping at shadows, Pecca was replaying the way he'd jumped in to protect her. And when he'd offered to stay and keep watch . . .

Heat tickled the apples of her cheeks.

As if on cue, Pecca's watch beeped. Time for her next patient. She grabbed the box Shirley had brought in.

"Gotta go."

"Make him work, baby."

Pecca left the girlish giggling of Shirley behind and headed for the gym. She found Colton sitting on a weight bench near the locker room—his shirt still on. *Head out of the gutter, Pecca.*

His eyes were closed. He had his earbuds in and his lips moved, but no sound came out. Was he singing? Meditating? Praying? Whatever he was doing, Pecca didn't want to interrupt. At least not right away.

Instead, she let her eyes roam the contours of his face. The jawline that stretched into the short, gruff beard that made him appear older than his thirty-two years. Creases in the skin near his eyes gave her the impression that, at one time, Captain Crawford had smiled a lot. Furrow lines crossed his forehead, and she wondered if they'd come about from the things he'd seen and done in the military. Or were they from his frustration over the movement disorder?

Her gaze slipped to his right arm and the twitching in his fingers. What would it feel like to lace hers between them? They clenched tight and then his hand jerked, shocking her out of her trance.

"Morning."

Colton's greeting drew her eyes to his. Heat sizzled across her face and neck. She'd just been caught staring at her patient. *So professional.*

"Good morning." She tried to sound extra perky, hoping that would distract him from her indiscretion. She looked down at the box in her hand and held it up. "I brought this."

He stood and closed the distance between them. "What is it?"

"A shaving kit." Pecca turned her attention to the box and opened it up to reveal a razor, a travel-size can of shaving cream, and a tiny bottle of aftershave. "I spoke with Chaplain Kelly about bringing in a barber to offer cuts and shaves for the residents—he thought it was a great idea—but they won't be here until next week. So I brought this, because I thought maybe you'd like a shave before then."

He took the box in his left hand, leaving the right to move at his side. "I, uh . . ." He took a breath. "I can't shave. Right-handed. But thanks."

"Oh, I know." She bit the inside of her cheek and met his eyes. "I'm going to do it."

Five minutes later, Pecca was beginning to second-guess her altruistic gesture. She'd just finished spreading shaving cream over Colton's face and hadn't realized what being so close to him was going to do to her pulse.

Pecca forced herself to breathe—act like the professional she was. "You ready to lose your furry friend?"

"Are *you* ready?"

"Me? Oh, sure! I've done this a time or two for patients. No big deal."

Colton's eyes flashed to her hand. The razor she held over his face shook slightly, giving her away. "Just go slow."

Slow. Right. Taking a breath, Pecca steeled her nerves and

pressed the razor to his cheek. Her eyes moved to his hazel ones gazing up at her in absolute trust. With a slow and gentle motion, she slid the razor across his cheek.

For the next several minutes, under his watchful stare, she continued to bring the edge of the blade tenderly across his face over and over until a basin of water was filled with cloudy water and the remnants of his beard. With every strip of hair removed, Pecca felt her heart pound in anticipation. *He's my patient. He's my patient. He's my patient. And he's hot.*

Heat bloomed in her chest, then stretched up her neck and into her face. "Okay, I think that's it." Pecca handed Colton a towel and stepped back so he could get a look at himself in the mirror. "What do you think?"

Colton stood, turned, and blinked at his reflection, running his left hand over his face. He looked so different. Younger. Stronger. His eyes found hers in the mirror, and she quickly looked down at the mess she needed to clean up.

"Next week you'll have a professional do it, and I'm sure it'll be a much better experience."

"It wasn't so bad," Colton said. "You did a good job."

"Thanks!" Pecca smiled at him. "After I get this cleaned up, we'll start on your PT."

"Is Maceo back at school?"

Pecca warned her heart not to read into his question. He was curious, that's all. Curiosity that was making her nerves tingle with energy. "Um, yes. And he was oddly excited to get back there today, though he still hasn't revealed what drove him to shove a kid to the ground in the first place."

"Maybe it's a family thing."

Colton's lip lifted into a smirk. Without the beard hiding his face, Pecca was finding it hard to get control of the fluttering in her stomach. He was attractive—oh, so attractive. And she was staring. At. Her. Patient.

Okay, this had to stop.

"So, we should get started on your session."

Pecca broke eye contact and put the basin and shave kit away—along with the crazy feelings teasing her heart. The affection was misplaced admiration and gratitude for the way Colton had come to her rescue on Friday and for the way he always brought a smile to Maceo's face.

While those were swoon-worthy qualities, they weren't everything. And after Pecca's last mistake, she wasn't going to allow herself to fall so easily for someone again. No matter how stinking cute he was.

Oh, this was going to be hard.

Watching Colton move to the mats to begin stretching, Pecca made a vow. She would keep perspective. Colton was her patient. She'd limit the amount of time she spent with him to *just* their sessions. And for the love of all that was good, she would do whatever it took to erase the memory of his shirtless torso from her mind.

Yeah, she could do this. No problem. Except she was already failing at one.

TEN

COLTON RIPPED THE CORD of the heart rate monitor from his fingers. His right hand spasmed, sending a sharp pain up his arm and into his shoulders.

"It's okay, Colton." Chaplain Kelly's voice was calm as he gathered the tangle of cords from the ground. "It's only the second day."

That should've made him feel better, but it didn't. Colton wasn't sure what he had expected, but not being able to even keep the electrodes on because of his movements was frustrating. The electrodes were supposed to monitor Colton's heart rate so he could practice techniques to bring the rate down, which would help him control the movements in his arm, but the only thing Colton had learned over the last two sessions was that this was just one more thing he couldn't control.

"How would you feel if we add another session each day?"

"Is that going to help?" Annoyance colored his words. Colton turned his angry stare to the wood floor. "What's the point if I can't even keep the wires on?"

"It's going to take time," Chaplain Kelly said, not taking his gaze off Colton's arm. Every twitch, jerk, and movement captured his attention as though he, too, was trying to understand why Colton's arm reacted that way. "Your disorder didn't get to this point overnight, and we can't expect that it's going to go away overnight. It's going to take practice and effort. A lot. And even with all of that, there are no guarantees."

Colton's eyes flew up to meet Chaplain Kelly's compassionate blue gaze. "The doctors at Walter Reed said you've helped cases like mine."

"No two cases are the same, Colton, but there's one thing all of my cases have in common."

"What's that?"

"Expectation. Expect your recovery—whatever that looks like for *your* case—to be challenging and without a timeline."

Heat seared the back of his neck. Colton could handle challenging. A decade in the Army with four deployments under his belt proved that. But no timeline? Colton couldn't give up any more time. This movement disorder had already stolen a year of his life and was progressing.

"I've lost"—he choked on the words—"everything because of this."

"When our mind has suffered greatly, our body's response is to restart—"

"My mind hasn't suffered greatly," Colton protested, sounding like an impertinent child. "I know what PTSD looks like. I've got friends who can't go into large crowds, who wake up in cold sweats, who—" His right hand jerked, sending his wrist into the corner of a table. His anger surged, forcing him to bite back the words that wouldn't alleviate the pain.

"Nurse Gallegos did a good job."

Hearing her name so unexpectedly felt like Colton was doused with cold water. He looked at Chaplain Kelly. "What?"

The chaplain ran his fingers along his own jawline. "Your shave. She asked me about the shaving kit. I'm assuming she did it."

Colton rubbed his hand over his chin as he gave a quick nod. He was still getting used to the absence of hair and the bittersweet feeling left behind. Beneath the beard, it was easy to forget who he once was. Now that the hair was gone, he was forced to look at the man he remembered being before his disability took over.

Colton found himself trying to figure out the feeling percolating in his chest every time he thought of Pecca. Or heard her name. Or the way his heart had almost thudded out of his chest when she leaned in close to his face, her minty breath tickling his skin, with every swipe of the blade.

The shave he had received at Walter Reed was efficient. The shave Pecca had given him was . . . intimate. Colton had willed—no, prayed—his movements to still so as to not interrupt the moment or to somehow make it last longer.

What moment? The question jarred Colton out of the memory and back to reality. She was a nurse doing him a favor. Doing her job. And when Charlie asked him to keep an eye on Pecca, Colton was sure he didn't mean in *that* way.

The ringtone on Chaplain Kelly's cell phone chimed, indicating their session was over. Colton was about to rise from his chair when the chaplain spoke up.

"Before you leave, Colton, I'd like to ask how you're doing coming off your meds. I know it's only been a few days, but I want to make sure you're not experiencing any side effects."

Colton swallowed. Guilt riddled him as he thought about the pill bottles tucked into his sock drawer. "Um, good. Except my arm keeps moving." He tried for a laugh, but it came out stilted—unlike his lie.

Chaplain Kelly smiled. "If you stay on course and work hard, I think we're going to see some progress over the next couple of weeks. But I want to make sure you understand that the progress may not be what you expect."

The chaplain's tone was humble. Simple truth offered in the humility of someone who appeared sincere in his desire to help but refused to make promises.

"As long as it's progress." Colton stood. A vibration rattled against his leg from the cell phone in his pocket. "I'll see you around, sir."

Outside Chaplain Kelly's office, Colton pulled out his phone and saw Kekoa's toothy grin smiling up at him from the screen. "Brother, I've been waiting for this call all weekend. You losing your touch now that you're out?"

"Pshh." Kekoa laughed. "They begging me to come back, but I'm waiting for the payday."

Colton stepped outside the Mansion and down the porch steps, taking a deep breath of the muggy air. "The Navy paying more for old intel guys?"

"Old? I'm barely thirty and in my prime."

"In intelligence, that makes you at prime retirement age."

"Well, this old man is considering not giving you information on one Javier Torres and Serena Gallegos if—"

"Okay, okay." Colton found a bench shaded beneath a Magnolia. His eyes shot over to the gym, where Pecca was working. He'd planned to go in after his session with Kelly to keep an eye on her, but he rationalized that someone who used a silencer under the cover of night to conceal their identity wasn't likely to walk into the gym and finish the job.

He shifted on the bench, bothered by the thought. "Tell me what you have."

"First, I'm deeply offended that you withheld the hotness level of Serena Gallegos."

Colton's expression pinched. Of course Kekoa would discover that and make it an issue. "She's very pretty."

"Very pretty?" Kekoa said in disbelief. "She's like the Latina version of a Hawaiian Tropic girl."

And thank you, Kekoa, for that visual. Colton didn't need any help recognizing how attractive his nurse was. What he did need help with was overlooking that fact in order to help keep her safe.

"Is that all you found out?"

"Besides that she's a hottie? Yes." Colton rolled his eyes over the sound of tapping computer keys echoing into the phone. "Serena is from El Paso, Texas. Born and raised up until six years ago when she relocated to Dallas for four years. She moved to Mobile, Alabama, for one year and then to Walton. She's the youngest of four. Has two older brothers, one's a law enforcement officer in New Mexico, the other is an accountant. One older sister who works for a Boston-based financial company—Loews, Ridley, and Scott."

So far Kekoa hadn't shared any information to give Colton pause. In fact, he was beginning to wonder how Pecca even got caught up with Javier. "What about Javier?"

"I'm not finished yet." Kekoa's tone tightened, and with it so did Colton's gut. "Serena was arrested at sixteen for shoplifting. She was put on probation and, according to the records, had to do restitution."

"She was a juvenile. How did you get access to those?"

"Her association with the South Side Barrio gang and one of its leaders, Javier Torres."

Colton's gaze flicked back to the gym. Pecca hadn't just dated a gang member, she'd dated one of its leaders. "Did she commit any more crimes after that?"

"No, but the local gang unit keeps photos of the area gangs and their members, which is probably why they had her photo and information."

"Tell me about Javier." Colton wanted to know how Pecca—the sweet, overly cheerful, fiercely protective mother—got pulled into the gang life. "What's he serving time for?"

"I don't have to tell you what a pain in my *okole* it was to find this guy, do I?"

"Got it. I owe you."

"I'll take a date with the nurse, please."

"Not gonna happen." Colton ignored the flutter in his chest. "Get on with it."

"Javier Torres is currently serving a fifteen-year sentence at Buckner Penitentiary for aggravated robbery. Except for that, his record is fairly clean, given his position in the gang. Seems a little odd to me."

"Odd, how?"

"Dude's supposedly running one of El Paso's prominent gangs and aside from some petty crimes, his record doesn't reflect a typical gangbanger's life."

"Maybe he had other people do his dirty work."

"Maybe."

There was some hesitation in Kekoa's voice. "What is it?"

"It's probably nothing."

If Kekoa was picking up on something, it was rarely ever nothing. "Tell me."

"It's just that I wasn't able to pull up anything else on him. With technology what it is, I've got your girl's"—Colton opened his mouth to correct Kekoa, but he was already continuing—"entire educational record, first driver's license photo, even her electronic signature on the Buckner visitor sheet, but Javier's info is gone like he didn't exist until he started breaking the law."

Colton was still stuck on the idea of Pecca visiting Javier in jail. She hadn't mentioned that the other night. Well, to be fair, she hadn't really offered anything more than Javier's name and her connection to the SSB, which made the new information he had on her sit in his stomach like a piece of lead.

"What about South Side Barrio?"

"Not good news, brah," Kekoa sighed. "DEA has them tied to some cartels outside the country. There's been some territorial violence that looks like it started shortly after Javier went to prison, and it's been escalating over the last year."

That might be incentive for the SSB to want Javier paroled early—bring back some control. Movement across the lawn caught Colton's attention, and he turned to see Maceo running toward him with a football in his hand.

"Look, I gotta run. If you find anything else, you call me—night or day."

"Shootz," Kekoa said. "Hey, maybe give your uncle a call. Didn't you say he was a cop in Texas or something?"

"Texas Ranger."

"Right. Maybe he can find something on this guy."

"He's retired, but it's worth a shot." Colton waved at Maceo as he approached. "Talk to you soon."

"Don't forget you owe me a date with—"

Colton ended the call. "Hey, Maceo, how was school?"

Maceo's breath puffed out of pink cheeks. "Okay."

Colton held up his hands for Maceo to toss him the ball, which he did. "Go long." Maceo started jogging backward, and Colton noticed the movement was hard on his prosthetic joint. Technology was amazing and prosthetics allowed those with missing limbs to do far more than they ever could without them, but they fell short of the real thing. "Here it comes."

With his left hand, Colton tossed the ball in a miserable attempt at a spiral. The ball wobbled through the air and was narrowly missed by Maceo's outstretched arms before it bounced on the grass.

Defeat furrowed Maceo's brow as he reached down and grabbed the ball. "Sorry."

"That's okay. It was a bad throw." Colton watched Maceo line the laces up against his fingers. He pulled back and let the ball fly through the air much better than Colton. "Nice."

"He still won't tell me why he threw the kid to the ground." Pecca's words came to mind, and Colton tried another left-handed toss. "You didn't tackle anyone to the ground, did you?"

"No," Maceo said, eyeing the ball in the air and adjusting his position. This time he caught it, but he didn't throw it back right away. Instead, he started walking to Colton. "Do you think someone like me will ever be able to play football?"

"What do you mean?"

"That's why I pushed Tobey." Maceo looked up, squinting beneath the sun. "He said it didn't matter how good I was, I wouldn't be allowed to play football on a real team because of my leg."

Maceo's words gutted Colton and simultaneously made him want to teach this Tobey a lesson. "Listen to me, Maceo. If you work hard enough, you can do anything." *False!* the voice in Colton's head shouted. *If that were true, you wouldn't be here.*

"Like when Vincent James busted his leg?"

An inflection of hope was in Maceo's voice. Colton clenched his jaw as his eyes went to the movement in his arm—mocking proof that it didn't matter how hard he worked. Some things just didn't work out. But was he really going to tell that to Maceo?

"How about we start with the Saint James Fake and you can show that Tobey kid who's boss?"

As the sun began its descent, Colton continued working with Maceo on the fake and the proper way to spiral a ball, until both of their faces were sweaty. Thankfully, Shirley had delivered a couple of water bottles earlier, which they had finished a few minutes ago.

"You boys look like you've had too much fun." Pecca crossed the lawn. She started to ruffle her fingers through Maceo's hair but pulled back. "Eww. You're sweaty."

Maceo rolled his eyes. "We've been working, Mom."

"I hope not too hard." Her brown eyes flashed to Colton. "You don't want to overdo it."

"Mom, do you want to see me throw a spiral?" Maceo was already running across the field, ball in hand.

"What's a spiral?"

Colton's lips pressed into a smile. "The way the ball spins in the air when he throws it."

"Oh, right." Pecca watched Maceo. "Yes! I can't wait to see the spiral."

Maceo made a face before he shrugged. He launched the ball into the air toward Colton in a nearly perfect spiral. A little more practice, and he'd have it down. Colton took two steps back just as the ball sailed into his left arm.

"Great toss, Maceo!"

They turned to see David, the Army sergeant Pecca had introduced to him the other day in the gym, making his way toward them.

"Hey, Pecca!" David gave Colton an apologetic smile. "I'm not great with names."

"Colton," Pecca said before Colton could. "Everything okay?"

"Oh, that's right. Vincent James's friend." Colton sensed a bit of a bite to David's tone, but as he hobbled closer, he was all smiles. "I stopped by to see if I could pick you and Maceo up tonight."

Colton sensed Pecca stiffen, and from the look on David's face, he noticed it as well and quickly added, "The bet. Maceo won't let me off the hook. Not that I would either when it comes to ice cream." He looked Colton in the eyes. "Just a double scoop this time."

"Oh, right." Pecca's shoulders relaxed. "Um, well, I'll have to check how much homework he has. You know, after the suspension and all."

"Of course." David nodded. "Education is the most important thing, my dad used to always say."

Maceo ran up. "Mister David, do you want to see what Colton taught me?"

"Absolutely."

"You wait here," Maceo said to Colton, handing him the football. "Pretend I'm Vincent and you throw me the ball like we practiced."

"Okay."

All three adults watched Maceo line up on the grass, pretending he was preparing for the snap of the ball.

"How long you been out of the Army?" David said, shifting his cane.

Colton watched Maceo fight off imaginary defensive linemen as he moved back, preparing for the ball. "Thirteen months, eleven days."

David whistled. "Down to the day, huh?"

When Maceo was ready, Colton pulled back with his left arm and let the ball loose. He sighed in relief that the throw wasn't half bad, considering it was his nondominant arm—and he was in front of Pecca.

And David.

"Great job, Maceo!" Pecca yelled, clapping. David clapped too.

Colton wasn't sure what to make of David, but he'd be willing to bet a triple scoop sundae that David had feelings for the woman standing between them. "What about you?"

David tapped his cane on the ground. "Oh, uh, it's been a couple of years."

"That from the war?"

"Yeah. Third Infantry Division, Bagram Air Base."

Colton's ears perked up. "Oh yeah? I have a buddy who was part of the 3ID Bulldog Brigade. Captain Helwig. You know him?"

"Uh," David tilted his head, his eyes searching as if trying to place the name. "I-I don't think I do." He shifted and peered down at his leg. "Since the explosion, there are some things I can't really remember."

Pecca put a reassuring hand on David's arm. "I think that's the brain's way of protecting us from remembering the bad stuff."

Colton might've agreed with her if his gut wasn't saying something else. The infantry division from Fort Stewart wasn't small, but it wasn't so big that David wouldn't know the name of a company commander.

"Maceo, it's time to go." Pecca waved Maceo over. "Tell Colton thank you."

"We're meeting again tomorrow, right?" Maceo looked up at Colton. "I still need to perfect the fake."

"How about we discuss the homework situation first?" Pecca said.

That reminded Colton of Maceo's confession about the kid at school. Should he say something to Pecca or let Maceo tell her?

"I'll walk you to your car," David said and then leaned close to Maceo. "So we can convince your mom to let me take you guys out for ice cream."

As expected, Maceo's eyes lit up. He spun around and stared up at Pecca with pleading eyes. "Please, Mom. Please."

Pecca shot David an exasperated look, and Colton didn't know why, but he really wanted her to say no.

"Fine. As long as you promise to do all your homework and eat all your dinner and"—she held up a finger to Maceo—"you only get one scoop."

"But—"

"One scoop is all you need."

"Fine." Maceo's shoulders hunched, and he mumbled, "But the bet was for two."

Colton hated the feeling snaking around his stomach. It felt a lot like jealousy—but what was making him jealous? It wasn't like Colton could take Pecca out for ice cream. He could barely throw a spiral for Maceo.

"Well, I guess I better get inside. If I don't get to the kitchen before Gunny, he makes me sing the Marine Corps song, which I don't know, while Sarge hollers something about the Marines being shark bait."

Pecca laughed. "Maybe I should stay for dinner. I bet that's a sight."

Maybe you should. Colton cringed inwardly. "So, I'll see you tomorrow."

"First thing in the morning." Pecca smiled, her eyes lingering on his before she looked away. "Say goodbye, Maceo."

"Goodbye, Maceo," Maceo mimicked.

Pecca rolled her eyes and then winked at Colton. From the corner of his eye, he could see David giving him a less-than-approving look. In fact, Colton felt like the man was sizing him up. Did David think Colton was competition?

"David." Colton gave him a nod before starting across the grass to the Mansion. He smiled. Part of him wanted to reassure the guy that he had nothing to worry about. Another part of him—a super tiny part that Colton could easily ignore if he wanted to—was sickly satisfied that David found him to be a threat.

ELEVEN

THE MOUTH-WATERING AROMA of cinnamon and sugar and all things deliciously unhealthy pulled Pecca into the staff kitchen at the Mansion.

"I knew this would work."

Pecca halted at the doorway to find Lane and Shirley sitting at the table with a box of cinnamon rolls in front of them. Lane slid the box forward an inch.

"Would you like one?"

Pecca glanced between them, feeling like she should be suspicious but unsure why. "What's going on?"

"Aw, nothing, honey." Shirley smiled and patted the table. "Lane brought over these delicious treats for the residents, and since you have a bit of time before your next patient, we hoped you might join us."

Something didn't feel right. Pecca shot a look at Lane, who was biting her lip like a teenage girl about to divulge her secret crush. Slowly, Pecca stepped into the room and sat, eyeing them both. Shirley took a paper plate from the table and scooped a roll onto it, the cream cheese frosting dripping over the side.

She set the plate in front of Pecca. "I just made a fresh pot of coffee too."

"Okay, that's it." Pecca leaned against the back of the chair and folded her arms over her chest. "What's going on here?"

The two women exchanged a mischievous look, and Pecca edged forward in her seat.

"Come on, guys. Spill it."

"We're sorta hoping you'll be the one doing the spilling," Lane said, a sparkle in her eye. "A little bird told us you had a date last night."

A date? Pecca could barely remember what she'd had for breakfast, so she had to think for a second. "Wait. With David? The ice cream? That wasn't a date."

"That's not what Mrs. Kingsley said," Shirley cooed.

Pecca rolled her eyes. "Mrs. Kingsley has been trying to marry off her grandson since Lane moved back to town."

"That's true." Lane rubbed her belly. "But why didn't you tell me you were going on a date?"

"Because it wasn't a date," Pecca said. "David made a bet with Maceo and lost." She reached for the plate and pulled apart a piece of the roll. "Y'all should know better than to listen to gossip."

"If it quacks like a duck . . ." Shirley made a face like she wasn't buying it. "David's been building the confidence to ask you out since he got here."

"Yeah, and he's not bad looking," Lane added. "Nice. I heard he's been volunteering at the elementary school. Meagan says he's agreed to man the jumping balloon at the fall festival."

Pecca sighed around her bite of cinnamon roll. She wasn't unaware of David's feelings. Lately, she noticed he was coming around the Mansion in between his volunteer days. And even though he wasn't as quirky as Ryan, David stepped into the friend role the former deputy had left vacant, winning Maceo over—even if it was with ice cream.

"So, do you like him?"

"He's nice," Pecca answered Lane. She slid the plate away. *What a waste of a perfectly good cinnamon roll.* "He's just not—"

"Lighting your fire?" Shirley raised her eyebrows. "Revving your motor? Sweetening your tea?"

"Colton?"

"What?" Pecca's gaze shot to Lane. "No, I don't . . . he's not . . . why—"

Shirley laughed. "Ooh, now she's got you, honey."

Just spit it out. Colton doesn't light my tea or rev my fire or— She shook her head. "Captain Crawford is my patient."

Lane shrugged, her hands cradling her belly. "So?"

Pecca widened her eyes at Lane. "So, there are rules." She looked to Shirley. "Right?"

"I wouldn't know, child." She picked a piece of lint off her peach blouse. "There's only one man who sizzles my bacon."

Lane made a face before she and Pecca burst into laughter. A second later Shirley joined in, and the hysterics continued until Pecca's side ached and tears streamed down Lane's face. Pecca's watch beeped, and there was a collective moan around the table. "Back to work."

"Oh, I almost forgot." Shirley tapped her fingernails on the table. "Chaplain Kelly left you a note in Captain Crawford's file. Said he'd like you to look at it before your appointment with him today."

"Okay." Pecca stood, purposely ignoring the expectant looks on their faces. She knew what they were waiting for and she wasn't going to give them anything—because there was nothing to give. "I'll see you two later."

"Have a good session, honey."

"Yeah, a *good* session," Lane said with a wiggle of her eyebrows.

Oh, brother. No matter what Lane claimed, she was just as bad as Mrs. Kingsley. It took Ryan kissing Vivian in the middle of the Peach Bowl this past summer for Lane to accept that he and Pecca would only ever be friends. Now that Colton was here, it seemed her romantic heart was set on Pecca making a choice between him and David.

And Pecca blamed Charlie.

Ever since Charlie had come to town and swept Lane into lovey-dovey bliss, she'd wanted everyone else to experience a Hallmark-worthy relationship like theirs—or apparently the bacon-sizzling kind like Shirley shared with her husband.

Walking across the gravel pathway to the gym, Pecca bit her lip. There was no choice. Colton was her patient and David was . . . not sizzling or revving anything. Pecca jerked to a stop, her eyes scanning the area around her as though someone might've heard her thoughts.

A friend.

David was a friend. Colton was her patient. And if Pecca didn't get her head out of the clouds, she wouldn't have time to read Chaplain Kelly's note before Colton showed up for his session. Pecca hoped it wasn't bad news.

Inside the gym, she opened her laptop and read through Colton's file, breathing a sigh of relief. It wasn't bad. It was a suggestion. A good one too. She looked around the gym, her mind making a quick list of options. After watching Colton with Maceo last night on the grass, she couldn't believe she hadn't thought about it.

"Morning." Colton's voice echoed from the doorway where he stood in a Dallas Mustangs T-shirt, the sleeves cut off, exposing his lean, muscular arms. The involuntary movement in his right arm triggered the muscles to flex, and Pecca couldn't help remembering what it felt like when his arms were wrapped around her. Safe and protecting.

Gracious. If she didn't want Lane and Shirley's romantic notions messing with her, she'd better stay focused.

"Good morning." Pecca added extra perkiness to her voice, hoping it would silence the traitorous thumping of her heart. She needed to keep perspective. She reached under the counter and grabbed a yellow tennis ball. "Think fast."

She threw the ball at Colton. His reaction was quick, but the movement in his arm slowed his response. He tried to grab the ball but missed, sending it bouncing across the room.

He frowned. "What was that?"

"We're going to try something new today." Pecca pulled out a bucket of balls and gave him a wicked smile before throwing another at him. This time he was ready and grabbed it with his left hand easily. "Don't drop that ball."

"Wha—"

Pecca threw another, this time harder. Colton's right hand swung up just before the ball would've smashed him in the face. She whooped. "Did you see that?"

Colton made a face. "What? Are you trying to—"

Another ball flew at him. Colton dropped both balls to grab it using his dominant arm.

"What are you doing?"

"Throwing the ball triggers your brain to respond instinctively, sending the signal to your arms to catch it before it hits your face."

"So you *were* aiming for my face?"

"I had to get your body to respond *naturally*."

Colton gave her a hard stare as though he was trying to figure out if she was crazy. She was about to explain further when a ball came flying at her. She ducked.

"Hey!"

"Just checking your natural response." The side of his lip quirked into an impish grin.

Pecca narrowed her eyes playfully. "Remember who's in charge here, Captain Colton."

Over the next half hour, Pecca threw balls at him. They laughed at the ones he missed, which he firmly blamed on her, pointing out that *he* was the one with a movement disorder in his arm. She tried to catch him off guard, but Colton was fast and Pecca couldn't help remembering how swiftly his instincts responded to protect her.

A flicker of heat swelled in her chest, distracting her.

"Heads up!"

But Colton's warning came too late and the tennis ball struck her in the arm.

"Ow!"

"I'm so sorry." Colton ran over and rubbed Pecca's arm. "Are you okay? I thought you were watching. I shouldn't have thrown it so hard."

There was no mistaking the guilt in Colton's eyes or the way his fingers were stoking the flame with every stroke against her skin.

"It's okay." Pecca brought her fingers to the sore spot, effectively forcing Colton to withdraw his hand. His expression shifted and she couldn't tell if it was hurt or disappointment, but it prodded her to convince him she was fine. She nudged him with her shoulder. "If you wanted a water break, you could've just told me."

Colton shook his head, but she saw him try to conceal the smile playing at his lips.

"You know, without your beard you definitely look less Unabomber-ish."

"Did you just compare me to the Unabomber?" Colton let his jaw drop in mock dismay. "I thought bearding was all the rage these days."

"Bearding?" Pecca snorted and then clapped her hand over her mouth. Did she really just do that? She spun on her heel in the direction of the minifridge, not wanting Colton to see the embarrassment coloring her cheeks. "How do you feel?"

"Bad."

She peeked over the counter. "You do?"

"About nailing you with the ball, yes."

"I already told you it's fine. I'm pretty sure I hit you harder the day we met."

Colton pressed his lips together. "Not my finest moment."

"Mine either." Pecca couldn't help smiling at his phony posture of defeat. "Guess that makes us even." She held up a bottle of water. Colton nodded and she tossed it at him, grateful when he caught it. "Nice."

"I'd never thought about forcing my hand to respond naturally."

"Hard to do if you're thinking about it." Pecca walked back. "The idea is that you don't think about it. Don't think about getting your hand to move in a specific way—just allow it to move."

Colton used his teeth to open the bottle of water. "What other things can we do like that?"

Pecca twisted her lips, thinking. She peeked outside and caught the reflection of the swimming pool. "Well, you've already started swimming. That's kind of the same thing."

"It is?"

"Yeah." Her eyes met his. "When you jump in the water, your body's natural instincts kick in to keep you from drowning."

"That's true."

He nodded, and it was unnerving how he could make her heart beat in a rhythm—rhythm!

"Do you know how to dance?" she asked.

"What?"

"Dance, you know"—she twisted her hips from side to side— "dance."

"I've taken a girl two-stepping before."

"That's great, but I think . . ." Pecca grabbed the little remote and started flipping through the satellite radio for the perfect station. Trumpets trilled against the staccato beat of the familiar music thumping through the speakers, making Pecca move her hips instinctively. "We need something that doesn't require you to think."

Colton shook his head, his eyes wide. "I-I don't know how to dance salsa."

"You don't *dance* salsa, you *feel* salsa." Pecca grabbed Colton's hands, but his right arm jerked so badly that she had to lightly take hold of his wrist. "Just let the rhythm move your body naturally."

Skepticism colored his hazel eyes, but she ignored it—and the warning that having him this close was a bad idea. Instead, she danced. Rolling her shoulders and bringing his arms up in the air, she let the music move her. Colton stood there like his feet were glued to the ground.

"Come on." She put her hands on his hips and then pulled them back when she realized what she'd done. "Sorry, may I, um . . ."

Licking his lips, Colton nodded.

Pecca put her hands on his hips, feeling his muscles tense at her touch. She started moving again, but Colton remained rigid. Okay. Maybe this wasn't such a good idea. She stepped back just as the song shifted into the pulsating melody. Time for drastic measures.

With as much gusto as she could muster, Pecca busted out her best moves. The running man. Cabbage Patch. She slid her hands to her hips and shuffled to her right, and then her left, and was about to moonwalk when Colton burst out laughing.

Breathing hard, she looked up at him, meeting his smile with her own. "You think you can do better?"

"I'm sure Gunny can do better."

She shot him a look. "But can you?"

Colton stood there for a second before his feet started to move side to side, matching the beat of the music. His eyes stayed trained on her, and she mirrored his movement. It took a minute, but soon Colton's body loosened up and she could see the rhythm travel through his body. His hips swayed, his shoulders bounced—even his arms swung in a controlled manner.

It was working.

And then the music transitioned into a romantic ballad. Pecca and Colton both stopped but neither stepped away.

"What if we try again?" Colton asked, stepping so close she could smell the laundered scent of his shirt.

He picked up her right hand with his left and placed it on his shoulder. Her pulse throbbed. The muscle in his jaw ticked as he glanced at his right arm, but Pecca quickly put her left hand over his shoulder and a look of gratitude filled his face.

He placed his left hand on her hip, and as the singer crooned about his love with every strum of the guitar, Colton let the music move him, guiding her body with his. He wasn't half bad. In fact, with every sway, she found herself liking the feel of his arms around her, his body close. Her breathing faltered. When was the last time she felt like this?

He's my patient. The thought was barely discernible over the fluttering in her chest. Fluttering that Pecca worried Colton might feel, they were so close.

"Oh, I'm sorry. Didn't know there was anyone in here."

Colton and Pecca quickly stepped apart, her hands slipping from his shoulders. They turned to see Gunny ambling toward them.

"Hey, Gunny." Heat flared into her cheeks as she clicked the remote, cutting off the music. "I was, um"—she glanced at Colton, whose cheeks were as red as hers felt—"dancing. I was using dance therapy with Colton, but we're done now."

"Sign me up," Gunny said with a slap to his leg. "You've been holding out on me, Hot Tamale."

Pecca rolled her eyes and turned to Colton. "Don't forget aqua therapy this afternoon."

"I'll be there." Colton gave her a half smile before grabbing a towel. He passed Gunny, and the man chuckled.

"Sorry about that, Cap."

Colton glanced over his shoulder and pierced Pecca with a look that said maybe he'd felt something too. A look that had Gunny chuckling even more.

A look that . . . lit a fire.

TWELVE

THEY WERE SAFE.

Colton picked up his pace as he rounded the corner to the next street, which would take him behind Pecca's home and in the direction of the Mansion. It had taken him a few wrong turns and some backtracking to figure out the best route to her house from the Mansion, but now that he'd found it, the route had become part of his nightly run. He felt responsible to ensure that she and Maceo made it home safely.

The nightly run also allowed him the opportunity to recon the neighborhood, get familiar with it so he'd be able to recognize if something was out of the ordinary. It had been only a few days, but Colton hadn't heard a single thing about the incident. There had been some whispering around town, concern that maybe some of the crime in Savannah might be stretching closer to home. Sheriff Huggins and Charlie were careful to hedge those rumors with assurances they were doing their jobs and would find answers. But what would they find? A raucous small-town resident who should be banned from owning guns or something more menacing?

His intuition still leaned toward a threat, but where was the intel to back it up? Colton crossed Ford Avenue, sensing the heaviness of his thoughts. It didn't help that his feelings had become involved. He instantly remembered their session that had somehow ended with Pecca in his arms—dancing. He could still feel the sway of her body next to his, the heat of her touch lighting something in him he hadn't been able to ignore or extinguish.

Just like the threat against her and Maceo.

Colton cut through town, jogging past brick buildings bearing plaques dating from the late 1800s. The glass storefronts, colorful

111

awnings, and iron lampposts reminded him of his grandparents'
hometown near Fort Worth.

Walton wasn't a big city, but it was far from the Podunk town
he had imagined. Before moving here, he'd done an internet search
and learned Henry Ford used to winter in town with his family.
He also learned that in recent months Walton had seen a couple
of bad passes with the murder of a teenager and the near death of
some actor, which meant it wasn't a stretch to assume the nature
of the shooting might be more sinister.

Was Pecca's ex coming after her? Would the South Side Barrio
send someone to find her and Maceo? What lengths would they
go to? And why would they shoot at her? He didn't have enough
intel. Nothing he could properly analyze and—

Colton slowed down.

What was he doing? It was like his instincts were trying to make
up for lost time, or maybe he was attempting to prove he still had
what it took. That his arm movements hadn't stolen everything
from him.

Finding a park bench, Colton sat. His arm jerked, and he swallowed back the frustration. His session with Pecca had been . . .
encouraging. She had been right. His arm moved instinctively
when necessary. It had given him confidence. Progress. Then it
all slipped away inside Chaplain Kelly's office. Once again the
movements and muscle spasms made it impossible to keep the
wires on his fingers. Why wasn't it working? Maybe he could in-
crease his medications? His doctor at Reed said the prescription
was as needed. He could take up to three a day, but the doctor
warned that there was a chance he could develop a dependency
issue—and that scared Colton. But the movements in his arm
scared him more. Not getting a chance to do the therapy he'd
moved here for scared him. If he wasn't going to get better, then
what was the point? He might as well pack up and head back to
Texas—and do what?

His phone chirped in his pocket, snapping Colton out of his

pity party. He considered letting it go to voicemail but remembered he was waiting for a call.

"Hey, Uncle Jack."

"Colton, how are you, son?"

Hearing his uncle's familiar weathered voice felt like a balm of comfort, and Colton's body relaxed against the wood slats of the bench.

"I'm . . ." Colton flexed his hand. He knew whatever he said to his uncle would be reported back to his parents. Though they hadn't said so, Colton knew they were just as hopeful as he was that his stay at Home for Heroes was going to lead to recovery. He didn't want to let them down. "I'm well."

A second passed, and Colton heard his uncle sigh. It was his way. Never one to speak when silence spoke louder. And his uncle's silence was hurting Colton's ears.

"I guess you're wondering why I called?"

"You made a decision?"

Colton squeezed his eyes shut, feeling a breeze pass over. The scratchy sound of leaves shuffling over the ground in front of him filled his ears, and if he tried hard enough, he could imagine himself sitting along the Brazos River, Uncle Jack next to him as they overlooked the ranch.

Colton opened his eyes and peered down at his arm again. How many more things would this disorder steal from him? "I-I don't think . . ." He didn't want to say the words aloud, fearing that the second he released them into the air, they would drift away on the breeze and be impossible to get back.

He exhaled. "My treatment isn't going as well as I'd hoped." Better to admit that than to admit he'd have to let another one of his dreams disappear. "My movements haven't gotten any better, Uncle Jack."

"It's only been a few days." Uncle Jack gave a soft chuckle. "You're a go-getter, son, but even Lazarus had to die before the Lord could do his work."

Colton blinked. "That's a bit morbid."

"I'm just saying that the best miracles come when all hope seems out of reach."

"It's gonna take a miracle, alright," Colton grumbled. "I just hope it comes to me before it did Lazarus."

"We all die different kinds of deaths, Colt, but they all lead to one truth. Do you trust him enough to bring you back to life?"

Colton bit back on his molars. He wasn't in the mood for a sermon and was rather surprised to hear it coming from Uncle Jack. Unlike his parents, Uncle Jack preferred a more thoughtful approach, speaking when he felt it was . . . important.

Sighing, Colton sat forward. "Uncle Jack, thanks for calling me back. I have a favor to ask. I need some help finding information on a prisoner at Buckner."

"Buckner, huh?" Colton imagined his uncle scratching his chin, which made him do the same. He had more than a day's growth and the barber would be coming tomorrow. "You in some kind of trouble?"

"No. There was a, uh . . ." Colton considered the effects of what he was going to say. Uncle Jack had retired a little more than five years ago from a lifetime of service as a Texas Ranger, but his mind was still sharp. Asking about a prisoner would warrant questions Colton would have to answer. "There was a shooting the other night. Three shots. Sniper style. The intended target has a connection to Javier Torres, a member of the South Side Barrio, who is currently serving a fifteen-year sentence for aggravated robbery."

Uncle Jack whistled. "Fifteen years?"

"A woman was killed," Colton said. "Another member of the SSB shot her. Javier is up for parole, and there's suspicion members of the gang might be looking for his ex-girlfriend to testify on his behalf."

"Seems like you have a lot of information already," Uncle Jack said. "You get that from one of your *friends*?"

Colton, understanding the implication, grinned. "Yes, sir, but he ran into a wall. He was only able to draw a limited amount of information on Javier, mostly about the crime that landed him in prison. Nothing personal."

"And for your friend, that would be impossible. Him not having access to . . . everything."

"Yes, sir." As a Texas Ranger, Uncle Jack understood the integrity behind intelligence.

"I have a buddy whose son is a prison guard at Clemmons. He might be able to get me access to the warden at Buckner, but I have a suspicion that if your friend couldn't get you what you want—"

"I understand, Uncle Jack. I appreciate your help."

"Sure, son. Now, if you have a minute, I'd like to ask you a favor."

Before his uncle even spoke the words, Colton knew what was coming. The ranch.

"Frank's expressed interest in purchasing the land. Wants to expand his property and asked if we'd be willing to sell."

Sell? Colton's gut twisted. He thought about the money he had sitting in his account—the money he'd saved through every deployment. He'd intended to have enough to purchase the property from his grandparents so he could—

The dream stopped at the tip of his thoughts.

"Is it a good offer?"

"He hasn't made an official one yet. I was hoping I wouldn't need to consider an offer from outside the family."

Colton's grandparents owned fifty acres of pastureland a few miles north of McKinley. Growing up, he had spent every summer there riding horses, fishing the Brazos, learning how to care for the land. He even brought Vincent James there so they could perfect the Saint James Fake. Every stargazing night, Colton let himself imagine a future there.

He snorted. There was no future there now. Not for him. Not when he could barely take care of himself, much less fifty acres.

Asking Uncle Jack to dismiss a genuine offer would be unfair to his family.

"If it's good"—Colton stood—"take it."

Silence passed between them, and Colton appreciated it. Uncle Jack wasn't eager to accept the truth, but there was no other choice. Colton was learning to accept it, and his uncle would have to as well.

Colton inhaled deeply. It was getting dark, and he needed to take his next dose of medicine if he had any hope of getting to sleep. "So, you'll let me know if you find out anything new?" If his uncle wanted to avoid the truth or hang on to some kind of Lazarus-worthy hope, he could. "I'll send you an email with the information."

"I will." A bit of defeat was in Uncle Jack's voice. "We're praying, son."

Emotion tightened Colton's throat so that he was barely able to whisper, "Yes, sir."

Ending the call, Colton started down the asphalt trail toward the Mansion. The weight of the conversation had sucked away any energy he'd had left. Next to his own father, Uncle Jack was the only other person he wanted to make proud. After that call, Colton couldn't help but feel like he'd somehow let him down.

How was he supposed to take care of a ranch? Colton had gone over a dozen different scenarios. Even though his grandfather only used land for cattle and had a team of hired workers to help, he still got up every morning before sunrise to supervise operations and pitch in where he could. Colton broke out in a sweat trying to tie his shoes.

The shrill sound of a whistle drew Colton's attention to the large field on the other side of the street. Beneath the bright field lights two groups of kids, one in blue jerseys and the other in red, were huddled on opposite sides of the field. Parents standing or sitting in folding chairs watched as coaches relayed plays to kids who looked too small for the shoulder pads and helmets they wore.

Was he ever that small?

Colton paused by the chain-link fence and watched them practice a single sweep formation and was impressed that more than half the kids ran in the right direction. Another whistle blew and the boys ran to their coach, who passed out high fives, along with words of encouragement to those who nailed the play and instruction to those who needed it. He thought about Maceo and the explanation behind his suspension. Twenty-plus years separated them, but he had no problem identifying with the anger and frustration of being told you couldn't do something.

Was there a way for Maceo to play football? Pushing back from the fence, Colton left the young footballers behind and started back on his way. There was something about being on a team. Having a brotherhood of friends with a singular focus.

The crunch of leaves beneath his steps gave way to the soft carpet of grass in front of the Mansion. A few hours ago, Colton witnessed Maceo throw a beautiful spiral. The kid had talent, but more than that he had determination. Colton didn't want to see that kind of spirit crushed because of some kid named Tobey.

He was almost to the front porch when an idea came to him. One that had him turning around to take in the lawn and picture the possibility. Maybe there was a way to get Maceo on a team. It just wouldn't be what he expected.

THIRTEEN

"I DON'T WANT TO, MAMA."

Juan watched Diego shake his head, not even looking up from the gaming device in his hand. Alicia pressed the phone to her chest and spoke to her son, but Juan could only hear her soft mumblings. He could tell she had already forgotten about the cameras that gave him a bird's-eye view of Diego's defiance. It would take a simple click and Juan would have access to their conversation, but he wasn't sure his heart could handle it.

A second later, Alicia's shoulders moved in a sigh and she pointed down the hall. Diego rolled off the couch, tossing the game against the cushion before stalking to his room.

"He's tired."

Juan brushed his thumb over his laptop screen where Alicia had collapsed onto the couch. "Mi amor, you have forgotten about the cameras already."

Alicia's eyes flashed up to the camera, which had been mounted only hours earlier. Her lips pulled into a small smile as though she could sense his pain.

"He is upset, Juan." Her voice was soothing, but not enough to wipe the memory of Diego's anger from Juan's mind. "Diego misses you. We miss you."

"I miss you, amor, and Diego too." Juan exhaled, pinching the bridge of his nose. He couldn't unsee the angry look on Diego's little face. "Everything I do is for him. For his future."

"And what of mine?" she teased. Juan saw her smiling up at the camera.

"Of course. You and Diego are my life. That is why it pains me to see him upset."

119

"Do not worry, my love," Alicia said. "Diego will get over it and all will be fine."

Juan watched Beatriz bring in a tray of coffee and set it next to Alicia. He clicked a button and the large screen split into nine smaller squares, showing him varying angles around his home. Another click, and he had nine new angles. The only way he wouldn't worry was if he did everything he could to make sure Alicia and Diego remained safe.

"Did they teach you how to use the security system?" There was a pause, and the hair on Juan's arm rose. "Alicia?"

"I know how to use an alarm, Juan." Alicia scowled up at the camera. "I don't understand—why the update to the system? The cameras are a little much, don't you think?"

"Not if I want to see your beautiful face."

Alicia stuck out her tongue. "Seriously, Juan. I can think of only one reason why you would be making changes, and that doesn't make me happy."

Juan sighed and leaned back in the desk chair so that it rocked back slightly. "I'm simply making sure you and Diego are safe."

"Why? What's happened?" With a single glance up at the cameras, Alicia pierced the distance separating them. "Are we in danger?"

"No, mi amor." Juan sat forward, wanting to take his wife into his arms and reassure her, but instead, he was left only to draw his hand into a fist of frustration. "It is only a precaution. I'm not there to protect you, and I want you and Diego to be safe in my absence."

"We *are* safe, but you are making me nervous, Juan."

Alicia wasn't the only one feeling that way. Juan hadn't been able to settle his nerves since his conversation with Señor. The man was impulsive and irrational—a combination that could equal trouble if he didn't get what he wanted, when he wanted it.

"I don't want you to be nervous, but you must be diligent when I'm not there. If something were to happen to you or Diego—"

The ugly thought drove his attention to the board on the wall. A new photo had been added. Colton Crawford.

Army captain. Military intelligence. Honorable discharge, according to his records, due to a movement disorder. *Honorable*. His actions the other night proved that, but one more second and the outcome wouldn't have been good. If Juan hadn't been quick, Señor would have had a reason to execute him.

"I will not forget, Juan." His wife's voice was soft, and it pulled him back to the computer screen. She looked up to the camera. "I know what to do. You don't have to worry."

Alicia was not naïve. She grew up in the business. Understood the risks but also believed in him. Juan would not let her down. Or Diego.

"Mi amor, you are tired. Get some rest. Tomorrow I want you to go out with your friends. Shop. Let your mind rest and let me take care of everything. I don't know how much longer I will be away, but I want you to be ready. Do you understand?"

She nodded at the camera but said nothing.

"Good." The fire he saw in her eyes told him she would be ready when the time came. He was counting on that. "Now, I must make another call. Have a good night, and tell Diego I will have a surprise for him soon."

"You spoil him." Alicia's lips split into a smile.

"It's my job." He ran a finger over the image of her face and wished he could draw her close to him. *No*. Drawing her close was temporary. What he wanted was to whisk her and Diego away as far as necessary so they would never have to worry again. That was his job. "But don't worry, you will have a surprise as well."

"I only want you."

"Soon."

"*Te amo*, Juan."

He ended the call with his wife's vow of love still lingering in his ear and watched her disappear down the hall to their bedroom. There were no cameras installed there. Alicia had limits.

Minimizing the screen, Juan pressed the video chat and a ringing tone filled his office. Then he rose from the chair and walked to the window and opened it. A clean burst of air funneled into the room, bringing with it the cadence of crickets. Next door the sound of the nightly news echoed from his neighbor's apartment.

"I was expecting you to call sooner."

"*Lo siento*, Señor." Juan stepped back from the window, turning on his heel to face the screen. Surrounded in hazy smoke, Señor sat at his desk, his fat fingers wrapped around a Cohiba 1966 Edition cigar. He was dressed in black and the collar of his shirt was unbuttoned, revealing a poof of gray chest hair and a thick gold chain with a scorpion medallion. "I know what today is, and I did not wish to disturb you. I waited for as long as I could so that you would have time to mourn."

Señor brought the cigar to his lips, which were hidden beneath a thick mustache, and inhaled slowly. The pricey Cubans were Señor's favorite, and he made sure those around him knew their value. It was a brazen display of power. He was smoking away hundreds of dollars with every puff.

"Is the problem taken care of?"

Once again, Juan found himself eyeing the photo of the Army captain. Before his arrival, only one other man threatened to get in the way, but now both had quickly exposed their weakness and Juan was ready.

"I'm taking care of it. It will not be long."

"It is already too long!" Señor slapped his hand on the desk, rattling the computer and distorting the video for a second. "*Promesas*. You made promises."

Juan studied the man. His black hair was parted neatly, and Juan could almost smell the distinct scent of *Tres Flores* hair gel. Señor's face revealed little emotion due to the enormous amount of money spent on plastic surgery to eliminate any sign of age. Youth, strength, and power were the only things the cartel baron wanted people to see.

But Juan saw more.

Behind Señor's smooth exterior, Juan saw a reckless and unyielding man. A man desperate to reclaim the position of power that had been stripped away from his family by a woman.

"She has made a mistake."

The pompous man sprang forward in his seat. "You have her?"

Juan had to be careful about proceeding. Too much information and Señor's expectation would escalate. "I have men in place. Soon the stakes will be too high for her to ignore."

"Soon?" Señor growled, pushing up from behind his desk. "Today I mourn a brother who has not even had the honor of a burial because there is no body, his family slaughtered by our enemies, and you sit there biding time you do not have?"

Juan tucked his chin in deference, though he felt none for the man barking at him. "Señor, it will not be much longer. You have my word."

Señor leaned across the desk, his face inches from the screen. "I will have much more than that if you do not deliver."

The computer screen flashed blank. Juan wanted to scream. To throw something. He fisted his hands, wanting to squeeze the breath from the man. He stared up at her picture. It mocked him. A reminder that he would have no rest until she paid.

Juan took in measured breaths, his gaze sliding to the rifle. He'd anticipated a response. The fact that he didn't get one demonstrated her arrogance.

It was time for him to raise the stakes.

This time she would respond.

FOURTEEN

"YOU BETTER HURRY, CAP!" Sarge hollered. "Team Army needs their leader."

It had taken Colton nearly ten minutes to put on his shoes. He didn't know if it was nerves, but the movement in his arm was worse than usual, making the task a preschooler could do that much more difficult. And now he was late.

"They're going to need more than that if they hope to win," Sticks said. "Go, team Air Force."

"Bah." Gunny swiped his hand in the air. "Go Navy."

"Sticks, correct me if I'm wrong, but didn't Navy get sunk by Army and Air Force this year?"

"You ain't wrong, Sarge."

Laughter echoed among the members of D-Wing sitting in the rocking chairs on the porch of the Mansion. They'd all claimed front-row seats, and Colton wasn't sure if he was appreciative of their support or doubly nervous because of it. He was about to run down the steps when he thought of something.

"Any of you boys play football?"

Sticks straightened. "Four years. Tight end for the Midlothian Tigers. Went to state."

Gunny wheeled around, his right pant leg folded at the knee. "He's not talking peewee league, Sticks." Gunny leaned back, pride puffing his chest, and squared his eyes on Colton. "Longhorn, two years before the draft took me out of the game. Coaches told me I'd probably have gone pro, given the chance."

Colton turned to Sarge. "What about you?"

"Baseball."

"But you know the sport? Watched it?"

125

"Haven't missed a single one of my grandsons' games. And I've got four of them."

"Good." Colton nodded. "You three have any plans for the next couple of weeks?"

"Was planning my escape," Gunny said. "But depending on what you're offering, I might stick around."

"I'm here until my wife decides she wants me back home again." Sticks smiled. "Hates my snoring, but that woman has no idea what she sounds like at night. Thought a Huey was landing to scoop me out of the rice paddies those first few years of our marriage."

They all laughed, and Colton couldn't help smiling.

"If you guys are up for it, I'd like you to officiate the games for the kids. From the sidelines, of course." The last thing he needed was these guys trying to outdo each other to the detriment of their healing.

The laughter quieted. Colton, wondering if he'd overstepped, glanced to each of them. Or maybe he was asking too much. He was about to tell them it was okay when Sarge rolled forward, Gunny standing behind him with Sticks.

"It'd be a privilege."

"Hooah!" Sarge added.

"Besides, the way Hot Tamale took you out, maybe she should be coaching the team," Sticks said, breaking the moment of solidarity.

Colton shook his head. "I'll let you know when we're ready." He jogged down the stairs, ignoring the new round of jokes being passed between them at his expense. Even though they were decades older and constantly ribbing him, it felt good to be in a brotherhood again—a new team.

Georgia had finally gotten the memo from Mother Nature that it was time to transition from summer to fall, and a crisp breeze curled around Colton's bare legs and arms. He walked across the lawn toward the gym and could feel the excitement building the closer he got. He'd had no idea what to expect when he pitched his idea to Chaplain Kelly, but he and the staff at Home for Heroes were excited and made sure to spread the word. The turnout was more than he could've hoped for and provided just enough kids to form two teams.

He found Maceo on the field with Noah and, like a magnet, his gaze went to Pecca, standing on the side next to Lane, in skinny jeans that hugged her curves, an oversized sweatshirt, and her long hair pulled back in a ponytail. This was the first time he'd seen her in anything other than scrubs. He was finding it hard not to stare—until she caught him.

Nice, Colton.

Pecca waved, giving him a tight smile that concerned him. He crossed the grass to her and Lane.

"Hey, Colton." Lane smiled. "You ready?"

"I think so." He eyed Pecca. "How about you?"

A whistle shrilled behind him, and Pecca jumped. Colton turned to see Charlie gathering all the kids around him. "I should probably go."

"Wait." Pecca grabbed Colton's hand, her touch searing his skin. "You promise no one can get hurt, right? It's flag football. Fun, right?"

Colton glanced at Lane, who looked just as interested in the answer. He smiled, his thumb rubbing her fingers. "I can only promise one of those things."

"What kind of answer is that?" Pecca stared after Colton as he jogged to the middle of the field in his Mustangs T-shirt and shorts, baseball cap flipped backward. The second she'd caught him looking at her, a flutter of butterflies took flight inside her stomach. It was nerves about Maceo playing football. At least that's what she was telling herself.

"Are you freaking out?"

"A little," Pecca said, rubbing her hands over her arms. "You?"

Lane ran a hand over her belly. "A little."

Pecca gave her a sideways peek. "You lying?"

"Mm-hmm. You?"

"Yep." For seven years, she'd been able to convince Maceo that sports weren't a big deal, and *maybe* she used comic books and action figures to further make her point. But last time she checked, there weren't pediatric concussion reports for Comic-Con nerds.

A whistle blew, and the group of boys and girls—yes, five girls showed up—broke away from their circle and formed two lines facing each other. One side wore a belt with red Velcro flags around their waist, the other side wore blue. Flag football. Colton had come into his session with the idea a few days ago, and the excitement shining in his eyes made it impossible to tell him no.

"I don't know who was more excited about this—Charlie or Noah." Lane sighed. "It was all 'football this and football that.'" Lane placed her palms on either side of her belly and whispered, "I'm really hoping this is a little girl so I can level the playing field."

Pecca laughed. Looking across the lawn, she found Charlie kneeling next to one boy and tying his shoe as another walked up dutifully and pointed at his untied laces. Her gaze followed along the sidelines to the parents either standing or sitting in foldable chairs while, off to the side, siblings not involved in the practice were somersaulting, picking grass, or chasing each other. Her eyes stopped on David, who had promised Maceo he would come today. He looked over, smiled, and waved. Pecca returned the wave and smile.

"So, have you decided?"

"What?"

Lane gave her an amused look. "Is it going to be Captain Handsome or Sergeant Good Heart?"

"Shh." Pecca searched the area around them. "You can't call my patient 'Captain Handsome.'"

"Fine." Lane shrugged. "But that doesn't mean I won't be thinking it."

And now so will I. Her eyes were drawn to Colton coaching on the side of the field.

"The way you keep staring at him like that, it seems like the decision has been made."

Pecca sighed. "There's no decision. I already told you that. He's my patient. Even if he wasn't . . ." Her thoughts transported her back eight years. She'd made mistakes with Javier. Been too stubborn to listen to her family's warnings until it was too late. She found Maceo making his way back onto the field. "There's only room for one guy in my life."

Thankfully, another blast of the whistle saved her from having to explain. The action before them drew everyone's attention as the kids scattered across the field chasing. "Is that Noah?"

Lane put her hands next to her mouth and yelled, "Go, Noah! Go!"

Noah rushed his way past two kids, narrowly escaping a third who lunged for the red flag attached to the belt around his waist but missed.

"Watch your back, Noah!"

Charlie's warning came too late as another kid sprinted out of nowhere and grabbed Noah's flag, ending the play.

Clapping and cheering filled the air as the kids circled Charlie and Colton again. Pecca searched the field for Maceo and found him bringing in the rear. His black hair was smushed against his forehead in sweat and his cheeks were splotchy, but he looked . . . happy.

That's all Pecca wanted for him—a safe childhood where he could grow up without worrying about who his father was. She shuddered. It had already been a week and there were no new leads. Rumors around town blamed some restless teenagers, and Pecca had allowed herself to hope it was the truth. She'd finally stopped jumping at every little noise in her house and even slept with all the lights off the last two nights.

Pecca inhaled deeply, feeling her body relax. Beams of sunlight pierced through the copse of trees, shining on the field and turning her focus right where it should be—on her son and his well-being. And of course Colton was standing right next to him.

※※※※※※※

The Warriors. The kids voted, and Colton couldn't think of a more fitting team name.

"The kids did great out there, don't you think?" Colton spun a football in his left hand. His throws were pretty abysmal, but the kids didn't seem to mind. And for the first time in a long time, he'd begun to feel like himself.

"I think they had fun and no one was hurt." Charlie loaded the footballs into the back of his truck bed and lifted the tailgate shut. "That means I'll be able to go home today."

Colton's eyes slipped to the sidelines, where Pecca was talking with a few other parents. "Pecca was worried for Maceo too. I'm glad she let him play."

"It took me nearly forty-eight hours of negotiations and a PowerPoint presentation to convince Lane to let Noah play."

"Forty-eight hours, huh?" Colton laughed.

"Actual missions have taken less energy." Charlie smiled. "I appreciate you keeping an eye on her and Maceo."

The shift in Charlie's tone and the subject matter pulled Colton's attention away from Pecca. He faced Charlie.

"Have you heard anything new?"

"Forensics is running labs on the bullets we pulled from the tree. The area across from the café is wooded, and without knowing where the shooter was at, trying to find anything out there is next to impossible." Charlie sat on the edge of his bumper. "Adrian isn't entirely convinced it was the SSB. His understanding is that the gang still doesn't know she's here."

"So, are you leaning toward it being a random shooting?"

"My gut says it's more than that, especially given the motive.

But it's hard not to give in to the idea that it might have been some teenagers messing around. I mean, why would the SSB try something so aggressive if they want her help? It's like we're missing something."

Colton tossed the football into the back of Charlie's truck, wondering if he should share what he learned from Kekoa or at least tell him he'd asked his uncle Jack to check into Javier. *"To find, know, and never lose the enemy."* The military intelligence creed Colton swore to uphold was ingrained in him whether or not he still wore the uniform. He didn't have all of the intel yet, and sharing fragmented information could be dangerous.

Charlie stood, tipping his head toward the field where Lane was waving them over. "Looks like if we want any of those cookies, we'd better get over there."

They both started over to where the kids and parents stood enjoying Lane's snack. Colton's eyes drifted back to Pecca, Maceo beside her with a football in one hand and a cookie in the other. Seeing them smiling, not worrying about a threat, reminded Colton of the days at the FOB. The forward operating base was a place his soldiers could relax and not think about where they were or the enemy waiting outside the gate. Colton's mission to protect his soldiers always started as soon as his boots hit the ground, and he wasn't any less invested in making sure Pecca and Maceo remained safe.

"I saved two cookies for our coaches." Lane smiled and passed Colton a cookie before handing the last one to Charlie with a kiss on the cheek. "Good job, guys."

Pecca walked closer, and Colton couldn't avoid the soft floral scent the breeze lifted from her skin. Not that he wanted to either. The sweet aroma reminded him of the honeysuckle growing around the porch at his grandparents' ranch and stirred a desire that felt less like a longing for home and more like a longing for the woman next to him.

Colton quickly shifted his attention to Maceo. He really needed to stop thinking of Pecca in that way. Their future was defined by their roles. She was his nurse.

"Did you have fun, Maceo?"

"Yeah."

Maceo didn't meet Colton's eyes, and there was something off in his tone. Colton looked to Pecca, who shrugged. He went to one knee, putting him at Maceo's eye level. "What's up, man?"

"I didn't play very good."

"What do you mean? I watched you play. You did great."

"No, I didn't." Maceo shook his head. "I didn't make one play."

Colton sighed. "One person doesn't make a play. It takes a team. Someone to pass, someone to block, someone to run, and someone to catch. You think one person can do all that?"

"Vincent James."

Colton laughed. "No way. Even Vincent James needs his teammates."

Maceo stared down at his prosthetic. "No one would throw me the ball."

Pecca shifted next to Maceo, and Colton could see that she wanted to comfort her son but wasn't sure whether she should. She looked to him, expectation in her expression. And he got it.

"Maceo, remember what I told you about Vincent? Me helping him?"

"Yeah."

"Well, when he finally got strong and his leg was better, he went back onto the field, and you know what happened?"

"What?"

"No one would throw him the ball either."

Maceo frowned. "Why not?"

"Because they didn't think he could run the ball. Make the play. He had to get out on the field every day and prove he was strong enough." Colton tapped his finger against Maceo's chest. "And that's what you're going to do."

"I am?"

"You are. And I'm going to help you every day, because I believe you can be just as good as Vincent James."

It was like Colton had said the magic words, because in an instant Maceo's little chest puffed a bit and his chin lifted a little higher than it had been before. Colton peered up and saw Pecca's smile was wavering. She mouthed "thank you" and swiped at her eyes.

Heat crawled up Colton's neck. His arm jerked and he tucked it close, as if he needed another reason to remind him why thinking about Pecca in any other way than as his nurse was a bad idea. If he couldn't take care of himself, what did he hope to offer her?

***

Pecca tucked a loose strand of hair behind her ear in an attempt to distract herself from her growing feelings for Colton. He was making it impossible to stick to her principle. Colton was her patient—and he was kind, gentle, generous, and spoke truth into Maceo that brought light back to his eyes. She was becoming as attracted to his character as she was to his good looks.

That undeniable truth brought a smile to her lips, forcing her to tuck her chin. Maybe she should check into the Mansion's rules for any mention about a staff member dating a patient. Her heart thumped a little harder in approval.

"What do you think, Pecca?"

Her eyes flashed up to find Lane, Charlie, Colton, and a brunette woman standing there looking at her. "Oh, I'm sorry, I was"—*daydreaming about my patient*—"trying to remember what I need to pick up from the grocery store."

Lane eyed her with all the suspicion of a friend who knew better. "You know Kristen," she said, gesturing to the brunette. "She's Emilia's mom and is the chairperson for the fall festival at the elementary school." Pecca smiled at Kristen. "She's hosting a meeting at her house, but Charlie's schedule changed and we had to reschedule our birthing class for that night."

Charlie made a face. "I don't know which is worse, birthing class or PTO meetings."

Kristen pouted. "Hey! My meetings are fun. I have wine and appetizers."

"A dozen women who love to gab," Charlie added with a smile before Lane playfully smacked him on the arm. "Kidding."

"There's not only women. We have a few dads who volunteer too." Kristen looked at Pecca. "You know David. He's always helping out at the school, and the saint doesn't even have kids. He'll be there."

Pecca's eyes darted to Colton in time to see a flicker of emotion wash over his face. Why she looked at him in the first place bothered her, but seeing what looked like irritation on his face made her feel funny. She sensed something was off between Colton and David the other day but figured it was because they didn't really know each other. Now it felt like there was more to it than that.

"Um, I don't know."

"Oh, please." Kristen pressed her hands together like she was praying. "If you don't come, then we'll have to reschedule because we won't make quorum."

"And that could affect the fall festival." Lane sighed. "We may have to cancel."

"There's no fall festival?" Noah looked like someone had just told him Disneyland was shutting down.

Emilia spun in a circle. "I'm going to be a princess."

"I wanted to be a football player," Maceo said.

Pecca shot Lane a look that she hoped said "Thanks for putting me on the spot." Then a thought occurred to her. "Oh, I don't have a sitter for Maceo."

"What about Colton?"

If Pecca was surprised by Lane's suggestion, Colton appeared shocked. They both looked at each other and then to Lane.

"Yeah!" Maceo cheered. "We can practice more, and I bet my mom will let us have pizza for dinner, right?"

"Um." She looked to Colton, trying to figure out what to say.
He shrugged. "Pizza and football sound good to me."

"Perfect. I'll put you at David's table." Kristen clapped her
hands. "I'll see you then."

As Kristen gathered Emilia to leave, Pecca spun around to stare
down her friend. Lane wiggled her eyebrows like she was in on a
secret, but with Colton right there, Pecca didn't dare ask. Instead,
she was left trying to figure out how she ended up agreeing to a
night out with David and why she was suddenly very jealous of
Maceo.

FIFTEEN

"OOOH WEEE, CAP, you sure the Army checked your brain?" Sticks said as soon as Colton stepped out of his room. The man was leaning against the wall, arms folded like he'd been waiting. Gunny and Sarge were there too.

Colton looked around. "I feel like I'm walking into an ambush."

"It's not babysitting. It's recon, right?" Sarge gave Colton a tight nod. "Soldier needs to know how to win the battle. Strengths and weaknesses of the enemy."

"It's not a battle." He looked at Sarge. "There's no enemy." He looked at Gunny. "I'm just helping her out." He looked at Sticks. "She's my nurse."

"Hot Tamale's more than that," Gunny said with a glint in eyes. "She's a good one."

"Yeah," Sticks spoke up, pushing away from the wall. "I know you're Army, but don't let that hold you back. She'll overlook it."

"Maybe," Gunny said with a laugh.

Colton shook his head. "I've gotta go."

"Don't make her wait, Cap," Sticks said. "Or a fly-boy is going to swoop in and show you how it's done."

"Or a Marine!" Gunny cackled.

Sarge squinted in thought. "Last time I checked, the wars were won with boots on the ground."

Colton left Sarge to defend his battle theory as he jogged down the stairs of the Mansion and out the door. It was a cool night, and he gave himself plenty of time to walk to Pecca's so that he wouldn't be sweaty when he arrived. It didn't matter if he was an Army soldier or not, his mama always taught him to arrive on time—and looking respectable.

Thirty-three minutes later, Colton stood on Pecca's porch and rang her doorbell. The sound of little feet echoed on the other side of the door before it swung open.

"Colton!" Maceo pushed the screen door open and pulled on Colton's right hand, bringing him into the house. "Mom's still getting ready, but she ordered pizza and said that if I got all of my homework done I could play a video game with you or watch a movie." Maceo tugged on Colton's arm. Colton leaned forward. "My bedtime's nine o'clock, but Mom said if there's only a few minutes left or we're really into the game I can stay up a little later."

Maceo speared him with his dark brown eyes and a look that said he had every intention of pushing his bedtime curfew. Colton gave him an approving wink.

"I hope you like plain old cheese pizza."

Colton straightened to find Pecca standing in the hallway, putting in a gold hoop earring. She blinked and then smiled.

"I don't think I've ever seen you in anything but workout shorts and a T-shirt."

He glanced down at his jeans and forest-green long-sleeve Henley. Colton hadn't expected to go on any dates while he was in Walton, so his wardrobe was limited to cotton shirts and two pairs of jeans. But Pecca . . . In a simple burgundy sweater, black skinny jeans, and flats, he was finding it hard not to stare. She looked amazing. Her long hair was twisted on top of her head, while a few tiny pieces framed her face, and he noticed she was wearing makeup. His eyes were drawn to the ruby color on her lips.

"You okay?" The skin between Pecca's eyes pinched. "Maybe I should cancel—"

"No," Colton said. "It's just, uh, you look . . ." Her eyes pinned him with expectation. "You look very nice."

"Is it too much?" She walked to a mirror hanging on the wall. "I rarely wear anything but scrubs these days, so getting to wear real clothes is a luxury. Lane's sister, Meagan, said some people apparently get dressed up for these PTO meetings."

138

"No. Nope." He shook his head. "You look . . ." *Perfect.*

The doorbell rang, saving him from his thoughts.

"That would be my ride."

"Ride?"

Colton looked over his shoulder in time to see Maceo let David in. From the look on David's face, he wasn't expecting to find Colton there but smiled quickly to cover it up.

"Colton, good to see you." He moved his attention to Pecca. "Wow, you look great."

Great. I could've told her she looked great. Beautiful. Stunning. Amazing. Who says a woman looks very nice, anyway?

"Thanks." Pecca gave him a smile and brushed by Colton, her body skimming his just enough to send a current of electricity spiraling through him. "Let me just give Colton a few last-minute instructions."

Colton followed Pecca into her kitchen, not missing the amused expression lifting David's eyebrows. Yep, from captain in the Army to babysitter . . . he was living his best life. Though, to be fair, pizza and video games with Maceo sounded way better than being the brunt of the jokes from the men in D-Wing.

"The pizza will be delivered in a few minutes." Pecca looked at her watch. "I already paid, and I told Maceo he could watch a movie or play a video game but not both. And no matter what he tells you, his bedtime is nine on the dot."

Colton shot a glance to the living room. David, in his slacks, collared shirt, and tie, looked every part a nervous date, shifting over his cane. He appeared interested in whatever Maceo was saying, but Colton caught him looking into the kitchen.

"Um, I left my number there." Pecca's voice turned Colton's attention to a piece of paper she was pointing to on the counter. "I also left Lane's, though she's going to be at birthing class, which is why I'm going to this thing in the first place."

Did he hear resentment in her tone? A small part of him was happy about that. Pecca was looking at this not as a date but as an obligation. Nothing was romantic about that. Not that he was worried. Or should be worried.

"Are you sure you're okay to do this?"

He met her concerned look and realized she must've asked him something or said something and he hadn't responded.

"I can cancel or try to see if Ms. Byrdie could watch Maceo—"

"It'll be fine." Colton smiled. "I promise."

Pecca made a face, her lips twisting into something like a grimace. "I hate to ask this, but have you, um, ever babysat before?"

Colton swallowed. "A kid, no." Pecca's eyes widened. "But I have commanded a troop of soldiers, and that's basically the same thing. Except a lot more of them. Annnd they get into far more trouble than a seven-year-old."

"Almost eight!" Maceo shouted from the living room. "My birthday's next week."

Pecca wrinkled her nose at Colton. "You haven't seen this seven-year-old in action."

"It's just a couple of hours. What's the worst that could happen?"

"How about we don't find out." Pecca pointed to the paper again. "I left Ms. Byrdie's number too just in case."

David limped over. "We should probably go if we don't want to be late."

"Right. Okay."

Colton watched Pecca make a mad dash to the closet to grab her coat and purse before hugging Maceo and whispering something in his ear that made him peek at Colton from the corner of his eye.

At the door, Pecca turned and gave Colton, Maceo, and the house a final look as though she was trying to remember what it looked like before chaos ensued. Maybe he should be worried.

"Thanks so much! I'll try to get back as soon as I can." With those parting words, she shut the door, leaving him in a wake of her perfume that was fueling an ugly flame of jealousy.

Colton turned to Maceo. "Cheese pizza? That's so boring."

Maceo laughed, and for the next hour and a half they enjoyed their pizza and talked about football, Vincent James, which Marvel movie Colton should watch first—*Iron Man* or *Captain America*—and the merits of movie order—chronological or by release date. In the end, Colton didn't care because he couldn't keep his thoughts from wandering to Pecca and David.

If he counted how many times he had to remind himself they weren't on an actual date, it would be pathetic. But he couldn't help himself. The idea of her sitting next to him, laughing at something funny he said—did the guy even have a sense of humor? Colton didn't know and shouldn't care, because maybe David was a good guy and maybe Pecca did have feelings for him. And maybe he should get a hold of himself.

"I'm going to grab a glass of water. You want anything?"

Maceo, eyes glued to the movie, shook his head. Colton rose and left Robert Downey Jr. waxing poetic about the dangers of a militarized army of robots. He flipped on the light to the kitchen and froze.

Taking in the scene, he blinked to make sure he wasn't imagining what he was seeing. A soapy blanket of bubbles a foot deep covered the entire kitchen floor. Colton looked at the dishwasher still whirring defiantly as a snowy river of soap spewed from the edges. Dread knotted the muscles in his shoulders. How had this happened?

Colton's arm jerked as he rushed toward the machine, but the floor was slippery and his feet split in opposite directions before he caught himself on the counter. "Maceo, we have a problem."

"Whoa!" Maceo hurried over. He stuck his foot in the suds, watching it cover his leg up to the calf. "Cool!"

"Not cool." Colton couldn't find the power button beneath the mess, so he just opened the door. He groaned when a wave of fluffy soap spilled out onto the floor. "What did you put in the dishwasher?"

"Soap," Maceo said, stepping the rest of the way into the soapy wonderland. He reached down and gathered the fluff into his hands and then blew it so the bubbles flew into the air.

"Don't do that. It's slippery."

As if on cue, Maceo's feet began slipping and sliding, and before Colton could do anything Maceo dropped to the floor, buried in bubbles.

"Are you okay?" Colton started toward Maceo, using the counter to hold him steady. "Maceo, you alright?"

"Yes." He giggled. Another spray of bubbles flew into the air. "What are we going to do?"

"Clean it up before your mom gets home."

Maceo's head popped up with a crown of bubbles covering his hair. "You're in so much trouble."

Mom come quick. Bubbles everywhere. Colton's in trouble.

Pecca read the text message from Maceo over and over, trying to make sense of what it meant and keep her panic in check. She tried calling Colton's cell phone, but it kept going to voicemail. Just like Maceo's. By the time she arrived at her house, she was expecting the worst—just not this.

"We tried cleaning it up," Maceo said.

Pecca couldn't believe her eyes. She stood gawking at her kitchen and the layer of soap so thick it looked like snow covering the floor. Colton and Maceo both stood there, heads hung in guilt, their clothes wet, as bubbles clung to their hair—and pretty much everywhere.

"What in the world happened?"

"He made me do it." Maceo looked up. A towel in one hand, the other pointed at Colton. "Said we had to do the dishes so you wouldn't have to worry about it when you got home."

Colton looked at her, a mop in his left hand, his right hand clutched to his side. "I don't know what happened. Maceo put the soap in, and it just started spewing everywhere."

Maceo slapped a palm to his forehead. "Throw me under the bus, why don't you?"

Pecca shot a look at her son. Where had he learned that phrase from? "Okay, you go get ready for bed." She pushed up the sleeves of her sweater and took the towel from Maceo. "I'll be there after I clean up."

"I'll do it." Colton shook his head. "This was my fault. I should've been watching better."

"And not done the dishes!" Maceo yelled from down the hall.

Pecca rolled her eyes and gave a little laugh. "Serves me right for not teaching him how to do them in the first place, I suppose."

"I'm really sorry."

"Don't be. I needed to deep clean this kitchen anyway."

"I mean for taking you away from your party or whatever." Colton's right arm twitched. "I hope David didn't mind leaving early to bring you home."

"He didn't. Leave, I mean." Pecca took a step toward the mess. "I took an Uber home. And believe me, I'd rather deal with a foot of soap suds than decide what flavor snow cone has the least amount of red dye #5 in it."

Colton smirked. "Still, I insist on cleaning this up myself."

"No way, José." Pecca stepped into the mess, and her foot slid out from under her. "Whoa!"

"Be careful." Colton held out a hand. "It's slippery."

No sooner had the words left his mouth than Pecca's foot slipped forward. She tried to regain her balance, but her back arched backward, arms pinwheeling in a wild, frantic attempt to right herself as she tumbled backward.

Scrunching her eyes tight, she prepared to fall, but a strong hand reached out and grabbed one of her flailing arms. She peeked through her squinted eyes to see Colton smiling.

"Gotcha."

Pecca latched onto his arm, feeling the bunching of his bicep beneath her grip. "Thanks. That really is sli—"

Colton's eyes went round, and they both did this jig of a dance. His legs scissored front and back until the momentum built and control was lost. Pecca started laughing, which was a huge mistake. Her legs began their own erratic movement, forcing her to hold on tighter to his arms, but they might as well have been a pair of newborn deer on a pond of ice for all the good it was doing.

"Just . . . stop . . ." Colton's face was red. Sweat lined his forehead. He was so determined not to fall and that only made Pecca giggle more. "Laughing."

"Arghhh!" Pecca slipped, landing hard on her backside and pulling Colton down with a loud *ooooph*. A cloud of bubbles flew into the air and floated everywhere. She tried to roll over, but her legs kept slipping side to side. Another fit of laughter took hold of her as she put a hand on Colton's arm. "Are you okay?"

"I told you to stop laughing." Colton remained on his back, his chest rising with heavy breaths and his face splattered with little poofs of soap.

Pecca gasped between laughing. Was he being serious? Maybe he was hurt. She should stop laughing—only she couldn't. She ran her hand along his arm to his chest, gripping his shirt to stabilize herself, when she felt the muscles in his stomach begin to bounce. A second later the low rumble of his laughter filled the kitchen.

Soap soaking her jeans, she crawled on her knees and leaned over him. "Are you okay?"

"Nothing hurts but my pride," Colton said, blowing bubbles off his nose with a breath.

"That's—whoa!" She slipped again, her face smashing against his chest. The quick thumping of his heart pulsed against her cheek. "Sorry."

Colton maneuvered her around and gently tugged her away from his chest so that she rolled into the crook of his shoulder. She bit her lip, not wanting the laughter to return and alter the moment. *So this is what it feels like to be snuggled up with Colton.* It wasn't exactly how she imagined it happening, but she couldn't deny how good it felt.

Too good.

So good it made her forget her place.

"Shall we try this again?" Colton asked, his voice vibrating softly beneath her head. "Or are you content to have your kitchen become a skating rink?"

Pecca carefully rolled to her side, taking with her the soft scent of Colton's cologne that had transferred to her sweater. "As much as Maceo would like it, I think I'll stick with just one dangerous sport this season."

"Hey." Colton rolled to his side and then, with one hand, pushed himself up to his knees. "Flag football isn't dangerous." His foot slipped an inch, but he remained steady. "This floor, on the other hand." Slowly, he straightened and then, gripping the counter with his left hand, held out his right, the tremor shaking his fingers. "If you can catch it, I'll help you up."

Pecca smiled and wrapped her fingers around Colton's right hand. She looked up at him and held his gaze, feeling the strength in his muscles tighten as he helped her up. Standing, Pecca didn't release his hand right away. Her fingers intertwined with his as they flexed almost like a pulse, and she took a careful step closer to him.

Colton licked his lips. Closing what remained of the space separating them, he lifted his left hand and brushed a soap bubble from her nose. She batted her eyes and smiled. His lips separated and everything in her wanted him to kiss her. Like *really* kiss her. Toe-curling, mind-numbing, take-her-breath-away kiss that she believed was the only kind a man like Colton could give.

His arm jerked, causing Colton to blink. When he looked back at her, Pecca could see the moment was gone. Pink tinged his cheeks, and he quickly pulled his fingers away from hers.

"Colton—"

"I think the, uh, best way to clean this might be to just use towels." He looked anywhere but at her. "Soak it up."

Pecca was embarrassed. She'd crossed a line. *So stupid.* "Um, yeah." She took slow, steady steps toward the hallway, using the counter as an anchor. "I have some old towels out in the garage. I'll just go get them."

Rounding the corner, Pecca stepped into the hallway and paused to catch her breath. She pressed her hands against her cheeks, feeling the warmth. What had she done? Colton was her patient. She muffled a groan and peeked her head into Maceo's room. *What if we had*— Her thought stopped midway at the sight of Maceo draped over his bed, asleep.

She lifted his comforter over him and then, brushing the hair from his forehead, she kissed him. Pecca closed her eyes, realizing how close she'd come to making another mistake. One that could cost her job. If keeping Maceo happy and stable was her priority, then she needed to stop letting her feelings get the better of her.

A noise in the kitchen urged her back to her task. She shut Maceo's bedroom door and walked to the front door. The only thing she didn't like about her cottage-style home was the detached garage. She flipped on the porch light and stepped outside. She was halfway to the garage when the floodlight popped on, illuminating something on the ground near the door.

It was a piece of paper. No, wait. She walked closer, squinted. A photo? Squatting, she reached down and grabbed the picture. She brought it up into the light. It was a picture from the flag football practice. The kids on the field—her eyes shot to the red X. Fear pulsed loudly in her ears. It was Maceo.

Her fingers trembled. Where did this come from? Pecca covered her mouth, stifling a gasp. The picture she was holding drifted to the ground like a dead leaf, landing on a dozen more photos. A big red X covered the faces of her parents. Siblings. Her. Maceo. She wanted to scream, but it was lodged against the fear stealing her breath when she saw a single photo standing out among the rest.

"Pecca, do you need help?" Colton stopped. From the corner of her eye, she could see him taking in the scene as she had. "You need to call the police right now."

Tears pooled in her eyes as she gasped for air. She couldn't deny it now. The South Side Barrio had found her. Her eyes locked on the image of a handprint with the letters *SSB* carved in red into the palm. It was a clear message—everyone she loved had a target on their head.

SIXTEEN

"I NEED TO LEAVE. We need to leave. How could I be so stupid to stay here?"

"Pecca, honey, you need to take a breath."

Sheriff Huggins put a warm hand over her trembling ones and squeezed just enough to pull her out of her panic. Sitting inside the conference room at the sheriff's station made the situation feel all too real. As did the photos lined up in front of her. She'd spent the last half hour identifying the faces of her family members that had been marked out with an ugly red X.

If she wasn't sure before, she saw clearly now that the SSB had found her. She bit down on her lip to keep it from quivering, her eyes moving to Colton.

Ever since he'd called the sheriff, he hadn't been able to sit or stand still. His arm was moving more than she had ever seen before, and she was worried. The features of his face that she'd longed to kiss earlier this evening had turned rigid. Standing tall, he narrowed his gaze on the conversation between her and Sheriff Huggins like he was trying to assess the situation and make a decision. He was in soldier mode and looked like he was ready for war.

"You don't remember seeing anything out of the ordinary when you got home from work today?"

"No." She closed her eyes, trying to remember, but all she could see were the faces of her parents, Adrian, Claudia, Luis, and Maceo with red X's marked over them. "I didn't even park my car in the garage because I was running late and needed to change before the PTO meeting at Kristen's. I don't think I even looked at the garage."

"What about before tonight?"

Pecca's thoughts went to the family photo that was missing from the shelf. "It's probably nothing, but ever since the shooting I've had this feeling that something was off inside my house. I thought it was just anxiety. A photo of my family had been moved from where I normally keep it, and Maceo swears he didn't touch it and I know I didn't move it."

Sheriff Huggins's forehead creased. "You keep your doors and windows locked?"

"After the shooting, yes." Pecca's eyes landed on Sheriff Huggins's blue ones. She wanted to cry. All those days when she felt like something was off. The feeling that someone was watching her. "Do you think someone's been in my house?"

Charlie came into the conference room carrying a cup of hot tea, which he put in front of her.

"We're not going to jump to any conclusions." Sheriff Huggins wrote something down in his notebook. "But I think it would be a good idea if you had the locks changed, and Charlie's got a state-of-the-art security system in his house that I believe Ryan Frost helped him install. Maybe we could get you one of those as well."

"It comes with a panic button that calls straight here to the station," Charlie said with a nod. "I'll get one tomorrow. Doesn't take much to install it."

"That'll work for now until I can make arrangements."

"Arrangements?" Colton paused. Pecca had found the rhythm of his steps soothing to her rattled nerves, but now she shifted under the pressure of his questioning gaze. "You aren't planning on leaving, are you?"

"I don't think that's wise," Sheriff Huggins added before she could respond. "Running puts you on your own. Away from help."

"And that might be exactly what he's driving you to do," Charlie said. "Run."

"We don't know what he's doing." Pecca's thigh bounced against the metal table leg. "Why would Javier do this? He was never like this."

At least not the Javier she knew when they were younger, but it had been eight years and he was in prison. That changed people. But coming after her and Maceo? Threatening her family?

"Can you tell us a little bit about Javier, Pecca?" Sheriff Huggins's voice was tender. "What makes you think he wouldn't go to such extreme lengths to get your attention?"

Pecca stared at the steam rising from her tea. She wasn't proud of her past with Javier, but after Maceo was born she'd worked really hard to forgive herself and move on from her mistakes. It seemed those very same mistakes were now coming back to haunt her. If—and that was a big if—Javier was behind all of this. But was he?

"The Javier I remember, the one I met when I was sixteen, was kind and compassionate. He had a good heart and never wanted a life in the gang, but he grew up in a rough neighborhood and made choices so he could survive."

"Is that why he was part of the robbery?"

"He was trying to stop Felix. His cousin." Pecca met Charlie's eyes. Her shoulders slumped. "I'm not making excuses for him, but Javier wanted to help his cousin. It just . . ." She glanced over to Colton and Sheriff Huggins. Both looked at her like they were trying to understand, and she appreciated it, but unless someone grew up in the Barrio it was hard to explain and even harder to understand. "Something went wrong."

Charlie walked over and pulled his phone from his pocket. "Is this Felix?"

She leaned over the table and cringed. Under the harsh glow of the fluorescent light, Felix looked as scary as he had when she'd first met him. It hadn't mattered what Javier had said, nothing could've stopped the shiver that danced down her spine at the look in his eyes. She rubbed her arms. "That's him."

Charlie twisted the phone around so Colton could see. "I spoke with Adrian while you were getting Maceo settled at the house." Charlie scratched the side of his face. "Your brother said Felix Garcia is missing."

A rush of breath escaped through Pecca's lips. "What do you mean he's missing?"

"After the shooting." Charlie put his phone away. "I talked with Adrian. He agreed to reach out to the gang unit in El Paso and they've put out a BOLO, but they're coming up empty."

"El Paso's a pretty big city," Colton said. "How long has he been missing?"

"Felix 'the Spider' Garcia is a ranking member of the SSB. According to Adrian's contact at the police department, his power is in his presence. They've checked all his regular spots and have a unit outside of his home, but so far he's AWOL."

"Do we think this Felix fella found out Pecca's here in Walton?" Sheriff Huggins tapped the photos on the table. "That he's responsible for tonight?"

The muscles in Pecca's stomach grew tight, making her feel sick. It wasn't hard to imagine Felix going to extreme lengths. He was always trying to prove himself, and that chip on his shoulder had ended up becoming a yoke over Javier's neck.

"Wait." Colton ran a hand over his face. "If Javier was trying to stop Felix, how did he end up behind bars while Felix walked free?"

"Felix never showed up," Pecca said, her voice monotone. "When Javier arrived, the other gang members thought he was there as backup. Javier told me he was going to leave but saw the store owner reaching for a gun behind the counter. He ran inside to stop him before someone got hurt, but it was too late. Another member of the SSB started shooting."

The weight of those days came rushing back, and Pecca wrapped her arms around her stomach. After Javier was arrested, her life felt like it was spinning out of control. And it was. She'd missed her period and thought it was due to stress, but a pregnancy test confirmed that it was not. It was the consequence of a bad decision that, by the grace of God—

Her mind went to Maceo.

Pecca turned her wrist to check the time. She'd missed another one of Claudia's messages. A pang of homesickness blossomed in her chest. She wanted to go home. Wanted her family near her. Tears burned the back of her eyes.

"Do you know how much longer I need to be here?" She sniffled and forced the tears to remain where they were. "I'd like to check on Maceo again."

Sheriff Huggins collected the photos of her family. They were now protected in clear plastic baggies wrapped in bright red tape with the word *EVIDENCE* stamped across it. "Okay, honey. We can get you home, but first I want to discuss your and Maceo's safety."

Pecca pressed her eyes closed, and a rogue tear slid between her lashes. She appreciated what they were trying to do, but the SSB had got to her. *"Be anxious for nothing."* The Bible verse she'd prayed over Maceo's crib after his surgery came rushing back. She clung to it then, feeling helpless, but this time she could do something about it. She could protect her son.

"I will talk to Adrian and maybe my sister, Claudia. She lives in Boston. Maybe we could stay there for a while until this all blows over."

"No." Colton's voice echoed against the walls of the conference room, drawing everyone's attention. His cheeks were a little pink, but it was the fierce look in his eyes that kept Pecca's attention riveted to the man flexing both of his hands in an attempt at control. "I think Charlie's right. If you leave, you'll only be putting yourself and Maceo in danger. Something is keeping you safe, and I think it's your routine."

"Safe? We've been shot at, and now my family is being targeted."

"Yes." Colton hung his head as though the guilt of that fact lay squarely on his shoulders. "But if you go to Boston, you'd be relying on a police force in a city with a population ten times the size of Walton. They won't know you or your case. You won't find a team better equipped to keep you and Maceo safe than the one in Walton."

Charlie nodded. "We can assign an officer to the elementary school. And Colton can continue to escort you between patients and keep an eye on you in between his appointments. Thankfully, you're surrounded by a group of heroes who I'm willing to bet will protect you and Maceo at all costs. We'll be able to watch for anything that seems out of the ordinary."

Pecca's gaze bounced between Charlie, Colton, and Sheriff Huggins. "Colton isn't at the Mansion to watch over me. I'm supposed to be helping him. He's my patient."

Colton shifted, his hazel eyes bearing down on her. "Can I talk to you alone for a minute?"

Biting the inside of her cheek, she nodded. Sheriff Huggins and Charlie stepped out of the conference room before Colton pulled out the chair next to her and sat. He inhaled deeply, and she could see a battle happening behind his eyes. He was warring with what he was going to say. The feeling she had earlier in her kitchen returned, and she longed to run a hand along his arm—to comfort him.

"Pecca, I've dealt with a lot of evil in my career, and if there's one thing I've learned it's that the enemy wants to get you alone. They want you to *feel* alone, helpless. Despite what those guys in D-Wing think, every battle won takes a team. You're not alone here in Walton. Sheriff Huggins and Charlie know who they're watching for now. They can keep you safe. And if you'll allow me." He looked down at his arm. "I know I can't offer much, but I'd like to help."

Her heart twinged with a deep ache for the man. Did Colton really believe that about himself? He had to know that his disorder was only a single part of him, and in the last several days even she'd been able to see how much more there was to him.

"Playing ball with Maceo is one of the highlights of my day." Colton spoke softly. "It gives me something to look forward to when everything else in my life feels like it's been taken from me. I really hope you'll stay."

154

Looking into his eyes, Pecca could see his request held far more meaning than someone wanting to help. But was it fair to ask that of him? The last thing she wanted to do was put him or anyone else in danger, but leaving Walton suddenly didn't sound as tempting anymore.

Colton's jaw ached. He clenched down hard, trying to keep the tremor crawling up his arm from getting worse. He hadn't had an episode since his first appointment with Chaplain Kelly, but the movements in his arm had grown steadily worse since Pecca discovered the photos.

Earlier that evening, he'd checked out her arrangement of family photos she had displayed around the house and realized it made him feel closer to her somehow. Now, after listening to her identify her family members, the threat against them felt personal and he was ticked.

"I didn't think she was going to stay," Charlie said as he and Colton watched Sheriff Huggins leave to drive Pecca back to Lane and Charlie's home above the café. "What'd you say to her?"

That I needed a chance to do something meaningful again. Colton swallowed the truth. "That I believed she was safer here." His arm jerked. "I hope I'm not wrong."

"I know it's late, but if you've got time I'd like to talk through how we're going to make sure you're not wrong."

Colton nodded, taking note of the time on his watch. Barely past ten and the day already felt much longer. As he followed Charlie back into the station's conference room, the image of Felix Garcia came to mind. He couldn't forget the tattoos inking the Spider's face and stretching over his shaved head, but it was the hatred emanating from the man's eyes that had Colton unnerved. He looked dangerous. "We need more information on Javier's cousin."

"When I spoke with Adrian, I got the indication he's doing his best, but he's gotta be careful. Too much interest in the SSB and Javier is going to draw attention, and that'll put his career—and possibly his life—in danger."

"What about Pecca and Maceo?"

"He knows what's at stake." Charlie sat. "The only way we're going to get insider information is if he keeps his cover."

Sitting in the chair once occupied by Pecca, Colton blew out a breath. "It's not the only way."

Charlie turned, eyebrows raised as he folded his arms over his chest. "How long before you called someone after the shooting?"

A ping of guilt radiated in Colton's chest, but the years he'd spent gathering and analyzing intelligence told him that good information in the wrong hands was just as dangerous as bad information in the right hands. He had to be sure he had good information before passing it on, and right now the only thing he was sure of was that he didn't have enough.

A cold memory—the faces of the soldiers from the 401st—sent a painful shiver over his shoulders. Their deaths would've been on his shoulders. Gritting his teeth, he took a measured breath. The last thing he needed was to let his past take his focus off what was happening right now.

"Colton, we both want the same thing—to keep Pecca and Maceo safe. I know integrity matters in the intelligence field, and I'm not asking you to divulge your sources, but the best way we can keep our promise to Pecca is to work together."

Every battle won takes a team.

Even if his earlier words to Pecca weren't enough, Charlie's reminder of the promise was. Colton had convinced Pecca to stay in Walton not only because he believed it was in the best interest of their safety but also because it meant a level of control that made him feel as though he had a purpose again.

"The information I have is shallow at best." Colton thought back on his conversation with Kekoa. "Besides the aggravated assault, Javier doesn't have the kind of criminal history one would expect from a gang member, much less a leader, which kind of confirms what Pecca said about him."

It was still hard to picture Pecca being involved with a gang member. What had she seen in him in the first place? She was smart and sweet and just not the kind of woman he could see getting caught up with a man like Javier Torres.

"Which makes it hard to understand why he would do this to her."

"None of this makes sense." Colton shifted, the muscles in his arm throbbing. "If the SSB wanted Pecca to testify on Javier's behalf, why would they shoot at her? Leave photos at her house threatening her family? If they really wanted to get to her, the opportunity was there. Why didn't they take it?"

Charlie nodded. "Unless they're trying to intimidate her into testifying."

"Yes, but how would she know that? The only reason Pecca knows that now is because of her brother's information. Take that away and you're left with threats."

"And why would someone be threatening Pecca?"

"To get to Javier."

"What do you mean? He's the one behind this."

"Unless he's not." Colton shook his head as the pieces of his theory began to fall into place. "Adrian told you the South Side Barrio lost some of their control when Javier went to prison. I've learned the DEA has connected them to cartels outside the country. What if Javier doesn't want to come out of prison on early release? Maybe that's the motive behind the threats. Get to Pecca, get to Javier."

A grim expression lined Charlie's face. "That might explain why Javier's cousin is missing."

Apprehension rolled through Colton. If that was the explanation behind Felix's disappearance, it meant the threat against Pecca was far more serious. If the SSB was behind the shooting and the photos, the message was clear—they could get to her.

SEVENTEEN

"LET'S DO IT AGAIN." Colton took a swig from his water bottle, emptying a third of it in a single gulp. The lights inside Chaplain Kelly's office had been dimmed, the shades on the window turned to subdue the sun's afternoon rays. It was supposed to infuse the space with a sense of calm to help Colton's brain relax, but at the moment he was feeling anything but relaxed. He eyed Chaplain Kelly sitting next to him, concern in his eyes. "We have time. Let's do it again."

"I think we should take a break."

"No," Colton said, almost shouting. Then he took a deep breath and exhaled slowly. "I want to do it again."

Chaplain Kelly pressed his lips together but nodded and tapped a button. The computer screen in front of Colton lit up. 178. 176. 177. He took another long breath, trying to bring the numbers down. 177. 179. 178. Why wasn't it working?

"Colton—"

"I can do this." 180. 183. Come on! Colton wanted to scream, but an outburst wasn't going to bring his numbers down. Sweat soaked his shirt, his breathing becoming shallow. 188.

"That's enough for today." The screen in front of Colton went blank, and Chaplain Kelly put the remote on his desk. "You did well."

"I can do it again." But the tremor in his arm said otherwise. "Maybe I can come back in for another session? After my pool therapy with Pecca."

"Colton, is everything okay?"

The events from the night before came hurtling back into his mind, twisting Colton's stomach into a knot. He pushed his chair

159

back from the machine. What was keeping whoever was behind the shooting and photos from harming Pecca and Maceo? And what about next time? Frustration nipped at his nerves. Colton needed information. Without it, he felt helpless, out of control. So he focused on the one thing he currently had access to—his strength.

By the time the sun had crested the horizon that morning, he was out the door for his morning run. Then he'd gotten to the gym early and was stretching by the time Pecca came in. During their session he'd noticed her mood had shifted. Her motivation lacked its usual cheerfulness, which only pushed Colton to work harder. He'd been so focused that Pecca had to put herself in front of the equipment to get him to stop.

"I'm fine," Colton said, slipping the wires off his fingers and holding them out to the chaplain. "I thought I was doing well. Didn't want to quit while I was on a roll."

"There's definitely improvement. You were able to control the numbers, which is good, but we have to be mindful not to push too hard. It can make the movements worse." Chaplain Kelly smiled and looked over his notes. "Now, you should be off your medications completely. Have you noticed any changes?"

Colton fixed his eyes on the ground. "I haven't noticed any changes."

"It'll take some time, but eventually your body will flush the medicine out."

He glanced up. "Are you sure the medicine won't help me? Why would the doctors prescribe it if it won't help?"

"I've spoken with your doctors and Dr. Bruno here, and all agree that the medications you were on acted more like a bandage. A short-term fix but potentially problematic in the long-term."

"Problematic how?"

"Dependency. At some point the dosage you're on won't be enough and the symptoms will come back, maybe worse than before. It'll require upping the prescription, and since your disorder isn't organic, it's unlikely the medicine is helping. Trust me, the sooner we can get it out of your system, the better."

A chill took hold of Colton's damp skin. He cast his eyes down at his hand, willed himself to make a fist. His fingers curled but didn't close completely. Had the medicine stopped working? Was he becoming dependent? He thought about the pill bottles upstairs in his room and guilt punched him in the gut.

"Tell me how physical therapy is going."

"Wha—" Colton's whole body jerked, his mind whirling with the ramifications of being dependent on his meds. "Um, yeah. Good. We started pool therapy. My arm doesn't jerk as much in the water. Pecca said it's because my brain is responding naturally to keep me from drowning."

"That's true." Chaplain Kelly set his pen on the desk and leaned back in his chair. "That's the goal here too. Using cognitive therapy, we're trying to retrain your brain to signal your nervous system without you thinking about it."

"Like when Pecca threw tennis balls at my head." Colton snickered. "I caught *most* of those."

Chaplain Kelly chuckled. "The flag football team seems to be really taking off. It's been a pleasure to see the kids out there playing."

"I think they're having fun."

"D-Wing fellas are too."

Colton smiled, his mood lightening. "I think they're rowdier than the parents."

"I used to think mealtimes were the highlight of their day, but I'm beginning to think those practices are what's getting them through their therapy sessions with Pecca. How's Maceo coming along?"

"Good. The kid's got a great arm and so much heart. He has to work a little harder than the other kids, but he's not willing to back down. I love that about him." Colton's shoulders slumped and his arm twitched. "Look at me. Here I am complaining about how difficult my life is and then there's Maceo. A seven-year-old kid with as much courage as guys I've seen take the battlefield. I have no right to complain."

"Why not?" Chaplain Kelly said. "What's happening to you doesn't feel fair. And what Maceo faces isn't fair either, but this is your journey. Your feelings are valid. What's the point in pretending they don't exist?"

Colton eyed the man behind the desk. "What's the point in whining about it?"

"There's a difference between whining about them and acknowledging them."

If that were true, Colton wasn't sure he knew the difference.

"Have you ever considered what you were going to do outside of the military?" Chaplain Kelly said. "I've read your file and you were on the path for a long career, but all soldiers eventually retire. Did you have plans?"

"Well, retire for one." Colton exhaled, the tension returning. "Then I wanted to move back to Texas and run my grandfather's ranch."

Chaplain Kelly shifted, his chair squeaking. "And now you don't want to?"

"And now I can barely brush my teeth or eat without making a mess. I couldn't even sign my name on a check to pay for the property much less take care of the land and house."

"I have a homework assignment for you." The groan escaped Colton's lips before he could stop it, and Chaplain Kelly smiled. "I promise it won't be too difficult. I want you to begin imagining what your future's going to look like once you leave here. Will you go back to Texas? Buy your grandparents' ranch? Or do something else?"

"No offense, sir, but I can't even plan what my day is going to be like with these movements, much less a future."

"I didn't ask you to plan your future. I said imagine. *The heart of man plans his way, but the Lord establishes his steps.*' Consider how God is establishing your future."

God? The only thing Colton considered regarding God was why this was happening to him. Was he being punished? Had he committed some horrible sin? And how could he make up for it? Living back at home with his parents, listening to them pray and talk about staying faithful to God, trusting his plans—Colton couldn't take it. He'd been faithful. Went to chapel. Prayed. Even read the Bible verses his mom sent him, yet somehow none of it was enough. If God would just tell him what he'd done to deserve this, he would change. Fix it. Repent. Whatever it took to get his life back.

Walking out of Chaplain Kelly's office, Colton wasn't sure he'd be able to complete his homework. How was he supposed to imagine a future when he didn't even know what the rest of the day would bring?

He paused by a window overlooking the manicured lawn. The grass had been mowed that morning, leaving a checkered pattern in the blades. He spotted Gunny, cane in hand, hobbling along the path. The veterans in D-Wing never stopped talking about their service in the military. Most had served long careers, but for some, like Sarge, whose leg was destroyed in war, their future probably wasn't what they'd imagined it to be, yet they were happy.

Could he be happy too? Colton glanced over his shoulder to the gym. His heart turned over. He might not be able to plan his future, but no one was going to stop him from his plan to keep Pecca and Maceo safe.

⁂

Pecca stared at her cell phone, trying not to cry. She had another missed call from her sister, and when she called back the phone call went straight to Claudia's voicemail. After everything that had happened last night, Pecca still wasn't sure going up to Boston was a bad idea. But that would mean leaving Walton—*and Colton.*

"Great catch, Maceo."

"Thanks, Coach."

Maceo beamed up at Colton, and Pecca's heart skipped a beat. She really ought to stop thinking of him in *that* way. Putting her phone away, she wrapped her arms around herself. The temperatures had dipped with a cold front, but the chills on her skin weren't because of the brisk October day.

Everywhere she turned, Pecca expected to see Felix's tattooed face—among the crowd of parents or in the car next to her at a stoplight or in the shadows of the trees outside of her house. She shuddered.

Tonight she and Maceo would be returning to their home. Charlie had spent the day overseeing the locksmith installing new locks for all the windows and rekeying the front and back doors. On top of adding an additional dead bolt, Charlie set up a video security system—the same one Ryan had recommended—that came with a portable panic button she could use to alert the sheriff's station immediately if she was in trouble.

Tugging the scarf around her neck, Pecca's eyes went back to Colton. He was standing on the sidelines a few feet away from her. He'd been like that all day—never far—hanging out with her in the gym as she worked with patients and scheduling his session with Chaplain Kelly around her lunch to make sure she was inside the Mansion.

Pecca, hating how much she was enjoying Colton's extra attention despite the circumstances, bit the inside of her lip. Being under his watchful eye made her feel more than protected—she was beginning to feel things for him that definitely crossed the line.

"I guess Colton didn't get the memo about the weather?"

Pecca, pretending she hadn't just been staring at Colton, gave Lane a hug and her belly a little rub before looking over at him again. Dressed in a T-shirt and workout shorts, a Mustangs ball cap turned backward over his head, he called out plays as he paced the sidelines. His muscles flexed and bunched as he mimicked what he wanted the kids to do with the ball. It was clear from the bright expression lighting the features on his face that he was having as much fun as the kids were. It was also clear why girls fell in love with the quarterback or defensive back or whatever position Colton played.

"He's hot—" Pecca snapped her lips shut. She turned slowly, hoping Lane hadn't heard that, but the smile on her friend's face said she had heard it and was already planning the wedding. "What I mean is, because of the movements his body temperature is always higher. Making him . . . hot." Lane's eyes sparked with amusement. "Never mind."

"Don't stop. Please keep telling me how hot Captain Handsome is."

Pecca's eyes went round. Colton was literally less than five feet away. She gave Lane a death stare, which only made her friend burst out laughing. Pecca relaxed a little and allowed herself to smile. She'd take talking about Colton's good looks over what had happened last night any day. Thankfully, Lane seemed to know that.

"Shh."

"What? He's not paying any attention to you right now. He's watching the kids play."

"Which is what we should be doing." Pecca pointed at the field where the kids lined up for a play. "Besides, you know things have shifted."

"Do I need to remind you how Charlie and I got together? You never know what God will use to bring two people together. Besides"—Lane bumped her hip against Pecca's—"I have exciting news."

Pecca turned. "You found out what you're having!"

Lane frowned, her eyes dimming. "No. Charlie's as stubborn as an ox." Her eyes lit up again. "But this is better."

"Better than knowing if your baby is a boy or a girl?"

"You can date him." Lane used her eyes to direct Pecca's attention to Colton. "Shirley checked into it, and while it's not encouraged, it's also not *discouraged*."

Heat flamed up Pecca's neck and into her face. She slid a sideways peek at Colton. The whistle blew and the kids broke their formation. Pecca followed the football, watching it get passed to another kid as Noah raced ahead and called for the ball. It was thrown but fell short and the play ended.

"Did you hear m—"

"Yes, I heard you," Pecca whispered harshly. "What does that even mean—'it's not discouraged'?"

"It means that if your patient . . ." Lane's brow wrinkled. "What did Shirley say . . . revs your engine, then there are no rules that say you can't enjoy the ride."

Oh, man. Lane's metaphors were as bad as Shirley's. "What happened to you pushing me to attend a PTO meeting with David?"

Lane waved her hand in the air. "Yeah, well, we all make mistakes." She winked. "Besides, when you ask me to be your matron of honor, this will make an excellent story for a great speech."

Pecca squeezed her eyes shut, but that only brought a vision of her in a white gown walking down an aisle with Colton at the end of it. Wow! That was fast. "So, um, what yummy snacks did you bring this time?"

"Double fudge chocolate chip cookies, but don't change the subject."

"Mmm, I bet the town dentist just loves you."

"Come on, Pecca. What's it going to hurt if you admit you like him? He likes you too."

"He does?" Pecca swallowed, remembering how much she had wanted him to kiss her last night. The moment felt like ages ago. "I-I can't. I have to think of Maceo."

"What's wrong with Maceo?"

Pecca found her son on the field. He looked like a little man, with his hands on his hips and an intense expression on his face as he listened to Colton. She didn't know what Colton was like on the battlefield, but on the football field the man was in his element. He had a way with the kids, speaking to them in a manner that filled them with visible confidence. Pecca saw it with Maceo. He'd come home after practice with Colton, and it was like he was invincible, believing there was nothing he couldn't do if he worked hard. She couldn't even remember the last time Maceo complained about his prosthetic.

That alone was enough to make her all swoony for Colton, but Pecca had to be realistic. She was in the middle of a mess caused by the last bad choice she'd made.

"Nothing," Pecca said quickly. "He's never been happier. I want to keep it that way."

"What about you?"

"I'm happy."

Lane made her eyebrows dance above her eyes. "But you could be *really* happy with—"

"Now that looks like the smile of a proud mom."

Pecca turned to find David walking over. He tilted his head toward the field, and Pecca saw Maceo charging after a little girl carrying the football. In the beginning, she had been worried about the girls on the team, but they quickly earned their place just like Maceo. They all just went out there and played.

She pressed her hands to her cheeks, feeling guilty that her smile had nothing to do with Maceo. "He does love football."

"He's good at it," David said. "I'm glad you decided to let him play."

"Oh, I forgot to ask." Lane slapped her forehead. "How was the fall festival meeting last night?"

It really felt like a lifetime ago. "Um, it was chatty. I had to leave before they really got started, but I think I'm signed up for the ring toss." Pecca looked to David. "Right?"

"Yes." David smiled. "Was everything okay at home?"

Pecca rubbed her arms again. "Yeah. Maceo put the wrong soap inside the dishwasher, and the whole kitchen was covered in bubbles."

"Yikes." David laughed, twisting his cane into the ground as he shifted his footing. "Sounds like something on one of those funniest home video shows."

The whistle blew again, and the kids were back at it. This time Kristen's daughter, Emilia, was running with the football but was being chased quite vigorously by two boys. She panicked and tossed the ball to the boy next to her, who wasn't expecting it. The ball hit his chest and fell to the ground, only to be scooped up by a kid on the other team who knew exactly what to do with it. Touchdown.

"Pecca."

"Huh?" David and Lane stared at her a second before Lane's eyes darted to David and then back. "Sorry, I was watching the play."

"I was wondering if, after Maceo's birthday party, I could take you both out to the new Marvel movie." David shifted again. "I heard it's supposed to be good."

"Oh, um." Pecca looked to Lane for help. "It's just—"

"She's already seeing someone." Lane gave a "sorry, that just popped out" look to Pecca before continuing. "It's still kind of a new relationship, which is why Pecca hasn't talked about it yet."

David's forehead creased as his gaze flicked to Colton and back. "Right. Sure."

He smiled, but Pecca could tell it was forced, and she felt bad. Really bad. David was a nice guy and had always been kind to her and Maceo, but Lane was right, there was no spark between them—no engine revving.

"I, uh, have a gift for Maceo for his birthday. The new Endzone video game. I can just drop it off here—"

"No!" Pecca said, her hand landing on David's arm. He glanced down as she quickly withdrew it. "Maceo wants you to come to his birthday party. I do too. You've been a really good friend to him, to us. Please say you'll come."

A few awkward seconds passed before David nodded. "A man can never have too many friends, right?"

Pecca smiled. "Right."

"Well, I promised Kristen I'd talk to her about the price I got for the jumping balloon. I'll see you around, then."

When David was far enough away, Pecca spun on her heel so fast she bumped into Lane. "What were you thinking?"

"I was trying to help." Lane made a face. "It did, sorta."

Pecca rubbed her forehead. "Yeah, now I just need to find a relationship."

"Lucky for you, you don't have to look very far."

Looking over her shoulder, Pecca's eyes were drawn to the only man on the field Lane could possibly be talking about. Colton flashed her a smile that sent a parade of tingles marching through her body. Why did he have to be so freaking cute?

Fine. If it wasn't discouraged . . . She bit her lip, coming to a decision.

If Colton asked her out, she wouldn't say no. She'd consider it, analyze the pros and cons. She'd also discuss it with Claudia, because her sister was the logical one, and that's if she could ever get hold of her. Then, if it seemed like a good idea, she might say yes, depending on her mood.

Pecca's cheeks ached, and she realized it was because she was smiling again. Who was she kidding? She'd already imagined them getting married, and they hadn't even been on their first date. *What was the harm in one little date?*

EIGHTEEN

PECCA CRINGED. *Please be careful. Please be careful.* That was her prayer all afternoon as she watched Maceo and his friends bounce, climb, swing, and fall all over the place inside the trampoline park. The giant warehouse kept the kids busy for hours. They barely sat still long enough to eat pizza and sing "Happy Birthday," even leaving the pile of presents on the table, forgotten.

"This party was a great idea," Lane said, scooping up a plate with a half-eaten piece of birthday cake left on it. "I think we'll do this for Noah's birthday."

"I'll pay you not to have it here." She looked over to the monkey ropes just in time to see Maceo racing through the air on a zip line. He made some *Lord of the Flies* noise before releasing his grip and dropping into a giant pit filled with huge chunks of blue and red foam. "I don't think my son realizes how much that prosthetic costs. If he breaks it . . ."

"Aren't they pretty durable?"

Pecca sat next to Lane. "They are, but he still needs to be careful."

"I think these belong to one of those boys." Shirley carried over a pair of socks and set them on the bench. "I thought I was done collecting smelly clothes."

"Ha." Lane licked chocolate icing from her finger. "I thought once I married Charlie I'd have some help." She quirked her lip. "Now I'm just picking up little-boy and big-boy clothes with varying degrees of smells I don't want to identify."

"It's called *man*, woman." Charlie planted a kiss on Lane's head as he straddled the bench. "And you know you love it."

Lane made a face that said otherwise, and Pecca sighed. She

171

glanced over to Colton, who was being pulled toward a dodgeball game Maceo and some of his flag football teammates were trying to organize. Did it make her sound pathetic to admit that she maybe wanted to be the one to pick up after Colton?

Claudia would say it was because she had a thing for broken and wounded souls. Said that's why she was drawn to Javier—wanted to fix him. But that wasn't entirely true. Javier was not like the guys he hung out with in the gang. Something was different about him.

And Colton was nothing like Javier.

"How's the new alarm system working?" Charlie said, massaging Lane's shoulders. "You're setting it every night? Even when you're home?"

"Yes. Maceo thinks it's fun." But for Pecca, it was unnerving. Most homes had alarm systems these days as a preventative deterrent, but she was relying on hers to warn her against an anticipated danger.

"I still think your best defense is a big, scary dog." Shirley shivered. "Or a Colt. Maybe a Smith & Wesson."

They laughed.

"I'm the only person in my family, besides my mom, who doesn't know how to shoot a gun." Pecca shrugged. "Not sure I'm missing out."

Lane raised her eyebrows. "Even your sister knows?"

"Yeah, she was on the rifle team in high school and got a scholarship to the University of Texas. Was even invited to the Junior Olympics."

Charlie whistled. "Remind me not to mess with her."

"Don't worry." Pecca laughed. "The only thing Claudia shoots now are after-hour cocktails with clients as she's trying to make the next great deal."

Pecca's throat turned raw and she quickly averted her eyes, running her hands down her jeans in an attempt to regain control of her emotions.

Lane put a hand on Pecca's. "Did she call?"

"Not yet." Pecca peered at her friend, appreciating Lane's heart. She knew how much Pecca missed her family and always made it a point to ask about them or their lives whenever possible. "But she'll call tonight. She never misses Maceo's birthday."

"I'm sure your family wishes they could be here." Lane squeezed her hand. "Bad timing."

"The worst." Pecca's dad got sick and couldn't fly. Adrian had work. Her sister-in-law was pregnant and due any day, and there was no way she could ask Luis to leave his wife to bring her niece and nephew to Georgia for Maceo's birthday.

Her heart ached. This was the first time no one from her family was there to celebrate his special day, but she had a lot to be grateful for. Colton, Charlie, and Lane were there, Shirley, Sheriff Huggins and Ms. Byrdie—all of them filled in the void. Even David had come.

Pecca watched David as he talked to the mom of one of Maceo's classmates. She had no ring on her finger. Maybe David had moved on. Good. She was happy for him. David was as good as they came. He'd honorably served his country and gotten injured, but he didn't let it stop him from still trying to find ways to serve his community. The staff at the school spoke highly of him, and he was a reliable volunteer at Home for Heroes. Any woman would be lucky to have a guy like him, except he wasn't Colton.

"So, have you decided who you're going to give the final rose to?"

"What?" She turned to find Lane and Shirley looking at her expectantly. She glanced back to David and then to Colton before rolling her eyes. "You guys are too much, but that does remind me, I have an episode of *The Bachelor* to catch up on."

Shirley tsked. "Honey, you've got your own bachelor over there, and you don't have to worry about thirty girls chasing after him."

"And that's my cue." Charlie, making a face, stood up. "I'm just going to do . . . man stuff." He hitched his thumb toward

Colton and the kids. "Sweat, compete in feats of strength—not talk about *The Bachelor*."

Pecca, Shirley, and Lane burst into laughter as they watched Charlie hurry away.

"Don't let him fool you." Lane held the sides of her belly. "If I'm watching it, he's like a moth to a flame."

This started another round of girlish giggles that left all three of them trying to catch their breath.

"Are you ladies okay?" David smiled at them as he approached. "Can I get you some water or something?"

"No, we're good, honey." Shirley wiped her eyes. "Would you like some more cake?"

"Oh, no thank you, ma'am." He pressed a palm to his flat stomach. "I've had my fill." His eyes shifted to Pecca. "It's getting late, and I promised my neighbor I would feed her cat while she's out of town. I wanted to say goodbye to the birthday boy and thank him for the invitation, but he seems a little occupied at the moment."

Pecca stood and turned to find Maceo climbing a huge rope ladder. He was struggling and slower than his friends, but he was smiling. "I'll let him know. I'm glad you came today, David."

"Me too." His eyes traveled to Maceo again, his lips parting into a lopsided smile. "He's a great kid, Pecca. Really special."

"Thank you." She started to reach for David's arm and then hesitated. He really was the whole package—just not the one for her. She touched his arm. "David, I know you're going to make a woman very happy one day."

David patted the top of her hand, his light brown eyes dimming. "Have a good weekend, Pecca."

Pecca cringed watching him leave. Alone. *"You're going to make a woman very happy one day."* Had she really said that?

"You okay?" Lane asked, her eyes following David out the front door before returning to Pecca. "You made the right choice. David's nice, but he's sort of . . . boring. Not in a bad way. Just not in a good way either."

Pecca began gathering shoes, jackets, and belongings, getting everything ready for parents to arrive and collect their kids. It had been three days since Pecca had decided to allow herself to feel something for Colton in the hopes that maybe he felt something too, but nothing had changed. He came into the gym for his session, hung out until his appointment with Chaplain Kelly, went back to the gym until his pool session, and then played football with Maceo outside the gym until she was done with work.

"I don't know. Is *now* really the right time to be thinking about any of this?" She rubbed her hands together. "I'm locking my house down like it's Fort Knox. My focus needs to be on keeping Maceo safe—not dating."

"Wait here."

"Where are you—"

Pecca tried to grab Lane's hand, but it was too late. Her friend was striding over to Colton like a woman on a mission. They looked over at her and she ducked her head, quickly busying herself with the mess of paper plates and plastic cups littering the table. Tossing the mess into the trash can, Pecca kept an eye on the conversation happening among Lane, Colton, and Charlie. *What is Lane doing?* A second later, she returned like someone who had just gotten their way.

"What did you do?"

"Gave you one less thing to worry about." Lane sat, leaning her elbows back on the table, looking completely pleased with herself. "Colton said he would be *happy* to help you get Maceo and all those presents back to your house."

"That's nice, but I don't really need help."

Lane sat forward. "You just said you need to be thinking about your and Maceo's safety." She tilted her head in Colton's direction. "Shirley thinks a dog is your best security. I say it's that six-foot hunk of muscle."

Pecca watched Colton, who was overseeing Maceo and the kids playing on the monkey ropes, and the familiar burst of attraction rushed through her. There was a seriousness to his posture—protective and alert. Pecca was beginning to understand that those traits were the cornerstone of who Colton was at his core, but she also caught glimpses of his quiet humor and tenderness that reached the places of her heart she'd long since closed off.

Was it time to open them up?

Maceo was toast by the time they got to Pecca's house. Colton finished unloading her car and carrying in the gifts while she got him ready for bed. He surveyed the cottage-style homes and dense tree line hedging the neighborhood. His nightly runs gave him a good idea of the places a person could hide and watch, waiting for the perfect moment to make good on their threat.

"You okay?"

Colton turned to find Pecca standing near the hallway, watching him. He gave her neighborhood one final survey before stepping the rest of the way into her house. "Yeah. I set Maceo's gifts on the table. I hope that's alright."

"Perfect. Thank you." She eyed the colorful packages. "He really wanted to open them, but he was so tired. I told him opening them up tomorrow morning would be like his birthday was two days instead of one."

"Smart."

She shrugged. "I have my moments."

Colton was sure she had many. Maceo was such a well-adjusted young man, no one would ever guess the hardships he'd faced in his short life—and that was all due to the woman standing a few feet away from him. She was strong and determined, and her joyful personality defied her circumstances in ways he couldn't understand. Those qualities and so much more made Pecca more beautiful with every passing day.

His skin grew hot. "So, I'll just head back—"

"I was going to make some quesadillas," Pecca said. Her cheeks pinked at her interruption, but she continued. "I didn't realize how bad that pizza was, and I'm starving. Would you, uh, like to stay?"

Yes. He wanted to very much, but was it a good idea? There was no denying his feelings for her were growing into something he needed to be cautious about, but at the moment he couldn't remember why. Besides, it was just cheese and tortillas.

"That kind of sounds delicious right now."

A sparkle returned to her eyes when they met his. "Yeah?"

He tipped his head toward her fireplace. "Would you like me to start a fire?"

"Oh, that would be great." Pecca disappeared into the kitchen. "There's wood on the porch."

Colton gathered some logs and kindling from the porch in his left hand and began stacking the wood next to the fireplace when he heard Pecca in the kitchen. Was she humming? He paused and listened. She was. He smiled and continued working on the fire. A few minutes later it was crackling, and Pecca carried a tray into the living room.

"I don't like to keep soda in the house, but I've got some juice, tea, and water."

"Water is good."

When Pecca returned, she handed him a bottle of water and then stopped. "Can you give me a few minutes? I'll be right back." She hurried down the hall before turning around abruptly. "Oh, the remote's on the side table. Go ahead and start eating, and make yourself at home."

And then she was down the hall. Colton sat on the couch and leaned back. His stomach rumbled at the sight of the gooey cheese pressed between the tortillas. He'd wait for Pecca.

Colton surveyed the room, remembering the last two times he'd been here. He sat up. Should he have checked the house first? No, she had an alarm now. But an alarm wouldn't stop someone if they were determined.

"Sorry."

He turned in her direction and his mouth went dry. Pecca had changed into a pair of black leggings and an oversized sweatshirt with— "Are you really wearing that?"

"What?" She smiled coyly and glanced down at the Navy sweat-shirt. "A patient gave it to me." She locked eyes with him. "You don't like it?"

"It should be burned," Colton said. He tilted his head to the fireplace. "We can use it if we need more fuel."

"Ha-ha."

Pecca plopped down on the couch close to him and tucked her legs beneath her. She'd let her hair down, and Colton realized it was the first time he'd seen it not pulled back. The long chestnut layers fell over her shoulders, and every time she moved the sweet scent of her shampoo wafted over him.

"Why aren't you eating?" She stretched across him, grabbing a triangle of tortilla and cheese, and his heart about thudded out of his chest. The heat of her body next to him made him swallow back an urge he hadn't felt for a long time. "It's good, I promise."

"I was waiting for you."

"Did you want to watch a movie or something?" She took a bite and then swiveled on the couch so that she was facing him. "I have Netflix, and we own every Marvel movie."

"Can I ask you a question?"

She tilted her head to the side, a nervous look in her eyes. "Um, sure."

"Are those tacos on your socks?"

Pecca let out a startled laugh. "Yes." She wiggled her toes. "Maceo got them for me for Mother's Day last year," she said around a bite, then wiped her lips with a napkin. "Okay, my turn to ask a question. But first you have to eat, because if you don't I will eat all of this—and I'm not joking."

Colton smiled, then picked up a quesadilla and took a huge bite to satisfy her. "You're right. These are good."

"It's the homemade tortilla." She lifted her shoulders and took another bite. "Makes all the difference." She licked her lips and straightened her shoulders. "Tell me about Texas."

Colton swallowed the last of his quesadilla. "What do you mean? You're from Texas."

"I know, but I miss it. And I want to hear you talk about it. Where you grew up. Your family home."

He grabbed a napkin and wiped his lips, his fingers twitching. Talking about home used to be one of his favorite topics, but now it was a painful reminder of a life no longer within his grasp. Chaplain Kelly's homework came to mind. *"Begin imagining what your future's going to look like once you leave here."*

"Jasper is a decent-sized town. Maybe a little smaller than Walton. We're just north of Dallas, so it feels more like a suburb. My dad is a lawyer and my mom is a homemaker."

"Any siblings?"

"No." Colton shook his head. "I always wanted a big family. Feels like I should've had brothers or sisters. Probably why I gravitated toward team sports and then the military. Instant brotherhood."

"I get that." Pecca sipped her water and then set down the bottle. "Siblings are not all they're cracked up to be." She smiled. "I was the youngest and tortured at their pleasure."

He cracked a smile. "But you talk so highly of them."

"I'm pretty sure I suffer from Stockholm syndrome," she said with a laugh. "They always made me feel bad so I wouldn't tell on them."

It wasn't hard to imagine. Pecca had a good heart. Maybe too good. "Does"—he didn't know if he should ask, but it was another piece of the puzzle—"does Maceo know about his dad?"

Pecca's expression shifted, her gaze growing distant. "I found out I was pregnant with Maceo after Javier was arrested. He pleaded guilty, so his trial was quick. His lawyer expected he'd get a two-to-five-year sentence since he wasn't the one who killed the store owner, but I guess the judge wanted to make a statement.

He sentenced Javier to fifteen years. I was shocked. Very upset. I started having contractions and ended up delivering Maceo early, but there were complications. I was young and didn't have health insurance, so there were no ultrasounds to warn me, but bands of the amniotic sac had been wrapped around Maceo's leg, cutting off his circulation. It's called amniotic band syndrome. When the doctors delivered him, the only thing they could do was amputate the leg."

Her voice shook, and Colton wished he'd never asked. He scooted closer, unsure how to comfort her or what to say. He was surprised when she moved so her body could lean against his.

"I visited Javier one time in prison to tell him he had a son. He told me to never come back. To move away from El Paso, away from the SSB, and do whatever it took to protect Maceo."

Colton's breath stilled in his chest. Javier told her to move and keep Maceo safe? That sounded eerily like something someone would say if they were expecting trouble, and it supported his and Charlie's theory about the SSB's motivations.

Pecca settled against him, watching the flames dance over the logs. "Maceo doesn't know Javier's in prison. I couldn't tell him the truth because it was an unfair burden to put on his shoulders. All he knows is that his dad went away to do his job and never came back." She turned to look up at him. "I don't want him to suffer for Javier's mistakes."

A piece of hair fell over her eyes, and Colton lifted his fingers to her face and brushed it aside. He gazed into her eyes, feeling his heart banging wildly against his chest. His thumb traced her jaw and she lifted her chin. He wanted to kiss her so badly, but he couldn't do it. Pecca was vulnerable and he wouldn't take advantage of her honesty. Colton pulled her closer to him and whispered, "I will make sure that never happens, Pecca."

NINETEEN

FOOTBALL WAS EXHILARATING. Pecca's voice was hoarse from all the cheering. Maceo was a rock star. No, he hadn't made any great plays, but watching her son play with the other kids like he was one of them made her heart soar.

And maybe it had something to do with the hunky coach.

Pecca smiled. She hadn't stopped since their one-on-one quesadilla date. And her heart fluttered in her chest every time she thought about it, which was clocking in at every other minute.

Movement at the corner of her eye caught her attention. Lane was waving, a huge smile filling her face as she half scurried/half waddled over. "I've been dying. Please tell me you got a rose."

"A rose?" Pecca pretended she was confused even though she wasn't. "I don't know what you're talking about."

"Do you want me to have this baby right now?" Lane put her hands on her belly before collapsing into the extra folding chair Pecca had brought. "Because I will if you don't tell me everything." She blew out a breath. "And thank you for bringing chairs today."

"Sure, but please don't have that baby here. You'll scar these kids for life." Lane stuck her tongue out playfully. Pecca laughed. "You realize you sound like a teenager, right?"

Lane's nose wrinkled. "No, I don't. Otherwise I'd be talking in letters. LOL. SMH. BRB. SOS—which, BTW, does not mean you need help."

"What does it mean?"

"Someone over shoulder." Lane raised her eyebrows. "Frankie taught me a few before she left for college. Said I'll need to know them when Noah gets a phone, which is going to be never."

"How's Frankie doing?" Pecca asked. "Is she coming home for the holidays?"

"She's good, and I think so, because she asked if she could pick up a couple of shifts at the café while she's home. Has Ryan said if he and Vivian are coming down?"

"Haven't heard, but I hope so."

"Okay, enough chitchat. Tell me about your date."

Pecca kept her eyes on the action happening on the field even as her mind drifted back to being snuggled next to Colton on the couch. She hadn't been sure how he would react to her answer about Javier, but his simple yet resolute response was the tipping point. She was falling for Colton—hard.

"We ate quesadillas in front of the fire and just talked."

"Just talked?" Lane eyed her, expectation lighting her face as she waited for more.

"That's it."

"Oh." Lane's face fell. She leaned back in the chair and gazed over the lawn, no doubt looking at Colton. "I expected more."

"More?" Pecca gawked. "That was technically our first date." She twisted her lips together. "Sorta."

"You've been working out with him every day for the last several weeks." Lane sighed. "I guess I just thought you would know by now."

Pecca found Colton on the field. Today he was wearing a pair of navy blue Adidas running pants, a gray T-shirt, and the Mustangs cap flipped backward as usual. Her nerves zinged with the anticipation of having him close again. To feel his fingers trailing a line over her shoulders, giving her that heady feeling of desire.

"I need to be careful," Pecca said. "His rehab here ends in a couple of weeks. I already know Maceo is going to be devastated."

"And you?"

Crushed.

"Blue forty-two, blue fifty-two. Hut."

Pecca watched the ball get passed to the kid playing quarterback. Her knowledge of the game and the positions was basic at best, thanks to Maceo's continuous discussion of the sport. He also took every opportunity to correct her with an animated roll of his eyes. Noah received the ball and started running, but the kids knew he was good, so several started for him.

"Pass, Noah!" Colton called out. "Maceo's open."

Maceo? Pecca found her son running ahead of the pack by several yards—completely open. She jumped out of her chair and hurried to the sidelines to see Noah throw the ball to Maceo. *Catch it, baby. Catch it.* It was like slow motion as Maceo made a perfect catch. He cradled it against his chest, pivoted, and ran toward the end zone.

"He caught it! He caught it!" Lane screamed. "Run, Maceo!"

The kids charged after Maceo and Pecca couldn't help herself as she followed, running along the sidelines. "Go, Maceo! Run!"

"Hang on to the ball, Mac!" Colton's voice echoed behind her.

Jogging, Pecca passed the roar of the other parents cheering Maceo's name. The veterans of D-Wing were on their feet, waving their hands, canes, caps. The rest of the kids standing on the sidelines joined Pecca and Colton, running toward the end zone.

One kid sprinted out of nowhere and was a hand's length away from Maceo's blue flag. The kid lunged, but Maceo sidestepped at the last second, putting him out of reach and across the goal line for a touchdown.

A touchdown. Maceo just made a touchdown. Pecca watched her son get mobbed by members of both teams, the kids congratulating him with high fives, fist bumps, and pats on the back. She covered her mouth, emotion blocking her from screaming his name.

Colton turned to her, a huge smile on his face, and without a second thought, she plunged herself into his arms, wrapping hers around his neck so that he scooped her up off the ground in an embrace so warm and tender it sucked what was left of Pecca's breath away.

"Thank you," she whispered against his neck. "Thank you so much."

Colton slowly released her back to the ground, his eyes remaining on her. "It was all him."

If the world had slowed watching Maceo run his first touchdown, it was at a standstill now. Colton's arm twitched and he started to pull it back, but she held on, firm. "It was both of you."

Pecca ran her hands to the sides of his face, feeling the muscle in his jaw tick. The gold flecks in his hazel eyes glimmered beneath the sun's reflection and she knew. That thing other women talked about—that Lane talked about—Pecca knew it in this moment, and all she wanted to do was extend the celebration and kiss Colton. Kiss him with gratitude for bringing so much joy to Maceo's life, and kiss him because she was falling for him.

"Colton, did you see that?" Maceo's excited voice pulled her back to reality. He stood next to them, holding up the football, his cheeks pink with excitement. He turned to her. "I made a touchdown, Mom!"

"I saw." She ruffled his hair. "You were amazing."

Maceo looked up to Colton. "I did the two-step. The one you taught me."

"You nailed it." Colton lifted his left hand for a high five. "But we still have more game to play. Go get on the field."

"Yes, Coach."

Colton backed up to the field, his gaze not leaving hers until Charlie blew the whistle, jerking them both out of whatever trance they were in. Charlie shook his head and said something to Colton she couldn't hear, but the pointed look Charlie gave her next said everything.

Pecca walked back to her seat and found Lane standing there with the same knowing smile plastered on her face. In the exuberant moment of a touchdown, something in Pecca's world had shifted and she wasn't the only one who saw it, which made it very real and very, very hard to focus on the rest of the game.

Colton's heart had begun racing the moment Maceo carried the ball into the end zone like a pro, momentarily causing his brain to lapse and sweep Pecca up into his arms. And now it wouldn't slow down.

Gathering the equipment, Colton let both moments replay in his head. The excitement on Maceo's face mirrored the emotion he'd felt having Pecca in his arms, whispering words of gratitude that fed his soul in a way that reminded him just how empty it had become since his diagnosis.

The sound of laughter pulled his eyes to the sidelines, where Pecca, her smile vibrant, was talking with Lane and a few other parents. His heart sank. David was there, his hand on Maceo's shoulder.

"What's up, brother?"

Colton spun around to find Charlie walking over with orange cones in his arms. "Nothing."

"I have an eight-year-old boy. I know what pouting looks like."

"I'm not pouting." Colton grabbed the net bag and started stuffing footballs into it. He looked over at Pecca. "I'm thinking."

"About how you're going to win her heart?"

"How I'm going to get mine back."

Charlie gave him a curious look. "Why would you want to do that?"

"Because it makes things complicated. I'm only here for a few more weeks, and my focus—our focus—needs to be on keeping her and Maceo safe." Colton's arm twitched. "I don't want to get distracted."

"I'm still not seeing the problem."

"The problem"—Colton sighed—"is that Chaplain Kelly asked me to imagine a future when I leave here. Where I'm going to go. What I'm going to do. Do I even have a future with this disorder? And honestly, since he asked, the only thing I've been able to imagine these last couple of days is a future with Pecca and Maceo in it, but . . ."

"But . . ."

He blew out a breath. "But I have no idea where I'm going to go or what I'm going to do. And without any purpose, what do I have to offer them?"

Charlie paused and looked Colton up and down, his eyes stopping on Colton's right arm. "You know, I stopped seeing your movement disorder about two weeks ago. When you brought up the idea of creating this flag football team, I had my concerns about why you were doing it." Charlie shrugged. "I mean, we do crazy things for the women we have feelings for. I tried brussels sprouts for Lane."

Colton chuckled and shook his head.

"My point is that you told Maceo he has to be on this field working twice as hard as everyone else, and I thought it was because you wanted him to prove his prosthetic wasn't going to hold him back, but what happened today, on this field, took place because Maceo stopped seeing his prosthetic. He stopped playing like he had a handicap and started playing like a kid with nothing to lose."

Colton looked down at his arm. It twitched and jerked and trembled. He had everything to lose and had lost so much already. He glanced over to see David still talking to Pecca. A flare of jealousy lit up inside him. "I don't want to get in the way of her finding someone she deserves."

"I won't pretend to know what you've been through this last year or what you've lost, but I will tell you that at some point you're going to have to stop seeing that arm as a handicap and start playing the game of life before it passes you by."

"I'm only going to say this once"—a gruff voice spoke up behind them—"but the Marine is right."

They turned to find Sarge, his Vietnam cap tipped up slightly to reveal blue eyes, rolling down the pathway in his wheelchair. "She doesn't like him, but she's just too nice."

"Maybe she's just being nice to me."

Sarge pierced Colton with a look that made him stand at attention. "Quit your pity party, soldier, and tell the girl how you feel." He shook his head. "I never thought I'd appreciate the draft, but at least it forced a man to put on his big-boy pants and grab life by the horns. You kids think life goes on forever." Sarge's age-spotted hands gripped the wheels on his chair. He pushed forward in the direction of the Mansion. "Life has an expiration date, Cap."

Colton's shoulders didn't relax until Sarge had rolled a good twenty paces away. He pivoted and let out a breath, noticing Charlie do the same.

"Think we'll ever stop doing that?"

Charlie scratched the top of his head. "Not if we don't want to get sent to the brig."

"That's why I chose the Army. No way I was getting on a ship."

"We all can't be heroes, now can we?"

Colton laughed, enjoying the camaraderie. He hadn't realized how much he'd missed it—the brotherhood. What was he going to do when he left? Even if he was the brunt of D-Wing's jokes, he enjoyed listening to the men banter and revel in the stories of their service. Cracking jokes with Charlie and forming this football team . . . Colton didn't want to imagine a future without them either.

"So now what?"

"What?"

Charlie rolled his eyes. "Are you going to tell her how you feel?"

"Right now?" Colton's heart raced. A few parents were still hanging around, but happily, David wasn't among them. "I was kind of thinking I'd take her on a date."

"Then go ask her out." Charlie took the net of footballs from Colton's hand. "Go, soldier. Make the Army proud."

Colton swallowed and then started across the lawn. *I'd like to take you out. Would you go out with me?* He flexed his fingers nervously. How was he going to take her out? He couldn't even drive. He turned around and saw Charlie urge him forward with a look that said it would be worse if he turned around.

A whistling noise drifted on a breeze from the porch, and Colton saw Sarge watching. The whistling was coming from him, and it wasn't noise—it was . . . the "Army Song."

Fighting till the battle's won, and the Army Goes Rolling Along.

The rest of the song played in the back of his mind, his steps matching the cadence as if he were marching, and suddenly a plan came together in his mind. Pecca turned and smiled as he approached.

"Hey, Colton."

"Pecca, I was wondering if you were free for dinner this evening?"

Several seconds passed, and Colton wasn't sure if he had said the words aloud or just in his head. She blinked up at him beneath long lashes, her lips wavering.

"You just going to stand there all lovestruck, Hot Tamale?" Gunny shouted from the porch. "Or you going to answer the boy?"

Colton frowned at the Marine's antics. Maybe he should've waited and—

"Yes." Laughter bubbled around her answer. "Yes. I would love to."

"Atta boy, Cap!" The shout of encouragement sounded suspiciously like it had come from Sarge, while the rest of D-Wing began hooting and whistling.

His chest expanded, and he didn't care that the peanut gallery was watching. "I'll see you tonight."

"I can't wait."

Neither could he. *Hooah.*

TWENTY

PECCA CHECKED HER MAKEUP in the rearview mirror for the hundredth time. Mush. Her insides had turned to mush the second Colton marched up to her and asked her on their first date. An hour ago, she had received a message to meet him at the Mansion. The flame from the gaslight lanterns lighting the porch danced in an exciting rhythm that matched the beat of her heart. Inside, Colton was waiting for her.

It felt like her heart craved him. Her nerves buzzed with an electricity that urged her to rush up the stairs, but her head was telling her to slow down. Biting her lip, she settled back into the driver's seat. How was it possible to feel something so deeply for a man she barely knew?

That was her way, according to her family. *"Pecca loves people fast—and hard."* "It's like she was born with a mission to love as many people as possible," her brothers used to tease. Her mother and father had both assured her there were worse things to do than love, but Claudia never let an opportunity pass to warn her of the risks—to guard herself so she wouldn't get hurt.

When Javier was arrested, Claudia had the decency not to say, "I told you so," but Pecca could see it in her sister's eyes—the disappointment. Especially after Maceo was born. Part of Pecca wondered if Claudia blamed her for what happened to Maceo, that maybe under different circumstances Maceo would've been born healthy. Different circumstances might've meant a different man and better prenatal care, but it also meant Pecca wouldn't have Maceo.

Tap-tap-tap.

Pecca jumped, her heart thudding against her ribs as she turned

189

to see Deputy Wilson standing outside her car. With her pulse pounding in her ears, she opened the door.

"Sorry, I didn't mean to scare you, but I wanted to make sure you were okay."

She *was* okay, but now she was close to having a heart attack. It wasn't Deputy Wilson's fault. Poor guy probably didn't join the police force thinking he'd be tasked to follow women on dates.

"Ah, yes. I was just, um, gathering my things." She reached for her purse with shaky fingers. "I'm about to head inside."

Deputy Wilson stood back and helped her with her door. "Would you like me to walk you up?"

"That's okay." Pecca smiled. "It's a quick walk."

"Have a nice evening, Pecca." Deputy Wilson tipped his hat and waited for her to head up the gravel path before he returned to his squad car.

A nice evening. Right. That's all this was. A simple date for her to get to know Colton better. It wasn't rushing. It was exactly how dating was supposed to go—or at least she thought it was. Javier was her first boyfriend, and after she had Maceo the last thing she wanted to do was date.

Pecca blew out a breath once she reached the front entrance. She caught a faint reflection of herself in the sidelight windows next to the door. Colton had told her to meet him there for their date and that she should dress comfortably.

Boys.

They had no clue that identifying "comfortably" was like picking out the correct shade of blue to describe the sky. So she chose her favorite boyfriend jeans that hugged her hips cutely but were loose enough that she could move around in them and a slouchy T-shirt she tucked in at the front. Her burgundy cardigan matched the shade of eyeshadow she was wearing, and leopard-print flats pulled the whole comfy, chic outfit together. At least that's what Lane said when Pecca dropped Maceo off at the café for the night.

In a last-minute decision, she'd decided to keep her hair down, but because of Georgia's inconsistent weather, the temperature was now in the balmy sixties, and after Deputy Wilson's scare, Pecca's armpits were sweating. Maybe just a quick twist up. She opened her purse to look for a hair tie when the door to the Mansion swung open.

Sticks stood there with a grin on his face. "Are you going to keep the man waiting forever or what, Hot Tamale?"

"I was just— Are you wearing a tie?"

"I am, thank you for noticing." Sticks released his cane and used both hands to straighten the tie. "Now, if you'll please come in, your date is waiting for you in the library."

Her date. Pecca pressed her lips together, trying to control the smile tugging at her cheeks. She stepped inside and waited for Sticks to close the door before he held his arm out to escort her down the hall and to the library.

Heart thrumming, she gasped when Sticks slid open the pocket doors. The entire library was lit up with twinkling lights strung along the windows and over the bookcases. The leather couch and club chairs normally centered at the middle of the room had been repositioned to the sides to make room for the blanket covering the rug.

"I hope you don't mind a picnic."

Pecca turned her head to see that Colton had come up beside her. His eyes sparked with something that made her knees weak. His hair had been cut, and his face no longer held the stubble from that morning. He smiled, and every warning she had given herself in the car seemed to evaporate.

"I love picnics."

Sticks cleared his throat, and Colton jumped like he was coming out of a trance. He looked at Sticks and then down.

"Oh, these are for you." Colton held up a small bouquet of red, peach, and yellow flowers. "The guys told me giving flowers on a date was still okay."

"We told him that if he didn't, we'd have him in the front-leaning rest position until he knew how to properly court a young woman," Sticks whispered over her shoulder. "That's push-ups, in case you didn't know."

She laughed and eyed Sticks. "I know what it is." Then she faced Colton. "Thank you. They're beautiful."

"Shall we?" Colton pivoted and gestured into the library. He took her purse and the flowers and set them on a table where a long board had been set up with cheese, grapes, crackers, and rolled slices of meat.

"It's a"—Colton scratched the back of his neck—"charcoal . . . charkuh—"

"Charcuterie board?"

"Yes, that's it. Shirley said it's all over Pinterest and perfect for picnics."

"Do you know what Pinterest is?"

"No idea," Colton said as he shook his head. "But I can eat these foods with one hand, so . . ."

Sadness pinched her heart as she began to understand how much Colton was having to make adjustments to his life just like Maceo did. She slipped her hand into his and squeezed. "It's perfect."

"I have a special treat for you."

"Ahem," a throat cleared from the doorway. Colton started to roll his eyes but stopped.

"*We* have a special treat for you."

Pecca hadn't noticed before, but two folding chairs were positioned near the back wall. Sarge rolled in with a trumpet on his lap, and Gunny followed behind. The two men went to the chairs where Sticks stood, holding two guitars.

"What are they doing?"

"Just wait."

A moment later, Sarge brought the trumpet to his lips as Gunny and Sticks strummed, adding to the tender harmony. It took only a few notes for Pecca to recognize the song—Louis Armstrong's soulful tune, *What a Wonderful World*—bringing tears to the edges of her lashes.

Colton used her hand to turn her. "May I have this dance?"

She nodded, afraid of the emotion balling in her throat, and let Colton draw her close. He placed his hand on the small of her back, and her body quivered in delight. Glancing up, she met his eyes. A touch of a smile played on his lips as their bodies swayed to the music.

She loved too fast and too hard, but Pecca didn't care. This was the kind of moment producers orchestrated on television for ratings, not because they had some inner desire to see two people fall in love. She pressed her cheek to his chest, feeling the *thump-thump-thump* of his heart beating.

Three war veterans, a vibrant receptionist, and Lane and Charlie, who had become family, had made sure this night could happen for no other reason than to give her and Colton a chance to discover love.

The song ended, and Pecca released Colton to clap for the men as they tipped their heads down in a bow. Colton watched her walk to each and hug them fiercely.

"That was beautiful. Thank you."

"Anything for you, Hot Tamale," Sticks said. "And the song choice was my suggestion."

"Only after he suggested the Air Force Fight Song," Gunny grumbled with a smile.

"Alright, fellas," Colton said, his hand gesturing to the doorway. He needed to get these old guys back to their rooms before their usual arguments got rolling. "I think I can handle the rest of the night on my own."

Each of the D-Wing veterans ambled out, making sure to give Colton a look that he guessed said he'd better not mess this up or he'd find his belongings on the porch with a one-way ticket back to Texas.

Colton started to slide the pocket doors closed and then paused. Pushing them open, he popped his head into the hallway. Sticks, Gunny, and Sarge startled and stumbled over one another.

"We were just, uh, waiting for the elevator," Gunny said.

"I can handle this, guys."

"Atta boy, Cap," Sarge said just as the elevator doors opened.

Colton waited until all three were inside the elevator and on their way upstairs before he shut the pocket doors.

When he turned, he found Pecca already sitting on the blanket, the char—whatever it was—next to her as she propped pillows against the bottom of the couch to lean on. When he saw her tonight, it was like he was seeing her for the first time and made him want to memorize every detail of her. Lately, he felt like that every time he saw her, and it reminded him of the look in his dad's eyes whenever he caught him staring at his mom. Colton asked him one day why he looked at her that way, and his dad said simply, "Never thought I'd be so blessed."

He took a breath and lowered himself next to Pecca. "If they leave us alone for the rest of the night, it might be a miracle."

"They were wonderful." Pecca sighed. "I didn't even know they could play."

"Me either, but they insisted music would woo you."

"Woo?" She giggled. "They said *woo*?"

"It's a little old-fashioned, huh?"

"I like old-fashioned. A lot." She wrapped her fingers around his, her touch warming his skin. "Consider me wooed."

Man, he wanted to kiss her. But getting D-Wing to agree to his plan tonight came with a lecture from Gunny, Sarge, and Sticks about date etiquette, *including* when it was appropriate to kiss a lady. It was a painful hour of his life, but he had to admit it was like taking lessons from a bygone generation, and all of them had been married over five decades, so their wisdom carried merit. Now, if he could just control the urge inside him to settle down. D-Wing might like him, but he had a feeling they liked Pecca a whole lot more.

If Colton messed this up, it would be like having to answer to three fathers.

"Is everything okay? Do you need anything else?"

"This is . . ." She looked up at the twinkling lights. "I'm not sure you could ever top this date."

Colton leaned against the pillows, taking in the library. "If we were in Jasper, it would've been different."

"Different how?"

"My grandparents have a ranch a few miles outside of town with the most spectacular view of the Brazos. Bluebonnets color the entire valley, and if you go just before sunset, you can watch the sky transform in a palette of colors ranging from the deepest peach to the softest lavender. My uncle Jack says it's like watching the brushstrokes of God painting his canvas."

"That sounds beautiful."

It was. And he missed it. More than he thought he would. More than he ever did when he was in the Army, but maybe that was because he always knew the ranch, and his dream of living there, was waiting. Now . . .

"What about the dancing?" Pecca said. "That was pretty magical."

"In Texas, we would've been serenaded by the cicadas and crickets, but I guess that unlikely trio of musicians was just as enchanting."

"Stop. They taunt you because they like you. Take it as a compliment."

"Is that so, *Hot Tamale*?"

Her cheeks pinked as she picked up a grape. "They're harmless."

"You realize they're trained killers?"

Pecca swallowed, her eyes locked on him. "You know, I always forget about that. I mean, I know they've fought wars out there and done who knows what, but in here all I see are their tender hearts."

She said it so matter-of-factly that when Colton's arm jerked, he watched to see if his disorder was something she noticed when she looked at him, but Pecca didn't even flinch. Was Charlie right? Maybe he was the only one who saw his disorder as a liability. If Pecca could see past Maceo's limitations, could she see past his?

"When I became a nurse, I thought for sure I'd end up in pediatrics because I love kids, but there's something about working here that feels so fulfilling. I can't imagine myself anywhere else."

Her statement felt like a punch to his gut. "You don't see yourself moving back to Texas?"

"Oh." Her eyes grew wide. "I mean, yeah, I would love to move closer to my family, but I feel like God's led me here for a reason and . . ." She took a slow breath and looked at him. "Where do you want to go, Colton?"

It was similar to Chaplain Kelly's question, and a minute ago he would've answered, "Texas. And Pecca, will you please consider moving there with me?" but now he wasn't sure.

"Texas, right?" She chewed another grape. "You talk about your grandparents' ranch with such affection. Would you go back there?"

"That was my dream once."

She stopped chewing. "It's not anymore?"

He thought about the answer he had given Chaplain Kelly. How he couldn't see running the ranch given his current condition. "Maybe. When I can get back to normal or—"

"What's your definition of normal?"

"What do you mean?"

Pecca shrugged. "I hear patients say all the time how much they want their lives to go back to normal, but who gets to define what normal is?"

Colton held up his right arm, tremors twisting his hand. "Well, this isn't normal." He laughed, trying to lighten the mood. "I just want some control back in my life."

"Don't we all." She scooted to his right side, taking his hand and all of its movements into hers. "You're facing a setback, Colton, and setbacks don't define you. How you respond to them does."

"Is that what you say to all of your patients?"

"Only the stubborn ones." Her right eyebrow lifted. "Now, tell me"—she snuggled into his side—"will you have goats on your farm?"

He tipped his head back. "Goats?"

"Yeah, like Chip and Joanna Gaines on *Fixer Upper*. They're so cute. I'd have goats if I had a farm."

"We have cattle."

"I don't think it's the same," she said wistfully. "What's the difference between a ranch and a farm?"

Colton thought about it for a minute. "Purpose, I suppose."

Pecca twisted to face him. "What would be your purpose on the ranch?"

He eyed her suspiciously. "Have you been talking to Chaplain Kelly?"

"No, why?"

"He kind of asked a similar question the other day. Gave me homework, in fact."

"What is it?"

"He asked me to imagine what my future held if my arm never got better or . . ." The words stuck on his tongue. "Got worse."

Pecca looked at him, an intensity lighting her brown eyes. She tucked a piece of hair behind her ear. "What do you imagine?"

You, the voice in his heart answered, but he stayed silent for fear that saying it out loud would jinx him and somehow this new dream would be stolen from him too.

"When Javier was arrested and I found out I was pregnant, it was hard for me to imagine what the future held. I sank to my knees and cried, angry at myself for letting it happen. But my grandmother took my hand and gently pulled me from the ground so she could embrace me. She told me life is a series of choices. We should always strive to make the right ones, but sometimes we don't. She said that when we face hardships, whether by our own making or through circumstances beyond our control, that's when we have to turn everything over to God—because only he has enough grace to turn our messes into blessings."

"Messes into blessings." It was hard to imagine how God could turn his movement disorder into a good thing, but he found it hard to disagree completely with Pecca's grandmother. After all, that night in the Zabul province, Colton was convinced his intel—or lack thereof—was single-handedly going to kill an entire convoy of soldiers. It was only by God's grace they survived, but that night changed him forever.

"With everything you and Maceo have been through, *are* going through, you really believe that? About God?"

"All I have to do is look around. I see God's grace every day." Pecca's thumb traced a line on his hand, bringing a shiver to his skin. She smiled softly. "He gave me Maceo, then protected him after he was born and through surgery. He brought us here to Walton, where I've met the most amazing people who have become like family to me. And tonight I was serenaded by war heroes as part of an unbelievable date with a charming Army captain who spoke words to my son that only someone who's *been* there could offer. You inspired him to his first touchdown.

"How can I not believe it?" She moved closer and brought a hand to his cheek. "It hasn't been easy, but if I keep my focus on God's goodness, it reminds me that no matter how difficult the journey, God's plans will lead me to where I need to be—I just have to trust him."

"I was told I'm supposed to ask permission to kiss you. So would it be alright, Ms. Serena Gallegos, if I kissed you?"

Her smile lit up her face, setting her eyes glittering. "Yes, Colton. I would like that very—"

He leaned in and kissed her before she could take another breath. Her hands went to the back of his neck, bringing him closer, deepening the kiss. The taste of her lips was intoxicating.

Pecca pulled back, her breaths quick. "Wow."

Colton grinned and kissed her again. He wasn't sure if it was because he asked her permission first, or maybe it was her words, but something had awakened his heart and sparked a more vibrant dream for his future. One that included Pecca, Maceo, his grandfather's ranch—and maybe a few goats.

TWENTY-ONE

COLTON, feeling as nervous as a teenager, stood on Pecca's front porch. Today was date number two, and it included Maceo, Noah, pizza, and as many Marvel movies as Colton could handle. He shifted the two bags in his hand as the sound of feet running to the door was halted momentarily by Pecca's reminder about the alarm.

Colton scanned the neighborhood. After the break-in, Charlie canvassed the neighbors on both sides of Pecca's house to see if they had noticed anything suspicious. Neither had. Colton watched a mom pushing a jogging stroller up the street, her baby sleeping as she looked down at her phone. She glanced up at Colton for half a second as she passed and offered a quick smile before returning her attention to the phone.

With their noses constantly in their phones, would anyone notice anything suspicious these days? Colton wasn't sure they would. All it would take was for someone to dress like they belonged—a delivery person or a neighbor out for a jog, making them appear inconsequential—and they could easily be overlooked.

"You're just in time." Pecca opened the screen door. "These boys are going to drive me nuts."

"Colton!" Maceo and Noah started sliding in their socks on the wood floors like they were on skis, bursting into laughter as they pitched back and forth, clawing at each other's shirts.

"What did you give them?" Colton whispered.

"Nothing," Pecca said, a bit of weariness in her voice. "But Maceo was at Lane's earlier, and I'm pretty sure she loaded them with sugar."

"Remember when we put soap all over the kitchen floor?" Maceo looked up. "Can we do that again?"

"No." This time it was Pecca's and Colton's voices colliding.

"I know it's late, but I just got Maceo's gift in the mail and brought it with me, along with another surprise I brought both of them." Colton spoke directly to Pecca but made sure his voice was loud enough to be heard. "But I guess it can wait."

"Well, technically, Maceo's birthday has passed." Pecca gave Colton a knowing look. "I can save it until next year."

"No." Maceo stopped. "Please, Mom, can I have it now?"

"I don't know." She walked around the couch. "Are you guys going to settle down?"

Maceo and Noah looked at each other, a silent debate passing between them. Finally, they looked at her and nodded.

Colton sat in the armchair and handed Maceo the big bag. "This is for your birthday. I'm sorry it was late."

It took less than three seconds for Maceo to tear through the bags Colton had found at the Mansion to roughly wrap the gift. A regulation-size football rolled into his hands. Maceo's eyebrows pinched as he spun the ball until his eyes landed on the signature penned in white marker.

"No way! No way! No way!" Maceo's eyes were as round as his mouth. "No way!"

"That's so cool!" shouted Noah. He touched the ball with light fingers. "You're so lucky, dude."

"What?" Pecca leaned over, looking confused. "What is it?"

"It's a football signed by Vincent James. To me." Awe filled Maceo's face as he pointed out the signature to Pecca. "See, right there, that's my name."

"Wow." Pecca smiled. "That is amazing. What do you say?"

Maceo launched himself at Colton, wrapping his arms around his neck as best he could while still holding the football. "Thank you, Colton. It's the best gift I ever got."

A strange sensation flooded Colton's chest, which felt like it was caving in but also expanding so wide it kind of ached. He hugged Maceo back. "You're welcome. Now, there's one more item for both of you, but you can't tell any of your teammates you got it first."

Maceo released his hold on Colton's neck, but not on the ball. Noah came up beside him. "We won't tell."

Colton handed them the other bag and the boys dug in.

"Awesome!" Maceo held up the Warrior jersey Colton had had delivered from Savannah earlier that day.

"Cool!" Noah held his against his chest. "Can I wear this for the fall festival? I want to be a Mustangs football player."

"Me too," Maceo chimed in.

"Will all the other players have their jerseys by then?" Pecca asked.

Colton nodded. "I plan on handing them out at our next practice."

"Then I think it should be fine." A ding went off in the kitchen. "You boys get the movie ready—"

"Mom, can we go in the backyard and play football instead?" Maceo's eyes moved to Colton. "We'll use my old football, not this one." He tucked the autographed ball to his chest. "Please?"

"Physical activity over tube time? Hmm, I don't know."

Noah's face scrunched. "What's a tube?"

"Mom."

Maceo gave Pecca a pointed look that said "please don't embarrass me," and Colton stifled his laugh.

"Fine." Pecca answered as though it pained her. "We'll call you inside when the pizza's ready."

"Pizza!" Both boys wiggled into their jerseys and hustled out the French doors leading to Pecca's backyard. Maceo carefully set his birthday gift on the patio table before picking a well-used football from a bin.

The last thing Colton heard as he followed Pecca into the kitchen was Noah asking to hold the ball if he promised to be gentle. "I think I might have to get Vince to sign another ball for Noah."

Pecca was staring at him.

"What?"

She stepped forward, closing the distance between them and increasing the heat in the kitchen by several degrees. "That was really nice of you." Her fingers grazed the edge of his, making his heart race. "But you didn't need to do that."

He put his hand on her hip and pulled her the rest of the way to him. "I wanted to."

"No." She grinned, leaning her head back, eyes narrow. "You *really* didn't. How am I ever going to compete with a gift from Vincent James?" She warbled Vince's name mockingly.

Her pout was cute and made him want to kiss it away, but they both agreed that in front of Maceo they would use discretion. The same went for when they were in public, just until they knew how they were going to proceed. Or at least that's what they agreed to between kisses last night, but right now he couldn't remember why he'd thought it was a good idea.

"Vince has nothing on you." He kissed her forehead and then along her cheekbone, until his lips finally found hers. She gripped the edge of his T-shirt at his waist, kissing him deeper, and it was like the first time all over again.

Excited shouting from the backyard caused Colton and Pecca to flinch and back apart. Colton ran his hand through his hair, trying to regain some control of his erratic heartbeat as they both looked through the kitchen window to see the boys calling out plays. Colton couldn't help feeling proud.

Pecca moved around him to get to the sink. "I thought we'd make our own pizza tonight." She started washing her hands. "Is that okay?"

"Perfect." He guessed she could've suggested liver and onions and he would've said the same thing. When she finished at the sink, he brushed by her, his skin tingling at their closeness, to wash his own hands. "How can I help?"

"I've got the ingredients ready," Pecca said as she started pulling bowls out of the refrigerator. "We're going personal size, so you can make whatever you like, and there's a note by the microwave with Maceo and Noah's order. I'll take care of the salad."

The two of them moved around each other in the kitchen like they'd been doing it their whole lives, and Colton thought about the conversation from their date. As they slid the pizzas into the oven, Pecca set the timer and suggested they sit on the back porch and watch the boys. He followed her out, and as they settled into the Adirondack chairs, Colton chose his words carefully.

"I've been thinking a lot about what you said on our date—"

"You're adding goats to the ranch?"

"No." He smiled, liking the excitement in her voice. "About God having a plan, and trusting." Colton kept his eyes on the boys but could feel Pecca watching him. "It reminded me of a situation I found myself in two years ago. My unit was deployed to Afghanistan, and my team was running intel reports in preparation for troops to move into Zabul province so they could help the Afghan forces reclaim the territory."

Colton was instantly transported back. "I didn't realize when I joined the Army how fulfilling it would be to serve our country. I felt like I was making a difference, that it was . . . within my control to keep America safe." Pecca's hand found his and she gave it a gentle squeeze. "That night in Zabul, my intel report was incomplete, but time was not on our side and my commander had a chip on his shoulder. Wanted to prove something. I wasn't comfortable turning in my report because I knew he'd jump to send the convoy out. Those soldiers' lives were in my hands.

"I'd never felt more out of control in my life. The whole night that convoy was out, I was inside the operations center working out every possible scenario. Fourteen hours straight until we got the call that they had made it. The mission was a success."

He could see the confusion in her eyes and knew he needed to explain. "When they returned, everyone celebrated, and I should've too, but instead I went back to my tent and wrestled with how different the atmosphere would've been had the opposite happened. My intel up to the second before they came back said they shouldn't have returned. It still haunts me. How could I have gotten it so wrong? I mean, I'm glad I was wrong, but what if I had been right? If something had happened to those soldiers—it would've been on me. I should've done more to make my case, made the commander listen."

"Colton, you know that had to be God protecting those soldiers. You did everything you could and—"

The doorbell rang. Colton and Pecca looked over their shoulders and through the house to the front window. "It's Lane and Charlie."

Pecca stood, looking at her watch. "That's weird. Their class hasn't even started yet."

"Maybe it got canceled." Colton couldn't help feeling a mixture of relief and disappointment. Their conversation had grown intense, causing the twitching in his arm to pick up. He wasn't sure why he felt the need to share that moment with Pecca, but it was like he had to explain himself, explain his shortcomings.

The oven timer went off. Pecca pointed to the kitchen. "I'll get the pizza if you'll get the door."

Colton jogged to the door. "Hey—" The grim expression on Charlie's face stole the rest of Colton's greeting when he opened the door. "What's wrong?"

"Aren't you guys supposed to be at your birthing class still?" Pecca said as she walked to the door, oblivious to her friend's body language. "Did it end early? You're just in time—the pizzas came out, but I think there's enough for—"

"Pecca, we need to talk." Charlie stepped inside the house, Lane at his side. "It's about Javier. Is it okay if Lane takes Noah and Maceo to the café?"

"What's happened?" Pecca's hand reached for Colton's arm, and he could feel the tremor in her body.

Charlie stared over their shoulders to the backyard where Maceo and Noah were still playing football. His eyes moved to

Colton for a fleeting second before he directed his attention to Pecca. Lane was already by her side.

"I'm sorry to be the one to tell you this," Charlie said, "but Javier was killed."

⁓⁓⁓⁓⁓⁓

The next several minutes were a blur, like Pecca was watching what was happening around her from the outside. She heard Charlie's words, then felt her knees grow weak. Colton escorted her to the couch while Lane got Maceo and Noah ready to go. She hugged Maceo before he left and told him it was okay to take his new football to the café.

"I've been working with Peter Jenkins, a correctional officer at Buckner Penitentiary, since the night of the break-in to gather information on Javier. He called me tonight to inform me that there was a fight this afternoon. Unfortunately, Javier's life was taken."

Pecca covered her mouth, stifling a cry. Javier's face popped into her mind, followed by images of their history. She felt sick, and nausea burned her throat.

"What happened?"

The vibration of Colton's voice radiated against her, and she leaned into him, unsure if she wanted to know the answer to his question. She blinked through tears and looked to Charlie, who seemed to be waiting for her approval. She nodded.

"Officer Jenkins said Javier was scheduled for a transfer to another facility, but sometime after lunch a fight broke out in the courtyard. Somehow, in the chaos, someone got to Javier."

Pecca thought of the afternoon she met Javier. She had been at her friend's house, sunbathing by their pool, when a ball popped over the wall. Javier's face peeked over and he made a joke she couldn't remember, but it made her laugh and take notice. It wasn't until a few weeks later that she learned her friend's neighbor was rumored to be a member of a Mexican cartel, but by then Pecca was infatuated with Javier and the idea that he would change.

"Wait, he was being transferred?" Colton shifted, bringing Pecca back to the present. "I thought he was up for parole."

"I asked the same thing." Charlie sat forward, elbows on his knees. "Officer Jenkins spoke with the correctional release coordinator, who said Javier was never up for parole. He was being transferred to a minimum security prison outside Birmingham, Alabama."

"But Adrian said he was up for parole." Pecca sniffled, wiping the stray tears streaming down her face. "That was why the SSB was coming after me and Maceo—to get us to go there."

Charlie frowned. "I don't doubt what your brother said, but Officer Jenkins emailed me a copy of the transfer request. Javier wasn't getting paroled early."

Pecca chewed on her thumbnail, unsure of how to understand what she was feeling. "I haven't seen him in eight years. I . . ." She sniffled. "That day at the jail, he told me to never come see him. That he didn't want to see Maceo. I was so mad at him." Her jaw tensed. "I thought the punishment fit the crime—Javier never seeing Maceo, but I . . ."

She was sad but also angry, and part of her felt . . . relieved. Did that make her a bad person? Maceo's father was dead.

"Do they know who did it?" Colton asked quietly.

Pecca looked at Charlie, who shook his head. "They're looking through surveillance footage and questioning the inmates involved in the fight. Officer Jenkins said it didn't look like Javier was involved."

Colton's arm jerked, causing his body to bump against hers. She could feel his muscles go rigid. His expression was tight. He moved his hand from her back and interlaced his fingers through hers, his grip strong.

"Yet he was killed."

Pecca inhaled sharply. Colton wasn't asking a question. Her eyes darted to Charlie, who rubbed his hands down his jeans and sat back in the chair.

Then he nodded.

"Wait, how does that happen? I mean, I know prison isn't summer camp and fights happen, but why would someone kill Javier?"

Colton took a breath. "There's not always a reason."

She watched his lips form the words, but something in his tone told her he believed otherwise. "But you don't think that's true in this case?"

Stress was straining Colton's features, and Pecca wasn't sure if it was from their earlier conversation or now. When he was sharing that part of his life, she could feel the anxiety radiating off his body and it made her wonder if that incident was the catalyst for his movement disorder. He was already carrying the weight from that moment—the last thing she needed to do was add to it.

"Charlie and I have been working a theory." Colton locked eyes with her. "We've been trying to figure out what the South Side Barrio gains from threatening you. Since you haven't been hurt physically, it feels like intimidation."

"Right, to get me to testify."

"Well, that's what we thought initially," Charlie said. "But it's hard to understand why they would go to such extreme measures to get your cooperation."

"Not to mention they haven't actually done or said anything to indicate that that's what they want from you," Colton added. "It's just threats at this point. Your brother was the only one who gave us any indication as to the reason."

"You think there's another reason?"

"We think it's possible that the South Side Barrio may have been trying to scare you to get to Javier."

Pecca lifted her hands to her forehead, feeling dizzy as her mind pieced together what Colton was saying. "Wait, if that's true, then we should be safe. Maceo and I, right?"

"Well"—Charlie shifted forward on the chair—"we don't have all the details, and until we do I'd still like to be cautious." He glanced at Colton. "I think you're onto something, but we need more information."

Colton nodded, and another silent message passed between them. But before Pecca could ask about it, Charlie stood.

"How about you have a sleepover with Lane tonight? And before you say something about not wanting to impose on us, I'm asking it as a favor. Those PTO parents have been calling in orders for the fall festival all week, and she could use some help."

Charlie was a good man, and Lane was lucky to call him hers. Pecca nodded because she would do anything to help Lane out, and truthfully, she didn't want to be home by herself tonight. "Of course."

"I'll wait for you guys outside." Charlie gave an embarrassed smile. "Lane took my car."

When Charlie closed the front door behind him, Colton turned to her. "Are you okay?"

She rubbed her arm. "I don't know. I mean, I think so. I can't really believe this happened. I feel . . . guilty."

"Why?"

A tear slipped over her cheek. "I think at one time I loved Javier, maybe. I mean, we made a baby." She watched for his reaction, but his face remained passive so she continued. "I'm not proud of the choices we made back then, but Maceo is one of the best things in my life. As hard as our lives have been, I look around at where I am and can't help but be grateful. But I never wanted Javier to die." She looked down at her feet. "I wish this could've ended differently, but I can't help but feel a little bit relieved it's over."

Colton gently tipped her chin up with his hand. "You are one of the most amazing people I've ever met, and Charlie and I will get the answers necessary to make sure Javier's death wasn't for nothing."

"Do you think it's over? That we're safe?"

"I hope so." Colton's fingers found hers. His lips brushed the side of her temple. "But I promise you that no matter what, I'm here, and I will do whatever it takes to make sure you and Maceo are safe."

Pecca pressed her cheek to his chest and wrapped her arms around his back, sinking into his promise and wanting nothing more than for him to be right.

TWENTY-TWO

JUAN'S PULSE POUNDED. His legs bounced with dangerous energy, fingers itching to put a bullet into someone's head, and right now he was leaning toward making the man staring at him on the computer that someone.

Too bad thousands of miles separated them.

"I did what had to be done." Señor leaned back in his chair and lifted a cigar to his lips. "You were taking too long."

Grinding his teeth, Juan forced himself to take a calming breath. Thankfully, Señor couldn't see his clenched fists.

"I did not hire you," Señor growled, launching forward in his chair. "You were favored by Hector because his blood runs through Alicia, but he is gone and you will earn your place by obeying my commands."

Hearing Señor speak Alicia's name made heat crawl up Juan's neck. He needed to tread cautiously. Any response outside of humble submission would lead to trouble, and Juan couldn't take that chance until he had everything in place.

Bowing his head, Juan thought of Alicia and Diego. "*Lo siento,* Señor. My apologies. I know you are only trying to bring justice to the memory of Tio Hector, and I am nothing but loyal to you, but"—Juan lifted his eyes back to the computer screen—"killing Javier will not bring her out."

Señor eyed Juan smugly and shook his head as though he pitied Juan. "Javier was killed *because* of her."

Juan's blood turned cold. How? It wasn't possible. He had men in place within the SSB, and they would've reported back to him.

"I can tell from the look on your face that you were not aware of her visit to Javier in jail. That suggests two things." Señor held up two fingers. "You are not as good as Hector believed you to be or two, you are wasting my time."

They locked eyes, the message as clear as if Juan were standing in front of Señor's desk—he was disposable. In a single move, the man had managed to get ahead of him. How? Juan had people in place. The news of Javier's murder came to him by another member of the SSB who was not pleased. There was not much to be done about that, but how had Javier reached her?

Her face beckoned from the photo tacked to his wall. Juan's plan was solid, even if it wasn't happening as quickly as Señor wanted. But speed didn't always guarantee results and— His thoughts stopped whirling.

Juan returned his attention to the computer screen. If Señor had what he wanted, he would not have called. There would be no outburst. Only arrogance, which meant . . .

"Do you have her?" The flash in Señor's eyes was quick but not quick enough. It told Juan everything.

"It seemed even facing his death, Javier remained unwavering. Under different circumstances, he could have been an asset to our company."

A shadow appeared at the edge of the screen. Someone had walked into Señor's office, causing him to look away for a second. He nodded slightly, almost imperceptibly, and Juan might've thought he was seeing things until the shadow disappeared. Señor's expression shifted, and Juan's gut told him an order had just been given. But to who and to do what? The thought rattled him.

"Am I to continue?"

"I'm willing to offer you the opportunity to prove yourself to me, Juan, to the organization. There will be no second chances. I do not have to remind you what the consequence of your failure will be this time." Señor puffed on his cigar, the bright orange ashes glowing as smoke momentarily hid his face. When it cleared, he leaned forward, a wicked smile carved into his face. "Give my best to Alicia and Diego."

The screen went black and Juan's blood ran cold. He slammed his wrist against the desk and cursed. He grabbed his phone and dialed while simultaneously pulling up the security cameras at his home.

"Juan." Alicia's voice rushed over him like a warm blanket of comfort. "Please tell me you're on your way home, because I'm not going to train this dog."

He tapped a few keys and found Alicia inside the kitchen leaning against the counter, barefoot and shaking her head. Below her, Diego was wrestling with the German shepherd he'd had delivered a few days after their last conversation.

"Train? I paid good money to make sure he was already trained."

"The barking, Juan." Alicia rubbed her forehead. "He scares me every night with that loud bark. I'm surprised the neighbors have not complained."

Juan frowned. Apollo came from a breeder who had spent months training him as a protector. The dog would not be barking unless there was a threat. "Alicia, it's time."

"Time for what?" She walked to the refrigerator and pulled out a bottle of vitamin water. "Diego, be careful."

Diego was on all fours, moving side to side, as Apollo leaned forward on his legs ready to leap. It was good they had bonded well, as the trainer said it would reinforce Apollo's training and make him a part of the herd.

"*Mi amor, escuchame.*" Juan opened another screen to pull up the bank's website. "I need you to listen to me. It is time."

Juan heard a quick intake of breath and hated the sound. He typed in his password and quickly transferred the money. He looked at the cameras and saw that Alicia had moved into the living room.

"Please, Juan, no." She stared up at the camera, assuming correctly that he would be watching her. "Diego has all of his friends here. I do too. Our lives cannot be disrupted over this . . . stupid business."

"I am sorry, mi amor, but we have no choice." He opened his email and sent a message to Victor, giving him notice to be ready. "Maybe we will be able to come back, but for now I need you to do as we planned."

"Diego's team made it to the finals. He's been working so hard. He can't miss the game."

Frustration needled at his skin. He didn't want to scare his wife and knew Diego would be angry about missing his game, but time could not be wasted. The type of death Javier endured was designed to send a message.

"Alicia, it is only a game. There will be more." Juan stood and began pacing. "Victor knows the plan. He will make sure you and Diego make it to the airport. Keep Apollo with you."

"The dog." Alicia's voice was soft. He paused and saw her pressing a finger to her lip. "You knew. This whole time—you knew?"

"There was always a possibility. I had hoped it would not come to this, but your uncle is not a reasonable man."

"He's a lunatic," she said. "When Hector died, the cartel should have died with him. It would have been better."

Juan wanted to agree, but they'd have to discuss it later, preferably at the guarded location he'd selected when Señor first called him about the job. He knew the cartel leader was a lunatic the second he used Alicia's and Diego's lives to coerce him into servitude.

And while Alicia may not have been willing to admit the riches of her life came from the deterioration of society, it was the truth. A truth her father and mother went to great lengths to protect her from as she grew up. Her life in gated subdivisions among country clubs told her that her family was just like every other law-abiding family.

Except they weren't. The legacy of the Perez family crossed generations, and when Juan married Alicia, he knew he was taking on the role of not only running operations from the United States but also keeping Alicia's conscience clear.

Juan could not afford to soothe his wife's contrived naïveté. Not this time. "Then you understand why it is important you follow the plan. *Ahora.*"

"Now? Like right this minute? We aren't packed. What about school?"

"You don't need to pack. Everything will be ready for you and Diego. Call the school and tell them there was a . . ." He almost said death, but that felt like a bad omen. "A family emergency. Tell them we will make an extra-large donation to the holiday fundraiser." He gripped his hair with his hand. "It doesn't matter, Alicia. What matters is that you and Diego are safe. Now, do as I ask. *Por favor.*"

Long seconds passed, and Juan prepared for a fight. He deserved it. He hadn't done his job. But all he got was silence, and it was killing him. "We will leave in the morning." She sighed into the phone. "I'm tired, and I want to pack a few things."

"Amor—"

"No, Juan. You are taking us from our lives for who knows how long. You will give me tonight. Tell Victor and whoever else that we will be ready tomorrow."

Putting his hand behind his head, he looked up at the ceiling and blew out a breath. Alicia had made up her mind and there would be no changing it. Juan had to trust they would be safe until then—but he didn't.

"I will see you soon, Alicia," he said quietly. "I promise this will be over soon, and we will return home."

She barely whispered a response before ending the call. Juan stared at the phone in his hand, tempted to smash it against the wall. He took another deep breath and sat in his desk chair. The plan was in place, and in a few days he'd be sitting with Alicia in his arms, watching Diego play with Apollo on a sunny beach far away from Señor's reach.

As long as nothing else went wrong.

TWENTY-THREE

"HE WAS BEATEN AND STABBED?"

"Pretty badly," Charlie said, tipping back in his chair. "I felt bad not telling Pecca all the details, but it seemed like the right thing to do."

"But Officer Jenkins told you Javier wasn't involved in the fight." Charlie nodded. "That's right."

Colton set his left elbow on the conference table and rested his forehead in his palm. Charlie had asked him to stop by the sheriff's station after his sessions were done at Home for Heroes. He'd guessed it was to discuss how the security around Pecca and Maceo would shift now that Javier was dead, but he was not expecting this.

"How does that happen?"

"It's got me baffled." Charlie tapped his thumb against the table. "Maybe the injuries were old?"

"There are cameras and guards everywhere. Doesn't make sense why Officer Jenkins would bring the injuries up if they weren't relevant. Does he think Javier was beat up before the stabbing?"

"That's what I understood when he first called, but today I'm getting the silent treatment."

Colton frowned. "What do you mean?"

"I tried calling Jenkins this morning because I've got the same questions you do. I want to tell Pecca she's got nothing to worry about as much as you do, but Jenkins wasn't as helpful today as he was before. Said the warden is investigating Javier's death and wouldn't offer any more information."

"I'd like to assume that's standard procedure, but my gut is telling me it seems awful convenient to get tongue-tied."

219

"I agree." Charlie rubbed the back of his neck. "Have you heard anything back from your uncle Jack yet?"

"Not yet."

Charlie's shoulders dropped. "I was hoping you'd have better luck."

"I didn't say I don't have luck." Colton straightened in his chair. "I said I haven't heard anything yet."

"There's a difference?"

"With Uncle Jack, yes. He doesn't speak unless he has something to say."

Colton pulled out his phone and dialed.

"I was wondering when I was gonna get your call." The raspy twang of his uncle's voice had an immediate effect, and instantly Colton was homesick.

"Hey, Uncle Jack. How are you?"

"Can't complain. You?"

"Therapy's going well." Colton slid a sideways glance to Charlie, who raised his eyebrows. "Uncle Jack, I'm sitting here with Deputy Charlie Lynch. I'm going to put you on speaker." He pressed a button and set the phone between them. "I was wondering if you've had any luck getting information on Javier Torres."

"I'm guessing you've heard what happened."

"Sir, I was working with Officer Peter Jenkins at Buckner." Charlie leaned closer to the phone. "He informed me about the fight but has gone radio silent as of late. As upsetting as Javier's death is, I'm hoping that with a little more information I can ease the mind of a friend."

"I'm not sure that what I've got is going to do that, son."

Colton shifted in his seat, feeling pinpricks of dread coiling inside his stomach. Charlie's strained features said he was feeling the same. Was Colton's promise to Pecca premature? Was she still in danger? He held his breath.

"Go ahead, sir," Charlie said.

"I took a drive south and met up with a buddy. Knows a couple of the guards inside Buckner. Warden's a fine fellow, but he's feeling the pressure of budget restraints and overpopulation. Having an inmate killed inside his house will garner attention. One killed the way Javier was has brought the spotlight of God down on him."

A smile tipped Colton's lips before he schooled himself. He wasn't pleased with the situation but always enjoyed his uncle's Southern slang. "Last thing we heard from Jenkins was that they were interviewing the inmates involved. Have you heard anything about why Javier was beaten and killed?"

"Wasn't privileged with that information, sorry. But I do have something else you might be interested in. Seems Javier didn't get very many visitors. No family. No friends. Just a few ladies from the church prison ministry. I'm told he was an exemplary inmate with no history of disorderly conduct. Usually kept to himself."

And yet he was beaten and then stabbed to death hours before being transferred to a minimum security prison. Colton pinched the bridge of his nose. He had a feeling this was going somewhere, just not fast enough. "Except?"

Uncle Jack chuckled. "Always had ants in your britches, didn't you?" Colton shook his head. Charlie smirked. "Except, the week before Javier was killed, a pretty young lady paid him a visit."

Colton and Charlie exchanged a look. "Who?"

"Well, here's the kicker. Woman signed in as Marissa Dominguez. Prison protocol is to take a photocopy of the ID for verification. After Javier was killed, they double-checked the visitor log and ran Ms. Dominguez back through the system to discover she doesn't exist and her ID was a fake."

"They didn't run the ID number when she checked in?" Charlie said.

"Guard swears he did, and the warden double-checked the surveillance camera and the computer log. Both show the guard followed procedure."

"So an unidentified woman—other than she's pretty—visits

Javier a week before he's beaten and killed." Something was missing. Colton played through the scenarios that had kept him up all night. "Why was Javier being transferred?"

"I checked into that too, but apparently it's above my buddy's paygrade."

Charlie scratched his head, his forehead creasing as he tried to string the pieces together, but from the shake of his head, Colton knew the deputy was coming up empty.

"The surveillance footage," Colton said, a thought occurring to him. "Is there a clear image of the woman?"

"Not a clear one," his uncle answered. "It's like she knew where the cameras were and avoided them." That did not sit well with Colton. And from the grim expression hooding Charlie's blue eyes, he didn't like it either.

"Sir, is there any way you can send us stills of the video footage?"

"I can probably make that happen. You boys don't plan on bringing trouble on yourself, do you?"

"Doing our best to avoid it," Colton said. Uncle Jack ran as straight as an arrow, but he never lied. If Colton's parents found out he had spoken to his uncle, they'd ask how he was doing, so it was best to give Uncle Jack an answer he could pass along. "But something's not sitting right about this whole situation, and an ornery old man once told me the most important part of the game is knowing who I'm playing against."

"That *handsome, wizened* man has proven he's pretty smart."

Colton nodded. He loved his uncle and missed him. "Yes, sir, he is."

"Call me if you need anything else, and I'll keep you posted if something new emerges. You boys stay safe."

"Yes, sir," Colton and Charlie responded.

A few moments after they disconnected the phone call, Colton's cell phone chimed with an incoming email from his uncle. The man was efficient. Colton quickly clicked through the images and blew out a breath. He handed the phone to Charlie, who did the same. "My uncle was right. She knew where the cameras were."

Charlie leaned back. "Do you think it's a coincidence that woman"—he pointed at the phone—"shows up to the prison with a fake ID, avoids the cameras, talks to Javier, and a week later he ends up dead?"

"No." Colton rubbed a hand over his chin. "You think she's SSB?"

"If she is, it doesn't explain why they were coming after Pecca." Charlie folded his arms over his chest. "If they could get to Javier in prison, why take a shot at her? Break into her house?"

Charlie was voicing every concern running through Colton's head. None of this was making sense. He picked up his phone and scrolled through the pictures again. The angle of the woman's face in each of the shots kept the cameras from getting a good view.

"It's not the SSB."

"What do you mean?"

Colton went through the pictures once more. "She *knows* where the cameras are. It's not a guess—it's a fact. Who would know the layout of the surveillance cameras inside the prison?"

"Staff." Charlie took the phone. "Maintenance, maybe?"

"Those people would all have access badges though. This woman walked in pretending to be a visitor." Colton shook his head. "Marissa Dominguez wasn't a visitor. She went to see Javier for a reason."

"To have him killed?"

"I don't think so. Why does someone talk to a person before they kill them?"

"For pleasure?" Charlie said with a grim twist to his lips. "To torture them? Get them to beg for their life?"

Colton's pulse slowed like it did whenever the information he was analyzing started to make sense. Before that point, it was like he was listening to a foreign language and only able to pick up bits and pieces of what was being said. Then the time would come when a key piece of intel would give him access to the whole conversation.

Was Marissa Dominguez the key?

"We need to find out who she is."

"I agree."

"I have a friend—" they both said and then looked at each other.

"What?" Colton asked.

"I was going to tell you I have a friend, deputy, I mean Agent, Frost, who I can send the pictures to and see if he can tell us who our mystery woman is. What were you going to say?"

"The same thing."

Charlie smirked. "You were going to say Agent Frost?"

"No. I have someone else in mind. He's been helping me and probably has better access than your agent friend." Not to mention that hearing Ryan's name had begun to trigger a little jealousy in him. It was stupid, because apparently he was seeing some reporter, but hearing Pecca and Maceo talk about him so admiringly struck a chord.

"My *agent friend* is a computer genius. Had his pick of government agencies, including the private sector, that were begging him to join their team. Sure, he works for the FBI now, but the guy hacked into a gaming conference when he was sixteen."

It sounded like Charlie was saying his friend was better than Kekoa. He eyed Charlie, who didn't flinch. "First man wins."

Colton would've enjoyed the unspoken wager between him and Charlie under any other circumstances, but the heaviness of why they needed the information hung over him. Was Marissa Dominguez involved in Javier's death? How did she know him? And what about her triggered a fear in him that Pecca's life wasn't out of danger yet?

The noise level inside Walton Elementary School was piercing. Kids in costumes ran around on sugar highs as their parents chased after them. Pecca was manning the ring toss game with Lane but kept an eye out for the blue and white Warrior jersey Maceo was wearing. The problem was, nearly half the members of Maceo's team were wearing their jerseys, making it nearly impossible for her to keep track of her son.

Relax. She had nothing to be afraid of anymore. Javier was . . .

She swallowed. Pecca still hadn't fully processed everything. It didn't feel real. She allowed herself to cry the night she learned the news. Javier's death, no matter what he did, was horrible. And Pecca still hadn't figured out how she would ever explain it to Maceo. One day he would ask about his father, and what would she say?

"I did it!" The exclamation of a little girl dressed like a ladybug snapped Pecca out of the chaos of her life and back to the fall festival chaos.

"Great job. Here's your prize." Lane handed the girl a chocolate bar and leaned over to Pecca. "How many more minutes do we have?"

Pecca looked at her watch. "Three."

"Whew." Lane blew out a breath that lifted her bangs. "Whoever said being pregnant after thirty was easy is a big, fat liar."

"Who says that?"

"I don't know, but they're a liar. Big. And fat." Lane rubbed her belly. "Like me."

A father and his son, Black Panther, were waiting for their turn. Pecca held up her finger and urged Lane to a folding chair. "Here, sit down and rest. I'll take care of the last three minutes."

Black Panther, it turned out, was not very good at the ring toss and burst into tears when all his rings bounced, rolled, or ricocheted everywhere but at the target. His father tried to console him as Pecca hurried to gather the rings for a second try, but the boy's wail only grew louder. She grabbed a handful of candy bars and handed them to Black Panther. "Here you go. You're lucky player number one hundred, and you get all the candy!"

Black Panther's tantrum shut off like a spigot, and he gleefully walked away with his loot and his father walking behind him looking less pleased. Oh well. It was already eight o'clock, and the school principal was making the announcement that the fall festival would be shutting down. *Thank goodness.*

Lane started to get up from the chair, but Pecca waved her back down. "I'll clean up."

"I already agreed to watch Maceo tonight so you and Captain Handsome can canoodle. I can help you clean up."

Pecca smiled. She knew it was a silly smile, because Maceo told her it was, but she couldn't help it. Every time she thought of Colton, it just . . . happened. Even after the tragic news about Javier, all Pecca wanted to do was be with Colton. And if they ended up canoodling, well, she wasn't going to turn him away. His kisses curled her toes.

"I might be changing my mind."

Lane tipped her chin toward the crew walking their way. Maceo and Noah were sluggish, their faces streaked with sweat. Charlie and Colton were deep in conversation that—from their expressions—looked serious.

"Did you boys have fun?"

"We got so much candy!" Maceo lifted his bag to answer her. "I only had a few pieces."

Pecca looked at Colton. His guilt-stricken expression said more than a few pieces of candy had been consumed.

"Dad said I could eat three pieces if I got out of the jumping balloon."

Lane looked at Charlie, who made a face and shrugged. Pecca laughed.

"I'm too tired to care," Lane said, shaking her head.

"Are you sure you still want to take Maceo home?"

"It's no problem." Charlie helped Lane out of the chair. "They're probably minutes away from a sugar coma. Come on, mama." Charlie guided Lane forward, rubbing her shoulders. "Thanks, Pecca."

Pecca hugged Maceo and made him promise to behave before waving to the others. "Night."

Colton began collecting the colored rings. "Did I ever tell you I have a thing for cowgirls?"

"Cowgirl?" Pecca looked down at her plaid shirt tied at the waist, jeans, boots, and straw sticking out everywhere. "I'm supposed to be a scarecrow."

He tugged on her belt loop, pulling her close enough that his minty breath was warm against her cheek. "You don't scare me."

Desire welled up inside, and Pecca dropped her eyes to his lips. He smiled and then backed away. "Wha—"

"Later." He winked, and her heart swooped at his flirtation.

For the next several minutes, they worked side by side to shut down the booth—their fingers brushing, "accidentally" bumping into one another, sneaking looks that spoke of a fervency to finish their job and get to their date.

Canoodling was most definitely going to happen.

"I just need to turn this in to Kristen." Pecca lifted a box of supplies. "Would you grab us some waters from the snack bar?"

"Sure."

She spun on her heel to hurry and drop off the box. After handing off the supplies to Kristen, Pecca walked past the jumping balloon, which was still occupied by a handful of kids unwilling to get out despite their parents' pleas. Pecca spotted David looking frazzled. Part of her still felt bad. She'd been seeing him less at the Mansion and hoped he was doing okay. If he hadn't already found someone else, maybe she could figure out who the single moms were in Walton and set him up.

"You ready?"

Colton was waiting for her at the doors, and just the sight of him sent her heart pounding. She smiled. "Definitely."

The cool air felt refreshing when Pecca stepped outside the gym, and the decibel level dropped so suddenly it was like her ears had lost their hearing. "Nothing like a bunch of crazy kids to make you appreciate peace and quiet."

Colton walked around her so that she was on his left side, a move she figured out was to put her on the side with his good arm. "I'm pretty sure mortar rounds are quieter than a bunch of kids fired up on sugar."

Moonlight peeked through the branches, lighting up the school playground as they crossed through. Since they had found out about Javier, Colton hadn't mentioned anything more about his time in the Army. "How are your sessions going with Chaplain Kelly?"

"I wish they were going better."

"What do you mean?" She looked him over. Something was definitely different about him. "I see a difference. You're less . . . rigid."

"Rigid?"

"Not in a bad way." She bumped into him playfully and he captured her hand in his, interlacing their fingers. Her breath caught. "It's like you've relaxed."

Colton gave her hand a little tug to bring her next to him. "I've been thinking about his question. About what I imagine happening after here."

Pecca bit the inside of her cheek. He was leaving in just a few weeks and she didn't want him to, but she couldn't ask him to stay. Home for Heroes wasn't a permanent treatment facility. Arrangements would be made in Colton's hometown for his continued treatment. She always hated the days her patients left, but watching Colton leave was going to be a whole new and painful experience.

As though he were reading her thoughts, Colton pulled her closer and kissed her forehead. "Odd as it sounds, I think it's because I feel at home here."

Her heart quickened. "In Walton?"

Colton tipped his head to the side. "I was thinking Home for Heroes, actually, and what we talked about the other day. The feeling of being back on a team. Chaplain Kelly is trying to find a place like it near where I live, but it's not looking good." His arm twitched. "Not sure how it'll feel to leave."

Pecca sighed, feeling the sadness return as they continued to walk the pathway leading them away from the school and toward Home for Heroes. A nighttime melody of bugs and bullfrogs from the river sang a chorus. It would've been super romantic if not for the reality she and Colton faced in the not-so-distant future.

Had this been a mistake? She sighed, imagining Claudia shaking her head in an "I told you so" fashion. Why had she allowed herself to fall for Colton when she knew he was going to leave?

"Would you think I was crazy if I said I was thinking of turning my grandparents' ranch into a Home for Heroes?"

Colton's question stunned her. She stopped walking and stared at him, the glow of the lamppost revealing an anxiousness in his eyes.

"It's crazy, right? I mean, with . . ." He lifted his right arm.

"No," Pecca said. "It's not a crazy idea. Is the ranch big enough?"

"The land is, for sure. We'd have to add some rooms, and I don't think I could offer what Home for Heroes does in the medical sense, but . . ." He stared ahead in the direction of the Mansion. "Gunny's going home to an empty house. His wife is gone, and his kids don't live nearby. What's he going to do when he leaves?"

Pecca heard the underlying question in Colton's tone—what was he going to do when he left? She closed the distance between them and reached her hand around his waist. "I think that would be amazing, Colton. And I believe you could do it." She pressed a kiss to his lips, softly, and pulled back. "You are amazing."

That put a sheepish smile on his lips, but it only lasted a second before he kissed her back. Long and deep and toe curling. Her hands slid behind his neck and she couldn't help feeling that this was where she belonged. With him.

Colton drew back, breathless. "You're pretty amazing yourself."

Putting her fingers to her lips, she could still feel the warmth of his kiss. "We should hurry up and get to our date."

They began walking again, this time a little more quickly, and it made her laugh. Colton too.

"Tell me more about your idea."

"I want to give veterans and soldiers a place they can hang out. Maybe a camp or something."

"With goats?"

Colton lifted her fingers to his lips. "You and your goats."

"You have to have goats. They're so much fun."

"Shh." Colton's grip on her hand tightened and she stopped walking. He released it, his body tensing.

"What's wrong?"

Colton narrowed his eyes. "That lamppost is out."

She followed his gaze to a lamppost down the pathway. Sure enough, it was dark. "It's probably burned out."

"I don't remember it being out when we walked here."

"It wasn't dark yet," Pecca said, hating the fear nestling inside of her. "Colton, it's fin—"

The branches next to them rustled as a dark figure emerged from the shadows.

"Pecca, watch out!"

The figure rammed into her side, sending her flying. She cried out as the asphalt bit into her skin, her head cracking against the ground.

"Pecca!"

She rolled to her side, dazed and in pain. *What is happening?* A loud thud jerked her attention to Colton.

He was on the ground, wrestling with the legs of the person standing over him. He kicked Colton in the ribs, causing him to yell in pain. Pecca turned onto her stomach and pushed herself up onto her hands and knees. She felt dizzy, but the sound of flesh hitting flesh, followed by Colton's painful grunts, forced her up.

Pecca launched herself at the person dressed in black, but they were ready and sidestepped. She caught a glimpse of his face and saw the man's wicked smile seconds before he brought his arms up and around her head. She flailed, her fingers grasping at his arms tightening against her neck, suffocating her.

Rage pulsed within her. She elbowed the man and then made her body go limp so that he was supporting her entire weight. He wasn't expecting it and lost balance, giving her room to twist in his grip and strike a blow to the parts that would have him singing soprano. He let out a growl as his knees buckled, and Pecca stumbled back.

"Pecca!" Colton clutched his side, crawling toward her on his knees. "Go. Run."

Blood poured from his nose, and she started for him. She wasn't going to leave him. "Colton, are you okay? Can you get up?"

Colton looked up, his eyes wide with fear. "Run!"

TWENTY-FOUR

PECCA'S CRIES were more torturous than the shooting pains radiating through Colton's ribs. His warning had come too late. The man grabbed Pecca's hair and yanked her backward. Colton gritted his teeth and shoved himself off the ground, charging their attacker, but skidded to a stop when he saw the flash of metal. The nose of a gun was pressed into Pecca's head, causing her to whimper and squeeze her eyes shut.

Nothing beat a bullet.

"What do you want?" Colton tried to raise his hands, but his right arm jerked awkwardly to the side. "I've got money."

It was too dark to make out much of the man's features, but the white of his teeth gleamed beneath an ugly sneer that said he wasn't here for money. *SSB*. Was he Javier's cousin? Colton took a step closer, searching for the identifying tattoos, but the man pulled backward. Pecca wasn't prepared for the abrupt movement and stumbled. The man's attention shifted to her, and that was all the distraction Colton needed.

Colton rushed the man just like he would a tackling dummy on the field. His quick sprint turned the attacker's focus back to him, but Colton's arms were already wrapping around the man's waist. Squeezing, Colton raised him in the air before twisting and dropping him to the ground with a heavy thud. The man's head snapped back, his skull connecting with the asphalt in a sickening crack that made Colton's teeth hurt.

The gun skittered across the path, landing halfway beneath a shrub. Breathing hard, Colton started for it, but the muscles in his body were fatigued and his steps faltered. *Please, don't fail me now*. He urged his body forward, trying to ignore the familiar pang spreading through his arm.

"Colton, watch out!"

Colton caught sight of the flash of fabric just before impact. The man's shoulder caught Colton in the ribs and sent him pitching sideways to the ground. His hip and elbow took the brunt of the impact, the pain screaming through him. He scrambled toward the gun, grabbed it with his left hand, and spun around.

Ahead of Colton's shaky aim, the man ran. His finger trembled near the trigger, but the exertion and adrenaline coursing through Colton's body messed with his line of sight. Too dangerous. He rolled to his side and pushed himself to his feet. The world around him swayed for a second.

"Are . . . you . . . okay?" He spoke through ragged breaths.

Pecca was still on the ground. She looked herself over and then nodded up at him. "Yes, I'm fine. Who—"

"Call . . . the police."

"No, Colton, let him go."

He scanned the area quickly before his eyes turned on Pecca. Her hair was disheveled, but physically she looked fine. If someone else was out there, they would've helped with the attack by now. He had to go after the guy.

"The man just tried to kill you. If he's a part of SSB, I can't let him go."

Colton turned and started sprinting in the direction the man took off. *She will be alright. Pecca will be alright.* He didn't want to leave her, but something was telling him their attacker had answers Colton wanted. And if that was true—it spun his entire theory upside down.

Rounding a bend in the trail, Colton, his senses alert, slowed to a jog. With concentrated effort, he forced himself to take steady breaths through his nose and out his mouth as he listened. Feeling the weight of the gun in his nondominant hand felt weird, but he tightened his grip.

Who was this guy? Javier was dead. If they were after Pecca to get to him, they shouldn't be interested in her anymore. He thought back to the woman inside the prison. Why had she gone to talk to Javier, and why had he been killed a week later?

The sound of a twig snapping gave him his direction. Colton rushed through the bushes on his left, the branches scratching at his skin. The live oaks surrounding him created a canopy overhead that blocked out the moonlight, effectively turning the space into a black hole.

Squinting, Colton scanned the area around him as shadows began to form. A noise to his right caught his attention in time for him to see the figure jump through the bushes in the direction of the elementary school.

Not tonight, buddy.

Colton growled and started running after him. The playground he and Pecca had passed was just ahead. Families might still be leaving the festival—he needed to stop this guy before he reached the school. Anger spurred Colton's feet to keep moving despite the burning in his lungs, but his body was giving up. He could feel the weakness spreading into his legs. Frustration welled up within him.

There. The path narrowed, and the man was only ten yards in front of him now. Colton surged ahead, his muscles begging him to stop. Sirens echoed in the distance, and the man looked over his shoulder as he picked up his pace. With his attention on Colton, he didn't see the curb until it was too late.

Colton watched the man somersault forward, crashing into the grass. Taking advantage of the man's position, Colton lifted the gun, his aim unsteady. "Don't move."

But he did. So swiftly, Colton wasn't prepared. The man twisted around, swinging his leg to the side in a maneuver that caught Colton in the side of the knee. Trying to catch himself, Colton released the gun right before he hit the ground and smashed into something sharp that stole his breath.

From the corner of his eye, Colton watched the man get to his feet. Where was the gun? He ran his hands along the grass and dirt searching for it.

"Looking for this?"

What was left of his breath whooshed out when Colton turned and saw the gun pointed at him. "Who are you?"

CRACK!

Colton flinched as the man's body crumpled to the ground in front of him. What? Chest pounding, he swiveled his head in every direction for any sign of law enforcement. Flashing lights of a squad car colored the sky. His eyes went back to the body.

Who fired the shot?

"Colton." A voice called through the cacophony of sirens echoing in his ears. It was Charlie. He was running over, weapon in his hand. "Colton, are you okay?"

Clutching his side, Colton tried to get up, but his knees turned jelly-like and a wave of nausea crept over him. The edges of his vision began to grow dark as he rolled to his back. The next second, Charlie's face appeared over his, but Colton couldn't speak. The spasm in his arm radiated up into his shoulder. *No.* He tried to breathe, but the pain was unbearable. His body shook, and Charlie yelled for help.

The muscles in Colton's back contracted, thrusting his chin upward as his spine arched as though he was having a seizure. He ground his teeth, fighting back the urge to scream against the pain. *Breathe.* It was Pecca's voice he heard in his head. *Breathe, Colton.*

Pinching his eyes shut, he took a shallow breath. Then another. And another.

A few minutes later, the muscles in Colton's chest and back relaxed.

"An ambulance is on the way," Charlie said. "Hang tight."

"Did you . . . shoo . . ." Colton swallowed against the dryness. He opened his eyes and stared up at Charlie. "Shoot . . . him."

Charlie blinked. Colton watched his eyes flicker to the gun, then to the dead man and back to him.

"It wasn't me, Colton." Realization dawned, and Charlie's demeanor shifted from helping him to searching the area and barking orders into his radio about an active shooter in the area.

Colton closed his eyes and took in a few more breaths, trying to focus on the therapy technique he'd been working on with Chaplain Kelly, but all he could see was Pecca's face riddled with fear. His arm twitched, throbbed, ached.

He'd failed her.

He figured the dead man lying next to him held the answers about why the SSB was still after Pecca. Answers that would've helped keep Pecca safe, and all he had to do was . . . what? Rage prickled his skin, and Colton fought to breathe. It hurt. It *hurt*.

"Where is he?" a frantic voice called out. "Is he okay?"

The sound of her voice should've been reassuring, but it only fueled the fire of frustration burning inside him. He wasn't okay. Never would be. He was lying on the ground—weak.

"Colton, are you okay?" Pecca's cold hands found his face. "Colton."

He opened his eyes. "Is it . . . him?"

Pecca blinked, confusion lighting her eyes as she searched his face. "Who?"

"We've checked the perimeter. No sign of the shooter." Charlie walked over. "Savannah Metro is sending over a K9 unit."

"An ambulance is on its way," Sheriff Huggins said. "Are you hurt, Colton?"

"Is it him?" Colton pulled his left hand back to help himself off the ground, but Pecca stopped him.

"Don't move. Wait until the ambulance is—"

"I'm fine." The bitterness in his tone was received as three sets of eyes looked at him with concern. Colton didn't care. He pushed himself up to a seated position, feeling his head rush with dizziness. He blinked away the stars at the back of his eyes and turned his focus to the body Deputy Wilson was guarding. "Is it Spider—Javier's cousin?"

Charlie's lips pinched into a flat line. He pivoted and walked to Deputy Wilson, who lifted the blanket. Colton watched Charlie kneel to get a good look. A minute later he returned.

"It's not him."

Anxiety rippled through Colton's body, causing his arm to jerk. He turned to Pecca. The memory of what happened flew through his brain in quick bursts. "Are you okay?"

"Fine. A few scrapes and bruises, but I'm good."

"You need to look." His eyes moved to the body. "You need to see if you recognize him."

Pecca bit her lip, her eyes flashing to the body and back. "I can't."

"It'll be quick," Charlie said, holding out his hand to her.

She reached for Colton's hand and squeezed it before rising to her feet to follow Charlie.

"The ambulance is here," Sheriff Huggins said. "Why don't you tell me what happened while they check you out."

"I'm fine, sir."

Sheriff Huggins gave him a fatherly look that said there'd be no arguing. He reached out, and Colton grabbed his hand and allowed the sheriff to help him up slowly. Between answering the medics' questions, Colton gave Sheriff Huggins the details of the night leading up to the moment someone had sniped their attacker.

A few minutes later, Pecca walked over looking paler. She met his eyes and shook her head. She hadn't recognized him. The analytical side of his brain felt like it was short-circuiting. None of this made sense. If the SSB was after her—why? Javier was dead now, so they'd have no reason to go through her to get to him. And if it wasn't the SSB . . . then who? And why?

Pecca's cold hand wrapped around his, and the fear from the last two years was back, churning Colton's gut. He had no control. Just more anger. More frustration. More bitterness.

Colton withdrew his hand and stared at Charlie. "Until you

figure out who's behind these attacks, you need to put security on Pecca and Maceo. At her house. At the school. At the Mansion."

"We don't have the manpower—"

"Figure it out." His sharp tone made Pecca flinch and Charlie's shoulders stiffened. "That's your job."

"Colton"—Pecca reached for Colton's hand again—"we're okay. I'm okay."

"It's not okay!"

Pecca stepped back, hurt carving lines into her face that seared his heart, but he couldn't go on letting her believe he could do anything for her or Maceo—least of all keep them safe.

"This was a mistake. I don't know what I was thinking." He glared down at his arm, the movements increasing. "Tonight was too close." When he looked up again, both Charlie and Sheriff Huggins had a questioning look in their eyes. "I can't be trusted with keeping her or Maceo safe."

"Charlie, Sheriff Huggins." Pecca's voice was soft. "Would you please give us a minute?" When both men stepped away, Pecca came closer. "What's going on?"

"Exactly what I said. You need protection." His pulse pounded so heavy in his chest, Colton could hear it in his ears. He avoided looking at her, afraid his feelings for her would betray his resolve. "I can't offer that to you. Or anything else. It was a mistake."

Pecca took another step forward. "What was a mistake?"

Colton didn't answer.

"Look at me, Colton." Her voice shook, and he couldn't help looking up. Her eyes glistened with a mixture of hurt and anger. "What happened tonight is not your fault. You did everything you could to protect me, and I'm fine. I'm safe. You can't blame yourself—"

"But I do," he snapped.

Pecca took another tentative step forward. She was so close he could breathe in her floral fragrance. The same one that only hours ago had made him want to believe that what she'd said about God might be true—that he had a plan that brought Colton here just for her. His heart plunged into his stomach. If that were true, then he wasn't failing only Pecca—he was failing God.

"It was ego, Pecca. That's all. I agreed to help Charlie because I needed to feel like myself again." He exhaled, his shoulders sinking. "The Army let me go for a reason. Those soldiers' lives were in my hands. Tonight your life was in my—" He shook his head. "I can't protect you any more than I can feed myself with a fork. All this did was reinforce that I'm the last person who should be promising you anything. Least of all a future."

"So, that's it?" She wrapped her arms around herself. "You're just going to give up because it's hard? Because you think protecting me is the only role you play in my life?"

"It's an important role," he said. "If I can't protect you, what good am I?"

"What good are you?" Her face was a mixture of disbelief and confusion. "You have a movement disorder, Colton. It's not the end of the line for you. You think the only reason I want to be with you is because you can protect me?"

"It was my job, Pecca. Protect. If I can't do that for the people I . . ." He swallowed the word and looked away. "I'm leaving in two weeks anyway. It's better if we just admit it was a mistake—"

"Stop saying it was a mistake!" Pecca's voice broke. "Wanting to be with you isn't a mistake."

"You've made bad choices before." Colton's heart shredded. "Count me as one of them."

Tears crested Pecca's lashes as she stepped back. What he said was a low blow that immediately extinguished the light in her eyes. He watched her swallow, the devastation of his words playing across her delicate features.

Colton wanted to take them back, but he couldn't. He loved her too much. So he'd let her walk away.

TWENTY-FIVE

FORGET CHOCOLATE. Cinnamon, sugar, and cream cheese icing were the cure for a broken heart. Pecca chewed on her cinnamon roll but found it hard to swallow over the knot in her throat. She set the plate down and grabbed a tissue.

"Honey, don't cry." Lane scooted closer on the couch and rubbed Pecca's arm. "You'll make me cry."

"I can't"—she sucked in a sob—"help it."

After Colton pulverized her heart, Charlie came to her rescue and drove her to the café. The boys were already asleep, and Lane had the café dining area near the fireplace lit up with candles. A tray with cookies and warm cinnamon rolls sat on the coffee table in front of the couch. *"And I have a pint of double fudge brownie ice cream in the freezer too."*

Pecca had burst into a fresh round of tears at her friend's compassionate gesture. Charlie took that as his sign to head upstairs, leaving Pecca to rehash the whole night all over again.

"He's upset, Pecca." Lane squeezed her shoulders. "I'm sure he didn't mean what he said. People say crazy things when they're scared."

"Then he must be terrified."

Lane laughed softly at her pitiful sarcasm. "He's going through a lot. I'm sure it's difficult."

"I *know* difficult." Pecca's eyes flashed to the ceiling, where Maceo slept in the room above her. "I'm not dismissing Colton's challenges, but over the last few weeks I had begun seeing changes. He was helping Maceo, started the flag football team. Even his attitude during workouts had become less focused on what he couldn't do, and I could see this light beginning to

241

shine in him. I'd hoped he was starting to see that his movement disorder didn't have to be the setback he believed it was. And then tonight . . ." She swallowed. The pain pierced her raw heart. "He talked about turning his grandparents' ranch into something like Home for Heroes." Tears sprang to her eyes. "And I was hoping he was going to ask me to go with him. Am I so stupid, or what?"

"You're not stupid," Lane said, her voice consoling. "If fear makes people say crazy things, love makes us *do* crazy things."

Pecca, sighing deeply, wiped her eyes. Tears began slipping over her cheeks again. She closed her eyes and could picture the look on Colton's face. Anger. He was angry at himself, his circumstance. And she understood. Every time Maceo had to be fitted with a new prosthetic, the days following were painful physically and emotionally, leaving Maceo questioning why he didn't have a leg and why he had to go through this. And he'd ask something that gutted Pecca every time—Was God mad at him? Had God taken his leg as punishment?

They were questions Pecca had asked herself a million times when the doctors told her Maceo's leg had to be amputated. Was she being punished for sleeping with Javier before they were married? Was it punishment because of who Javier was?

"You've made bad choices before."

Colton's words had ripped a hole in her heart. Was he a bad choice?

"Maybe Claudia was right." She gave a stiff laugh. Lane frowned. "My sister is always telling me I have a heart for the wounded. That I'm a fixer. Says it makes me a great nurse but not a great judge of character—at least when it comes to boyfriends."

Lane nodded. "I've dated a troll or two."

"Javier was already in prison when Maceo was born. Dealing with his medical issues took up every ounce of my energy those first few years. I had no time to think about dating in between school, work, and taking care of Maceo, and I was fine with that.

As lonely and hard as it was, I felt it was the amends I needed to make for my part." Pecca's shoulders slumped. "Then I came here and Maceo was doing better, and I watched Ryan fall in love with Vivian and you with Charlie, and I . . . I began to wonder if maybe I had done my time. Ms. Byrdie says that God likes it when we pray for specifics. So I started praying specifically for God to lead me to the right man. I thought that man was Colton."

"He still could be."

"Not if my sister is right."

"Is she? Are you with Colton because you want to fix him?"

"No," Pecca said. "I'm with him because he's kind and generous. A little rough around the edges, but I like that because it makes the sweet parts of him so much better. I don't want to fix him, I want to love him."

Wow. She wanted to love Colton. The last several weeks she'd been there as he struggled, and all she'd wanted to do was encourage him. When Maceo got that touchdown, it was Colton she wanted to celebrate with. In her fears, when the reality of her mess overwhelmed her, it was thinking of Colton that brought calm back to her life. Pecca swallowed. She didn't want to love Colton—it was too late for that. She was already in love with him, which made this whole situation worse.

"Have you told him that?"

A stray tear rolled over her cheek. "I don't know if he'll listen. He's so stuck on seeing his arm as a weakness—as this roadblock to the life he once had—it's like he's using it as an excuse to stop living. I just wish he knew that I don't see him as weak. When I look at what he's going through, how his life was basically stripped from him, and yet he's still fighting . . . He's like—like Tony Stark or Bruce Banner."

Lane shifted back. "Did you just compare Colton to the Avengers?"

Pecca lifted her head, turning to Lane. "We've been watching a lot of movies, trying to catch him up." She sniffled. "But you know what I mean. Tony Stark has that electric heart thing and still wants to marry Pepper Potts."

A vibration tickled Pecca's arm, and she looked down at her watch. Claudia was calling.

"It's my sister."

Lane sat forward. "Ooh, you better answer that."

Pecca dug through her purse and retrieved her phone. "Leave everything. I'll put it away."

"Thank you." Lane hugged Pecca before sliding off the couch. Hands on her belly, she waddled to the stairs. At the first step, she paused. "Everything's going to work out, Pecca. I know it."

Pecca nodded because the emotion welling in her throat made it impossible to speak. Oh, how she hoped Lane was right.

Looking down at her phone, she wondered why her sister was calling so late. "Hello?"

"I wasn't sure I was going to catch you up at this late hour."

The sound of her sister's voice cut deep into her soul, and Pecca started crying again, muffling her mouth with her hand.

"Are you there?"

Pecca sniffled. "Yeah." She grabbed another tissue and wiped her nose. "Why are you calling so late?"

"I couldn't sleep."

"So you think, *I haven't talked to my sister in ages, so let me call her in the middle of the night and see if she's awake*?"

"No," Claudia answered defensively. "I've been worried about you."

Claudia had impeccable timing. Of all the nights to be worried. She shook her head, replaying the events of the evening and debating whether to tell Claudia what had happened. What would be the point? It would only worry her, and besides, Charlie had already called Adrian and Pecca assured him she was okay. All she could do now was wait for the medical examiner to identify the man who attacked her. Sheriff Huggins hoped with that information, they'd be one step closer to figuring out who was behind this and how to stop them.

Pecca shivered. She looked over her shoulder and out the window of the café. A squad car was parked out there, but she couldn't see who the deputy was. "Did Adrian tell you about Javier?"

"He left me a message."

Like usual. Pecca leaned back into the couch, pulling her knees to her chest. Claudia was always so busy that Pecca and the rest of her family ended up having a relationship with her voicemail.

"I'm sorry."

Claudia's tender support stripped away Pecca's disappointment in her, and the ache to have her sister here, sitting next to her, was enough to start her crying again.

"I wish you were here."

"How's Mac?"

Pecca rolled her eyes, not surprised by her sister's aversion to emotion. The fact that she got those two words out of Claudia in the first place was a miracle. Of all the Gallegos children, Claudia was the most reserved, which was strange because she was the third child. Maceo was the only person who could get her to show any emotion.

Part of Pecca didn't want to give Claudia any details. If she wanted to know about her nephew, she could come see him. Spend some time with him. "He's fine."

"Did you tell him?"

"No." Pecca, thinking about Maceo, closed her eyes. "I don't even know what I would say."

Several seconds of silence spread between them. Pecca's thoughts went back to when they were little girls. Well, Pecca was little. Claudia was five years older, and there was a big difference, according to her sister, between a seven-year-old and a preteen. Most days, Claudia made it clear the age difference meant they had nothing in common, but at night there was no escaping. They shared a room, and with only the moon, the stars, and a bedful of stuffed animals as witnesses, Claudia and Pecca would lay awake talking and staring up at their ceiling. Usually, they were making up stories, but sometimes they would *really* talk. About important things like school or when either of them felt like their parents were being unfair. For Claudia, that was a lot of the time. And they'd also talk about boys.

"Do you really think I fall for the wrong guys?"

More seconds passed before Claudia finally answered. "You have a good heart, Pequeña."

"That's not an answer."

Claudia sighed. "What I said doesn't matter anymore."

"It does," Pecca said, her voice louder than she expected. "It matters because I'm wondering if there's something wrong with me. Do I make bad choices? Pick men who are wounded so I can try to fix them, only to learn after my heart is broken that it was never going to work anyways?"

"What happened? Did someone hurt you?"

Yes. Pecca opened her eyes and stared at the ceiling. Colton had crushed her, but she was partly to blame. She had ignored her intuition and let herself cross a line, taking her relationship with Colton where it never should've gone.

"I just keep making mistakes."

"We all make mistakes, but we learn from them. Try to do better the next time."

"I don't seem to be learning from mine."

"Now, I'm being serious. Do I need to come over there and hurt somebody?"

Pecca smiled halfheartedly. "I don't need you to hurt anybody, but I'd sure love it if you'd come down here for a visit."

When Claudia didn't answer right away, Pecca found herself holding her breath. She was already imagining waking up to watch the Thanksgiving Day Parade with a box of Lane's cinnamon rolls. She'd even learn how to start a fire in her fireplace so they all could snuggle on the couch in their pajamas. Maybe she'd cook the dinner and invite Charlie, Lane, and Noah over. And—

"Work's been really busy lately."

Tears stung at the corners of Pecca's eyes. This night needed to end before she cried herself dry. "Right. Okay." She wanted to challenge her sister and say, "Even for Thanksgiving? What about Christmas? Didn't know you were working for Scrooge." But she didn't. There was no point.

"Look, I should probably get to bed. I have work in the morning, and it's been a long night."

"Oh, yeah, sure," Claudia said as though she just realized how late it was. "Give Mac a hug for me."

"Okay."

"And if you're not going to give me a name, then I'll just remind you that the most important man in your life is Maceo. He's not a mistake, and you're a good mom."

"Thanks."

"I love you, Pecca."

Hot frustration tightened the muscles in Pecca's throat so that she could only manage a weak "You too" before ending the call.

Curling up on the couch, she rested her head against a pillow and let the tears go. Holding them in was only going to make her feel worse, and right now she felt bad enough. Whenever Maceo was having a hard day, she allowed him a limited amount of time to wallow in his misery and then he'd have to decide if he was going to let it hold him back or make him better. So tonight, here on the café's couch, Pecca was going to allow herself to do the same.

Claudia was right—Maceo was the most important man in her life. And no matter how badly she wanted Colton to be in the running, she had to remain focused on Maceo's safety. That was one area in her life where she could not afford to make a mistake.

TWENTY-SIX

THE RINGING NOISE shook Colton out of his slump. He swiveled in the desk chair to face his laptop. Someone was trying to open a video chat with him. Using his legs, he scooted across his room and hit a button.

His screen lit up with the most adorable face Colton knew next to the face most of America knew.

"Man, are they not feeding you in Georgia?"

Vincent James's dark brown eyes narrowed at the screen a second before he had to maneuver it away from the grabby hands of his one-year-old daughter, Daesha.

Colton leaned back in his chair. "Brother, I'm consuming close to four thousand calories a day and can't keep the weight on."

"It sounds like rookie camp."

Daesha babbled, her chubby fingers reaching for Vince's lips. He smiled, pretending to eat them, much to her giggling delight. Colton still couldn't believe his friend was a father. It suited him well.

"She's getting big."

Vince set the phone in front of him so he could hold up Daesha. She was wearing some kind of pink shirt with ruffles on the bottom. Her little socks looked like ballet shoes. Vince made her legs bounce side to side in a dance.

"I'm teaching her the St. James Fake."

Colton raised an eyebrow. "Oh yeah? She going to be a future Mustang?"

"No way," a feminine voice called out from off screen. A second later, Shaunette, Vince's wife, walked into view. She leaned over the couch and tickled Daesha's chunky thighs. "This little girl has the legs of a track star, like her mama."

Daesha squealed, bringing her hands together. A string of drool dripped from her gummy smile, and Vince made a face.

"Looks like baby girl is ready for her mama to show her some moves." Vince lifted Daesha overhead, and Shaunette grabbed her.

"Tell Uncle Colt bye-bye." Shaunette took one of Daesha's hands and waved it at the screen. "Say, 'Bye-bye. Come visit us soon.'"

"Nice seeing you, Shaunette." Colton waved. "Bye, Daesha."

Shaunette walked off screen, and Vince's attention was on them for a few seconds before he turned back to the phone and picked it up.

"That little girl is going to be the end of me."

Colton smiled. "Isn't that the way it's supposed to be?"

"Yeah, but I never thought I'd have it this bad."

A tiny stab of jealousy pricked Colton's soul. Vince was living his dream. Colton was proud of him—couldn't be prouder—but it only made his own situation feel that much worse.

"Hey, man, the reason I was calling was to let you know I talked to my financial advisor and I've got the go-ahead for the investment. I'm all in."

The investment. Right. When Colton began *imagining* his future for the ranch as a retreat for veterans and their families, he knew he'd need investors to help him. Asking Vince was humbling, but his friend had always supported the military, and if Colton could get him on board, he figured other investors would see that and want to help too. But last night his vision for the ranch died right alongside the man who attacked him and Pecca.

"Yeah, about that—"

"And guess what? I spoke to a couple other players on the team, and they want to invest too. They asked if maybe they could come out. Have dinner and visit with the families. I know I didn't ask, but I figure that would be pretty cool, so why not, right?"

"Vince—"

"Oh, hey, did your friend's little boy like the football? I hope it wasn't too late?"

"Maceo loved it." His heart ached. "I appreciate you helping me out."

"And with his mama?" Vince's eyebrows danced. "Did she fall into your arms and profess her—"

"Look, Vince," Colton said. "I wanted to talk to you about the ranch. I, um, don't think it's going to happen, man."

Vince straightened. "Why not?"

The last thing Colton wanted to do was get into the details of last night and the mess he'd made with Pecca. The first thing he did this morning was cancel his sessions with her, because the idea of facing her was too much. His heart was too vulnerable.

"I don't know. It's probably a lot of work, and I'm not as far along in my therapy as I'd hoped to be. I think it's too much. Too soon."

"What can I do to help? Once my season's over, I can come to the ranch and help with construction. I can bring some players too. Do you need more money?"

"No." Colton shook his head. "I don't need money or anyone helping with construction. It was an idea I was toying with, and now I've realized it was too much."

"Talk to me, Colt." The corners of Vince's eyes pinched. "Is everything okay?"

"Yeah, good." Colton tried to sound convincing. "It's just . . ." He rubbed the back of his neck. "I never really thought this would be my life, ya know. It's been hard trying to imagine a future outside the one I worked for."

"I get you, brother, but that's the way of life." Vincent settled back. "Nothing is promised. Shaunette and I are always coming up with different visions for our future. All it takes is one hit the wrong way and I'm done. Toast. I have to consider alternate options. I've done that ever since I busted my leg in high school."

"You're still doing what you love." Colton hated how pathetic he sounded, especially in front of Vince.

"Brother, hear me out. What I'm saying is I like playing football. A lot. But I *love* my wife and my daughter. As great as it is to live my dream on the field, it's the dream I'm living at home, with my family, that means the most." Vince pointed at the screen. "You convinced me in high school not to give up, even when it hurt, and I'm telling you to do the same. Just because you're not wearing a uniform anymore doesn't mean you don't have anything to offer."

Vince's words echoed Pecca's, making Colton's chest hurt. He checked the clock. It was time to go.

"I appreciate that, Vince. I'll let you know what I do."

"Hang in there, Colt. You've got this."

Ending the call, Colton felt drained. Maybe Vince should consider being a therapist, like Chaplain Kelly. After one short video chat with his friend, Colton could see the pathetic reasoning behind his tantrum last night. Maybe his appointment with Chaplain Kelly would go better.

"You had a bad night."

Bad night. Next to the night following his diagnosis and departure from the Army, last night was the worst one of Colton's life. Pecca's heartbroken expression had haunted his dreams. He did that to her. He hurt Pecca.

"Pecca told me you canceled your sessions with her today." Chaplain Kelly leaned back in his chair. "Why?"

"I'm only here for another week and a half. I can go to a gym anywhere, but I want to make sure I have a good grasp on the cognitive brain therapy before I leave." And if hearing Pecca's name felt like a stab in his heart, seeing her would only cause him to bleed out. Colton tapped an electrode. "Can we start?"

"Sure, but I want to talk about what happened last night."

"I already told you."

"Yes." Chaplain Kelly pushed his glasses up his nose. "You gave me a report. Concise. Organized. Impassive. Exactly what I would expect from an intelligence officer."

"What else do you want?"

"To know how you're feeling. You said you had another episode. You hadn't had one since our first meeting. Do you realize that was five weeks ago?"

Colton shrugged. "I hadn't thought about it."

"You should." Chaplain Kelly smiled. "You've made progress."

Progress? Colton's gaze drifted to the window as he thought about how his body had failed him again. He could barely see the edge of the parking lot and the squad car parked there. He was grateful Charlie had listened and gotten Pecca more protection, but it was a painful reminder of his own shortcomings.

"Why don't we talk about your homework? You told me about your idea for your grandparents' ranch. What steps have you taken to make that happen?"

Colton scoffed, turning away from the window. He thought about his earlier conversation with Vince. "It's not going to happen."

"Why not?" Chaplain Kelly frowned. "It's a great idea."

"It's too big of a project. And I'm not ready for it."

"May I speak to you a moment as a chaplain rather than your therapist?" He smiled. "I have a bit more experience on that side."

"If I say yes, can we start the CBT?"

Chaplain Kelly's smile grew bigger. "Yes."

"Then fire away, sir."

"I want you to consider for a moment why God may have brought you to this point in your life."

Colton rolled his lip between his teeth. "Maybe I'm being punished for something?"

"Do you believe that?"

He shrugged. "I don't know. Maybe. Can't think of why else this is happening to me."

"Do you believe God has a plan for your life?"

"My parents seem to think he does, but I'm struggling to understand why God would allow this to happen."

"That idea about the ranch. Do you think you would've thought about that if you hadn't come here?"

Colton's fingers bounced with the tremor. All he'd planned to do on the ranch was retire after a long career in the Army. "No."

"And what about Maceo? You started a flag football team just to give him a chance to play a sport you both love. Did you ever think you'd get the privilege to coach and mentor a team of kids and inspire them to look beyond physical limitations?"

"You make me sound much better than I am."

"What I'm trying to do is make you look past your own narrow vision, Colton." Chaplain Kelly shifted in his chair. "You can't see the value of what you're currently bringing to the lives around you. Even *with* your movement disorder. You look at yourself as less than. Is that the message you want your life to reflect? Those kids on the field don't see Maceo's prosthetic because *he* stopped seeing it. Those guys in D-Wing have lived rich, full lives, not because they haven't seen hardships but because they *have* and are choosing to focus on what is better. When are you going to make that decision, Colton?"

"What was wrong with the life I had hoped for?" Colton looked at his arm. "Did I mess up and choose the wrong path or something and now God is using this to get me back on track?"

"I think God is using *this* to get you to trust him completely." Chaplain Kelly's voice was gentle. "Give your plans over to the Lord and trust him. Allow yourself to believe that even though this isn't how *you* planned your life, it doesn't mean it's not exactly where you need to be."

Taking the stairs two at a time, Colton feared running into Pecca. He wasn't sure what he would say to her if he saw her and was even more convinced that maybe Chaplain Kelly was right.

Chaplain Kelly's words had challenged Colton throughout the remainder of his session. It was like Pecca, Vincent, and the chaplain had all conspired to point out the same exact thing. His mother would call him stubborn and remind him that a wise word spoken once is easily ignored, but when it's spoken again the listener should pay attention. Reflecting back on the last year, Colton realized he had used his movement disorder as an excuse to give up. It was a foolish, prideful, stupid response, and he was ashamed of himself.

He scanned the hallway and lounge on the second floor. It was quiet. Good. Running into Gunny, Sarge, or anyone on D-Wing would be just as bad as running into Pecca. Worse. They would call him out on his cowardice. Remind him that women like Pecca didn't come around often, and he was making a mistake.

Brrring.

Colton stepped into his room and tugged his cell phone out of his pocket, closing the door behind him. Kekoa's mug popped up on the screen.

"Brah, we've got a problem. I don't know who that *wahine* is, but she's cursed. I was able to use a program to piece together enough of her face to run through a couple of facial recognition programs and sent you a copy. If she had a criminal record, it'd pop pretty quickly, but brother, this woman is hot, and I ain't talking about her good looks. My computer is fried."

Kekoa was amped up, his words running together—and there wasn't a lot that got the Hawaiian on edge. Colton put his phone on speaker and checked the message. The pixelated image was grainy at best, but Kekoa did a good job piecing the photos together. "Was it a virus?"

"Fried, Colton. Like Texas State Fair fried." Kekoa blew out a breath. "Something or someone turned my five-thousand-dollar computer into a paperweight."

Colton's mood grew darker. "You didn't get anything on her before then?"

"Brah, this wahine doesn't want to be found. She faked her way into a federal prison, knew how to avoid the cameras, and somehow discovered I was looking into her." He whistled. "I have a feeling we've stepped into a hornet's nest and met the queen."

What had he gotten his friend into? Who was this Marissa Dominguez? Something wasn't sitting right in Colton's gut. He needed to talk to Charlie. Maybe Agent Frost would have better luck.

Movement from the corner of Colton's eye spun him around. The shades in his room were still drawn, but there was no mistaking the silhouette of a person standing in the corner. Colton's shoulders tensed, and he took a step backward toward his door.

"Kekoa—"

The shadow moved and Colton's muscles strained, readying for a fight, but his arm jerked and he was right back to that night. The shadow continued stretching toward his window, and a second later the blinds twisted open a little, letting in some light.

Colton squinted and then his eyes widened. Marissa Dominguez. Standing right in front of him. *What is going on?*

"Brah, you okay?"

"Best to tell him all is well, Cap," she whispered, shifting so she was leaning against the desk.

He eyed her. Dark jeans hugged curves that led to a black sweater just bulky enough so that most wouldn't notice the bulge at her hip. Wait—she called him Cap. Her eyebrows lifted as though she were waiting for him to figure it out.

"I-I gotta go. I have an appointment with a queen."

TWENTY-SEVEN

THE DAY COULD NOT FEEL ANY LONGER. Pecca turned her wrist and checked the time—10:25 a.m. She sighed. Lane had woken her this morning and asked if she wanted to call in sick for the day, but Pecca couldn't do that to her patients. And part of her had hoped maybe Lane would be right.

Colton would get up this morning realizing, like she had, that their emotions were in overdrive last night and the situation had made them act irrationally. Imagining Colton walking into the gym and sweeping her into his arms, covering her face with a hundred kisses and apologizing for what a fool he'd been, was what drove her to get to work.

Finding out he had canceled all his appointments with her for the day had crushed her. Even Gunny had taken notice and asked her who he had to kill for stealing the smile off her face. Pecca had done her best to assure him she was just having an off day. She knew if D-Wing found out about last night, even though they'd mean no harm, they'd make Colton's life uncomfortable, and she didn't want to be the cause of that.

Would Colton's withdrawal from her affect his relationship with Maceo? Just the idea that it would made her hurt. Would Colton stop helping Maceo? Stop coaching the Warriors? She rounded the corner toward the staff kitchen, desperate for a third cup of coffee if she had any hope of surviving the day. Shirley, with a motherly smile on her face, stepped out. She lifted up a cup of coffee.

"How'd you know I needed one?"

"It's a dark roast mocha," Shirley said. "I only bring it out when a heart needs to be mended."

Pecca breathed in the heavenly aroma, not caring to know how Shirley knew about her fractured heart. She was about to reach for the cup when her watch pulsed in rhythm with the vibration inside her pocket. She pulled out her cell phone and answered.

"Hello?"

"Is this Ms. Gallegos?" a woman's voice asked.

"Yes, it is." *Great, a marketing call.* She should've checked the number before she answered.

"Good morning, ma'am. This is the attendance office at Walton Elementary, and we were calling to verify Maceo's absence today."

Pecca's heart lurched. "His what?"

"His absence. He's not here to—"

"What do you mean he's not there? I dropped him off this morning."

"I'm sorry, but his teacher marked him absent from morning class, and he wasn't marked present during P.E. I can—"

"I'm on my way."

Pecca's pulse jackhammered in her ears, drowning out the woman's voice. She rushed past Shirley and out the door, her feet barely touching the steps leading down to the lawn. Her thoughts tumbled through their morning. Lane woke her up. Maceo and Noah ate cereal. She forced him to also eat a banana. And yes, she drove him to school and dropped him off. She even waved to Deputy Wilson, who'd been assigned to watch the school. This had to be a mistake.

The trail was the fastest way to get to the school, so she took it, but the events from last night came spiraling back into her mind. When she passed the spot where she and Colton were attacked, a strangled cry caught in her throat and propelled her forward. Sheriff Huggins and Charlie were still searching for the shooter. Would he go after Maceo? Why? Why was this happening?

Every single headline about a child abduction flashed through her mind, and she urged her legs to move faster. *Please, God, let him be there and it be a mistake.* Yes. It was a mistake. Maceo must've been in the bathroom when attendance was taken or moved seats or . . .

The school came into view, and Pecca sprinted through the playground, skidding to a halt near one of the side doors. She reached for the handle and tugged, but it didn't budge. A curse rolled through her mind. The school kept all the doors locked but the main one. That should've reassured her, but it only aggravated her.

She ran to the front of the school and entered the building, heading to the office. Her frenzied and sudden appearance shocked the secretary and another woman standing near her. They stared at her, mouths open.

"Where's Maceo? I dropped him off this morning." Pecca huffed. "They called me. I dropped him off."

The secretary stood, concern etched into her face. The principal, Ms. Webb, came out of her office as well. "Ms. Gallegos, what's wrong?"

Pecca held up her cell phone, her chest heaving. "The attendance office called me and said Maceo was marked absent"—tears sprang to her eyes and her voice shook—"but I dropped him off."

Ms. Webb came around the counter and put a consoling hand on Pecca's arm. She turned to the secretary. "Call Ms. Johnson and see if Maceo's in class."

The woman moved like molasses, and Pecca's fears mounted. Unwilling to wait, she pivoted and raced out of the office and down the hall toward Maceo's classroom.

"Ms. Gallegos!"

Pecca ignored Ms. Webb's voice and ran down the main hall. A kid using the water fountain looked up and stared after her as she made her way to the second-grade hallway. Turning the corner, she halted abruptly when she saw Deputy Wilson walking toward her. Heart plunging, it took all her strength to remain upright.

"Ms. Gallegos."

"Wha—" Her voice cracked as she stared up into his dark brown eyes. "Where's Maceo?"

"Mom?"

Pecca swung around and saw Maceo standing outside the boys' bathroom, his forehead squished in confusion. She dashed toward him, dropped to her knees, and squeezed him to her chest. "Are you okay? I'm so glad you're here." She pushed him back and looked him over before meeting his eyes. "Where were you?"

"In the bathroom."

His sober response burst the balloon of emotion filling her chest, and Pecca sank to her heels. "The whole morning?"

Deputy Wilson walked over. "Ms. Gallegos, is everything okay?"

Maceo's eyes flashed with fear. "Ms. Johnson said I could." He looked down and back up, his eyes growing wide. "I left the hall pass in the bathroom." Freeing himself, Maceo went back into the boys' room and returned with an empty milk carton with Ms. Johnson's name and the room number written on it in red marker. "See?"

Ms. Webb jogged over to join them, along with Maceo's teacher. The commotion had also drawn the attention of several more teachers, who were opening their doors to peek out. "Ms. Gallegos, I stopped by the attendance office. Maceo wasn't marked absent."

"What?" Ms. Johnson frowned, her eyes passing between everyone. "Of course not. Maceo's been here all morning."

Pecca stood. "Then why would someone from the school call to tell me he wasn't here?"

"I don't know," Ms. Webb said. "It must've been a mistake."

A mistake. Pecca inhaled sharply. She glanced around at everyone until she found Maceo. It was a mistake. He was here. Safe.

"I've been here the whole time, ma'am." Deputy Wilson towered over them—his presence formidable but also comforting. "Your boy is safe."

"Thank you. I'm sorry I panicked. It's just—"

"Don't apologize, dear." Ms. Webb consoled her with a pat on the arm. "This was a terrible mistake, and I'm going to make sure I find out what happened."

"Can I go back to class now, Mom?"

Maceo's eyes darted to where the door of his classroom stood ajar, his classmates standing there, watching.

"Oh, yes, of course." She started to reach for him, but he shot her a "please don't embarrass me" look, and against her instinct, Pecca refrained from smothering him in hugs and kisses. It was probably for the best since she wasn't sure once she got her arms around him if she'd be able to let go. "I'll be here to pick you up after school."

Pecca peered up at Deputy Wilson, who read the worry on her face and gave her a reassuring nod, before she allowed Ms. Webb to walk her back to the front of the school. The frantic principal assured her the matter would be looked into and corrected. Pecca thanked her and did her best to pretend that the last twenty minutes hadn't stolen several years off her life.

When she stepped outside the school, Pecca barely made it to the parking lot before she completely lost it. Wrapping her arms around her waist, she bent over and released the sob that had been building since she got the call that Maceo was gone. Her shoulders shook like her body was trying to expel the dread of what she had imagined had happened to Maceo.

"Pecca?" She lifted her head and, through her tears, saw David standing there. "Are you okay?"

She shook her head. "No."

David put a hand on her back. "What happened?"

It must've been the emotional turmoil, because Pecca couldn't resist turning into David's chest, where she buried her head against his shoulder and cried again. He rubbed her back for a few seconds until Pecca finally got control over herself.

"I'm sorry," she said, pulling back. "I had a bit of a scare, but everything is fine now."

"Is Maceo okay?"

"Yes." Pecca said it firmly. Maceo was okay. She sniffled. "Everything is good."

"Are you headed back to work?"

Pecca looked at her watch. "Yeah."

"Here." David stepped aside. "Let me give you a ride."

She looked over at the trail and realized how stupid she was to take off from the Mansion. She looked back at David, who shifted on his cane and smiled. She bit the inside of her cheek. Crying on his shoulder suddenly felt very foolish. "Uh—"

"Come on, Pecca." He nudged her arm playfully with his. "We're friends, and friends help each other out."

Looking at her watch once more, Pecca sighed. "Okay, sure."

They walked toward his car, and Pecca climbed into the passenger seat. A woman was pulling Hula-Hoops from the back of her trunk when she glanced over and waved. It was Kristen, Emilia's mom. Pecca waved back.

"I appreciate the ride, David."

"It's no problem." He reached between them to set his cane in the back seat, and she noticed his hands shaking. "I was going to volunteer in the art lab today."

Pecca leaned back in the seat. "You're a really nice guy, David."

He gave a shy smile before it twisted into a grimace. He bent over and clutched his side. "Arghhh."

"David? Are you okay? What's wrong?" She leaned over the middle console to check on him and he looked up, his eyes wild. Chills shot down her spine. "David?"

"I'm sorry, Pecca." David lunged toward her, and his right hand snaked around the back of her neck. He jerked her head toward his face.

"David, stop!" She pushed her hands against his chest, trying to stop his advance, but he was too strong. "Sto—" His left hand went over her mouth, and it took her a second to realize he was pressing a cloth to her face.

Fear rippled through her and she gasped, trying to breathe, but with each intake of air noxious fumes filled her lungs. She kicked her legs and clawed at him, but he was strong. Very strong. The edges of her eyes grew dark as she scratched at his face, but her attempts were feeble. Her arms became heavy and dropped to her lap as her head lolled forward against David's shoulder. His grip on her relaxed, and he started the car. From the corner of her eye, Pecca saw Kristen still unloading her car.

Help! she screamed, but no noise escaped her lips. Feeling the car begin to roll forward, Pecca willed herself to move—to do anything—but her body felt like it was trapped in sand, leaving her helpless to fight against an enemy she never saw coming.

TWENTY-EIGHT

COLTON ENDED THE CALL and slipped the phone into his back pocket, taking his time so he could assess the situation. Though it was hard to see for sure, the woman hiding in the shadows couldn't be anyone else but Marissa Dominguez. His arm jerked outward, smacking a bottle of water off his nightstand and across the floor. The sudden movement brought Marissa to her feet, quick as a cat and poised for a fight.

That told him everything.

"You know who I am?"

"I'd say Marissa Dominguez, but we both know she doesn't exist." Colton recognized something—or thought he did. Her light brown hair was pulled back in a short ponytail. The angle of her chin . . . lips. Maybe it was his imagination playing tricks on his mind, but there was something more familiar about her than the memory of the photo Kekoa had just sent him. "Why are you here?"

"You were looking for me." She lifted her arms out. "Here I am."

Dread crawled over him. If this woman had something to do with Javier's death, and she was here . . . Pecca. Rage colored his vision. "My daddy taught me to never hit a girl, but if you think you're getting past me to go after Pecca, I'll tell you right now I've been known to disobey."

A smirk crept onto her face and Colton's world tilted. *No.* He blinked, trying to take in what he was seeing. Same color eyes and hair, but it was the smile. They shared the exact same smile.

"I'd have you pinned before your second step, but I appreciate your humor."

So many questions began swirling in Colton's brain that he thought he might get dizzy. She hadn't changed much from the family photos. Did Pecca know she was here? And why was she here? And *why* did she visit Javier in prison? He was about to ask when there was a knock on his door.

"You should get that." She stepped aside, her hand never far from the bulge on her hip. "I invited a guest."

Colton hesitated for a second. Would she shoot him the second he turned his back? Who had she invited? There was another knock, and she raised her eyebrows. He went to the door and cringed, expecting to hear the blast of a gunshot. When it didn't come, he let out a breath and opened the door.

"Charlie?"

"I'm glad you called. The ME is having trouble identifying your attacker." Charlie strode into the doorway and then paused. "Why's it so dark—" His hand flew to his weapon.

There was a blur of movement, ending with the sound of the hammer being pulled back. "Ah-ah-ah, Deputy Lynch. Just take a breath and come inside." The feminine voice spoke.

Charlie barely moved, and Colton wondered if he was breathing at all. He finally stepped inside and quickly closed the door. Colton wasn't sure why he was complying, but it was better this way. They didn't want anyone to get caught in cross fire.

"Who are you?" Charlie's voice was tight.

She looked at Colton. He crossed the room with a sigh and twisted the blinds open all the way so light filled his room. "Charlie, meet Claudia, Pecca's sister."

Charlie blinked several times, and then his eyes grew wide. "You're Marissa."

"I'm Claudia, and if you'll move your hand from your weapon, I'll put mine away."

Neither Charlie nor Claudia moved. Both stared at each other like they were in a showdown, unwilling to drop their guard. Colton had to do something.

"Did you kill Javier?"

Her dark eyes never left Charlie. "No."

"Strange. He doesn't get a visitor in years and you show up—a week later he's dead." The standoff continued, so Colton sat on his bed. "Why are you here?"

"For Pecca."

"It's a little late for moral support," Colton said. "Pecca's been shot at, threatened, her home broken into, and last night . . ." He swallowed, his chest aching. "Last night someone attacked her." He speared Claudia with a pointed look. "You can't find time in your schedule to be here for your sister, but you made it to Texas to see her ex?"

"It's complicated." Claudia's posture shifted, her eyes looking to the ground. "That's why I'm here. I need your help."

"You need my help?"

"Both of you, actually." Claudia lifted her gaze. "And time is not on our side, so I'm going to put my weapon away and keep my hands where you can see them so we can talk."

Charlie didn't budge as he watched Claudia do what she said she would. Then she pulled the desk chair over and sat. Only then did Charlie take a step back and holster his weapon before looping his hands in his gun belt. A purposeful position that wasn't lost on Claudia, who nodded.

"I paid a visit to the medical examiner before I came here," Claudia said. "The man who was shot last night was Manuel Lopez. At my direction, the ME is running his tattoo through the system and will soon discover its affiliation with the Valle Colombiano cartel. He was sent here to do the bidding of Salvador 'Señor' Perez, who is trying to reclaim control over the cartel and—"

"Wait. Are you telling me Javier or the SSB sent someone from a cartel to go after Pecca?" Charlie asked.

"It wasn't Javier. Or the SSB," Claudia said.

"How do you know that?"

Claudia looked up at Charlie. "When Adrian told me about

Javier's parole hearing and the shooting outside the café, I began my own investigation. My visit to Javier triggered some alarms, which is exactly what I needed it to do to find out who Javier really was and why Pecca was being targeted. He swore to me that he didn't know where Pecca or Maceo were, and he had no idea who was going after her."

"You believed him?"

She turned to Colton. "At first I was skeptical, but his body language told me he was telling the truth, and he was . . . scared." Claudia shook her head. "But he wouldn't tell me anything else. The next day I got a call from the DEA—Javier Torres was an undercover informant and had been for the last eight years."

Colton shook his head. Had he heard her right? "What?"

"All those years I spent hating him for dragging Pecca down . . ." Claudia dipped her chin to her chest. "My sister was right. Javier tried to avoid the gang life, but it was hard. His family, friends, and neighbors were all involved, and at some point he decided the best way to help them was to help the police. The gang situation inside the prison system is lethal. Gang leaders can still operate from behind bars, only now they're able to recruit and even combine forces with other gangs. When Javier was arrested, he made a deal with the DEA."

Pecca had been right. Colton thought back to the first attack, when she insisted Javier wouldn't harm her or Maceo. Even though he made her life more difficult, she never stopped seeing the good in him—his potential.

"Was that why he was killed?" Charlie's question broke into Colton's thoughts. "Was he informing on the SSB?"

"Javier became an integral part of Operation Gunsmoke—a joint mission between the DEA, Border Patrol, and the ATF to stop weapons and drugs from crossing the border. This directly impacted the SSB, as they were behind most of the runs. Over the last several years, the agencies have apprehended smugglers thanks to Javier."

Colton frowned. "How was he able to help from inside the prison?"

"His cousin Felix was feeding him information. The SSB had assumed a lackey was ratting them out to the Feds. It wasn't until a few months ago that they got wise and started looking at the ranking members. They began setting traps, so the DEA pulled Felix."

"Was Felix an informant?"

"No," she answered Charlie, "but soon after the attacks on Pecca escalated, the DEA put him in a safe house until he can testify."

A safe house. Clarity was beginning to burn through the fog. He stared hard at her. "What agency are you with?"

"I can't tell you, but—"

"Why not?" Colton stood and started pacing. "You may not have killed Javier directly, but I'll bet you're the reason he's dead."

"Because of the operational security of the mission."

From the corner of his eye, Colton saw Charlie's stunned expression and imagined he looked much the same way. "What mission?"

"We believe the cartel may have another man on the ground. Interpol has been helping us keep track of anyone entering the United States who's associated with the cartel. I've personally gone through the family lineage of Salvador Perez to make sure we're tracking every possible suspect, but I only recently learned of someone living in the US—Juan Pablo Rojas, Salvador's nephew-in-law."

"This doesn't make sense." Colton's arm jerked. "Why is the cartel interested in Pecca? If they're upset about the SSB or Javier or Felix, it doesn't explain why they would come all the way here to get to her. Do they think she knows something?"

Claudia's silence was confirmation enough.

Dread curled its way through Colton's body. "What does she know?"

"She knows me."

Colton jolted to a stop, his gaze swinging to Claudia. He narrowed his eyes on her. "What do you mean?"

"We believe Perez commissioned members of his cartel to go after Pecca as a way of getting to me."

"What did you do?"

"It's safer if you don't know," Claudia said, her tone softer. "It's the only thing keeping Pecca safe right now."

"The only thing?" It took a single step and Colton was in her face, towering over her. She backed into the chair, her hand going for her weapon. Charlie stepped in, pressing his hand against Colton's chest to get him to back up. "All this time you let her believe it was the SSB and Javier threatening her. Making her think she somehow brought this on herself, and it was *you*."

"It's . . . complicated." Claudia spoke through gritted teeth. There was a warning in her eyes that said he should tread lightly. "We weren't sure it wasn't Javier and the SSB. That's why I went to see him."

"You got him killed," Colton said. "Is Pecca next?"

"You said there was someone else," Charlie said calmly. "This Juan Pablo guy. Do you know where he is?"

Claudia nodded at Charlie. "We think he's here in Walton."

A ringing noise interrupted the confrontation. Charlie took a slow step back, eyeing him and Claudia. "I'm going to answer this. Don't kill each other."

Colton shoved back, turning to look out the window. His eyes went to the gym, and the urge to find Pecca rose within him. He needed to apologize to her, especially after hearing what Claudia said regarding Javier. His words had only driven her fears deeper.

"You think protecting me is the only role you play in my life?"

Pecca's words echoed in his ears. Chaplain Kelly was asking him to adjust his perspective—to see the good God could bring out of a bad situation if only he would adjust. For so long, Colton only imagined one role for his life. Well, that wasn't true. He'd wanted to play for the NFL, but his combine numbers weren't good enough for a draft pick—so he adjusted and joined the Army. Why was he struggling to adjust to the movement disorder?

Because it makes me weak.

Colton's eyes drifted to the lawn, and he thought about Maceo. That kid was anything but weak. Emotion clogged Colton's throat, his warm breath fogging the window. Maceo was strong because he had the support and love of a mom who could see potential.

"Colton."

He turned to find Charlie putting his phone away, concern lining his forehead.

"That was Deputy Wilson. He's at the elementary school. He said there was a situation with Maceo a little bit ago. Pecca ran over there because someone called her from the school saying Maceo was absent."

Claudia shot up. "Where is he?"

"He's there. Deputy Wilson said he's been there the whole time and that it was a mix-up or something—"

Colton raced out of his room and down the stairs. He saw Shirley at her desk. "Did Pecca come back from the school yet?"

"No, honey. Gunny came in—"

Colton was already halfway out the door and jogging in the direction of the elementary school, leaving Shirley's explanation trailing behind him. *Breathe.* But he couldn't over the tightness growing in his chest. He replayed everything Claudia had told them. Her job, whatever it was, had put a target on Pecca's back—and it had put one on Javier's.

That's why Claudia didn't object to his accusation. Javier wasn't killed by the SSB—he was killed by the cartel. Somehow they knew about her visit to the jail and then beat Javier to find out where she was. Nausea clawed at his stomach, but he couldn't think about it, he needed to get to the school. Make sure Pecca was okay.

Rounding the front of the school, Colton almost crashed into a father holding his daughter's hand. The father tucked his daughter behind him and Colton could appreciate his wariness, but at this moment he didn't have time to explain. Passing the man, he pulled open the glass doors to the school and ran in.

A woman jumped up from behind a desk. "Can I help you, sir?"

"Pecca . . . Gallegos." Colton huffed. "Where . . . is . . . she?"

"And you are?"

"Colton Crawford."

Remaining behind her desk, she arched an eyebrow in a look that asked if his name was supposed to mean something to her.

"She was here," he said in one breath. "To check on her son, Maceo. There . . . was a . . . mix-up." Something flickered in her expression that made him believe she knew what he was talking about. Colton took a step toward her. "Please, I'm a friend."

"Stay there." The woman squared her shoulders, positioning herself like she was a defensive lineman, ready to tackle Colton if he made any sudden moves toward her. Colton ran a hand through his sweaty hair and could only imagine what this must look like.

"Yes, ma'am. If you could just tell me if Pecca Gallegos was—"

"Coach?" A woman Colton sort of recognized stepped out of the library.

"Do you know this man?"

She smiled at Colton. "Yes, he's Emilia's flag football coach. One of them."

Emilia's mom. Yes. Karen, no, Kristen. He nodded at her. "I'm looking for Pecca."

The door behind him opened, and Colton turned to find Charlie walking in. Finally. Outside he could see Claudia on her phone. "They won't tell me if she's here."

"If you're talking about Pecca, she left," Kristen said. "Just a few minutes ago with, um"—she gave Colton an apprehensive look—"David."

Colton frowned. "Where did they go?"

"Maybe he gave her a lift back to the Mansion," Charlie said. "I'm sure she was upset."

"She's not at the Mansion." Colton and Charlie spun around. Claudia had walked into the office. "She's traveling west on Ford Avenue. Home for Heroes is east."

"How do you know—"

Claudia lifted up her phone, twisting it around. "Do you know this guy?"

Jealousy flared up in Colton's chest. "That's David."

"No," Claudia said. "That's Juan Pablo Rojas."

The world tilted, and Colton's knees started to buckle. He would've hit the ground had it not been for Charlie grabbing him. The truth crashed over him like a violent wave, sending his heart rolling and thrashing in his chest.

"He's got her. He's got Pecca."

TWENTY-NINE

IT WAS IMPOSSIBLE. The plan was in place. All Alicia had to do was let Victor drive her and Diego to the airport. His wife and son should have phoned to say they'd arrived at the villa in Côte d'Azur this morning, but their call never came.

Juan's heart writhed inside his chest as he pulled up the security camera images from his home, only to find an empty, ransacked house. His calls to Alicia went unanswered, as did his calls to Victor.

Where are they?

He glanced down at his phone again, the trembling in his fingers growing uncontrollable with every passing minute. What had Señor done? How had he gotten to her and Diego so fast? Juan should've known better. After Javier was killed, he should've reacted quicker. He turned and looked at Pecca. This was not what he wanted. He had tried to avoid it, but his delay—his temporary compassion for her—may have cost him his family.

A small groan escaped her lips. Pecca would be waking up soon. Juan paced, grinding his teeth. It shouldn't have come to this. Before his plane landed at the Savannah airport, he had already created David Turner. It wasn't hard. Identity theft wasn't nearly as hard anymore. And since Juan wasn't actually stealing anything but the Army sergeant's name, military record, and injury, there was no crime to make anyone suspicious enough to look into him.

Arriving early enough to build up David's life in Savannah and Walton had been vital. He'd been worried that the local residents would question his sudden presence, but they were so wrapped up with the Watcher case and the death of some newspaper owner that they barely noticed him.

Fitting into the community wasn't hard. Everyone loves a volunteer, and most people only look for the boxes marked for a criminal record when they run a background check. Sergeant David Turner was an exemplary citizen. Not even a parking ticket.

Movement from the corner of his eye caught his attention. Pecca's head hung forward against her chest but was slowly moving side to side. Juan had been prepared for a lot of scenarios, but not for the way Pecca Gallegos and her son, Maceo, had reminded him of Alicia and Diego.

Señor's wrath did not discriminate against mothers or children. Juan's breath caught in his throat, emotion burning. He looked at his phone and tried calling Alicia's number again. He cursed when she did not answer. He tried Victor's, vowing to kill him first if something happened to his wife and son.

The phone came to life in his hand, and Juan almost dropped it. He answered.

"Alicia?"

"No."

Juan shoved his fist between his teeth and bit down, fighting the scream he wanted to release. His heart felt like it was going to explode out of his chest. "Wh-where is she? Diego?"

"They are safe for now."

"I want to speak to them."

"You do not give me orders!"

Removing the phone from his ear, Juan took a breath. He needed to stay calm. Alicia and Diego were alive. He needed to keep them that way.

"Why have you involved them?"

"You involved them the second you told them to run. You think I wouldn't find out that my niece was going on a trip?" Señor gave a short, derisive laugh. "I know everything that happens in my family. That is my job now that Hector is gone."

Juan balled his hand into a fist and slammed it against his thigh. The physical pain was not even worth recognizing compared to what lay ahead emotionally if something happened to Alicia and Diego. Señor took it upon himself to lead the Perez family, but shared bloodlines did not guarantee their safety.

"Please let me talk to them. I'll do whatever you ask of me. Por favor."

"You will do what I ask, because I have found the proper incentive. Their lives rest in your hands, Juan. Now, I assume my little acquisition has spurred you into action, yes?"

"I have her sister." Juan turned to Pecca, who was stirring more. "Claudia will be here soon."

"How do you know this?"

Anger boiled beneath his skin. *Because I have a plan*, he wanted to scream. Bringing Manuel Lopez to Walton had been his ace. A disposable decoy he knew Claudia wouldn't be able to resist. All he had to do was wait for her to show up, and he would deliver the precious asset to Señor.

But when he couldn't get hold of Alicia—time had run out.

"Unlike you, Claudia is loyal to only two things in this world— her government and her family. She will come to save her sister."

"You better pray she values one of those things more than the other." Juan could hear Señor's lips smacking over a cigar. "For your sake and for the sake of your family, Juan. I hope you are right."

The line went dead and Juan screamed his curses into the air, the angry vulgarities echoing against the walls. He went to Pecca. For *her* sake, Claudia had better not fail to show up.

THIRTY

PECCA'S HEAD felt as heavy as a bowling ball, the weight of it tugging at her neck muscles. It took a great deal of effort to lift it up. *What happened?* She was at the elementary school. Maceo was marked absent but was there. She was upset. David was there—*David!*

Her eyes flashed open, and she immediately squeezed them shut to block out the bright light. The throbbing in her head was awful.

"Nice and slow, Pecca. I didn't use much but enough that you're going to feel dizzy and maybe a little sick. Your head is going to hurt."

David's voice echoed around her, sending a painful vibration through her brain and a shiver racing down her skin. *He didn't use much?* David was talking about the cloth he pressed over her nose and mouth. Was it chloroform? In nursing school, she studied the compound's effects and was shocked to learn how dangerous it was. The movies made it look like some simple solution bad guys could use, but the number of cases where people didn't wake up and died from the inhalation . . .

Dizziness swept over her, and she began to sway. Something was keeping her upright, squeezing her chest and arms. Pecca opened her eyes slowly, allowing them to adjust to the light surrounding her. Where was she?

Squinting, she looked around the vast space. Cement floors. Huge yellowed windows reached high into the ceiling over corrugated walls of metal. Steel beams crisscrossed overhead—it looked like an old warehouse.

Her head rolled downward and she saw the reason why she couldn't move. Ropes wrapped around her body, arms, and legs, strapping her to the chair she was sitting in. Bile rose up her throat. *I'm going to die.*

"This isn't my fault, you know."

Pecca lifted her eyes and found David pacing in front of her. "What?"

"There was a plan. All he had to do was give me a few more days, and I could've delivered. I know she's out there. All she has to do is show up." He snapped his gaze to her, and Pecca flinched. "And when she does"—he gritted his teeth—"I may kill her myself."

Kill? Her breaths came in short intakes, barely enough to fill her lungs. If she didn't slow down, she was going to hyperventilate and pass out—and she couldn't do that. She had to get away. Wiggling her arms against the constraints sent tears to her eyes. They were tight. Too tight to slip free.

"Now, don't think you're going to be getting out of those any-time soon." He shook his head as he walked over, then he stopped and stared at her. "I'm afraid there's only one way you're going to get out of them—well, two, if you count dying."

She swallowed. Who was this man? He wasn't the David she knew. The one who volunteered at the Mansion and the school, the one who had a tender heart for kids. Her eyes flickered to his legs. He was . . . walking. Without a cane. Her brain fought for purchase of what she was seeing. David walking. Standing. Drug-ging her. Threatening her. Panic surged through her with a rush of adrenaline, and her body immediately began to shake.

"Promise me you're going to do what I say, Pecca." David pro-duced a gun from his back pocket and pressed the muzzle against her forehead. She whimpered and nodded her head quickly. "Good girl."

David, curses slipping from his lips, stalked to a table and picked up a phone. He pressed a button and lifted the phone to his ear. A few seconds later, he ended the unanswered call. "If he has touched them. A single hair on their heads—" David fisted the phone in his hand, his knuckles turning white. He cursed before twisting to look at Pecca. Pointing the gun at her, he said, "You better hope she shows up."

"Wh-what are you talking about?"

With beads of sweat covering his forehead, David grabbed a metal chair and dragged it over the concrete, the legs causing a screeching noise that hurt Pecca's ears. He spun it around in front of her and then straddled it backward. His eyes were bloodshot and a vein throbbed in his neck.

"You must have a lot of questions." He used the tip of the gun to scratch at his temple. "First, I can walk." He did a little stomping dance. "A miracle, yes?"

Pecca detected a Spanish accent, and her pulse accelerated. South Side Barrio. It wasn't over. They'd found her. But why? "Javier's dead," she said, the words bittersweet on her tongue. "What else do you want?"

"Oh." David stilled. "You think—" He narrowed his eyes. "That was *him*." David shot out of the chair and kicked it across the room.

Her body shuddered against the restraints. "Who?"

David ignored her and pressed a button on his cell phone. Pecca took advantage of the distraction and began twisting her wrists, careful not to draw any attention. The ropes burned into her skin, but she kept moving them. She searched around for anything she could use as a weapon if she could free herself.

"Arghhh!"

Pecca froze.

"Where are they?"

Her lips trembled. "Who?"

David's light brown eyes grew dark. It was like he was transforming in front of her eyes, and she had no idea who this man was—except that he was a liar. Whatever was the goal of his elaborate hoax, Pecca needed to figure out how to stop it.

"Tell me why you're doing this. Maybe I can help."

"The same reason you ran from El Paso, *mi amiga—protege a mi familia*."

Protect his family? A flicker of something passed over his face. Regret? Was he being forced to do this? A burst of hope blossomed in her chest. She may not know the whole truth about David, but it couldn't have all been an act—right?

"You have kids, don't you?"

David narrowed his eyes. "How do you know?"

Pecca licked her lips. "Because there's nothing a parent won't do to protect their children." She glanced down at her restraints. "Even the unimaginable."

"*Entonces entiendes.*"

No. She didn't understand, but she kept quiet. If she could keep David talking, then he wasn't hurting her—and that would hopefully give someone enough time to figure out she was missing.

"I understand." She gave him a sympathetic look. "Who are you protecting them from? SSB?"

David gave a wry laugh. "Ha. That would be as simple as running away, wouldn't it?" He looked at the cell phone gripped in his hand. His knuckles turned white. "Do you know what he will do to them?" He ran a hand down his face. "All they had to do was leave. I set everything up. It was ready because I knew he . . . I knew he was a monster."

He glared at her. "You couldn't make this easy, could you? Señor found the picture, and there you were. It wasn't hard to track you down. The internet makes everything easy these days, and you're in the system. Did you know that?" He walked over and brushed the tip of the gun over her face, causing her body to tremble. "Because you're a nurse. Your name and information are all right there. An easy hack, but I had to set the stage."

David began pacing again. "I was worried when Colton showed up, but he was too concerned with his own weakness to pay attention to the details."

"He's not weak," Pecca snapped.

"There's something about you, Pecca, that makes people want to be better."

282

"Except you. You've drugged and kidnapped me. For what?"

"To protect Maceo!" David roared, his voice echoing loudly around her. "Don't you get it? They are going to keep coming after you and Maceo until they get to her. Maceo would be dead if it weren't for me. Last night after the fall festival, it was because I stayed behind that Maceo made it to Lane's home safely. I traded in my family's safety for you!"

Cold dread washed over her. David was the shooter.

David stormed to the table and picked up another phone. *Her* phone. He returned and thrust it into her face. "Call her."

"Who?"

"CALL HER!" Spittle landed on her face and she recoiled. "Tell her your life and the life of her nephew depend on it."

She was afraid to ask who he was talking about when her mind latched onto the words. *Her nephew*. Her—did he mean Claudia? Why would he want to talk to Claudia? Frowning, she opened her mouth, but the strike came quickly and snapped her head backward.

"*Ahora*," he whispered in her ear. "*Aprenderás la verdad.*"

Feeling the blood drip down her chin, Pecca began to cry, afraid to learn the truth.

THIRTY-ONE

IT FELT LIKE A BOMB had detonated inside Colton's chest, and he was still reeling from the effects. His mind was numb as he, Charlie, and Claudia rushed from the school office to the parking lot.

"You're tracking her?"

Charlie's question snapped Colton out of his daze. "How?"

"I bought Pecca her Apple Watch for a reason." Claudia looked at her phone and then frowned. "They're somewhere outside of Savannah, but"—she used her fingers to adjust the screen—"I can't see what street they're on. It looks industrial."

Colton looked at Charlie. "Where does David live?"

"I don't know, but I'm sure the school keeps a record of all their volunteers. They may have it."

"Good. Get that and get over to his house. Claudia and I will go to the location—"

"Wait a minute." Charlie held his hands up. "I know you're freaking out, Colton, but I can't allow a civilian to go running into trouble."

Colton lifted his chin. "You going to stop me?"

"I will."

"Listen, guys, we don't have much time. If Juan Pablo has her, it's because the game has shifted. We have to go now."

Charlie looked around like he was trying to come up with a solution, but with a final sigh, he said, "Fine. If you get to her before I do, don't engage." His eyes flashed to Claudia. "I don't know what kind of authority you have on this case, but it'll be my butt on the line if something happens to either of you."

"Call us when you get the address." Colton was already hurrying to the parking lot, Claudia at his side. They walked to a black Charger. He turned to her. "Tell me we have time."

She flattened her lips. "I have to make a call."

Colton's nerves thrummed along with the Charger's engine as Claudia raced down I-95 like a Formula 1 driver. She was steering with one hand while holding a cell phone to her ear with the other. His body lurched forward, straining against the seatbelt, and Claudia cursed the semitruck that had pulled in front of them. Swerving into the left lane, she narrowly missed a BMW, whose driver offered a choice hand signal.

His arm twitched and jerked, but he didn't care. He kept his eyes glued to the pulsating dot on the GPS screen on the dashboard—the lifeline to Pecca. The dot hadn't moved, which filled him with a mixture of gratitude and concern. If David and Pecca remained where they were, according to the GPS tracker—and Claudia's lead foot—the two of them would be arriving at Pecca's location in six minutes. But if the reason Pecca wasn't moving . . .

"Thanks, Nate, I appreciate it."

Claudia dropped the phone next to her. Her free hand went to the steering wheel, and with a burst of acceleration, she zipped across all three lanes on I-95, barely making it to the exit before Colton ate guardrail for lunch.

Colton's hand gripped the dashboard, his shoulder slamming into the door. "I'm pretty sure we need to be alive to save Pecca."

"One of us does."

He scoffed. "That's an agency joke, right?"

"You hurt her, you know."

This? This was what they were going to talk about right now? Colton shifted in the passenger seat, unsure if what she had said earlier was a joke. He studied the blur of Georgia marshland they were racing past. *She's gonna knock me off in the middle of the swamp and let the gators get me.* He pushed the ridiculous, he hoped, morbid thought from his mind and answered honestly. "I was stupid."

Claudia nodded. "You'd be lucky to have Pecca."

"I agree." Claudia took a hard right, and the Charger hit a berm, sending them bouncing hard along a side road. He checked the GPS to make sure they were headed to Pecca. "And I intend to make it up to her for the rest of my life."

"That's fast. Are you sure? Wouldn't want you to make any *mistakes.*"

Her sarcastic dig wasn't lost on him. Had Pecca told her about their last conversation? Colton pushed out a breath. He deserved it. His mind went back to his conversations with Vince and Chaplain Kelly. "I was reminded today of something I had forgotten. I had the chance to play for the NFL. Dreamt about the opportunity my whole life. When it didn't happen, I was lost. Felt like I'd spent my whole life preparing for that and then—poof—it was gone.

"It was hard to imagine my life outside of football, but my mom reminded me that things happen for a reason—she said *divine* reasons—and that God needed me for something else. I joined the military, and a new dream was born. I thought she was right. And then this happened." He looked down at his arm. "It felt like dreams kept getting snatched away from me, but today I finally realized that if those things had never happened, I wouldn't be here. I never would have met Pecca and Maceo. Or the guys at D-Wing. I wouldn't be dreaming of opening up a ranch for military veterans and their families." The Charger hit a bump, and Colton's knees knocked into the glove compartment. "Or on Mr. Toad's Wild Ride with you." Claudia smirked. "I can imagine a dozen new futures for my life, but none of them will be complete without Pecca and Maceo in it. More than anything, that's what I want her to know."

"Let's hope you get your chance."

In front of them, several dilapidated metal warehouses appeared. The Charger bumped and jostled down a narrow dirt road with deep ruts carved out by the rain. The rusted chain-link fence surrounding the area leaned at a precarious angle, waiting for the next storm to put it out of its misery. They passed a burned-out shell of a car, and fear wrapped itself around his gut and squeezed.

"Take a breath," Claudia whispered. "The damage on that car is too old. It's not theirs."

From the look on her face, she was answering his fear as much as her own. Claudia, driving slowly, continued toward the neglected buildings. Colton scanned the area, instinct kicking in as he watched for any indication of trouble.

Colton ran his palms down his pants. David was Juan Pablo. His stomach turned. They all missed it, but how? And what had made David react now? *The game has shifted.* He turned to Claudia.

"David—or Juan Pablo—had plenty of opportunity to get to Pecca. Why now? What's changed?"

"Has Charlie texted you yet?"

Colton slid his phone from his pocket and checked. "He's headed to the address on file for David. That was three minutes ago."

"I'm going to take a wild guess that when he gets there, he's going to find the rifle used to kill Manuel Lopez."

Colton frowned. "You think David was the shooter? Why would he kill the guy trying to attack Pecca if the plan was to get to her all along?"

Claudia pulled in behind a long dumpster overflowing with scrap metal, cardboard, and pipes. She turned to him. "That's how I know something's changed. Juan Pablo has been here for months, setting up whatever plan he had, which says he's methodical. But last night someone interfered, and I'm guessing he wasn't expecting that." She turned the key, shutting off the engine, and grabbed her phone. "Manuel's arrival in Walton to do what I assume was Juan Pablo's job means his time ran out."

Claudia got out of the car and shut the door silently behind her. Colton did the same and met her at the back of the vehicle. She had opened the trunk and was unzipping a long nylon case.

"That makes him desperate, then." Colton kept his voice low. "Juan Pablo."

She removed a Colt M4 carbine out of the case, opened the chamber to check for a round, and then grabbed the magazine. "Which is why I'm not waiting."

There was a glint of fear in Claudia's eyes that unnerved him. Her demeanor read cold and determined, mission focused, but the emotion in her glazed expression told him how personal this was to her.

Colton's thoughts went back to Charlie. He'd asked them not to engage, but if David, or whoever he was, was desperate, could they afford to wait? "We need to call this in."

Claudia put her hand on his. "We can't take that chance. If Pecca's alive inside there"—her eyes moved to the large warehouse looming in front of them—"and he hears sirens or gets any indication we're here . . . he'll react."

"If Pecca's alive." Bile climbed up his throat. Colton didn't want to consider the possibility that she wasn't, but the only thing they were going on right now was that her watch led them there. That didn't mean she was alive.

"How—" He swallowed. "How do we know she's—"

"Heat signatures." Claudia pulled out her phone and checked a message. "Thermal imaging captured the heat signatures of two people. That means she's still alive. For now."

Colton assumed she had that information courtesy of her friends at the agency, and he was grateful. He watched Claudia lift a Sig Sauer from the case, check that it was loaded, and slip it into the back of her waistband. What else did she have in there? He peeked into the trunk and spotted a football. "Think you'll need that too?"

"That's for Maceo."

Colton's arm twitched. It was clear by the way Claudia handled her weapons that she wasn't an amateur, but they were walking in blind. What if David had set up traps? His eyes searched the ground. "You can't go in without backup."

SILENT SHADOWS

"Are you going to stop me?"

They were the same words he had spoken to Charlie. The tilt of Claudia's lips and the flash of defiance in her eyes was uncanny. This was Pecca's sister in the flesh.

"No, but"—he reached around her with his left hand and lifted the weapon from her waistband—"you're not going in alone."

"Didn't think I was," she said with a smirk before turning on her heel. "You've got my six."

Colton, his nerves itching, fell in step behind her. Claudia's choice to pull out an assault-style weapon told him who they were up against, but it didn't ease the trepidation that this could turn bad really quick.

THIRTY-TWO

"WHY DO YOU WANT MY SISTER?" Pecca trembled. Her lip had swollen, the skin around it tight with the dried blood. "She has nothing to do with the SSB—"

"It's not the SSB!" David raised the cell phone in the air. The vein in his forehead looked ready to burst. "You're always talking about how close you are to your sister, yet you pretend that you don't know what I'm talking about. Do you take me for a fool? The SSB had nothing to do with any of this. It was all me."

"I don't understand, David."

"My name is not David, it is Juan Pablo, and the reason I'm here is the very same reason you are here—because of your sister. I did not come to hurt you, but if I have to in order to get her attention, then I will do what I must."

Pecca could barely hold her head up over the nausea roiling in her stomach. She was going to be sick. Fear and confusion warred within her mind, making her dizzy. David dialed Claudia's number and held up the phone, and Pecca prayed her sister would answer for once. When it rolled to voicemail, a small breath of relief filled her. She didn't know what David was talking about, but the last thing she wanted to do was get Claudia involved.

"Please, David," Pecca cried, still wiggling her wrists. They felt wet, which she assumed, by the pain, was her blood, but the ropes were loosening with her efforts. "You don't have to do this. We can get you help—"

"If you want to help, then stop lying for your sister." Darkness hooded David's eyes and a shudder curled down Pecca's spine. "Maybe I should have gone after Maceo." He released a sigh, his

291

forehead creasing in a determined expression. "If I lose my son, you should lose yours. That would be an even trade, yes?"

"No!" Pecca screamed, her voice hoarse. "Leave him alone. I'll do whatever you want. Try her number again. Call her job. She may be there." She stumbled over the words, willing to say anything to take David's mind off of Maceo. "She works at Loews, Ridley, and Scott. In Boston."

David breathed through his nose, his face growing red. He stalked over to Pecca and yanked her head back. She yelped, feeling him shove the gun beneath her chin. "*Tu hermana es una mentirosa.* A liar."

"Wh—" Her scalp burning, Pecca blinked back tears. "What do you mean?"

"Your sister works for the C-I-A." Hot breath hit her cheek as he emphasized each letter. "She killed Hector Perez, and now she must pay."

Pecca flinched. Claudia . . . CIA . . . Who was Hector Perez and why would David think her sister killed him? She squeezed her eyes shut to keep the room from spinning. The sound of a phone chiming jerked her eyes open. Claudia?

David's hands fumbled over the phone, but it wasn't Pecca's. It was his. "Hola, Alicia?"

She watched his face morph from hopeful expectation into fury. His eyes flashed to Pecca, and she jerked backward as though he had slapped her. An alarm bellowed inside her head—she needed to get out. *Now.*

At the other end of the warehouse were two sliding doors. She looked over her shoulder and saw another door, but an old desk was in front of it. Heaviness settled over her. Even if she could get out of these ropes, she'd have to get past the psychotic man she once knew as David. It was impossible.

". . . *donde esta mi familia . . . hablar con Señor . . . la tengo a ella . . .*"

David spoke Spanish so rapidly, she had no doubts it was his native tongue. Someone named Señor had his family—and David had her. Pecca's skin crawled. She had to assume he was talking about her, but was it true what he said about Claudia?

A jolt to her chair shook her attention back to David, who was standing in front of her, a mixture of pain and rage etched into his features. Thrusting Pecca's cell phone in her face, he spoke through his clenched jaw.

"If you want to keep Maceo safe—if you want him to live—you have no other choice. They will not stop. *He* will not stop until she's dead—until her head is presented to him on a platter."

Tears streaked from the corners of her eyes. "Th-there has to be another way."

"There's not!" A string of expletives in Spanish trailed from David's mouth, and Pecca squirmed against her restraints. "Señor will not be stopped. He'll use whatever it takes to avenge his family's honor. It's your son or your sister."

Colton's gaze shot to Claudia. The woman was seething—body tense, finger trembling next to the trigger, looking like she was ready to explode. Colton understood why after she whispered a quick translation of David's phone conversation. Salvador Señor Perez had David's family and was threatening to kill them if Claudia didn't show up.

"*I'm* going to kill *him*." Her whisper was rough. "Slowly and painfully."

From the crazy look in her eye, Colton believed Claudia could make that happen. And, apparently, she had killed some guy named Hector—the catalyst to this nightmare. They had found a decent-sized hole in the corrugated metal siding near the rear of the building that gave them a good view of both David and Pecca, but it wasn't big enough to breach the building without drawing attention.

"We need to come up with a plan," Colton said. He tucked the

Sig Sauer into his waistband and wiped the sweat from his hand. His right arm was still twitching, but not as bad as he expected. That was a good thing since he couldn't afford another episode. "We need to contact Charlie. Get him out here."

"We don't have time." Claudia set her jaw. "There's two of us—one of him."

Colton ran a hand over his hair, which was damp with sweat despite the chilly November wind swaying the weeds around them. How did he get here? He left the battlefield overseas to find himself battling a diagnosis he once believed stole everything from him, and now the battle in front of him felt like the most important one of his life.

He wanted to be ready.

And he wanted it to be over.

If what Claudia translated was true, they were already on borrowed time. Colton let the fact roll through his brain. Somehow Claudia's involvement with Hector Perez ended up with him dying, either at her hands or someone else's. Not important. What was important was that it led to Hector's brother, Señor, taking the reins and coming after Claudia in revenge. How he found her was a whole other matter, but for now it was safe to assume that whatever his methods, they had brought him into Pecca's and Maceo's lives through David.

"What are we waiting for?" Claudia hissed. "Let's go in and take him out."

"Do you know where Señor is?"

"What?"

"Salvador Perez. The guy who wants your head on a platter. Do you know where he is? Right now?"

Claudia studied him for a second before shaking her head. He was afraid of that. It meant David was probably right—there was only one way to end this, and Colton had an idea about how to do it. But first he'd need to convince a CIA officer to agree to his plan.

"You still have eyes in the sky?"

She narrowed her eyes. "What do you mean?"

"Your buddy with the thermal imaging. Had to happen by drone, right?"

Her jaw flinched and she nodded.

"Contact them and find out if they can trace a call remotely and how long it'll take."

"Why?"

"You just admitted you don't know where Señor is, which means if you take out David, it'll be only a matter of time before Señor sends someone else to get you—only he won't go for you first. He'll go for Pecca and Maceo. Your parents. Siblings. He already knows who they are and where they are. There's only one way to end this—and it's through Salvador."

Claudia hesitated for a second before grabbing her phone and typing the message. Colton pulled out his own phone. He had silenced it, which was good since Charlie had lit it up with calls and messages.

"Five to seven minutes to get a location once the call comes through."

With Claudia's reckless driving, it had taken them less than seven minutes to get there. With sirens, Charlie could maybe do it in less.

"What about David's family?"

"They're not my problem."

"They are your problem." Colton challenged her. "His wife and son are in this mess not by their choice. They're innocents." He eyed her and could see the resolve in her eyes soften. "And you're not heartless. No matter what David's done or does, his family shouldn't have to suffer because of it."

"You know, it's his wife's family that's behind all of this. Señor is *her* uncle. You really think he's going to hurt his niece and her child?"

"I don't know, but do you want to live with that on your conscience?"

Colton could see the battle warring in Claudia's mind. He understood her dilemma. She must choose between exacting justice or mercy. It was the same decision his commander had faced in Zabul. And all Colton could do right now was trust.

"Fine," she said, letting out a frustrated breath. "Give me a minute."

Claudia yanked out her phone again and typed a message. She snorted and muttered something under her breath, which Colton assumed meant someone else probably agreed with her initial response.

"It's done. A team is going to do their best to track down David's family."

"Good. Now we need to come up with a distraction."

"Me." Claudia began pulling the rifle sling over her head. "He's waiting for me anyway."

That was not what Colton was thinking, but it was a good idea—albeit one with great risks. It put two lives on the line. "What if David shoots you on the spot?"

"He won't," Claudia whispered, setting down her rifle. "He'll need to make sure his family is safe. Assurance. Which will buy my team the time they need to locate his family and Charlie enough time to get here." Her brown eyes shifted to the phone in Colton's hand. "Once the call comes in, you'll have five minutes."

"You said it's going to take five to seven minutes for your guys to get a location."

Claudia shrugged. "Señor isn't going to allow himself to be tracked and will be watching the clock. My guy is good and knows what's at stake." She licked her lips. "Five minutes and then you guys move in."

Colton quickly typed out a message to Charlie and sent it. A second later his phone vibrated with a response. They were on their way. He gave a tight nod to Claudia.

There was another vibration, this time from Claudia's phone. She looked down at it and smiled. "It's from Pecca's phone. Looks like it's time I make my appearance." She leveled her brown eyes on him. "My sister doesn't make mistakes, Colton."

Colton swallowed, the meaning clear.

"You want the rifle?"

"This'll do." He slipped the gun from his waistband. It still didn't feel right in his left hand, but hopefully he wouldn't have to use it. Hopefully, Charlie and the others would get there in time.

"If things don't go as planned, you take the shot no matter what. Pecca's life depends on it."

Suddenly, Colton wasn't so sure of his plan, but before he could change his mind Claudia was already making her way toward the front of the warehouse. She paused, closed her eyes, and did the sign of the cross over her chest. A burning reminder that Chaplain Kelly was right—there was only One who could turn what was going to happen next into something good.

THIRTY-THREE

PECCA JERKED AT THE SCREECHING METAL, the sound causing her pulse to soar. She spun her attention to the large warehouse door sliding open. Sunlight shone against the figure, shadowing their face as they approached, but it didn't take long for Pecca to recognize the familiar gait. It sent a parade of chills marching over her skin.

No!

Pecca blinked, unsure if her brain was playing tricks on her, but then Claudia smiled and she knew it was real. Claudia was there. David aimed his gun at her and she raised her hands, unfazed.

"Hola, Pequeña." Claudia winked. "Are you okay?"

"I'm—" *Speechless.* Pecca couldn't believe her eyes. Her sister was right in front of her. "I don't understand."

"Maybe we can talk about it over one of those famous cinnamon rolls you're always raving about."

"Shut up." David pressed the gun to Claudia's temple. "You armed?"

"No." She rotated in a slow circle, her eyes landing on Pecca. "*Todo irá bien.*"

It was going to be okay? Pecca couldn't believe what she was seeing. Her sister was getting an intimate pat-down, and judging by the tick in her jaw, she wasn't pleased with David's thorough search. But he wouldn't be searching unless . . .

Was it true? Pecca looked at her sister. Dressed in a T-shirt, jeans, and hideous-looking motorcycle boots, nothing about her screamed secret agent.

When David was done, Claudia shrugged. "You have me, so you can let my sister go now."

"You probably thought I was a monster." David looked at Pecca.

"That *I* was the one lying, but now you can hear it from your sister." Using the gun, he pointed between her and Claudia. "Go on, tell your sister the truth. It can be your final confession."

"David, please," Pecca begged. "You're not a monster. Don't do this."

"Ask your sister whose fault this is."

Pecca looked to Claudia, and without speaking a word, she could see the truth in her sister's face. "What did you do?"

"It doesn't matter." She turned to David. "Call your boss so we can get this over with."

David grabbed Claudia's hair and yanked her backward so that her back arched. "Tell your sister who you are and why all of this is your fault."

"Stop, David. You don't have to hurt her."

He turned his cold gaze on her. "Don't you want to know the truth? How we got to this point?"

"I want to go home, David. Back to Maceo. Please, let us go."

"And I want my family back!" Using his foot, he swept Claudia's feet out from under her, causing her to fall hard to her knees against the concrete. Claudia winced but didn't make a sound. "Do you know how long I have worked to secure the safety of my family? I gave Hector everything—"

"Which is why Señor owns you now," Claudia said. "You double-crossed your own family in Colombia. Betrayed them to their enemy. Did you really think the Zaragosas were going to forget about you? That Hector was going to protect you forever? He was only waiting for the right opportunity to use you, but it looks like Señor will get that honor."

David struck Claudia across the face, pitching her sideways. "You don't know what you're talking about. Hector would never do that. I was loyal."

"Loyalty can be bought." Claudia straightened, blood dripping from her lip. "One call from Señor to Zaragosa and you're dead. Your family too."

He raised his hand to strike her again, but Pecca screamed.

"Stop!" Pecca couldn't make sense of what was going on and who betrayed who, but she wasn't going to sit by and watch her sister die. "Are you with the CIA, Claudia? The truth."

Claudia spit out blood before her eyes met Pecca's. The truth was in them, and Pecca didn't realize how much it was going to hurt. How long had her sister been lying to her? The last several years played through her memory in quick bursts. Claudia's random work hours, always traveling, too busy to visit. Every excuse she gave Pecca and their family—was it all an elaborate lie?

"Then fix it." Pecca narrowed her eyes on her sister. "If you caused this mess, then you fix it. Help David get his family back and end this so I can get back to my son."

Claudia's shoulders lifted with a breath. She looked at David. "You're wasting precious time, Juan. The lives of your child and wife are in the balance. I'm here. Make the call to Salvador before it's too late." She pinned him with a scathing glare. "Unless you don't care about your family."

The *thwack* against the back of Claudia's head sent her tumbling forward. She landed at Pecca's feet and groaned.

"David, stop!"

He walked over and pressed the gun into Claudia's spine. Pecca squeezed her eyes closed, unwilling to watch. *Please, God, don't let him shoot.*

"You do not give orders, *entiendes*?"

Pecca opened one eye and saw David walking away, cell phone to his ear. She scanned Claudia. "Are you okay?"

Claudia rolled to her side, her hand going to the back of her head. When she brought it in front of her, Pecca cringed at the sight of the blood.

"Ouch."

Ouch? Claudia's dry wit was one of Pecca's favorite parts about her sister, but now was not the time. She was bleeding, Pecca was tied up, and David was teetering on the edge of full-blown mania.

"Can you untie me?" Pecca shimmied.

"Not yet."

"Wha—" But before she could finish her sentence, David, phone in hand, was already marching toward them.

"Señor, I have someone you've been waiting to speak with."

"*Lo encontraré.*" Claudia spit the threat out of her mouth. "I will find him, and I will kill him."

Pecca gasped. She'd never heard her sister speak like that. The glare etched into Claudia's brow was so threatening, it scared her. It was like she didn't even know who her sister was.

David tapped a button and raspy laughter echoed from the phone's speaker. "Isabel, it is good to hear your voice," Señor said.

Pecca frowned. Who was Isabel?

"I could've gone without hearing yours." Claudia snickered. "Give me time, and I'll silence yours just like I did Hector's."

What was Claudia doing? She'd always had a smart mouth, but she was only fueling the fire.

"Not this time, Isabel. This time, you are mine."

"Why don't you ask about your family, Juan?" Claudia whispered. "Ask to speak to them."

David yanked Claudia back to her feet by her hair, then brought the phone to his mouth. "I have her, Señor. My debt to you is paid, now where is my family?"

"When you bring Isabel to me, you will have your family."

"That's not the deal." David clenched his teeth. "I want to speak to them now!"

"Hold that thought." Claudia reared her head back and swung it forward, smashing David's nose with the front of her forehead. The sound of his nose breaking reverberated in the room, making Pecca sick.

Screaming, David dropped the phone and lunged for her, but Claudia was quick. She ducked, swinging her leg around and catching both of his legs. In a single move, she swiveled and brought him crashing down to the ground next to her.

Pecca wriggled beneath the ropes. She had no time to wonder how her sister knew to do that, only that she had to help. If she could just break free—

A guttural scream cut through the air, and she froze.

Turning slowly, Pecca saw David back away from Claudia, her face ashen. She looked down at her side, touched it with her hand, and when she brought it up, Pecca saw the crimson stain.

"No, Claudia!"

David, breathing hard, backed farther away as blood poured out of his nose. He scooped up the gun and pointed it at Claudia. "*Estás muerto.*"

Claudia took in a sharp breath, her brow furrowing. With a pained exhale of air, Claudia extracted herself from the rusty, metal fencing David had pinned her against. Clutching her side, she dropped.

"We . . . are looking . . . for your family, Juan." Claudia spoke carefully, as though it strained her to talk, and Pecca ached to go to her. "Señor will not honor his word to you, but I can—"

"Shut up!" David slapped Claudia across the face and then raised the gun to her forehead. "You are a liar, and you have cost me everything."

"David!" Pecca struggled against the ropes, the chair rocking. She had to stop him. A cry escaped her lips. She could not watch her sister die. "Stop! Please don't!"

There were several sounds that became unforgettable to a soldier. The sound of a SCUD missile sailing through the air. The sound of a soldier crying over his fallen brother in arms. And the sound of a gun slide being pulled back to send a bullet into the chamber.

It was like a whistle being blown on the field—game time.

Colton felt the steel of the gun pressing against his back. It was easy for Claudia to tell him to take the shot, but doing so would put her and Pecca in danger if the bullet went astray. He couldn't take that chance.

Hurtling out of the shadows, Colton dug his feet into the concrete, trying to gain as much momentum as possible. From his position, David didn't see him coming until it was too late. A growl escaped David's mouth as his body crunched beneath Colton's tackle.

Pain sliced through Colton's body, but he ignored it. He crushed David beneath him, his fists landing blows along the side of the man's face when they weren't slipping in the blood still pouring from his nose.

David landed a quick strike to Colton's ribs before connecting another on the side of his jaw that sent stars flashing in the back of his eyes.

"Colton, the gun!" Pecca said.

In the scuffle, the gun from Colton's waistband had fallen out. Both he and David looked to the gun lying a few feet away. David twisted, freeing his hand from Colton's grip long enough to get a solid punch to his kidneys. The breath rushed out of Colton's chest.

Taking advantage of his positioning, David smashed his fist into the side of Colton's head. Colton rolled, trying to protect his head, and David crawled toward the gun. Colton searched for the one David had been holding against Claudia, but he couldn't see it.

"Colton!"

The terrified emotion in Pecca's voice made his blood run cold. Colton turned in time to see David wrap his fingers around the gun and push himself up to standing. With a hand on his side, David turned to Colton with rage in his eyes.

"Who do you think I should shoot first?" David pivoted, aiming the gun at Claudia, who was lying on the ground looking pale. "This whole mess is her fault, so a slow death seems appropriate." He turned the gun on Pecca, and Colton clenched his teeth. "I really didn't want to have to hurt you, Pecca. Truly."

Colton searched for something he could use as a weapon. His eyes landed on the cell phone. His right arm jerked, and Colton knew the only chance he had was to use his left hand. Tucking the phone into his palm, he rolled to a seated position. The move grabbed David's attention.

"I'm sorry it's not going to work out between you two."

David twisted to look at Pecca, and it was all the distraction Colton needed. Gripping the phone, he pulled his left arm back and prayed all of those practice throws with Maceo were going to pay off. He released the phone just as David turned back.

It was a beautiful spiral—for a cell phone—flying straight into David's chest hard enough that it caused his shoulders to buckle forward slightly. The gun he had aimed at Pecca lowered—

CRACK!

A piercing ringing filled Colton's ears as he watched David drop to the ground. The harsh smell of cordite filled his nose, and he turned to see Claudia holding a gun in her hand. The doors of the warehouse screeched open and a team entered, shouting, "Savannah Metro Police, hands up! Hands up, now!"

Chest heaving, Colton raised his hands, keeping his eyes on Pecca. Two police officers ran to her and began untying the ropes. She was shaking and her face was drained of color, except for the dried blood on her chin and lip.

She turned to him.

"Are you hurt?" His voice was raspy from the strain of the last few minutes.

She shook her head. Her gaze fell to David, who was lying motionless on the ground. "Is he dead?"

"Have I ever missed a shot before?" Claudia wheezed, leaning into a pair of police officers who were holding her up. "I could've gone to the Olympics."

"Ma'am, we're going to get you some help," one of the officers said before two paramedics rushed in with a gurney.

"Is she going to be okay?" Pecca called out.

Claudia waved a hand as if she were brushing the question away, but Colton could see from the spread of blood that she needed immediate treatment.

Charlie, shaking his head, jogged in. "The only reason I'm not going to be angry about this is because you saved me from having to explain to my pregnant wife why I was involved in another gunfight." He helped Colton up. "She blames me for Walton's recent uptick in crime."

The second Colton had finished giving his statement to the police, he rushed to Pecca. A medic was already assessing her wounds. "Is she okay?"

"I'm okay," Pecca answered. "Rope burn, mostly."

The medic stepped aside after telling her they would bandage her wrists in the ambulance. Colton reached for her hands. The skin on her wrists was red and bloody, evidence of her struggle to break free. Emotion burned his eyes.

"I should've . . ." He cleared his throat and traced the outside edges of her wounds with his fingers. He looked up. "I'm sorry."

Tears edged her soft, black eyelashes. "For what? That was the greatest tackle in football history."

Colton exhaled the breath he'd been holding and brushed a stray tear from her cheek. He wanted to tell her all the things filling his heart, but at the moment, he was afraid all he would be able to do was cry tears of gratitude that God had taken care of her—of them.

"Well, that was quick."

Colton turned to find Charlie next to him. His eyes were directed on the suits filing into the warehouse. Two of them went to Claudia. The others headed for the police officers, who, up until this point, had probably assumed they would be in charge of the scene.

"Better take some mental pictures of this moment," Colton said. "Because I have a feeling what just happened . . . didn't."

Forty-five minutes later, the isolated warehouse was still teeming with federal agents, state police, and several deputies from Walton, including Sheriff Huggins, who were all trying to get the story straight. In the end, Colton knew from his experience in intelligence that government secrecy would prevail. This day would survive only in a redacted file tucked away in some storage room in Langley—and in the memories of those who witnessed it.

"You're all good, Captain Crawford," the EMT announced. She tilted her head to the ambulance where Pecca was seated, watching Claudia being tended to by another team of paramedics. "You can check on your friend now."

Colton hopped out of the ambulance and then swayed. His body felt like it had been run over by a truck. He took his time walking toward the other ambulance. He stopped a few feet away, unwilling to impose on the privacy of the moment shared between sisters.

There was a large welt, purpling with each passing minute, on Claudia's forehead from when she'd used it to break David's nose. She was receiving IV fluids and when she shifted, her attention pinning him, he caught sight of her bandaged side, the blood already soaking through.

"I told you to take the shot." Claudia's directive was jolting.

Pecca's gaze swung to meet his, a relieved smile cresting high into her cheeks. *Man, he missed that smile.*

"At least you can tackle."

Colton took another step forward and addressed Claudia, ignoring her jab. "Are you going to be okay?"

"Apparently." Claudia flashed a smile at Pecca. "At least I'll have a personal nurse to help take care of me."

"Were your people able to get a location on Salvador?"

"Yes."

"Did they get him?"

"If I tell you that, I'll have to kill you."

Colton smiled. "Ha, another one of your agency jokes, huh?"

"Want to find out?"

"What about David's family?"

"They'll be okay."

He wasn't sure if he was going to get much more of an answer out of her, and he'd have to be content with that. His eyes flashed to Pecca. At least she was okay. Or would be. The day's events had sucked the color out of her face and left shadows beneath her eyes.

"Ahem." Claudia, her eyebrow arched, pressed her lips together. "I think I remember you had something to say to my sister."

Pecca looked to him, anxiousness wavering in her eyes. Colton licked his lips, wishing he was going to be able to have this conversation in private. His arm twitched, and Pecca put her hand on it.

"I told you last night that I thought you'd made a mistake." Colton ignored the derisive snort coming from Claudia. "That I don't have anything to offer you." Her hand tightened over his arm. "I'm the one who made the mistake. This whole time I've been looking at my movement disorder as a life sentence. I've been angry at God. My family has been telling me God has a plan, and like a child, I've been unwilling to accept that maybe his plans for my life are better than my own. After all, his plans brought me here—to you and Maceo."

Pecca rolled her lower lip between her teeth, and he could see the energy lighting her eyes. It took everything in him not to blurt it out, but he had a plan—one he hoped to get some help with.

"I guess what I'm trying to say is that I'm sorry, and I hope you will give me the second chance I don't deserve."

THIRTY-FOUR

THE FINAL WHISTLE BLEW, and the kids roared with victory. The Warriors had played their last game. Pecca eyed the wide lawn in front of Home for Heroes. Family, friends, neighbors, Chaplain Kelly, Shirley and her husband, even the kitchen team had shown up to cheer on the Warriors.

The veterans from D-Wing had come out in full force, cheering more than officiating as they waved homemade banners and pennants. There was even a band. Okay, so it was a few of the team members' older siblings who also happened to play in school band, but they played all the football game favorites, with only a few errant notes.

"That was the most exciting game ever." Lane wiped her eyes.

"There's no crying in football."

"That's baseball," Claudia mumbled, and Pecca noticed the glassy haze covering her sister's eyes.

"Are you crying too?"

Claudia scowled. "I just watched my nephew play football. Give me a moment."

Pecca laughed, grateful Claudia had decided to ask for some time off. It was still hard to believe her sister was a CIA officer. After spending several nights in the hospital, Claudia revealed what she could about her career, and Pecca couldn't be prouder. Though she still wasn't entirely at ease about keeping Claudia's career a secret from the rest of the family, she understood that it was a matter of safety and security.

"Thank you for being here today." Pecca wrapped her arm around Claudia's waist, careful of her still-healing injury. She rested her head on Claudia's shoulder. "You always know when I need you most."

Claudia looked away, her lips tight, expression unreadable. She cleared her throat a couple times before turning her attention to the field.

Colton walked across the field in a hoodie and a pair of sweats, the legs pulled up at his calves. His Mustangs baseball cap was flipped backward, and he gave Pecca a boyish grin that charmed her into giddiness but also weighed heavy with the reality he would be heading back to Texas in just a few days.

In the week since the warehouse incident, they'd been trying to come up with a plan. Pecca had already coordinated Thanksgiving dinner with her family back in El Paso, and Claudia's medical leave gave her no excuses not to be there this year. After that, Pecca and Maceo would fly to Dallas and meet Colton for Christmas in his hometown of Jasper.

A nervous tingle danced through her. He would be meeting her family and she would be meeting his, but beyond the holidays they weren't really sure how they were going to do the long-distance thing yet.

"I can have him eliminated, you know."

Pecca snorted. She turned to Claudia, who was folding up the chair Lane had been sitting in.

"I warned him if he broke your heart, I'd make him disappear."

"Serena."

Pecca, caught off guard hearing Colton use her given name, spun around. His hand fell to hers, interlacing their fingers. Her heart raced. *What's happening?*

"Serena, I'm going to be leaving for Texas in a couple of days, and as much as I'd like to stay"—his eyes locked on hers—"I believe the plan for my life is back there."

Don't cry, Pecca, don't cry. As much as she'd been trying to console herself with their plans to see each other, the fact that he wouldn't be here every day made her heart sink.

"You know I've been making plans with Uncle Jack to buy the ranch and hopefully one day turn it into a retreat or camp for ornery old vets, like D-Wing, or young veterans with families who need a place to recuperate. It's a plan I never imagined for the ranch or myself, but I feel like God has led me to it."

Pecca's insides were shaking. "I'm so proud of how far you've come, and I can't wait to see what God has planned for you."

Colton smiled and tugged her a little closer. She breathed in the tangy soap scent and tried to memorize it.

"But—"

The sound of people *awing* around them pulled Pecca back. She peered over Colton's shoulder and saw Charlie carrying something brown and white and small. Was that an animal?

"The only way I see my plan working," Colton continued, bringing Pecca back to him, "is if you and Maceo are there with me."

"What?"

Colton stepped back, and Pecca's eyes rounded. It was a goat. Charlie handed Colton a small brown-and-white baby goat, then he stepped back to where Lane stood on the edge of the growing crowd.

Dropping to one knee, Colton set the goat beside him, and Pecca noticed the blue ribbon tied around its neck and the—

Her eyes shot to Colton, and he smiled wider than she'd ever seen him smile.

"Serena Gallegos, God may have led me back to Texas, but he led me to you first. I've spent the last thirty years not realizing my life was missing something." He winked at Maceo. "Two somethings. I know this seems fast, but I can't imagine living another day without both of you in it. Will you do me the honor of becoming my wife?"

"Yes!"

Colton jumped up and pulled Pecca into his arms. Dipping his chin, he whispered, "I would've asked you sooner, but I wanted to get your father's permission." His eyes darted over Pecca's shoulder to Claudia. "And hers."

Pecca smiled, and before she could take another breath, his lips were on hers. His arm wrapped around her waist, tucking her body into his as he deepened the kiss. Pecca closed her eyes, allowing herself to melt into the kiss further, her fingers clutching the front of his shirt. It felt like she couldn't get enough of him. She felt his right hand trail down her back, the tremor in his fingers sending a shudder of bliss coursing through her. It sounded like people were cheering—her eyes snapped open.

Pulling back, Pecca bit her lower lip, glancing around them. Not only was the team whooping and hollering, the parents had even joined in with cheers of their own. Her eyes met Colton's, and he smiled, looking only slightly embarrassed.

"Atta boy, Cap!" Gunny hollered.

Sarge waved his pennant. "Hooah!"

"There's definitely crying in football." Claudia wiped her eyes, her smile wavering with emotion. "Congratulations."

"Well, what are you waiting for?" Lane said, and she leaned against Charlie with tears streaming down her smiling face. "Put the ring on."

Colton untied the ribbon on the baby goat as it nibbled on the grass and, slipping back to his knee, he took her left hand and placed the diamond ring on her finger. Unable to believe what was happening, she pulled Colton up and planted another kiss on his lips.

A painful rendition of the "kissing in a tree" song started, and Pecca would've ignored it, but Maceo was behind her making gagging noises.

She giggled. "I guess I know how Maceo feels about that."

Colton shrugged. "I suppose we could work on it later," he whispered.

"For the rest of our lives."

EPILOGUE

"MAKE IT STOP! MAKE IT STOP! MAKE IT—"

The last of Kekoa's pleas were drowned out by the laughter of those witnessing the large Hawaiian jostling around in the saddle, his muscles bulging as he clung desperately to the saddle horn in an attempt not to be tossed from the mare's back.

"I reckon it's time you get ready." Colton's uncle Jack tipped the edge of his cowboy hat up. "Don't want to be late."

Colton wiped the tears of laughter from his eyes. He'd give anything for another five minutes watching Kekoa on a horse, but his uncle was right. He gave a short whistle and the horse pulled to a stop, pitching Kekoa forward with a curse.

Two ranch hands, laughter still spilling from their lips, hopped off the fence and stepped into the arena to rescue Kekoa and the horse.

"That was cruel, brah," Kekoa said, walking with a slightly wider gait. "I thought we were friends."

"I think I remember you putting me on a surfboard and laughing yourself silly watching me get rolled by a wave."

A mischievous smile filled Kekoa's face. "That was funny."

"Not as funny as you on a horse."

They ducked beneath the railing and walked out of the arena and across the freshly cut grass. Colton gazed at the rugged Texas landscape that stretched in every direction. The sun was nearing its descent, taking with it the heat and leaving the familiar lavender sky Colton had grown to appreciate the last six months.

"The place looks great." Kekoa scanned the ranch house in front of them. They'd already added a new addition to the west

313

side, giving the home four family suites, complete with bunk beds. "I'd pay to come here as long as I didn't have to ride the horses."

Colton laughed. "The whole idea is that no one will have to pay. I had no idea this was even a possibility." He swallowed the emotion that seemed to come unexpectedly whenever he thought about where he was a few months ago and how he'd cursed his existence. *Now, look*, the voice in Colton said. *Look at what I can do if only you trust me, your Lord.*

When Colton left Georgia, he had only one expectation: regain full control of his arm. He watched the ever-present tremor in his fingers. His movement had gotten better, but it was always there and on especially bad days—worse. But instead of seeing it as a hindrance to his life, he could finally look at his arm and see blessing.

"You nervous?"

"No," Colton said, even though a tiny niggling was in his chest. He surveyed the newly formed Warrior Ranch and smiled. "I've been waiting for this moment my whole life. I just never knew I wanted it."

<hr />

"Well, if that ain't the prettiest sight you ever saw."

Pecca spun around, the hem of her lace gown draping at her feet. "Sarge, you came!"

"Of course I did, darling." The old man's eyes twinkled as he rolled into the bedroom. Pecca hugged him. "Had to be sure Cap was ready."

"I'm going to go get Mom and Dad," Claudia said and then slipped out of the room.

"You better wipe that pretty grin off your face, otherwise Cap will think he has nothing to work for."

"Isn't that the best part of grace? It doesn't have to be earned."

Sarge's lips tipped into a loose smile, his pale blue eyes growing distant. "Grace. That was my sweetheart's name." His smile turned melancholy. "She had enough moxie to put up with me, but it was grace"—he looked at Pecca—"like you said, that she showed me every single day. I didn't deserve her, but I made sure I lived every day grateful to the Lord that he saw fit to think I did."

Pecca batted her eyelashes in an attempt to keep the tears from ruining her makeup. Sarge had a gruff exterior, but by the time he'd left Home for Heroes, Pecca had seen he was tender, kind, and deep down a hopeless romantic. She leaned in, picking up the scent of his Old Spice, and whispered, "Your Grace must've been a very special gal to snag a gentleman like you."

"Honey, it's time." Pecca's mother stood at the door. "Are you ready?"

She nodded. "Very much."

"I'll see you out there, darling." Sarge turned his wheelchair around and rolled out the door to where the rest of the guests were waiting.

Pecca grabbed her bouquet, her heart swelling when she saw Maceo in his navy suit. He looked so handsome and grown-up. It was so hard to imagine a moment like this happening for the both of them, and yet God was good. So good.

"Don't cry, you'll ruin your makeup," Claudia whispered. "Think about monkeys or something. No, wait. Those creep me out. Think about unicorns."

Pecca smiled. *All I want to think about is the man waiting for me at the end of the aisle.* The music started, and Pecca's heart began fluttering.

"You look beautiful, Mom," Maceo said as he took her arm. "Stunning."

There was no stopping the tears now. Pressing her lips together, Pecca smiled at her son. With her dad on the other side of her, Pecca lifted up a prayer of gratitude to God for giving her both of the men in her life. As they escorted her out of the house, she thanked him for Colton.

Colton stood beneath the cedar pergola at the edge of his property overlooking the Brazos River. It was one of his favorite spots, a place his grandfather, dad, and uncle Jack brought him as a boy when they wanted to get away from the busyness of life.

Colton loved it because it felt sacred, spending unbridled time with the men in his life. He hoped it would offer the same to those who came to stay at Warrior Ranch, and one day he desired to share with his own son the sage advice that had been passed to him.

The sweet scent of jasmine tickled his nose, and he gazed toward the house just as she stepped through the French doors. Colton's breath whooshed out of him, and he willed time to stop so he could take in this moment for as long as possible. Pecca's dark hair was swept up into a low knot, revealing the feminine lace detail of her gown. It hugged her curves in all the right places and made Colton want to sprint across the lawn, sweep her into his arms, vow his life to her, and kick everyone off his property so he could properly lavish Pecca with the love and passion that had been growing for her since the day he left Walton.

Her gaze met his, and it was like she could read his mind as a blush spread across her cheeks. Pecca walked toward him, her father on one side and Maceo on the other. Next to Colton, Kekoa let out a low whistle of appreciation, and all Colton could do was grin like a fool who realized he'd won the lottery.

<hr>

Walking down the aisle, she passed the faces of friends who'd become family to her over the last few years—Sheriff Huggins, Ms. Byrdie, Charlie, Lane, Noah, and their new baby girl. Even Ryan and Vivian had flown in from DC and soon would be planning a wedding of their own. Pecca was trying to rein in her emotions, but when she saw Gunny, Sticks, and Sarge sitting among the guests, she couldn't help but let the tears spill down her cheeks.

Ahead of her Colton waited beside his groomsmen, Vincent James and Kekoa Young. She smiled at their beaming faces and was excited to get to know them more, but for now her gaze remained on Colton. Her heart stirred within her chest as she closed the space between them. Their eyes met, speaking messages of excitement, anticipation, and love.

Chaplain Kelly cleared his throat, and Pecca blinked. It was time for the vows.

She cleared her throat. "Some say you know love when it knocks you to the ground like a linebacker." Colton smirked, and the guests who knew of her and Colton's first meeting laughed. "But for me, I knew love when I saw it through your courage to keep fighting, through your dedication to honor your word, through your willingness to sacrifice in order to become the man God wanted you to be."

Emotion getting the better of him, Colton rubbed a hand over his mouth and Pecca squeezed his arm. He smiled and said, "You are the woman I never even dreamed of one day marrying, because how could I get so lucky? Thankfully, God is good." He smiled and Pecca blushed. "I could spend hours telling you how much you mean to me, but our guests might get bored, and truthfully, having the privilege to remind you how much I love you every day of our lives from this day forward is one of the things I'm most excited about. I still don't know how I got here, but I know I wouldn't change a single thing—except maybe you tackling me in front of decorated war veterans who still won't let me live it down."

"Atta boy, Cap!"

The guests burst into laughter, and Colton and Pecca joined in. Chaplain Kelly blessed the rings and then announced they could seal their covenant with a kiss. Colton pulled her toward him, taking her face into his hands, and gazed down at her with hungry eyes. Their lips met, and with closed eyes, she allowed Colton's kiss to sweep her off her feet.

It took nearly an hour for them to say all their farewells. The wedding reception couldn't have gone any better, and when the final car had pulled away with Claudia and Maceo in it, Pecca and Colton stood beneath the vast Texas sky and held on to each other.

"I didn't want it to end," Pecca whispered against the collar of his shirt.

"I love them, but I'm not going to lie—I'm glad it's just us now."

Colton grasped her hand and spun her outwards before spinning her back close to his chest. Their lips met, and it was the sweetest taste he'd ever known.

With the melody of night serenading them, Colton and Pecca swayed as one. Colton closed his eyes and let the memories of the last two years flicker through his mind until he returned to the moment they were in.

"I never could've imagined a more perfect ending than this."

Pecca's gaze traveled over his face before she kissed his neck, and then his jawline, her lips moving slowly up until they met his lips. She kissed him gently, running her fingers through the hair on the back of his neck. It was the kind of kiss that woke up every desire, and he longed to take her into their home.

Unhurriedly, and much to Colton's dismay, Pecca drew back. "This is only the beginning, my love. We have a whole future ahead of us."

Colton swept his bride into his arms and started for their room, kissing her forehead. He turned his face to the stars and gave thanks for what the future held, because he knew it would be better than anything he could've planned or hoped for himself.

Acknowledgments

PECCA AND COLTON'S STORY CONCLUDES the Harbored Secrets series, and I still pinch myself as a reminder that this wasn't a dream but a dream come true. This book and series wouldn't have been possible without the amazing team at Revell. Andrea, Amy, Karen, Brianne, Gayle—y'all are literally the champions behind this book and series. I couldn't do this without your support, encouragement, and hard work to make my dreams a reality.

Tamela—there's no agent in the world like the one I've got! I'm so grateful for your belief in me as a writer with a story to tell and for the love and encouragement you've showered on me over the years.

Emilie—you know all the things my heart wants to say to you, yet there really are no words to truly express what you mean to me. Thank you for EVERYTHING!

It takes a tribe of friends and family to bring sanity to my life. Jaime Jo, Christen, Esther, Tom, Melanie, Chris, Danny, Lisa, Matt, Erin, Mom and Dad, Aaron, Julie, Phillip, Lorisa, and Sandy—y'all are the best, and I love you for your undying support!

My G.I. Joe and three bambinos—y'all are the greatest blessings I'll have on this side of heaven. Thank you for supporting my dream and almost never growing tired of breakfast for dinner. I love you guys so much!

A special thanks to my street team, who continue to bless me with their support, encouragement, and friendship. And a shout-out to Lilah Mast, who helped me name Maceo and Noah's flag football team. GO, WARRIORS!

A huge heart of gratitude to Becky Wade, who graciously allowed me to use the Dallas Mustangs in my story.

Finally, but most important, I thank my Lord and Savior. Much of this writing journey has occurred during the most difficult moments in my life. The day I sent this manuscript to my editor, I cried, feeling like it was inadequate, that I was inadequate. The day she emailed me telling me she loved it, I cried. If there's one thing I've learned, it's that God is faithful and good. Even in the hard stuff, he's never forsaken me or my dream. And he's turned the difficult into the beautiful.

> And we know that in all things God works for the good of those who love him, who have been called according to his purpose.
>
> Romans 8:28

Natalie Walters is a military wife of twenty-three years and currently resides in Hawaii with her soldier husband and their three kids. She writes full-time and has been published in *Proverbs 31* magazine and has blogged for *Guideposts* online. In addition to balancing life as a military spouse, mom, and writer, she loves connecting on social media, sharing her love of books, cooking, and traveling. Natalie comes from a long line of military and law enforcement veterans and is passionate about supporting them through volunteer work, races, and writing stories that affirm no one is defined by their past.

"Its FAST and ENTWINED plot lines, EXCITING TWISTS, and ELECTRIFYING conclusion will appeal to fans of suspenseful INSPIRATIONAL ROMANCES."

—*BOOKLIST*

When journalist Vivian DeMarco's boss dies under suspicious circumstances, her only hope for finding the truth is Deputy Ryan Frost. But the deeper they dig, the more twisted the truth becomes.

Meet Natalie...

www.NatalieWaltersWriter.com

f Natalie Walters, Writer

🐦 NatWaltersWrite

📷 nataliewalters_writer

Author Photo Credit: © Emilie Hendryx